City of Blood

By
Dominic Scott

Prologue

Dragos stood on the temple steps, facing the woods with his face upturned so he could feel the warmth of the glorious afternoon sun on his cheeks. He was savouring every second. In just a few moments he would achieve his destiny, the future of Bellum would be forever changed.

He wanted to recall every single detail, capture every single moment before entering the temple. The gentle breeze that cooled the sweat on his brow from the brisk walk through the woods, the birds chirping to each other in the trees, he drank it all in, etching everything into his mind. His gaze swung to the ground, his fierce blue eyes finding a colony of ants trudging past the temple steps. The whole colony worked so tirelessly to feed their queen, carrying food back and forth all day. He sympathised with the ants and the weight they carried on their backs. A similar burden would soon become his own, the immense weight of an entire kingdom. He was on the cusp of becoming Bellum's first ever king; no, he would become Bellum's first ever emperor. He liked the sound of that better. He would put an end to the two brothers' childish squabbles and unite them under one banner; his own. Mirron would have no choice but to then recognise his power. That left the desert dwelling Kidoshians, they'd no longer be allowed to roam the Kidesh sand sea in freedom. He relished the task. They would worship him as a god.

The walk had not been as arduous and taxing as he feared it might have been which pleased Dragos. He would need all his energy for the upcoming struggle. At first he'd found it hard going, manoeuvring his tall muscular frame through the brush and trees until he came across a game trail. It was much easier going than working his way through the tightly packed trees. He'd traversed the trail, and those branching from it, for a couple of hours before finally stumbling across the path to the temple.

Although to call it a path was kind. The majority of pavestones were missing and those left were pitiful moss ridden lumps, stubbornly refusing to be swallowed up by Mother Nature. As he squashed those remaining stones into the mud, Dragos wondered how long it had been since those pavestones had first been laid. At least two hundred years by his reckoning. He wondered what the masons who had constructed this path would think if they could see the fruits of their labour now. Would they be bitter? Would they smile ruefully? Time had won out in the end, it always does. It was inevitable, wasn't it? Dragos wondered.

He'd already surpassed everyone on the Council, commanding powers and abilities they couldn't even imagine existed. After today, there would be no limit to his power. Uncharted territory stretched before him, waiting to be explored. Could he attain immortality? Beat time and Mother Nature? It wasn't inconceivable. All his victims so far paled in comparison to the combined power of the Council, yet his abilities had grown tenfold from absorbing theirs.

Every single drop of life had been squeezed and sucked from their still beating hearts leaving their bodies as withered husks. Taking another man's lifeblood, his soul, into oneself was no easy task. Dragos had learned this the hard way but he had overcome. He had triumphed. To think he used to be in awe of those on the Council, hanging on their every word, borderline worshiping them. Doubting his burgeoning power, doubting his worthiness to be tutored by the Council members. Dragos vowed to himself that one day, he would wield the power to grant him a seat on the Council. What a fool he'd been back then. If only he could have seen himself now. The Council members were no match for him. They were weak, gullible, so easy to deceive and manipulate, dancing franticly to the tune of his fiddle.

His amusement had known no bounds watching them squirm and suffer. Their disquiet growing with each victim. He'd delighted in the panic, the distress, the arguing, the accusations and the mistrust that had grown so rife towards the end. A pity they finally figured out what was going on, cutting his amusement short, but it was already far too late. Dragos had grown to a level they could not comprehend. The spineless cowards had fled in terror, right here, to the very temple he stood outside. He spat on the temple steps in disgust of his former idols. Not a single one had stayed to oppose him, flight had been their only thought, trying to save their worthless, wretched lives.

Still, he owed the Council a small debt of gratitude. His eagerness, his need to prove himself to them, to show them he could become Council material, that he could become powerful enough to one day sit amongst them had set him down the path that had led inevitably here. To these crumbling temple steps. To his moment of triumph. Today he would have each and every one of the Council members. He would have their lives. He would have their power. Today he would take his first real stride towards becoming a god.

He noticed, with a wry smile, that he didn't look or smell like a god. The journey to the temple combined with the sun's blazing rays had conspired to ruin that. His padded, heavy cloak had been discarded long ago, yet he was still soaked from perspiration. Dust that covered his moccasins had steadily climbed up his breeches before falling just short of his mid-thigh tunic, which clung unrelenting to his back.

He ran his fingers through his long, thick black hair. They came away slick with sweat. He realised he was nervous. The long awaited day was finally here. Just moments away. He gazed down upon his upturned palms and once again felt the strength surging within them. He closed his eyes and let himself be carried away by the power that swept through his veins. He revelled in it. The nerves were banished. Gone. Never to return. In their place stood equal measures of anticipation and excitement.

Dragos had come so far, it was hard to believe it had all started with one of Essers stories. It had struck a chord within that reverberated endlessly in his mind. Always there. Constant. The seed planted by his tutor had been unwaveringly watered by his subconscious until it had grown too large to ignore. Blood magic! The very words sent ripples of delight through his body. Blood magic. The key to unlocking his potential. Unlocking his path to godhood. His mind wandered back to Esser and the fateful story he'd told that day.

'Blood magic is a very old, powerful magic. It's thought that the very first Gifted of Bellum all used Blood magic.' Dragos sat, enthralled, before his tutor. 'It's not like the refined magic Gifted use today.' Esser continued, 'it's raw, wild… primal!' He paused for effect, knowing Dragos hung on his every word. 'If used without care, it could even cause terrible harm to the user. That's why several of the Gifted assembled together to set strict rules in place for the use of Blood magic; they evolved into what we now know as the Council. Most Gifted sided with the early Council, seeing the wisdom of their rules and the benefits of compliance. But a small few ignored the wishes of the Council and continue to use Blood magic without restraint.'

Esser stopped to pull a pipe from one of the sleeves of his robe with a flourish. His leaf pouch appeared from the other and he started to pack his pipe, carefully, with Red Leaf. When the pipe was packed to his satisfaction, he slipped the pouch back into the secretive folds of his sleeve and lit the pipe with a match that appeared from where Dragos knew not. Esser leaned his portly frame back contentedly in his chair and started puffing away next to the fire. Dragos often wondered if there was anything his tutor couldn't tuck away inside his robe. He waited for what seemed like an eternity, but in reality, was only a dozen heartbeats, before he blurted out 'What happened to them!?' Esser stared into his student's imploring eyes and smiled. 'Put another log on the fire then lad, and I'll tell you.' He watched his most promising pupil scamper off to complete the task. He was fond of the boy - no, young man he corrected himself.

    Dragos was no longer the wide-eyed novice he had taken under his tutelage all those years ago; he had matured into a competent Gifted and had a promising future ahead of him. Possibly even a seat on the Council. Esser knew he was biased, but that didn't negate the fact the boy had potential. What endeared Dragos to Esser most was his willingness to learn, and more importantly, he enjoyed listening to Essers stories. His tutor loved nothing more than to weave a good story, taking his listeners on a journey down multiple strands of thread, leaping nimbly from one to the other.

    Dragos unceremoniously tossed the log he had brought back from the pile onto the fire and settled once more cross-legged before his tutor, waiting for him to continue. Dragos knew Esser was attempting to build tension in the tale and tried to wait patiently, but his impatience grew with each plume of smoke that escaped from the corner of his tutor's mouth. Finally, in between inhalations, Esser continued.

    'Those who ignored the rules were a danger! Not only to themselves but to those around them. The Council decided it was their duty to protect the people from harm and so waged war on the Wielders of Blood! Lives were lost on both sides, the Council had superior numbers but the Wielders commanded powerful and destructive Blood magic.' Dragos' mind carried him far into the past, to the plains of the battlefields. He tried to imagine the scale of destruction and bloodshed caused by such powerful forces pitted against each other, knowing he fell short of the mark. 'It became a war of attrition, with neither side willing to give ground but eventually the Councils superior numbers told and they were able to wipe out the last of the Wielders of Blood. The scant members of the Council who survived, created a safer way to access and use their gift. Blood magic was deemed too powerful and dangerous to wield and was banned from ever being used again.'

Esser had no way of knowing that with the completion of the story his fate was sealed. He would have been proud of how meticulous his pupil researched Blood magic, how hungrily he devoured any scraps thrown his way from unsuspecting Council members. Dragos had spent every waking moment he could in the grand library pouring over old tomes and scrolls, gleaning information, piecing it all together in his mind. His first mistake was to approach Cipric, the oldest and most learned of all the Gifted. The cantankerous goat had reluctantly answered Dragos' questions at first but quickly reproached him as soon as he thought Dragos was pushing too far, scolding him for taking too much of an interest in Blood magic. Shortly after, Esser had collared Dragos in the library, telling him to stay clear of Blood magic and leave Cipric alone.

'I told you about Blood magic to help you in your learning, so you could avoid past mistakes, not repeat them! The Blood war was the most violent and dark time in Bellum's history, many young and promising Gifted were lost. This is the last of Blood magic I will hear, unless I bring it up in lessons, are we clear?'

Dragos made a show of bowing to his tutor's will, but inwardly he seethed. Blood magic was the way forward, the key to unlocking his potential, his true power: his destiny! They had no right to stand in his way, to block the path he was meant to walk. The old fools had let fear get the better of them. Well, underneath, pressing his own cut into the slippery flesh. The knife, which had been poised above the rib cage, sprang forward like a hound slipped from its lead. It grated in-between two ribs and sank into the heart. Power unlike any other Dragos had known before surged into his body through the cut in his palm. It pulsated and seared through his veins. His body was on fire, as if burning from the inside out. Excruciating pain erupted in his brain, the pressure building until he thought his head would implode. He crumpled onto Essers body, unable to withstand the onslaught of pain. His body was racked by spasms. Moans escaped from behind clenched teeth. Then, as suddenly as it arrived, the pain dispersed. Panting, Dragos stood upright, wrenching his arm free of Esser's chest. A dozen tense, uncertain heartbeats passed in eerie silence before Dragos cocked his head back and let out maniacal laughter. The pain had gone, but the power, the power had stayed!

Cipric had been next. The old goat had been suspicious about Esser's death but instead of alerting the Council he'd brought his concerns straight to Dragos. Hardly able to believe his luck Dragos rushed the fool right there and then, overpowering the frail, older man. Cipric had taken his power to euphoric new heights, Dragos felt indestructible, he was unstoppable. Every Gifted, every Council member would lay before him, chest cut open, innards exposed, just like Cipric, just like Esser.

Dragos hauled his thoughts back to the present before he lost himself in the nostalgia of the blood ridden havoc he had wrought. He bounded up the last of the temple steps and approached the entrance. The temple had fared no better against time's onslaught than the path leading to it. Cracks and moss weaved a worn tapestry across its surface. The top left of the roof had crumbled and collapsed, leaving a gaping hole which birds used to build nests in. A dreary, but fitting place for the old relics of the Council to meet their demise, Dragos mused.

He paused on the brink of entering the temple, turned and swept his gaze once more over the peacefulness of the outside world. A menacing smirk played across his lips when he thought about how stark a contrast it was to the maelstrom he was about to unleash inside. He strode confidently into the temple.

Chapter 1

The hooded figure stole his way through the murky darkness, darting from corner to corner, allowing the night to envelop him, embrace him as a lover. He turned into an alleyway, where his nose was quickly assaulted by the acrid smell of stale urine and refuse. Swift, sure steps propelled him away from the barrage and to the alley's entrance which opened onto a broader street. A quick glance either way told him that not a single soul was in sight, so he continued on his way. The soft padding of his footfalls was the only sound defying silences complete rule. A small market square loomed before him. Bereft of life, the market stood dead, awaiting the resurrection that dawn would bring. Wooden stalls lined the way on either side, almost like soldiers standing smartly to attention, saluting him on his way.

    Leaving the Poor Quarter behind him, the figure arrived at a crossroads, which even in the dead of night, bustled with activity. The Docks were to his right, where the stone path turned to earth. Endless processions of wagons had left their mark over the years, hauling cargo back and forth, leaving parallel ruts in their wake. One such wagon trundled past him now with a group of drunken sailors stumbling behind. Most likely just arrived from Drethelstan, they were clearly enjoying making the most of time spent ashore, drinking and whoring whilst their Captain concluded his business. To his left, the Citadel rose ominously into the nights sky, dwarfing the adjoining barracks with its accompanying parade ground. Guards patrolled the outer rim whilst others stood at the entrance, no doubt grumbling about the cold, wishing they were inside rolling dice with their comrades. The Emperor no doubt slept soundly behind those secure walls. The Heralds gate was locked shut for the night and the only other entrance was through the Soldiers gate, which would require fighting your way through the barracks. Not a welcoming thought.

    Fortunately his destination didn't require such drastic feats to reach. The way lay open before him, on the opposite side of the crossroads. He drew back his hood and emerged into the flickering light given off by the bracketed torches for the first time since setting off from the tavern. He flattened his short, wavy brown hair which had become tousled inside the hood. Hazel green eyes swept the crossroads, looking to unearth any potential problems. No one paid him attention. The sailors remained in drunken bliss, whilst those heading up from the Docks were eager to begin the night's festivities. The guards scrutinised those who came within reach of their spluttering torches, but left everyone else alone. He set across, trying to look inconspicuous. He wondered if by trying to look inconspicuous, he unwittingly looked conspicuous.

    How do you look conspicuous anyway?

    He reached the other side without confrontation. It was like stepping into a different city. The street was well lit and maintained; almost pristine. There were no run down houses shared by large families, each estate stood in its own splendour. Gardens running from gate to door began appearing, each more colourful and lavish than the last. The estates grew in size as did the holdings inside them. Mansions that could fit fifty normal houses inside, the show of wealth was staggering.

    The grandeur of Tydon. It's what makes our city the most vibrant in all of Bellum, yet no one ever talks about the flip side of the coin; the beggars, the disease, the squalor of living conditions in the Poor Quarter. No one sees beyond the opulence. Beyond the towering architectural marvels, beyond the fetes, beyond the feasts. Tydon festers while you gorge yourself on wine and sweet meats. He'd known both sides of the coin and couldn't decide which he abhorred more. Those

'Reeva here,' Drak gestured to the woman sitting opposite him. 'Got a terrible nosebleed and sneezing fit all at the same time.'

Sarfina glanced questioningly over at Reeva, who like always, remained silent. Reeva never spoke. Ever. She was a mute. They all had bets going on as to whether this was from birth or if she'd had some kind of accident as a child. No one had a clue how they were going to settle the bet, but none of them were willing to back down, as over the years the stakes had grown significantly until there was a considerable amount of coin riding on it. Her clear blue eyes usually conveyed everything she needed to say but on this occasion they gave away nothing. She tucked a stray strand of her short blonde hair behind her ear and twiddled it until Sarfina looked away.

'What about those two?' she accused, pointing to the two bloody faced bodies sprawled on the floor. No one had thought to drag them away. 'Looks like your handiwork.'

'They've… err… obviously had too much to drink… they was dancing together swinging each other round n' round and smacked head first into each other…'

Tense moments passed before Sarfina said: 'Fine, I'll choose to believe that.' The whole room breathed a collective sigh of relief. It was a well-known secret that the Assassins Guild ran a Hand from the tavern and that Sarfina ruled both with an iron fist. She leant forward and it took all Drak's willpower to maintain eye contact. 'Need I remind you,' she hissed, 'That we have a contract tonight! Thran'll be back soon and Zel will be down any moment. So sit here quietly and don't cause any more trouble.'

'I didn't cause nothin.' Drak protested.

'That's a double negative, which means you most certainly did. Now be a good little boy and do as you're told!' Sarfina strode away without waiting for a reply.

Drak glanced at Reeva, the half smirk she wasn't even trying to hide cut more deeply into him than any of her knives ever could.

'Ah bollocks! I don't understand that double negative shit. Go get us some wine, Sarf didn't say we couldn't drink while we waited.'

* * * *

Thran was bored. This was one part of his job he disliked. *Stalking and then assassinating my target is what I'm good at, not sitting idly around waiting for them to arrive. C'mon old man, surely you've had enough to drink by now?* He stood up and tried to stretch the stiffness out of his muscles.

Why do I always get stuck with scout duty? He already knew the answer of course. Drak was the brawn, Zel the tactician and whilst Reeva was equally as stealthy, if not more so, her ability to communicate, or lack of, limited her usefulness as reconnaissance. *Reeva, it's a good job no one can best you with knives.* So he was lumped with scout duty. Stuck with this boredom. *By the gods I need to kill something!* Blood and death had held an unexplainable allure to Thran, ever since he was young.

He'd been a pretty normal child coming from a wealthy family. The birthmark on the back of his left shoulder, which looked like an angry red welt shaped water droplet, was the only uniqueness to distinguish him from any of the other children. That and his obsession with blood. He'd never cried out when scraping his knees or elbows like most kids. Instead he'd been enthralled by the way the thin red rivulets had run down his skin, forming intricate streams before dripping onto the floor. Loneliness had been his constant companion. His mother had died giving birth to him and his father wanted as little to do with his bizarre offspring as possible. His older brother blamed him for their mother's death, leaving only the servants to tend to the young master.

There was no love there, they simply did their job. It was almost a relief when his father grew sick and was consigned to his bed as Thran was unable to cope with his indifference any longer. His father's illness had prompted clumsy attempts at reconciliation, as years of regrets and guilt flooded forth. As death drew near and with the knowledge that Carrion would soon collect his father's soul, battlements erected over years came crashing down between father and son.

You selfish bastard! You died and I was left without a father again, days after finding out what having one was like. I almost wish you had remained distant.

After his passing, the elder brother had taken over as head of the household and the very next day Thran was thrown out and told never to return. The following two years found him living on the streets of the Poor Quarter, fighting off hunger and other homeless kids to survive. The streets stripped away his upbringing and brought forth an inner resilience he'd never known existed. It was the only way he kept going, through the beatings, through the disease, through the hunger.

Then one day during a brutal fight, Sarfina found him. She had a maturity about her, a self-assurance that set her apart from the crowd who had amassed around the two combatants. She'd watched the vicious fight unfold with interest.

Ducking and dodging Thran frantically tried to find a way to turn the tide in his favour as the stronger lad rushed in, trying to pin his opponent by using his superior weight to his advantage. Thran was tiring, having not eaten for days his malnourished body was running on pure adrenaline, he could feel his concentration slipping away. In one last desperate gamble he took his opponent by surprise, dashing forward inside his outstretched arms. Using the lad's filthy garments to haul himself up until their eye's locked, Thran lunged forward, viciously sinking his teeth into flesh. Ignoring the fists pummelling into his body, Thran worked his teeth deeper into the bloody mess, until with one final wrench, his rival's ear tore free. The circling children scattered in horror leaving all but one; Sarfina. Thran stood triumphantly over his defeated foe who knelt, screaming uncontrollably, hands clasped around what remained of his ear.

'How would you like to be put to good use?' Sarfinas question hung in the air as Thran regarded her with open suspicion. 'Well?' she demanded. Just when it appeared she would receive no answer, Thran spat out his bloody trophy. The earlobe landed at her feet with a wet splat, saliva mixed with blood. Thran looked from it to her, licked the remaining blood from his lips and smiled. Without another word she turned and strode from the scene. He followed, leaving the poor boy alone with his misery.

Thran's bored musings were abruptly interrupted when an ornate carriage sped past him, screeching to a halt in front of the guards who scrambled to open the gates at the hounding cry from the driver. The carriage was past the gardens before the occupants could even so much as glance at the sweet smelling plants. Stopping outside the massive wooden front door, the driver hastened to get down from atop his perch and open the carriage. An older gentlemen emerged and if not for the steady hand of the driver he would have sprawled head first onto the ground. Blind drunk, he staggered his way to the twin oak panelled doors which opened before him and swallowed him whole.

The driver lead the team of horses still attached to the carriage around the side of the huge mansion to the stables. He untacked the powerful beasts, brushed them down, and fed them before locking them in for the night. Duties finished, the driver disappeared in to the servant's quarters. Satisfied there

Chapter 2

They waited around the corner from their target's estate. Waiting to start the contract. Waiting for Zel. Reeva was the personification of calm and collected. She leant against the wall, arms folded across her chest, eyes fixed on the vibrant gardens opposite her. It was impossible to tell what she was thinking. The two men with her were quite the opposite, both were clearly attempting to keep themselves occupied to alleviate nerves. Drak shifting from one foot to the other, glancing around the corner every two seconds. Thran sitting cross legged, scraping dirt from the sole of his boots. Finally, Zel, dressed up as a noble, approached the guards from the opposite end of the street, singing loudly.

'About time.' muttered Drak

'Come on.' said Thran as he got up and set off around the corner. They followed.

'My girl's waiting for me there,
With bright blonde hair and alluring pears
My girl's waiting for me there,
With a cold shoulder and an icy stare
My girl's waiting to kill me,
'Cos I kissed another lady when she wasn't there!'

Zel finished the ditty as he drunkenly staggered towards the guards.

'S'cuse me gentleman-men, even. Sorry. I was just wondering maybe perchance you may be of some assistance to me?' Zel broke into a beaming smile. The guards glanced at one another.

Drak set his back against the estate wall and cupped his hands together. Thran set his right foot into Drak's palms and was boosted up, he grasped the stone parapet and scrambled over, dropping down into the dirt with a grunt. Reeva was next.

'Naul's hairy balls, have you put weight on?' He moaned as she stepped up. In response she took another step, the heel of her foot pushing down solely onto his forehead as she propelled herself up and over, landing silently on the other side. He grinned. 'Guess I deserved that...'

'And so you see in my stupor? Splendour? Stupendous! Yes! In my stupendous state of affairs I currently find myself in, I cannot seem to find my way back to the house I live in, my very own home. Actually, not very stupendous at all, scary I guess would be the right word beginning with S, if I wanted to continue that trend ha-ha, but I digress, in my distress. Can you point me in the right direction to my estate? It's big and it's got gardens in it, probably walls n' windows too hahaha. Houses usually dooooo. Ah never mind here comes my servant of the man variety to the rescue. My bodyguard manservant. Come along Drakorae, I must be home at once!'

'Of course, Lord Zelonius.' Drak said giving the guards apologetic looks. Grabbing Zel's arm he started to guide him back down the street to the imagined estate. 'Let's get you home, sir.'

'What was that all about?' asked one guard.
'Not a clue. Bloody nobles.' replied the other.
'You got plans for the festival yet?'
'No not yet. You?'
'I've got it all laid out, this year I'm finally going to get picked by the maidens to enter Oros' temple for the celebrations.'

'Every year you try this, you're obsessed with those celebrations. Why do you care so much?'

'Because they're having orgies in there, everyone knows it.'

'No they don't, nobody knows it, because all who enter never utter a word about it to anyone.'

'Oros swears them to secrecy, but it's obvious. They're kept in the temple until they've impregnated all the maidens.'

'I'll give you that, the maidens usually give birth around nine months on from the festival.'

'Exactly, so why all the secrecy? I tell you why, because at these orgies they use forbidden sex acts known only to the maidens of Oros.'

'You can keep fantasising all you want, it don't make no difference. You're never getting picked by the maidens. You're far too ugly.'

'True. Which is why I've devised a cunning plan that's been in motion for almost a year now.'

'Another one? They never work. What have you come up with this time?'

'So, they're looking for someone to impregnate the maidens, right? So I've been going to the temple every day this past year and making donations.'

'The maidens are not prostitutes…'

'Yes I know that! So every time I make a donation I thank the goddess for answering my prayers at last year's festival.'

'Go on then, I'll bite. What prayer did she answer?'

'I'm to be a father. All six women I've been sleeping with got pregnant. I became the most virile man in Tydon. The perfect candidate to impregnate the maidens. Oh and I also made it clear that the goddess had endowed me with a big dick too, thought it couldn't hurt my chances.'

'How much money have you given to the temple?'

'That's not important.'

'With all the money you've wasted, you could have had countless orgies with prostitutes.'

'Yes but they don't know the forbidden sex acts like the maidens. Nor are they as beautiful and pure.'

'They're pure, yet know forbidden sex acts? How does that make sense?'

'The gods move in mysterious ways, who are we to question them.'

'I'm worried about you. Genuinely…'

'Just you wait and see, I'm getting picked at this year's festival.'

Whilst the guards conversed, Zel and Drak had turned the corner and broke apart from each other laughing.

'Did you think I was believable? I thought I was pretty good!'

'You were lucky they didn't give a shit about you. Nobody talks like that when they're drunk, not even a noble!'

'I thought I was stupendous haha. I chose the wrong career, maybe I should become a thespian.'

'What's a thespian?'

'An actor you dolt!'

'Oh right… what's a dolt?'

* * * *

Thran, with Reeva in tow set off towards the enormous building, working their way through trees and bushes. They halted on the edge. The main path was to their left, the servant's quarters directly before them whilst the gardens ran round to the back of the house to their right. Thran looked to Reeva, she nodded. They broke cover and set off towards the servants' quarters, keeping low.

They reached the door and paused beneath its arch. No cries of alarm, no warning bells sounding. Thran gently tried

Reeva couldn't comprehend how he could possibly work all this out in his mind, reel off information and statistics like he was reading them straight off the page. He retained everything. Filed away for safe keeping, ready to be re-examined if the need arose. She'd lost count of the amount of arguments he'd won by recalling perfectly what someone had said two months ago. Backed up by flawless logic and reasoning.

Sometimes, I swear he's not human.

She followed his instructions. "At the top of the stairs, head right. Go to end of the corridor, turn left. Head down it until you get to the fifth door on your right." So here she stood, outside the fifth door on her right. Her bows furrowed in annoyance when she tried the door only to find it was locked.

You're lucky it's me, otherwise we'd have been having words Zel

She thought as she closed the door softly behind her.

She could see now why the door was locked, the room wasn't in use. Blankets had been draped over the furniture, a thin layer of dust covered everything. She crossed the room and drew back the curtains, letting pale moonlight in. She unlatched the window, pushed it wide open and felt the cool night air on her face. The branches of the tree within touching distance swayed gently. Everything was ready. Reeva went back over to the couch, peeled back the blanket and sat down to wait.

* * * *

Something was wrong. Three figures laid asleep in the bed. There was only supposed to be one. *Shit!* Zel had assured him that Pemtil slept neither with his wife or mistress.
Tonight of all nights they decide to re-connect, just my luck! Maybe The Lady looks out for him after all.

Thran approached the bed. He found clothes scattered on the floor. It was obvious which items belonged to each individual. The colourful patterned pieces belonged to Pemtil, only the aristocracy would deem them fashionable. Everything else was a drab, black colour. They were uniforms. One male, one female.

Pemtil you old lech!

He lay in-between the two servants, snoring contently.

Not surprising. Can't think of many better ways to spend my last night.

Still this posed a major problem to Thran, especially with the clients specifying only Pemtil to die. He didn't want to lose out on any money and face Drak's wrath. His refraining from extra killing would mean the big man would be able to afford two whores tonight instead of one.

He could try climbing onto the bed, slice open his throat and be gone before the two were ever the wiser, but if they woke up in the middle of the act, he'd have no other choice but to kill them as well. Thran knew it was a massive risk, but he had to wake the two and get them out of the room. He approached the side of the bed nearest him. The woman lay on her back, the covers bunched together at her waist. Thran's gaze flew to her breasts.

By the gods, they could belong to Brioth herself! No wonder you couldn't control yourself, she must have cost a fortune in the market. C'mon Thran, concentrate. She's not the woman for you.

He reached for her, grabbed her by the arm and gently shook her awake. 'Wha...?' She mumbled rubbing the sleep out of her eyes.

'Shhhh! You'll wake the Master.' Thran admonished her. 'Now get up, get your things and get out. You know he doesn't like waking up to servants still in his bed.' Thran hoped this was true. She seemed to accept it anyway, scrambling out of the bed, bending to pick up the clothes on the floor. Thran bit back a moan.

She could rival Sarfina. Shame I won't get to see her in the light of day.

'And take him with you.' Thran said gesturing to the figure still asleep on the far side of the bed.

'We're sorry, please don't report this to the Master.' She pleaded, head bowed before him.

'Leave in the next ten seconds and I shall ask him to be lenient.'

She rushed to her friend and all but dragged the poor guy out of bed and out the door before he was awake. Than spared them only a glance as they exited but he couldn't help but notice how well-endowed the male servant was.

By all the gods! How can anyone find being pierced by that "thing" enjoyable? It'd be like taking a spear up the arse!

Thran waited till their footsteps disappeared from the antechamber and down the hallway before he went over and shut the door behind them. Pulling his knife free, he made his way back over to the bed. Pemtil was still laid on his back, deep in sleeps oblivion. Thran stepped up onto the bed and laid his knife against Pemtil's throat. He paused.

He didn't want to rush. He wanted to savour. His birthmark grew warm, heating up until it was like a hot brand pressed against his flesh. It burned into his shoulder, setting his whole body ablaze. His soul felt like a chasm of fire, crying out to be released. His body thirsted for blood. It wanted him to slit the throat: it needed him to. It needed him to drink deep from Pemtil's lifeblood.

He struggled to control his breathing and heart rate. He was sweating.

Finally he could bare it no longer and drew his knife across Pemtil's throat. Blood gushed from the wound, spraying the sheets. Pemtil's throat gurgled and spluttered as he tried in vain to draw breath. Thran let the blood pool on his free hand. It acted like a balm, soothing his body, cooling it. Caressing the fire in his soul to acquiescence. He closed his eyes and began to call upon his powers.

Focus. Form the shape in your mind and project.

The blood on his palm twitched. Strands shot up and entwined, forming together in accordance to Thran's will. He could feel it, like it was a living part of him, an extension of his arm, of himself. Thran formed the one thing, the one person that he could recall intimately, every single feature of her face. He'd been with her ever since she recruited him all those years ago, ever since he'd spat the ear down at her feet. He opened his eyes to find a miniature Sarfina standing upright in his palm.

It was beautiful. She was beautiful. She stood hands on hips, head titled back to look at him, defiant. The blood was still circulating, making it look as if she were alive. As if he'd shrunk the real Sarfina into his palm and she stood berating him, telling him to make her right again. He couldn't look away. He was afraid if he did, she'd be gone. His own little Sarfina. So hauntingly breath-taking.

He'd lost track of time, there was no telling how long he'd been here, gaze locked with the blood statue in his palm. Finally, with great reluctance, he released the statue from its hold. It liquified before him and flowed into the other pools of blood on the bed. Gone, as quickly as that. Like it had never existed. He felt a twinge of sorrow, yet mini Sarf would live on, forever etched in his memory. He was exhausted, using his power always drained him of his strength. That was the longest he'd ever been able to hold an object before. His crowning achievement. He could reflect later, right now he needed to get out before he was discovered. He rolled over and sat on the edge of the bed, gathering his wits and remaining strength. A few minutes passed before he was ready to get up. He was back to the front of the house in no time, turned left and headed down the passage Reeva had gone down.

'You know what the best thing about having a penis is?' Drak paused. 'Sharing it with those that don't.' A pleased grin split across his face, then he was gone, sauntering off behind the bar to his room upstairs.

Thran laughed. 'He must have worked on that one for quite some time. Wonder where he heard it?'

'It was amusing, but nonsensical.'

'Ah c'mon Zel don't ruin it, even Reeva cracked a smile!'

'But how is that the best thing about having a penis? Can he back that statement up with research? Facts? I doubt it! All those whores are doing is stimulating one of his pleasure centres.'

'Wow, you even make sex sound so… contractual.'

'How would you know? How much sex have you had without paying for it?'

'Okay, you've made your point. What about, you know, feelings?'

'What about them?'

'Where do they enter into this equation of yours?'

'They don't. Man or woman, it doesn't matter who stimulates me. Granted I have certain people who I know will stimulate me better than others. But if they are unavailable, I can find another mate willing to copulate with me.'

'By the love of Brioth, that's a bleak outlook Zel.'

'On the contrary, it's the most logical way to go about things.'

'Love defies logic.'

'And look what it has brought you, nothing but pain. Nights spent mulling over whether your feelings were reciprocated or not. Having sat across from you Thran, I can tell you, you looked pretty bleak to me.'

'You can't experience actual intimacy with these random people. Passion perhaps, but not intimacy. Not love. They call it making love for a reason.'

'Look Thran, after all you've been through I think it's great that you still hold onto this notion of-'

'To experience true happiness, we must first experience despair. Otherwise what can you gauge it against? And I've experienced my fair share of pain. Maybe it's my turn to experience joy.'

'And I'm the one with the bleak outlook apparently. Thran you need to act upon it and tell her, everyone knows anyway, even me. Speaking of, we need to talk. Excuse me.'

Zel promptly got up and strode off in search of Sarfina. Thran leant forward, elbows propping him up on the table, thumbs rubbing tired eyes. Adrenaline could only carry him for so long, he was exhausted. Reeva laid a comforting hand on his shoulder.

'You'll be awake, right?' She nodded. 'Okay, I'll try get some sleep.' He left her sharpening one of her many sets of knives.

That'll keep away any unwanted guests alright.

* * * *

'I don't like it,' muttered Zel, pacing back and forth in front of Sarfina. They were in the storeroom off from the kitchen in the back, away from prying eyes and ears. 'The city is flooded with rumours of an imminent war with Shulakh.'

'When is it not?' snorted Sarfina.

'This is different, all my informants are saying the same.'

'Looks like there's finally going to be war then.'

'Tensions' been high ever since the Emperor's coup. Peace was never going to last. I'm surprised we've gotten this far with just minor border skirmishes.'

'Shulakh's new Warrior King will change that, he's out for blood. Why is it young males lust so violently for power and glory through battle?'

'They're fools who need an ego boost. It spells trouble for us, no matter which way you look at it.'

'Skrenn is remaining tight lipped. If the Faceless Man has issued orders, or has a plan, he's yet to share. I have no idea what the Guild is planning and I hate it, I'm not used to being outside the loop. What about your sources at the palace?'

'I'm in the dark just as much as you are. Only the Emperor and his inner circle seem to be in the know. We could try the Captain?'

'No, not yet. I have the feeling we shall have to call upon his services for other matters.'

'As you wish, however I do not appreciate not having all the facts.'

Sarfina's answering grunt was a mix of agreement and frustration. 'One thing is for certain, things are going to get interesting.'

'One hundred percent.' Agreed Zel.

* * * *

Once more, he stood inside the temple. Darkness swirled ominously all around him apart from one beam of light which illuminated the corpse laid before him. It had been thoroughly hacked to pieces and then dumped upon the altar. As always he began assembling the body, treating it like an intricate puzzle, every piece belonging in a specific place and he would find each one its home.

Experience had taught him to start with the trickiest parts first before progressing onto the larger, more solid pieces of flesh. His practiced fingers moved deftly, sliding entrails and organs roughly into their appropriate place. Next came the limbs, matching up hands to forearms, forearms to biceps and triceps, before locking it in to the shoulder joint. The legs he found straightforward, it was all about working from the kneecap. Up to this point in the procedure he was making good progress. Fingers and toes however, were a nightmare, most of them being chopped into two or three pieces, which caused him to move at an agonizingly slow pace. Low growls of frustration marked the passing of time and his growing impatience, yet still he persevered, bent over the altar. His diligence was finally rewarded as he fitted the last digit. He leant back to admire his handiwork, allowed himself a little smirk before his expression became serious once again, he still had work to do.

The head, the final puzzle piece, had been left intact for the most part. Only the eyeballs had been gouged out, leaving two bloody pits that seemed to bore into him more than any pupils could have ever done. He scooped them up off the altar, they were as slippery as eels squirming underneath his inquisitive fingers. Their texture sent a shiver down his spine. Grimacing, he slid them back into the gaping sockets, they slotted in easily enough and he was done. Finished. His nightmarish task was at an end. He took a step back from the altar, gazing at the grotesque, but now fully assembled figure upon it. He had no idea what would happen next, if anything at all. He stood transfixed for what seemed like an age, staring at the corpse which had tormented his nights for so long.

His vigilance ended abruptly when he noticed the eyes staring back at him. When he'd slotted them in they'd been bog eyed, he was sure of it. It wasn't his mind playing tricks on him, they were staring straight at him with a burning intensity.

Took you long enough, boy.

The voice made him jump, yet the corpses lips had not moved, not uttered a single syllable. It had spoken directly into his mind. He took a step backwards. He'd been wrong, that stare was worse than the bloody pits, far worse. *Hahaha!* Laughter boomed through his skull, he cried out in surprise and took another step backwards, then another, and another before he turned and fled from the beam of light into the darkness, away from that *thing*, that abomination with its haunting laughter. It was no use, it rang inside his head clearer than any bell. *Hahaha! Hahaha!* If anything it intensified until he could stand it no longer, flinging himself to the floor. The darkness rose to claim him.

* * * *

Covered in sweat and breathing heavily, Thran jolted awake. He peeled the blanket from his sticky skin and sat up on the edge of the bed. He tried to regulate his breathing to calm himself but his heart kept thumping so loud and fast he thought he must surely be having a heart attack. He could still hear that laughter faintly echoing around his head. The room suddenly felt constricting, he had to get out, no, needed to get out. He quickly put on some pants, yanked his bedroom door open and escaped into the corridor.

Once the door was shut behind him, he took a moment to gather his wits. He could hear Drak's contented snores from the room opposite over the sounds of revelry that echoed upstairs from the bar below. He was back, he was safe. This was the real world. He focused on those sounds, hoping they would drive the laughter away. It helped. He finally felt recovered enough to work his way down to the end of the corridor to Reeva's room. He didn't bother to knock, she was expecting him. She was sat on her bed, still cleaning and sharpening her knives, although onto the last set by the look of it. She looked up at him, arched an eyebrow. He nodded.

'Bad, worst it's been. I have no idea what'll happen next time.'

Thran wasn't entirely sure why he trusted Reeva the way he did, but he only showed her this side of him. Maybe it was to do with her being mute. At first the silence had been unsettling, but now, after spending so much time with her and going through countless contracts, he found it reassuring. He could unload on her without fear she would spill his secrets. She was always willing to listen, and he never caught judgement in her eyes when he talked.

She scooted up closer to him so he could curl up on the bed with his head resting on her lap. Reeva began to gently stroke and run her fingers through Thran's hair. It was the one thing that always calmed him, that was ultimately therapeutic for him. It transported him back to his childhood before he was thrown out onto the streets. When he couldn't sleep, when he was troubled by strange nightmares, one kind hearted maid used to sneak into his room and stroke his hair, telling him stories until he finally drifted off into a peaceful slumber. Years later, minus the stories, Reeva was doing the same thing with the same effect.

* * * *

As Reeva consoled Thran to sleep, as Zel and Sarfina debated, as Drak slept sandwiched between two whores, a figure stepped onto the docks of Tydon. He'd waited patiently on board the ship he'd stowed away on until the dead of night, then slipped overboard. Swift sure strokes took him quickly to shore and it wasn't long before he was shimmying up the wooden poles of the dock and standing on dry land for the first time in what felt like an age. He didn't like boats. It wasn't that he got sea sickness, motion sickness, any kind of sickness at all, they just made him feel uneasy. It was the length of time in the same place, granted the place itself was in motion, but he was still trapped, with very limited escape routes, and escape routes were vital to his trade; it was his trade he was here to practice.

He let out a low whistle. Tydon's reputation as a wealthy, opulent city was well founded. The city sprawled out before him in all its splendour, a monument to human graft and engineering. It would be a terrible ordeal to try and take the city. It'd take a lengthy siege with heavy losses on both sides but it could be done. Humanity's grand ability to create could always be outdone by its greater ability and appetite for destruction.

Stubborn bastards us humans. Tell us not to do something and what do we go and do? It's the making of some yet, the breaking of most. Especially those not chosen by the gods.

Yet there was another side to this city and it was that side he now sought out, the beggars, the crippled, the homeless and drunks. They'd put him on the right path. He'd have to work his way up the food chain, but that was fine, he wanted them to know he was coming. Wanted them to be desperate.

Can't stand here all night! he chided himself, *things to do, plenty of people to see.*

He set off at a measured pace towards the rougher areas of Tydon to be about his business, to make sure Thran's nightmares continued.

The hunt had begun.

Chapter 4

A lull hit Sarfina's Tavern. The Tavern itself was still busy with hungry and thirsty customers but the Assassins Guild members found themselves without a contract. After successfully carrying out Pemtil's demise they had taken on three more contracts and had seen them all to completion. Then, nothing. Everything had gone quiet, no more clients, no more contracts.

 Sarfina was worried; with war on the horizon the Guild should have been at its busiest, spying on everyone and rooting out potential agents from other cities. Rich merchants either paid them to take out rivals so they could then swoop in and claim their holdings and belongings for themselves, or to plant false evidence so they were taken away and tortured for being an undercover informant. They should be making the most of these uncertain and distrustful times but instead her Hand, the cell entrusted to her by the Guild, sat idle. The entire city seemed to be collectively holding its breath.

 She instinctively knew it was the calm before the storm, a storm they would be soon vehemently cursing, wishing they were once more safe inside the lull. For now though, they all wanted the calm to end as quickly as possible. She knew from experience that the longer the calm, the longer the storm brewed for, the worse it hit. She made sure they were all braced: ready for impact. Running drills and mock contracts kept them busy and out of mischief for a little while, but Sarf knew the Hand was growing increasingly impatient. They were restless and bored out of their minds, a deadly combination. When a Hand grew bored fights started to break out more frequently and people inevitably ending up dying. Consequently, she'd have to clean up the mess and explain herself to her Guild superiors. Not exactly something she looked forward to. Two weeks stretched by without incident but when the third arrived, still without as much as a sniff of a contract, a local bar ended up needing refurbishment.

It all started when the gang tried to alleviate their boredom. Thran had spent the first couple of days brooding about his Gift. Curse? He still hadn't quite decided due to the fact that every time he used his power that same nightmare returned with a vengeance. Except this time, he'd finally re-assembled the full corpse and it had spoken to him, well, laughed at him. He was scared to use his power again without knowing what would happen. He usually confided in Reeva but it wasn't a subject he could just bring up. He wouldn't even know where to start. He'd told no one about his powers and he wanted it to stay that way. A nasty little surprise up his sleeve, if he could learn to fully command his abilities, but that meant practicing, and that meant nightmares, and facing it again.

No thank you!

So he sat and brooded, rivalling Reeva in her silence and grunting if anyone asked him if he was okay. Zel and Drak both agreed he was being a moody little shit and that something needed to done.

So Drak decided to take Thran under his wing and show him around all of his favourite haunts. The next week and a half they spent their nights performing Drak's favourite three past times; drinking, whoring and gambling. Although much to Drak's bafflement Thran abstained from the women, claiming that he just wasn't in the mood. Drak would just shake his head before heading off with that nights purchase. He didn't seem to have any preferences, other than that the whores were female. During the fourth night of merriment Drak finally confronted him.

'What's the matter lad? Why are you passing up perfectly good prostitutes? You're offending them quite frankly.'

'You just wouldn't understand Drak, I mean I want to, I really want to but… I just can't.'

'Look, if it's a performance issue, I understand, we've all been there. I may know someone who can supply something to help with that, make you stand to attention like you're on the parade ground being examined by the Emperor himself!'

'Imagining the Emperor is hardly going to put me in the mood, Drak.'

'The saying holds true, "you can lead a horse to water, but you can't make it drink". I won't be long!'

Thran held his tongue as Drak headed away with tonight's chosen delight.

I'm not like you, I can't just quench my thirst in any old watering hole anymore!

The gambling however he did take a liking to. It wasn't as thrilling as killing another man, but gambling turned out to be quite fun and exciting in its own right. They played a lot of different games and bet on all sorts, from lowly cock fights right up to bare knuckle boxing. The game Thran enjoyed the most though was Around the Table, each gambler had a certain amount of dice in their cup (it changed depending on the amount of players) and after slamming your cups down you peeked at your dice and then bet on how many of a certain number would be face up on everyone's dice. They won as much as they lost but they had fun doing it and Thran's gloomy disposition slowly began to fade until it disappeared altogether. He pushed his troubles to the back of his mind and after a few nights in Drak's infectious happy go lucky company he forgot all about the corpse and its haunting laughter. Then, at the start of the third week, as the sun set at the beginning of their latest nightly outing, Zel joined them.

Zel had been keeping himself busy by going over contingency plans and theories, mapping out how the impending storm could happen in a hundred different situations and how they could counteract it. His sharp mind was always hungry and he did his best to keep it happy and fed. His spent all day upstairs in the Guild's meeting room at the end of the hallway, venturing out only to eat, drink and piss. Although some days he got so caught up in this intricate web of theories he'd created he forgot to feed himself. Reeva, who disappeared during the day, would come back and drag him downstairs and force him to feed his stomach as well as his mind. Nobody knew where she went but, as regular as the sunrise, she always left at the same time in the morning and came back at the same time in the early evening. They didn't bother to ask her, it's not like they would have gotten a response. Following her wasn't an option either, if Reeva didn't want to be followed, she could effortlessly slip away from them at any given moment, vanishing into thin air. They just added it to the long list of mysteries that surrounded the mute woman. So Zel would take the opportunity to use her as a sounding board for that days musings while he ate. Yet even his brilliant mind was beginning to fatigue after two weeks straight and Reeva looked ready to plunge one of the knives she kept sharpening into his gut, so he decided to take a break and join Thran and Drak.

It soon became apparent that Zel was a very good gambler. Most believe that gambling is all down to luck and having a good poker face, but he knew in reality it's all about numbers and percentages. If you could do the arithmetic, which of course Zel could, you could work out the percentage of what card would most likely be next, or what dice would be rolled. No chance involved when Zel came to the table, just pure calculations. He cleaned up wherever the trio went on the first two nights. On the third night he suggested something a little different.

'Drak I want you to take us to where the big boys go to play, I want to earn some real coin tonight.'
'Sure.' Drak replied 'But your luck won't last forever.'
'I keep telling you it's not luck, its maths. I simply use my superior intellect.'
'Well if they catch you using that, there'll be trouble.'
'Why?'
'Cos people don't like cheats.'

Zel just looked at him. He couldn't be sure if Drak was joking or not, sometimes it was hard to tell. Zel knew that underneath he wasn't the loveable fool he pretended to be. He suspected it was to do with Drak's past. He was lying low from someone or something from his past if the latticework of scars on his back were anything to go by. There was a high percentage that whoever had caused those criss-cross patterns regretted their actions and were now deceased. Zel's narrowed eyes held Drak's own for a few moments longer. 'Just take us there.' he snapped. Reeva watched as they filed out of the Tavern. She quietly followed from a safe distance, instinctively sensing there would be trouble.

* * * *

He watched the three figures exit the Tavern, quickly followed by a fourth who slinked silently behind, almost like their protective guardian. They knew she was there though, without turning. He grinned to himself. Sometimes, every so often life just worked out perfectly. The four of them made an odd-looking quartet; a great hulking brute, a blonde Grellon and two very average looking males, one over average height, the other smaller. In another life they would have never crossed paths, living their normal, separate lives. But they had been called to a purpose bigger than themselves. All four were possibilities and it was his job to whittle away the false three until he was left with the Descendent. Two of them were Gifted, of that there was no doubt, he could feel them. Especially when they awakened their powers. Were the other two that far advanced that they could cloak themselves? He didn't think so.

He stood up and stretched out; it felt good. Disguised as a beggar he'd been camped opposite Sarfina's Tavern for the better part of a week in anticipation. His excitement quickly diminished after three days of absolute nothingness. Sure, members of the four had come and gone but not on a contract. He'd yet to see their mettle tested, something he was about to change. He'd followed them, well the ones that ventured out of the Tavern anyway. Tall average seemed a recluse. Hulking brute and small average went out most nights but always came back drunk. He'd followed them the first two nights though it soon became clear that they were only out for some fun. The woman was a mystery, every day she came out and headed in the same direction and every day he tried to follow her only to lose her. He thought she was headed in the general direction of the Citadel but he couldn't be sure.

He'd got up this morning feeling very grotty and irritable and decided that tonight he would do something to change the monotony of the slowly passing days. He went to a nearby Inn and got himself a room. He bathed and changed into considerably cleaner clothes. Feeling human again he laid on a proper bed for the first time in days and immediately fell asleep. He awoke a few hours later refreshed and ready for tonight's entertainment. He set off to Sarfina's Tavern feeling his excitement return, he was finally going to make some progress with the mission. His Brothers would be most pleased, he'd be labelled the hero that brought in the Descendant, which was in its self its own reward. His name would go down in history.

It was still too early to reveal himself to the four, he wanted to leave meeting them face to face as late as possible in case any of them was sensitive to other Gifted. Knowledge of the Gift and Gifted was extremely limited, you couldn't be sure what an unknown Gifted was capable of. It was a far cry from the glory days of the Counsel when knowledge and training were both around in plentiful abundance.

They would bring those days back, him and his Brothers. The Gifted Council would once more be in power, running things, the way it was supposed to be. If he needed anymore validation that his cause was just, it soon became transparent, when he arrived at the Tavern and saw the four potential Descendants heading out together. The Lady smiled upon his mission despite not being the god he served. He waited for them to round a corner, out of sight, then waited a little longer for good measure before heading across the street and into the Tavern.

* * * *

Sarfina clocked the newcomer as soon as he ventured through the door.

Finally!

He'd been loitering around the Tavern for days and she was beginning to wonder if he would ever make his move, it would seem he'd finally plucked up the courage.

Let's see if he was worth the wait...

He was good; but not good enough. He glanced around the Tavern, scoping out entry and exit points and potential trouble causers.

Little late for that. You've come here all alone. Oh dear!

This suggested he was either arrogantly confident in his own abilities or just plain stupid! Both got you quickly killed in the world of the Assassins Guild, a world of harsh realities. Sarf operated one of the best Hands in Tydon, if not the best, yet she always made sure to keep them in check.

Sarfina knew he was an outsider even though he tried to hide it. There was no getting past the scrutiny of her experienced eye. He was a mixed blood, Shulakh and Tydonii with the Shulakh part slightly more dominant. Shulakh and Tydon shared a common ancestry. Lore spoke of two brothers who led their tribe west out of the Kideshi desert in search of more fertile ground. They had big plans for creating a stable community set in one place, an imitation of Mirron. They would no longer aimlessly roam. They would build houses out of new resources, in order to stake their claim permanently on the land. A concept most alien to the former tent dwellers of the Sand Sea. Nobody is quite certain as to why the brothers separated, although most sources speculate to underlying tensions between the siblings, leading to a final altercation, resulting in total separation.

One brother started a settlement that would one day become Tydon, the other Shulakh. They stood in the closest proximity to one another out of all the cities in Bellum. They both shared a history full of ever shifting states of alliances, war and uneasy peace treaties, each city never quite having enough of an advantage to conquer their rival for good. Shared bloodlines combined with captured slaves being integrated within their populations meant they shared very similar appearances, yet the Shulakhii were just that little bit smaller and stockier. His appearance, the way he walked and held himself gave him away.

A Shulakh spy perhaps?

She dismissed the idea straight away, their counterparts in Shulakh would be better trained than this. Sweeps of the room done his gaze finally settled on Sarfina. He strode over to the bar and sat down on the stool opposite her.

'Good evening. You must be the beautiful Sarfina I've heard so much about.'

He flashed her what she assumed he thought was his most charming smile. It came across as slimy. She smiled back regardless, acting like she didn't hear clumsy attempts at flattery a hundred times a night. She found it always helped to flirt with men, the key was to get them thinking about the stiffness in their pants and not what was coming out of their mouths. Physical contact worked best, brushing her bosom against them while squeezing past, touching fingertips when serving them drinks, laying a hand on their forearm whilst laughing at their stupid jokes, they loved it, lapped it up. She almost pitied them with how easy it was.

'-quite famous you know.' He was still speaking. 'Rumours abound about this Tavern and its voluptuous proprietor throughout the city, although they fall short of doing you justice.'

Voluptuous proprietor? Cleary out of practice if you think proprietor is a complimentary word to use after voluptuous. Although, it's more eloquent than the usual "busty maid" I get but I'd have even taken that over proprietor!

'You're too kind.' She replied broadening her smile and leaning down on the bar so he could get a good view of the swell of her breasts yet he didn't so much as glance in their direction.

Interesting.

The other customers sitting near enough to get a good view were all but drooling at the sight.

'There are other rumours too, about, err, other services your Tavern provides.' Those ogling Sarfina's breasts suddenly found better, more interesting things to stare at. It was not a good idea to overhear Guild business.

'Are there now?' Her tone playful yet with a hint of steel.

'Indeed! There are, and I would be very interested in acquiring those services.'

'Straight to the point, aren't we?'

'I find it's the best way to get things done.'

'That's funny seeing as though it's taken you a few days to come in and have this conversation with me.'

Flirting didn't seem to be working but her jibe certainly hit the mark. His face paled, then went bright red as he blushed.

Not as careful as you thought you were.

He recovered quickly, Sarfina gave him that, and chuckled softly to himself.

'Ah you have me. To be expected from a professional such as yourself. In a way it's reassuring, I know I'll be paying for the very best.'

A different tact but flattery none the less

'Speaking of payment…'

* * * *

'You lucky son of a bitch!'

This was aimed at Zel who sat counting his winnings after the latest victims of Around the Table mourned their losses. One gentleman was more upset about it than the rest.

'It ain't luck, it's superior intellect!' Drak replied on Zel's behalf. He stood up to his full height, itching for a fight and oozing violence. The gentleman gulped, took a step back but ploughed on anyway. It's amazing how far a man will go when he feels he has been wronged. The drink he'd steadily been consuming all night helped too, added fuel to the fire.

'I ain't accepting that, he's cheating!'

'How's he cheating?' Drak shot back.

'Cos he has an unfair advantage on us!' Murmurs of agreement greeted this statement from the surrounding losers.

Zel replied whilst counting the coins he'd been putting into stacks of ten, there was at least fifteen stacks already and he'd barely made a dint in the pot. 'It's not my fault you are too stupid to understand basic mathematics and how to apply it to gambling.' Drak and Thran who stood behind Zel readied themselves, no way things were going to end amicably now.

The man's face went purple with rage.

'Not only a cheat, but an arrogant prick!'

'It's not arrogance if it's the truth.' Zel replied matter-of-factly.

'Why don't you apologise or I'll apply my fist to your face.' Later as they trudged back to the Tavern, it was unanimously agreed that given the man's overall intelligence, it was a decent retort. 'Even I can work out that we out number you two to one.'

'Three actually but trust me, the odds are not in your favour.'

'That so?'

'Indeed, it is. I'll let you in a on a little secret too, the chances of you leaving here alive-'

Zel was interrupted mid flow by a growl of rage as the man grabbed his stool and swung it back around his head. When the stool reached its zenith the man inexplicably stopped, the stool slipped from his grasp and clattered on the floor behind him. He eyes widened in shock and fixed themselves to the far corner of the room. He staggered back, fell over the stool, arms flailing before finally landing sprawled out on the floor. It was only then they all noticed the small throwing knife protruding from his throat, it had gone straight through the Adam's apple. Everyone froze. As the dying man struggled to breath, the gurgling of blood created a morbid backdrop as they all turned to look at the far corner, following his last view before death. A blonde woman sat there staring innocently back at them, yet there could be no mistaking the throwing knife had come from her.

The man sitting beside her stared open mouthed in disbelief. He'd been about to take a sip of his ale when a knife suddenly launched like a blur next to him, and had hit that poor soul in the throat. The tankard still held at an angle was now slowly emptying its contents into his lap. He didn't seem to notice. If he had, he would most likely have been grateful as it masked the urine stain that had quickly spread there only moments before. Nobody could move that fast? Surely? A dozen heartbeats went by, still nobody moved.

'Now everyone… let's all just calm down.' Beseeched the barkeep who held up his hands in a placating manner. The peace held a few moments longer: then chaos. Fists, seats, even tables flew everywhere. The barkeep had to duck underneath the bar's relative safety as a tankard whistled past his head. Drak waded straight in, he was in his element. Zel and Thran followed in his wake, taking out the stragglers who'd not been permanently put down. Reeva remained seated, content with watching the spectacle as it played out before her. However, she was forced into action twice when someone ventured too close to her; both taking a throwing knife to the chest for their troubles.

The barkeep was praying fervently to The Lady that his Inn would survive the night. It did, but just barely. One unlucky gambler was tossed straight through the window into the street outside. Drak ripped a section of the bar off and slugged anyone who passed across the face before discarding it to dual wield two stools. Thran slammed another disgruntled participant head first through a door, leaving him crumpled over it like drying clothes. Zel's next opponent lunged at him with a knife, however Zel deftly sidestepped him before grabbing his arm and bringing it down across his knee. The bone snapped, slicing through flesh to protrude at a sickening angle. The sound it made was worse, just like the snapping of a twig. Zel winced. It seemed the whole bar was involved now with only Reeva staying aloof. The brawl spewed out onto the street where men battered each other until the soldiers on guard duty that night finally came to break it up. The trouble causers were nowhere to be found; at some point during the altercation they had slipped surreptitiously through the back unseen with their winnings.

'We seem to get into an awful lot of bar fights.' mused Thran.

'I didn't even start this one!' Drak seemed rather proud about that fact. He clutched the coinage tightly to his chest but he still jingled with every step. Despite him brazenly showing off a fair sum of money nobody seemed inclined to try take it from him. They'd ducked and weaved through back streets until they were clear of the ruckus. They now walked calmly back to the Tavern acting like they hadn't just beaten up a bar full of people.

'On average once every four days. That's not including the ones we start or get into for work purposes though.' Of course Zel kept track, just another tally among thousands of others that kept whirring along at the back of his brain.

'Is that high?' asked Thran.

'For normal people, yeah that's pretty high.'

Thran seemed quite perturbed by this so Reeva gave Zel a nudge.

'Well,' he added hastily clasping Thran on the shoulder. 'To say we kill people for money, I'd say it's not too bad.' Another jab in the ribs from Reeva. 'In fact, on average, it's less than your standard bar crawler.'

Thran seemed to accept this but a certain man mountain with a confused frown on his face leant in close to Zel's ear and whispered, 'Is that really true?'

'Don't be daft, of course not, it's nonsense I just made up. When you're as smart as I am-' (he held up a knowing, wagging finger) '-people just tend to accept whatever you say as truth and agree with you.'

'Huh...' Drak chewed on that for a few seconds. 'I guess you're right.'

They continued on in silence for the rest of the way back, filed into the Tavern one by one, heads down, unwilling to make eye contact with Sarfina who stood, hands on hips, glaring at them from behind the bar. They shuffled up and took four stools at the bar opposite her. Drak dumped the winnings down on the counter top where they scattered and spun all over the place. Sarfina waited, making them squirm, till the last coin had stopped rolling and spinning along the wooden surface. If any of them had been paying attention, they would have seen all the coins had landed on the same side showing the face of the Emperor, except for one. The odd one out instead showed the smirking visage of The Lady. Even Zel would not have been able to calculate the odds of that happening.

'Well?' Sarfina demanded.

'We're sorry.' The lads mumbled their apology all together whilst still not making eye contact. Reeva nodded in agreement.

'At least our winnings should pay for all the damages.' Drak added lamely.

'*My* winnings. Although I guess that's a moot point at this moment in time.' Zel hastened to add when he saw the look on Sarfina's face. She let them stew a moment longer.

'Well I hope you've enjoyed yourselves tonight because tomorrow we have proper work to do.' Heads lifted in interest. 'That's right, good news. I've secured us a contract.' Pleased grins spread along their collective faces, they finally had a new contract! 'Those smiles are a little premature, I haven't explained what you have to do yet and it's, ah, well… a little different shall we say.'

Under normal circumstances Sarfina would have never accepted the contract, but almost three weeks idle wasn't normal circumstances and tonight showed her just how badly the Hand needed one. Still, she didn't trust the man who'd hired them. There was something odd about him, she just couldn't put a finger on what exactly. And he was definitely hiding something too, she was certain of that. Certain too, that the storm had finally arrived.

Chapter 5

Drak woke up with an excruciatingly painful headache to find himself naked and tied down by his wrists and ankles. Not circumstances to be unduly worried by as he'd found, and would find himself in similar situations again. The problem was he didn't remember drinking last night. In fact, he didn't remember much at all. Usually he at least remembered getting to the point of no return, when his legs struggled to hold him up, and the room swam in and out of focus. After that point his memory got a little hazy, but never before. He couldn't have been drinking last night but his head suggested otherwise.

Sweet Jagreus give me strength!

'Don't worry, the pain will ease soon.'

Drak's eyes fully opened for the first time and he took in his surroundings. The room was small and sparsely furnished with two things; the straw mattress he was tied down on and a stool by its side which was occupied by the man who'd spoken. A solitary small window afforded him enough light to spot his clothes and belongings in a pile by the door. They were near the docks, Drak could gather that much, there was no mistaking the extra salt in the air mixed with the sickly sweet smell of decay, a smell to which he was very much accustomed to. He couldn't hear the distinct swell of the tide however which meant they were still a distance from the sea.

The man was correct, the pain was easing, but it was still distracting as he tried to collect his thoughts. He had a rough idea of where he might be but that still left many unanswered questions. Drak wasn't sure quite how to play the situation, he'd only been held captive once before but not alone. He'd had others to find solace in, help ease the burden. The man waited in patient calmness, he was letting Drak come to his senses. He used this opportunity to openly examine the man who returned his gaze steadily. He seemed familiar, yet Drak was sure they had never met. Then as the pain finally lifted it came to him, he looked exactly as Sarfina had described him from two nights ago when he'd first walked into the bar. He was their current employer, and the son of a bitch had laid a trap for them. Drak knew exactly how he was going to play this.

'You jealous? Why don't you commission a painting, it'll last longer.' he growled.

The man looked at him with distaste.

'There's no need to be so uncouth. I apologise for your state of undress but it was necessary.'

'It usually is for sodomy.'

'I have not inappropriately touched you, nor will I. I was simply looking for something.'

Drak shrugged, or attempted to given his restraints. 'However you want to justify stripping another man naked and tying him down while he's unconscious. I mean, I once asked this particularly limber whore to-'

'If you must know,' the man snapped, cutting Drak off mid-sentence. 'I was searching for a certain mark. And while you have plenty of interesting scars upon your back, none of them match the one I was looking for. Which brings us here. I will ask you some questions, and you will oblige me with an answer.'

Got under that calm exterior pretty quickly didn't I.
'Will I now?'

'Yes you will. You seem the type of guy who could handle torture, mayhap you've seen your fair share before. But your friends, will they hold up so well? I have no wish to inflict unspeakable horrors on them, but I will. I will do whatever it requires, do you understand?'

Drak nodded, he believed him. The man spoke calmly but with plenty of steel. He wasn't physically intimidating but he had an aura of confidence about him. What he sought was worth killing over and he was prepared to do it for this "mark". Drak concluded this man was extremely dangerous.

Why's this mark so important? Can't be money, a tattoo ain't worth shit. Just what does it signify? It was times like this Drak wish he had Zel's mind.

'Are you Gifted?'

Gifted. The word made his hairs stand on end. He'd met a couple of Gifted before, briefly back in his sea faring days, but long enough to know they were trouble. He groaned inwardly, this made the situation a whole lot worse, not to mention complicated.

'My Ma used to tell everybody I was her special little boy.'

'Stop trying my patience.' barked the stranger.

The man was at his limit, push him any further and he might just start cutting.

Can't be putting on the fool façade no longer.

'What god do you serve?'

The man half smiled. 'So you finally reveal your true nature, sharper than this lummox you purport to be.'

'Sollun? Naul? Reth?'

'I serve no *god*.' He spat the last word out with contempt. 'Now answer my question.'

'I ain't Gifted and glad about it too. Don't want nothing to do with it.'

They stared silently at each other as the man weighed Drak's words. Eventually he nodded to himself. 'I suspected as much. Thank you for your time.'

The man stood up, picked up his stool and walked over to the door, opened it a fraction then turned back to Drak. 'Now be a good little boy and lay there until I get back and no harm

will come to you or your friends. I will set you free once I have my answers.' Then he slipped through the door closing it firmly behind him. Drak was alone with his thoughts in the cramped little room.
    If we have to face off with Gifted, well, we're well and truly fucked!

* * * *

Zel awoke to find himself in the exact same situation as Drak; naked and tied down. His mind had been whirring through possibilities and solutions for two hundred and ninety six seconds when a man carrying a stool entered.
    'Please, take a seat.' Zel motioned to his left as best he could. The man set the stool down where he'd motioned and settled on it, clasped his hands together and leant forward.
    'Is being clever something your group specialises in?' he sighed.
    'You do me a disservice. Unlike my colleague I wasn't being facetious. There's no reason why we can't be civilised now is there?'
    The man regarded Zel with guarded eyes. Zel extended his hand as best he could to offer a handshake.
    'I'm Zelonius, Zel to my friends.'
    The man made no attempted to take his hand but acknowledged it with a small nod.
    'Herrick.'
    'So Herrick, mind elaborating on my current circumstances?'
    Herrick leant in closer and spoke in a low, almost confidential tone.
    'Tell me true, are you Gifted?'
    Zel couldn't contain his laughter, it burst from him and echoed through the room. Herrick looked disappointed.

'I'm sorry but you don't seriously believe those old wives tales? All that nonsense about The Grand Council, Gods who grant power through patronage. The Gifted. Are you one of those Temple Cultists?'

'I pity you. Your mind is sharp, but you are blind to much.'

'Definitely a Temple Cultist coming out with that philosophical, pretentious horseshit.'

'To think this conversation started with so much promise.'

'Twas not me who brought it to ruination.'

'I look forward to shattering your beliefs and seeing your world crumble. Unfortunately such pleasures will have to wait.' He stood up taking stool in hand. 'Next time we meet, I don't think you will hold me in such contempt.'

Herrick spoke with utter conviction, as only someone who wholly believes what he speaks is the truth can. Zel would have done well to heed the warning but he had already retreated inside his furiously working mind before the door closed behind his captor.

* * * *

Herrick was excited. This was where the real fun began. He'd been pretty certain those two hadn't been Gifted and the conversations he'd just held with them confirmed those suspicions. Talented yes, but not Gifted. Perhaps they could still be put to work towards the cause: one was incredibly strong, the other incredibly smart, but for now though he put them from mind and concentrated on the next two prisoners. Both were Gifted, he could feel it, sense it. It was more than just intuition, whenever he was around other Gifted he just knew. His Brothers and Sisters didn't have this sense, which is why he'd been chosen for this most important mission, why it could only be him and no one else. The "Quest for the Descendant" as he liked to call it, and his quest was nearing completion. The Descendant was waiting for him to step through the door and deliver his destiny, but first the other remaining Hand member.

He knew he was stalling, building up enough confidence to talk to the one who'd been his reason to live for so long. He'd worked on what to say, how to deliver his grand speech and inspire the Descendant to his purpose, but now the time had come, it had all slipped from mind, every last word.

Herrick had fallen into the age old trap of romanticising his objective. He held the idea of the Descendant in such high regard that he couldn't possibly live up to his expectations. He'd always pictured a tall, well-built man with an imposing aura who could make you quiver at the knees just by casting his piercing eyes upon you. A handsome hero the bards always sung about in their epic ballads, slaying endless foes and marrying fair maidens. Not a small plain looking assassin who'd likely hadn't set food outside Tydon. Herrick had taken this in his stride though, you didn't have to be tall and handsome to wield tremendous power. He was no muscular brute himself, yet he could wield the Gift in force. He smiled.

The Gift: the intellectual's way of levelling the playing field. Now focus your mind on the next task at hand... her.

The one he'd attempted to follow but always lost, she was a mystery indeed. He looked forward to speaking with her, unravelling some of those mysteries. He would approach her carefully for she was the most dangerous of the four, of that he was certain. When he'd stripped and disarmed her the amount of weapons she had secreted away had been staggering. Enough to equip a small garrison! Each weapon was very well maintained, oiled and razor sharp. Any one of them would cut through flesh as easily if it were butter. He shuddered at the very thought.

Approach her with caution. She's dangerous and surely has the Gift.
He kept repeating it to himself as he approached the next small room containing her. *Approach her with caution.*
He reached the door.
She's dangerous and Gifted.
He opened the door.
Approach with caution.
He edged through into the room.
She's d- gone! She's gone!
The room was empty, no one tied down on a straw mattress, no pile of clothes in the corner, no stack of weapons next to it. He let out a steam of curses, most of them directed at himself. How could he have been so stupid!?! Leaving an unknown Gifted to her own devices for that long, he was asking for trouble. He'd been so focused on the Descendant he'd not been thinking clearly. There was no telling how much time he had, she may already be waiting in ambush or have freed the others. He turned and made haste to the last room.

* * * *

Drak strained against his bonds, using every sinew of muscle in vain attempts to work loose the knots of rope that held him. His wrists and ankles were red raw from all the friction but he carried on. He needed to free himself before that odd man came back and the situation really became dire. He grunted in exertion as he tried one final heave but he was bound too tightly. Drak's chest heaved as he lay panting, regaining his strength. He was so focused on escaping that he hadn't noticed the figure leaning against the far wall just next to the door, watching his mighty struggle. With a start Drak caught the person now, how had they gotten in? He hadn't seen or heard the door open. The figure held a dagger in their hand and looked ready to use it. Their eyes met. Drak tensed. The dagger twirled. Finally he broke out into a grin.

'Took ya bloody long enough!'

Of course, Reeva didn't reply. She just remained casually leaning against the wall, a ghost of a smile playing across her lips as she eyed Drak up and down in all his glory. He was, after all, a fine specimen of mankind. His grin broadened.

'As impressive as I am lass, we've got more important things to be doing so cut me loose already.'

The smile vanished, she was once again all business. It scared Drak how quickly Reeva's demeanour could change in the space of a heartbeat. He knew they were yet to get beneath the mask she constantly wore but they were wearing it down. It was cracking, slowly but surely. She'd been a true stoic when she was first inducted into the Hand. Though over time, little by little she had opened up to them so now they were able to distinguish between what amused her and what she found displeasing. They had gotten used to reading the subtle shifts in her facial expressions that spoke volumes. In the end she'd fit right in with the rest of their ragtag group and they'd come to trust her completely, despite knowing very little about her. They had all shared snippets about their pasts with each other but not in great detail. It was best not to pry, they all kept their own secrets, and that suited everyone just fine. Some things were better off not being dredged up. He thought about the scars on his back.

My past is a little harder to hide than most.

She walked over, the dagger flashed and in a matter of seconds Drak was free and stretching off. He winced as once more blood started circulating to his hands and feet. He quickly tugged on his clothes and boots. While Drak was making himself decent Reeva had sidled up to the door and had opened it ever so slightly so she could peer through the crack. It seemed clear. Drak joined her at the door. They looked at each other, nodded in unison and went through.

* * * *

Herrick composed himself before opening the door, he let out a huge sigh of relief as the Descendant was still inside, safely bound. Unlike the others Thran had only been stripped to his waist. Herrick had found the mark on his back almost instantly so there'd been no need to go any further. He'd discarded the stool in his rush to get here, so now, instead of sitting he stood awkwardly gazing upon Thran with a nervous smile. Thran returned his scrutiny with open hostility, he was seething, more at himself and the others for being duped so easily and getting caught whilst carrying out their sole contract for weeks. Now this smarmy, sweating man stood over him looking at him with a fervent look in his eyes. It made him uneasy, the gods only knew what this man wanted with them, but it wouldn't be anything good. The man opened his mouth to speak, but hesitated. Then after what seemed like an age, as if he needed to pluck up enough courage, he spoke.

'It's an honour and a pleasure to finally meet you…' He hesitated again, before adding. 'Descendant.'

Descendant?

'I apologise for having to restrain you like this, it was an unfortunate necessity as I couldn't be sure how you would react-'

'You hired the Guild for a contract, then ambushed us as we went about your business, all because you weren't sure how I would *react!?!*' He uttered the last word with such scorn the man seemed to shrink into himself. He had to forcibly rally himself.

'This isn't going how I would have hoped. I'm sorry but time is short and what I have to say is urgent.'

Thran realised he'd somehow managed to get the upper hand so far and decided to press his advantage.

'Your time is short alright. You've crossed the Guild of Assassins. You're a dead man.'

'Death does not scare me.'

'We'll see if you feel the same when you have a knife stuck in your gut, mewling like a baby as your life slips away through your fingertips.'

Herrick was floundering, he knew time was of the essence, the Assassin's companions could arrive to rescue him at any moment. So in desperation he blurted out:

'I know about your powers!' he was encouraged by Thran's shocked silence, so he ploughed on hurriedly, lest he be interrupted and side tracked again. 'I myself am Gifted. My powers are different but they are nothing compared to yours. You have inherited our Lords unique power that holds the key to his revival. *Blood Magic.*' He spoke the words with such reverence it sent a chill down Thran's spine. 'You've already met him, my Lord that is. Well not physically, but in your dreams you've met him.'

Now Thran was really shaken. 'How do you know about my dreams?' He asked in a quiet voice. Their roles had been reversed and now it was Thran who was suddenly unsure of himself.

'Don't worry.' Herrick replied sympathetically. 'We all had them to begin with.'

'Who are you?'

'My name is Herrick, and I'm a member of a secret Gifted group called the Small Council. Our mission is to revive the real Grand Council and restore them to the power that they once ruled with. Please do not get us confused with the Cults from the Temples, we have uncovered truths and reached a state of enlightenment that they could only dream of.'

'What does this all have to do with me?'

'As I said, you have powers we are incapable of.'

'But I can barely use it, let alone control it.' Thran replied weakly.

'Fear not, my Brothers and Sisters and I will help train you. We all struggled to begin with. It's your destiny, what you were born to do, Descendant.'

'Thran, my name is Thran.'

Herrick tensed and cocked his head. He stayed like this for a few seconds before frowning.

'Your friends are on their way. I would have liked to have longer to talk with you. I fear instead of making things clearer, I have just muddied the waters.'

He walked over to Thran, cut his ropes and handed over his clothes. Thran sat up but made no effort to stand or put on his shirt.

'Please Descendant, you must come with me.' Herrick beseeched, tugging at Thran's arm.

Thran shrugged him off. 'I can't.' he replied distractedly.

'Please, you must, you must!'

'I can't and I won't!' Thran responded more forcefully.

Herrick could see he wasn't going to win this particular fight so tried another tack instead.

'Then please use your powers tonight and speak to our Lord. He will explain everything, it will all become clear.' Thran still seemed unresponsive, so Herrick pressed him again and again until he capitulated.

'Okay, okay I'll speak to him.'

It was as though a great weight had been lifted from Herrick's shoulders and he beamed at Thran. 'Wonderful.'

'Just who is this Lord of yours?'

'He has gone by many names over the years but this generation knows him as Carrion – the god of Death.'

Thran gulped. 'You… you serve the god of Death.'

Herrick laughed. 'Don't worry, he's not as bad as the name implies. Besides,' he added cryptically. 'He's no god.'

Herrick went over to the door, placed an ear to it and listened.

'Thran, I must go now, but do not worry I shall visit you again after you have spoken to Carrion.'

Without another word he was gone, leaving Thran in a dazed state, trying to process all that had been divulged. It just didn't seem real, couldn't be real. He'd always wondered where his powers had come from, but it just sounded so absurd. Inherited from the god of Death who wasn't a god that was supposedly unique and all powerful. He didn't know what to think: how to feel. He placed his index finger on the stone floor and began to trace little patterns. He could feel the rough grooves and contours of the stone and they helped to sooth him, ground him in reality. And that's how Drak, Reeva and Zel found him. Sitting half naked tracing patterns in the ground with his finger, a perturbed frown on his brow.

Chapter 6

As Captain of the Guard, Zakanos rarely had time to himself, a time where he could unwind and relax, not worry about his responsibilities. Tonight was one of those nights, and he was determined to make the most of it. He'd spent the morning standing watch with his men before leading them through numerous exercise drills on the parade ground in the afternoon. He was of the opinion that a leader of men should be able and willing to go through the trials and tribulations he put his men through. Needless to say it was not a popular opinion shared amongst his peers. He would lead from the front, as all good Captains should.

A good Captain pulls his men from the front, not pushes them from the back.

This was his mantra, one that he made sure to remind himself of every day. So he finished the afternoon's exertions lathered in sweat, just like all of his men.

He was fiercely proud of his Company. Despite being the youngest ever Captain of the Guard at the age of thirty-two, Zakanos knew he was more than capable of doing the job and was determined to show everyone that he could. His first challenge had been winning over his men, many of them veterans older than himself. Admission into the Guard required years of service in the regular Companies, or an outstanding feat of bravery in battle. That was how it was supposed to be, however more recently under his predecessors, commissions into the Guard had been bought, bribed or leveraged.

My promotion may have come through unscrupulous means, but I earned this post. I will make the Guard what it once was, the pride of Tydon!

Ever since his promotion Zak had worked his men hard, and himself even harder. He knew every single name of the soldiers under his command. He knew their likes, dislikes and temperaments. Gradually and begrudgingly, he'd won their respect, and then their hearts. He knew they would follow his orders implicitly and hold their nerve in battle. Over the last two years he'd shaped his Company into one of the best Tydon had to offer. His was a rising star, and he knew it would continue to rise, as long as he didn't upset the wrong apple carts. In a few years he might be in a position to make a real difference. Clear out the lazy, corrupt, incompetent officers and replace them with quality, dedicated ones. He knew Tydon edged closer and closer to war and it scared Zakanos how unprepared his city was for the coming hardships.

He quickly washed before returning to work, he would spend the next couple of hours filling out and then filing paperwork. He always made sure to keep up with the more mundane tasks of running his Company. Finally the evening bell sounded six times; that was his cue to start his drinking. He didn't bother to change, instead just headed straight out of the barracks and into The Haven, a local watering hole popular amongst garrison soldiers. He sat on an empty stool at the bar and ordered an ale, nodding greetings to the soldiers around the room he recognised, a couple of them his own men. He took a long sip of his drink when it arrived and smacked his lips in appreciation. He nursed the drink for the better part of twenty minutes, just savouring the taste, listening to the conversations around him and occasionally offering a comment. He finally drained the tankard, deliberating whether he should order another, before deciding that he would. It wasn't even the seventh bell yet, he had plenty of time before he was expected home. It was one of the perks of his Captaincy, being able to officially take a wife and have his own home. Zakanos loved his wife and young son dearly, but he needed his own personal time and sitting at the bar, drinking ale, helped him unwind.

He was halfway through his second ale when he heard whistles and catcalls sound from all around the room. He didn't bother turning around, anyone who entered got the same treatment, male and female alike. He still didn't turn around when he noticed the woman halt in his peripheral vision, he just wanted to be left in peace to drink for a couple of hours.

Apparently it's too much to ask for.

'Excuse me Captain.' A feminine voiced asked him rather demurely. 'Please may I sit on the stool next to you?'

Only then did Zakanos turn around to see who addressed him. The blood drained from his face leaving it as pale as milk. He asked in a meek voice:

'W-w-what do you want?'

'Now, now Captain.' Sarfina replied in mock indignation as she sat next to him, crossing her legs. 'That's no way to talk to a lady.'

* * * *

'Are you alright lad?' asked Drak with genuine concern.

'Yeah I'm fine, don't worry.' Thran mumbled back, convincing no one.

They stood in a warehouse that was half stocked with crates waiting to be taken down to the docks, loaded onto ships and sent overseas to destinations far and wide. The last third had been converted into separate rooms where the crew could house themselves till the next voyage. It was in these rooms Sarfina's Hand had been tied down.

'It's just that you've barely spoken a word since we found you shirtless staring off into space.'

'Seriously, I'm fine.'

'Given that it was his first time being ambushed and held captive, his reaction is understandable.' Zel offered,

'See.' Thran attempted a reassuring smile.

'In fact I'd say he's taking it quite well all things considered.' Zel continued. 'Now, let's make some sense of this mess.'

Drak's and Zel's stories were almost identical. The last thing they remembered was entering the premises of their target only to wake up naked and tied down. Herrick had come in and questioned them about being Gifted before Reeva had freed them. When Zel was happy with Drak's version of events he turned to Thran.

'Did he ask if you were Gifted too?'

'No.' He spoke too quickly, a little too sharply, incurring a sceptical look from Zel. 'He didn't get the chance. Introduced himself but then Reeva must've got free cos he left in a hurry.'

'How did you get free?'

'What?'

'How. Did you. Get free?' Zel made sure to slowly pronounce every single syllable. 'It's a relatively straightforward question.'

'I broke free.'

'You broke free?'

'Yeah, I broke free. So what?'

'Drak struggled against his bonds in vain while you miraculously break free. With consummate ease apparently seeing as there are no friction marks on your wrists or ankles.'

'Well maybe mine were looser.'

'How convenient.'

Reeva stood up from the crate she'd been sitting on and headed towards the entrance. Clearly she'd had enough. Drak followed. Thran made to but was stopped by a firm hand on his chest.

'You need to sort yourself out. Lying to the group accomplishes nothing, just isolates you from us. She'll give us the tongue lashing we deserve then ask the same questions. I suggest you tell her the truth. For everyone's sake. With what's to come, we can't afford to be divided.'

Thran nodded and Zel let him go. Despite having the worst social skills of anyone he'd ever met, Thran had to admit that sometimes he could be eerily insightful. They joined the other two at the entrance and cautiously made their way outside even though it was unlikely Herrick was still around. They emerged between two warehouses to find themselves a long bow shot from the docks. There was little activity around them which spared any unwanted attention and questions. Thran judged it to be around the eleventh bell, which meant they'd been unconscious for a worrying amount of time. He fell in behind the others as they trudged back to the Tavern in silence. He wasn't quite sure why he'd lied to Zel and not mentioned all this Descendant business. A calculated deceit? No, more like instinct, a sudden impulse. Zel was right about one thing, Thran needed to organise his thoughts and sort himself out.

* * * *

Everyone in The Haven was jealous of Zakanos as he led Sarfina to a booth where they could talk more privately. He wasn't surprised, even with no cleavage on show and a full length skirt which covered her long legs, she was strikingly beautiful. She could have easily been mistaken for a Nymph the bards sing tales of. Perhaps from the woodlands, a fair creature who lives at the heart of a great forest, bewitching and ensnaring men who wandered too close: doomed to live the rest of their life in servitude to the Nymph's desires. Zakanos knew better. He knew under that pretty face lived a demon. A demon from his past come to torment him again.

Not too long ago she had tried to use her Nymph like charms and seduce him. When Zakanos had shown no inclination towards her she'd quickly switched tack, instead tapping into his ambition. Despite all the deal had brought him, Zak wondered if he would now regret making it. At the time he'd believed the ends justified the means. How could he have been so stupid? They'd left him alone since that night and part of him hoped they had just forgotten him and he'd be allowed to get on with his life. The bigger part knew the truth though, and now he was about to lie down in the bed his past-self had made. He hated cliché expressions but for once they adequately summed up his position.

I finally understand what blind ambition means, he thought wryly

Neither had spoken since they'd sat down. Zakanos glared at her with open hostility. Sarfina met his stare, unflustered. Finally she decided to break the silence.

'How's your wife and baby boy? Both healthy I trust.'

She doesn't even treat me with dignity. Straight to the barely veiled threats.

It galled him that his only fault, his only weakness, was loving his wife and child. *This time I can't be bought, but I can be coerced. Shit this beds' uncomfortable.*

'Are you forgetting I'm Captain of the Guard now? I could have you thrown in a prison cell so small you barley fit inside. You'd never see the light of day again. You'd be fed enough to keep you alive but pretty quickly you'd see that body wither away to nothing, just skin and bone. I'll burn your precious Tavern to the ground, with your Hand inside. But don't worry, there will be room inside your cell for their ashes!'

'I suggest, *Captain*, that you lower your voice. Lest we draw unwanted attention.'

'I suggest that you crawl back into whatever refuse pit you emerged from.'

'Finished?'

'Fuck you!'

'Need *I*, remind *you,* how you acquired your title?

'Of course not.'

'I think I do.'

'Don't patronise me.'

'Then stop acting like a petulant child. Treat me with just a little decorum. You may despise me, my Guild, and what we do, you may look down on us yet you willingly struck a deal to further your own ambitions. I'm sure you found a way to justify your actions so you could live with yourself, sleep at night. I don't care. The truth is you're no better than us, if not worse. You threw aside your beliefs, your ideals for the chance of a promotion. I think that's quite telling about the kind of man you are. You were contaminated with the stink of the refuse pit long before you shook hands with the creatures it spat out. Shall I continue?'

'Our dealings together are concluded.'

'Spare me, you're smarter than that. It's one of the reasons you make such a good Captain of the Guard.'

Zakanos sighed and brought his hands up to his face and used his thumbs to rub his temples. He could feel a headache brewing. He knew Sarfina was right but, damn, it had felt good to vent all his anger and frustration. Zak wasn't about to see his star crash and burn over this so for now he'd play their game, but as soon as he could he'd turn the tables.

Another damned cliché.

'What would you have me do?'

For the first time since they'd sat down at the booth Sarfina smiled. There was no humour or warmth in it, only cold satisfaction.

* * * *

When the Hand arrived back at the Tavern they found Sarfina absent. "Out on business" was the curt reply they received from the stressed man tending the bar in her absence. So they headed to their usual table at the back of the room and waited. They sat in silence, each member lost in their own thoughts, thinking of different ways Sarfina would punish them: each more harsh and creative than the last. Drak didn't even bother to go get a drink. Half a bell stretched by, then a full one before finally Sarfina entered the bar. She looked straight at them, letting her gaze linger on each one of them for a moment then she was gone, through the kitchen and upstairs. Her face had been unreadable.

'Well, let's get this over with.' said Drak with all the enthusiasm someone resigned to their fate could muster.

They followed her up the stairs, past their living quarters and into the room at the far end of the corridor, their operations room. A large table with the main streets and quarters of Tydon carved into it dominated the centre of the room. Sarfina was leant over it, knuckles white, pressed down into the wood.

'Zel. Tell me what happened tonight. Be thorough.'

Zel cleared his throat and began. He left out no detail. At the end of his recounting he had the good sense to look sheepish

'Look, Sarf-'

'I'm sorry.' This stunned them more than any tongue lashing. Had Sarfina really just apologised!? 'I should have properly vetted the client before accepting the contract. Circumstances were dire but that is no excuse. I will deal with the consequences from Skrenn and the Faceless Man. Having said that, I'm extremely disappointed in all of you. How could you let one man get the better of all four of you? That is unacceptable. Far below the high standards this Hand has set for itself. Drak, Thran, I want your versions of tonight's event.'

So they each recounted their own version of events, except Reeva of course, who just nodded at parts relevant for her. Despite Zel's advice, Thran stuck to his altered version. Sarfina didn't say a word, saving all her questions for the end. She didn't have many and Thran was relieved when none of them were directed at him.

'You still have not explained how he came to capture four well trained assassins.'

'The truth is Sarf, I don't know. I have not figured it out yet, but I will. One minute we were about to kill, the next we're waking up prisoners.' Answered Zel. This clearly bothered him and Drak the most, but Thran knew it was to do with Herrick's Gift.

'And what do you make of all this Gifted talk?'

'It's a load of horseshit! This Herrick fellow is quite clearly deranged, indoctrinated by those fools in the temples and by old bard tales. Absolute nonsense!'

'Okay Zel, I think we get the point.' She addressed the whole group. 'I have already set plans in motion for Herricks capture, by dusk tomorrow we shall have him hung upside down by his ankles, his skin being flayed piece by piece.'

'Zakanos.' said Zel. It was more of a statement than a question.

'Yes. I met with him after you'd not returned on time.'

'The right choice.'

'I know. Zel stay, the rest of you leave. Eat, sleep. Make sure you are well rested for tomorrow.'

* * * *

'Pleeeease, please don't do this.' The man whined desperately. 'Please I beg you!'

'Quit your pathetic snivelling!'

He pressed the knife harder against his latest victim's throat so that it cut him slightly and a little droplet of blood trickled down from his neck. The man was determined to keep his mouth shut but couldn't help letting out little whimpers.

'The only way you get out of this alive and in one piece is by answering the questions to my satisfaction. Do you understand?'

'Y-y-yes.'

'Good. All you have to do is give me names. That's it.'

'I don't know any-'

The knife pressed harder, the trickle became a stream. The man squealed.

'You're going to give me those names. Right. Now.'

'Okay okay okay, the guy I report to, don't know his name, it's the truth I swear, but I can tell you his whereabouts, and what he looks like.'

He screamed as the knife plunged into his shoulder, breaking his collarbone. A hand clamped his mouth shut, muffling his cries of pain. His whole body was shuddering as tears streamed down his face. When he finally calmed a little the hand released its grip.

'Please, please stop.' He pleaded, his hoarse voice barely audible.

'Then give me what I want.'

Three fingers and an ear later, he did. He finally gave up names, places, anything the man with the knife wanted, only to be rewarded by having his throat cut. The killer let the blood spurt all over him like a fountain spraying cool water on a warm summer's day. He licked his cheek to taste the salty metallic goodness, and then cleaned his weapon on the dead man's clothes, that is the parts that weren't already soaked in blood. He left the body where it lay, in a dark alley where it would no doubt be found come daylight. He whistled a lively tune as he walked away. He was happy; his employers would be happy.

For he was almost at the top of the food chain.

Chapter 7

Thran stood silently outside her door. He'd been there for half a bell. It was very late, or rather, very early but he had barely slept. The couple of hours he'd managed to get had been fitful and he'd woken up wearier than before, so he'd come to Reeva's room seeking his usual comfort. Yet he could not bring himself to enter, so he just stood there in indecision. Time made up his mind; everyone would be up soon so he retreated back into his room and slumped onto his bed. He closed his eyes but sleep still eluded him; he lay like a star just staring at the ceiling. After what seemed like an eternity he heard the others get up, one by one and go about their morning routines. He wanted to join them, yet he couldn't bring himself to get up. He wasn't just physically tired, but mentally exhausted as well. He lay there for a while longer until, with great effort, he willed himself into a sitting position before finally standing. Splashing water on his face from the wooden basin next to his bed did little to help liven his mood.

    When he finally made it downstairs he slumped into the chair opposite Drak who was shovelling bread and stew into his mouth with gusto.

    'Smells good.'

    'It is. Grab yourself a bowl lad, plenty left in the kitchen. It'll do you good, you look like shit.'

    'Thanks.'

    The stew didn't taste particularly great but it was wet and warm and after a few mouthfuls Thran did start to feel a little better. He mopped the last few morsels with a bit of bread and popped it into his mouth.

    'You were right, it did me good.' He concluded.

Drak didn't answer right away; he was far too busy lifting his bowl to his lips, slurping down his third helping. After wiping away the overspill with his forearm, he looked at Thran with a grin and said:

'You look better. Almost alive.'

'You're always smiling Drak, no matter what happens, whatever comes your way; you greet it with a smile.'

'You make it sound like a bad thing.'

'It's not. It's something about you I admire, but...'

'But what?'

'How do you do it? How can you stay so happy?'

'I dunno really.' The big man leant back in his chair and folded his arms. 'I just don't let stuff get to me and I don't over think things.'

'How can you not over think things?'

Drak just shrugged.

'Well that doesn't really help me does it?'

'Okay then lad.' Drak leant forward onto the table, Thran leaned towards him giving them the appearance of two plotting conspirators.

'Before the Guild, I was Captain of a ship, well a couple of ships actually. I had wealth, respect and brilliant crews to command.'

'Wait, you were a commissioned officer in Tydon's navy?'

'No lad, don't be daft. I was a bloody pirate.'

Thran laughed. 'I was about to say, can't see you addressing anyone as sir.'

'Like most pirates, Drethelstan was our base of operations. A man can go from rags to riches and back again in a matter of days in that cesspool.' Drak spoke with a fondness only nostalgia could bring. 'I was small time for quite a long time, but all it took was one big haul, a merchant ship full of spices bound for one of the great cities no doubt and suddenly I had men flocking to join the crew. They wanna get in while the getting's good ya see, they can smell the loot. Pretty soon I was commanding two big ships, each with a full complement of crew. I was becoming a big influence on the island, getting tribune from smaller Captains who wanted to keep me on their good side. Everyone wanted my approval and thoughts on ventures. But with power comes problems, I had to keep my men fed, busy and drowning in bounty. I had the upkeep of two ships to think about. But I managed, and managed well.' Drak paused, his eyes staring into the distance as though we could stare directly into the past.

'But?' Thran prompted.

Drak's eyes focused back on Thran. His smile now rueful, voice barely above a whisper. 'But I still lost it all.'

'How?' Thran found himself whispering too.

'Because power also attracts rivals. Because with men it all comes down to dick size, if we believe someone else's is bigger, then they gotta go.'

'Crudely put, but I take your point. We're egotistical buggers.'

'Me and Ratham practical-'

'Wait, Ratham as in-'

'Yes, that Ratham. As I was saying, we practically ran the island fifty-fifty but he wasn't happy with that. He wanted it all. Ratham's cunning as a snake and just as deadly. He started bribing men, spreading rumours and turning men against me, whittling down my support. I could see it happening right before my eyes yet I did nothing, because I was indecisive. If I confronted Ratham it would lead to a fight that would mean high casualties and I was uncertain of victory. It wasn't cowardice, why I didn't go down that road, I cared for my men. I didn't want to see them needlessly endangered so I tried to think of a better solution. One that wouldn't end in bloodshed.

All the while I was losing ground to Ratham until he was in a position to move against me outright. So I surrendered.'

'You just surrendered!? For Saul's sake Drak, why?'

'My indecision had already cost me, I wasn't about to let it cost my men their lives. I'd spent an entire week fixating on the problem, and that was the root of it, I couldn't see past the problem and find a solution. I was over thinking things, I'd trapped myself in a sorta, mind prison of my own making instead of trusting my gut which had gotten me so far. I let myself be overwhelmed. I wasn't fit to lead those men anymore, so I surrendered. Ratham claimed everything and sold me into slavery. The Lady surely favoured me from then on otherwise I wouldn't be sitting here, alive and healthy.'

'That was... surprisingly insightful.'

'When a man is sold into slavery, all he does is fixate on how he got there. But now I'm free, and I've decided to just trust my gut, and do what makes me happy. Why waste your life worrying about what will or won't be when tomorrow you could be dead and tonight you could be out enjoying yourself.'

That's all well and good but you don't have strange abilities, you don't have strange dreams and a madman who serves the god of Death taking an interest in those abilities.

'Don't you want to go back and get revenge on Ratham?'

'Of course! To begin with anyway. That hatred and need for revenge kept me going for a long time while I was shackled to other men rowing for my life. But now? Where would that get me? I'd end up dead most likely. That hatred sat in my gut for a long time, poisoning me from the inside, turning me bitter. Besides he's turned that pirate port into a real force to be reckoned with and proclaimed himself King of the island. I couldn't have done that. I still dislike that conniving weasel, but by the gods, I can't help but admire what he's done. Besides, I have a life here, without the responsibilities, without the pressure but with plenty of rewards. Look, the point of me telling my life's tale, is, I guess, trust your gut even if you must over think things.'

'I'll think about it.' They shared a smile and shifted into more comfortable positions. 'What about Zel? All he does is think about things.'

'He's different, that man's not normal. Zel's an emotionless bastard.'

'Actually gentlemen,' Zel interjected as he plonked down into an empty chair. 'I was born in wedlock. Sorry to disappoint.'

This elicited an amused grunt from Reeva who'd snuck in unnoticed and claimed a seat beside Thran. Surprised, Thran and Drak turned their heads toward her in unison.

'How long have-' Drak began but was interrupted by Zel.

'If you two have quite finished story time, we have a busy day ahead.'

Thran turned a little to make a sly comment to Reeva but she wasn't facing him. In fact, it was as if she was making a point of not looking in his direction at all.

She knows I wanted to come to her last night but didn't. Please Lady grant me some time to think about how to mend what I've done.

'I've spent the night divvying the city into sections which we'll be working through. We're not the only Hand working on this. You should use all contacts, Guild or otherwise. We'll be going in pairs, it's too dangerous to go alone. Drak you're with me.'

Bollocks!

* * * *

The streets of Tydon bustled with afternoon activity. Merchants called out to anyone who would listen, enticing them to purchase their wares. Groups of women gossiped as they browsed the goods on offer. Servants weaved their way through the crowds, hurrying to complete their masters business. Homeless children patrolled the corners and alleyways looking for easy marks that could be relieved of their valuables. Thran was crouched next to one such urchin, seeking information.

'Nah, ain't seen nuffin, ain't eard nuffin bout anyone matching dat description.'

The boy hawked and spat, as if to emphasize his point. Thran rose and slipped into the crowd, blending into the steady stream of people that trickled its way through the streets. Reeva followed, five or six paces in his wake. Wherever he glanced the city teemed with life, people going about their daily lives. They seemed generally happy and at ease to be where they were right now. Thran was neither. His mood had gradually worsened as the day had progressed. They'd been in countless Inns and Taverns, spoken to numerous informants and urchins, yet they were no closer to locating Herrick's whereabouts than when they had started. As the boy had so eloquently phrased it: nobody had seen or heard "nuffin". It had been a long and frustrating day and promised to continue in that vein.

To make matters worse, his usual companionable silence with Reeva now only served as a reminder of the schism he had created between them, that widened with each step they took. He had no idea how to approach her, how to mend things. It was an area he lacked experience in. On the street his fists had done all his talking for him. Besides, finding Herrick and trying to sort that mess out came first. Except the man had vanished, almost like he hadn't existed in the first place. Tydon had plenty of places to hide and plenty of people willing to hide you for the right price, but there was always a trace, always a way of being caught. The Guild maintained a very thorough weave of informants throughout the City, in all levels of society, yet they were all proving unfruitful. Thran wanted to speak to Herrick again, he had so many unanswered questions. He needed time alone with him, away from the other Guild members. How he was going to work that opportunity, he hadn't a clue; it was going to be difficult to say the least. He slipped through the crowd, eyebrows knitted together as he mulled things over.

Deep in thought Thran barely noticed the stranger who sidled up to him and kept walking alongside him until the man spoke in hushed tones.

'Time grows short Descendant; you must hurry and speak to my master.'

'Herrick?!' Thran turned but did not recognise the man standing next to him. 'How...'

'I am using this man as a conduit, but my hold won't last much longer. Please Thran, there are other forces in play, speak to my master I beseech thee.'

'Why can't you meet me?'

'It's too dangerous. I will contact you again after you've spoken to my Lord Carrion.'

'Wait!' Thran grabbed the man by his shoulders and shook him with urgency. 'Wait!' But Herrick had already released his hold and the man's normal consciousness resurfaced. He shoved Thran away, swearing at him, telling him to back off. Thran backed away apologising and after a few seconds the man was happy that he was no longer a threat and went on his way. He didn't need to turn around to feel Reeva's gaze boring into the back of his head, he could picture the questioning arch of her eyebrow and the slant of her lips as they worked toward a half frown. So instead he ploughed ahead, on to the next informant and a welcome break to the already stifling silence.

* * * *

They both stood silently over the body. It was the second such body they had come across today. Zel was not happy. He stood over the deceased informant with furrowed brow. Drak was worried about Zel. He hadn't spoken in quite some time, which was very unusual for the tactician. Instead he'd adopted a brooding silence.

'Everything okay, Zel?'

'Oh yes Drak, everything is just brilliant. Couldn't be better! Two dead informants is exactly what I wanted to find when we set out this morning.'

'You've repeatedly told me that sarcasm is the lowest form of wit.'

He received a stony glare and Drak had to bite the inside of his cheek to stop a cheeky grin from spreading across his features. He didn't want to receive a lecture as to why this wasn't the right time for banter. Zel's gaze swung back to the body, piecing the situation together from the information he could glean from the body. Drak allowed himself a half-smile at actually having bested the arrogant prick for a change.

More satisfying than the majority of sex I've had.

Eventually Zel became aware of his surroundings once again and set off at a brisk pace.

'We may have a bigger problem on our hands than Herrick.'

'You don't think he was responsible for this?'

'No, I don't. Even if he is somehow involved, he didn't commit these murders.'

'So who did?'

'I have a few suspicions, but right now I just don't know.' If Drak had been a little worried about Zel before, he was now very concerned. He couldn't remember Zel ever admitting to not knowing something, now it had occurred twice in the same amount of days.

'Come on, we need to get back to the Tavern. Someone is targeting the Guild with a ruthless efficiency.'

Chapter 8

A malicious grin spread across his face as he watched the assassin work her way through the crowd. There'd been an influx of them scurrying around the city lately and he fancied it was all to down to his handiwork. He'd repeatedly smacked the hive, now the bees were a buzzing and he was about to get his first taste of honey. He almost licked his lips at the thought. His target quickened her pace, he matched it. The assassin knew she was being followed, had done for some time. Now it was just a case of seeing which one of them would make the first move. The age old battle of cat and mouse. Except on this occasion two highly trained predators squared off against one another. He relished it, the anticipation, the nerves, both churning around inside him just waiting to be turned into pure adrenaline. It was hard to explain this feeling to anyone who didn't take lives for fun. The closest thing he could liken it to was the moment just before climaxing during sexual intercourse. You know that euphoric moment is on its way. In some ways it's almost as good as the climax. Almost. In this case the climax was butchering the unfortunate assassin who had been the first to set out from their hidey-hole alone. A stupid mistake in normal circumstances: fatal in these.

  The assassin once again quickened her pace then abruptly stopped, appearing to take interest in some trinket at a merchants stall. He hovered two stalls down, unsure what his target was up to. The problem was he couldn't be sure which merchants were in the Guild's pay or not. He had a fairly lengthy list of names due to his previous excursions but he wasn't fooled into thinking it was anywhere near complete. The other advantage she had over him was knowing the city inside out. While he had mapped a fair amount of it during his short time here, the majority remained uncharted. It would help prolong her survival but that suited him just fine, nobody wanted the climax to arrive too soon. He glanced over his shoulder to make sure he wasn't in turn being followed. It was only momentary yet the assassin somehow sensed his gaze absent the back of her head and so took off sprinting. He sprang after, admiring the way she slalomed through the crowd, so lithe and graceful. He thundered after her, sending anyone who got in his way sprawling, steadily making ground, until he was almost within touching distance. Tantalizingly close. He stretched his fingers out, brushing the hem of her garment. He stretched out again, this time she would be within reach of his grasp. His fingers closed around thin air as she zigzagged left then right down a side street. He would not be deterred as he skidded into the turn and kept right on her trail.

They were both breathing hard by this point, yet neither seemed inclined to slow their pace. Fear often adds extra incentive and speed to those being chased and it was certainly helping the assassin keep that little gap between them from closing again. However his blood was up and the adrenaline was pumping hard, he would not be denied his quarry. The "thrill of the hunt" it is often called, especially by those in the upper classes who could afford the luxury. Yet he wasn't hunting some scared animal, no today he hunted the greatest game of all; a human being. The top of the food chain. So far, she wasn't disappointing. She shot down another alley, this time to the left. As he rounded it he saw her leap into the air and plant off the wall, leg muscles straining with effort, she propelled herself through the air towards a low jutting balcony. For a moment it seemed as though she would fall short but then her hands slapped against the stonework and she began to heave herself up. From there it would be a quick scramble up to the roof and that was something he could not allow. The rooftops and sewer systems of Tydon belonged to the Guild through and through, if she made it up there her escape was pretty much guaranteed. He wouldn't be able to follow, even in broad daylight it would be suicidal.

His anger at potentially losing his prey spurred him to greater speed and he surged down the alley after her. She had one leg over the balcony but the other still dangled down enticingly. He leapt towards that leg, his own two scissoring as he arced through the air, arms desperately stretching toward her. He managed to grab her ankle, but that was all it took as his weight brought her plummeting back down to the cobbled floor. Thankfully he landed on his feet, still the impact sent a jarring pain up his legs. The assassin wasn't as lucky, she landed squarely on her back, violently winding her. He went to press home his advantage while she still struggled to suck in air, launching himself at her, aiming to clasp his hands around her neck and slowly strangle the life out of her. The assassins training saved her. Instinctively rolling away she showed great reflexes and agility to swivel her body around and boot him in the face with the heel he'd grabbed momentarily before. As he staggered back, blood already beginning to gush from his nose, she hauled herself up and began to stumble down the alley, breath still not fully recovered. He wiped the blood away, resisting the urge to have a taste of the coppery delight. There'd be plenty of time for that later.

Once again he set out in pursuit.

She was struggling now; the fall must have done some interior damage for one hand clutched her back while the other held on to the wall for support. He deftly drew his knife as he closed the gap, sensing that the climax was imminent. She'd given him a good chase, made sure it was entertaining, so he would reward her with a quick death. But not before he squeezed information from her. The assassin turned to face him, drawing twin blades which she held out defensively before her. He slowed, cautiously advancing as even wounded, his prey was still extremely dangerous and it wouldn't do to underestimate her now. Such mistakes had been the downfall of many a hunter. He also suspected she was playing on her injury, making out she was weaker than she actually was. The gap was now closed and she settled into a half-crouch, balancing on the balls of her feet, poised to strike. He didn't think she would attack but it gave him a moment's pause none the less. He feinted at her a twice but both times she stayed well inside her defences. Their eyes were locked, each trying to gauge what the others next move would be.

Two men came around the corner deep in conversation which stopped abruptly when they spotted the two figures before them with weapons drawn. One with a vicious grin spread across his face, the other with a defiant grimace. They quickly made themselves scarce.

Neither combatant spared them a glance; a break in concentration at this moment would be fatal. He was just about to launch an attack when he noticed the corner of her mouth turning up into a ghost of a smile. She obviously had a trick up her sleeve, one last desperate throw of the dice. It would not matter. This time when he made his move towards her she shuffled backward, giving him ground. He was starting to get a little frustrated, she was only delaying the inevitable, but she kept shuffling back regardless always keeping him at arm's length, biding her time. Almost as if she was waiting for something. An opening perhaps? Well he would not present one. He lunged at her, driving her further back. All the while they had maintained eye contact but for a split second her gaze darted past him before snapping back.

That split second saved his life.

Had he not thrown himself to the right the knife would have plunged into his kidney, instead it sliced into his side. Pain flared up the left side of his body. He spun around to face a new opponent, inwardly cursing for allowing himself to be so easily duped. Of course she had a partner, the bastard had probably been waiting on the rooftop all along ready to ambush him. That's why she'd been waiting; for him to clamber down from his vantage point and finish the job. The new attacker lunged at him but he was fast enough to deflect with his own blade, he attempted to counter but the man stepped back so his knife slashed harmlessly through thin air. He glimpsed a flash of steel as the woman launched one of her daggers whirling towards his chest, he tried to jerk out of the way but wasn't quite quick enough. It slammed into him just below the collarbone. He staggered back a few steps, gritting his teeth against the fiery pain, and forced himself to focus.

Her companion lunged at him again, now aiming for his throat, however he managed to duck below, bringing his own weapon down onto his opponent's outstretched knee. The man screamed in anguish as the blade bit deep into his flesh. He tried to pull it out in order to strike again but the knife was firmly lodged in the knee joint, so instead he grabbed the handle of the blade jutting from his chest and pulled. It slid free with a horrible wet squelch, followed by a thick spurt of hot blood. His entire chest burned in agony. He sprang up, wielding the newly acquired weapon, and slammed it up into the jaw of his second attacker. His cries of pain turned to gurgles as blood filled his throat. The woman was now upon him, her second dagger arching dangerously. He grabbed her dying partner, twisting the body around so it was in-between the two of them, buying him precious recovery time. But she was quick, very quick. Darting around the falling body she tried to plunge her knife into his face but he'd bought enough time and space, he was outside her reach. She wasn't outside his. His hand clamped onto her wrist, she tried to wriggle free but as much as she struggled it was impossible to break his vice like grip. He sent a fist crashing into her face, she wobbled but stayed upright so he punched her twice more. Her hand slackened and the dagger slipped from her fingers, he scooped it up and slammed it into her gut, twisting it for good measure. She gasped and looked down at the weapon protruding from her stomach in disbelief. He finally let go of her wrist and without him to hold her upright she stumbled back and fell against the wall. He staggered over to her slumped form and knelt beside her.

He looked down, met her fearful eyes and couldn't control himself. He pressed his lips hard against her bloodied ones. He withdrew but kept their faces inches apart. The fear had been replaced by anger and it further flamed his passion but he reined himself in. He had a job to complete.

'Oh darlin.' He whispered, his voice hoarse. 'Thank you.' He cleared his throat and continued in a steadier voice. 'That was one of the best hunts I've had in a long time. As a reward I'll give you a quick death, that is, providing you answer my questions.'

She didn't answer and for a moment he thought death had claimed her but then he felt her faint breath on his cheek. He'd get his answers, and then he'd get healed. The cut to his side wasn't too bad, but the one just under his collarbone would be a major hindrance going forward. However he'd planned for situations like this, he knew exactly where he could go to find the healing he needed and he was confident he remembered how to get there.

But first things first he thought as his hand gripped the dagger once more.

* * * *

'It makes no sense for Herrick to take out our informants when he seems to know so much about us already, and has made direct contact with us. Besides, he hasn't killed anyone so far, so why start now?' Sarfina's question was rhetorical. She'd been in her room pouring over the map of Tydon exquisitely carved into the table when Zel had reported back with his unsettling news.

'My thoughts exactly! Herrick is not our killer. But I do think he is connected in some way. Maybe he's hired or brought help? Would have to be from outside the city. We'd know if anybody this good was operating in Tydon without the Guilds consent, or they'd belong to the Guild. You think the Faceless Man is clearing house? Purging any dissent in the ranks?'

'No. Skrenn would've given me a heads up. He knows we're loyal, he would have assigned us the task.'

'What if he's part of the dissent?'

Sarfina laughed. 'I guess we have to consider every possibility, but no. Skrenn would never betray the Faceless Man. I don't know their history but I get the feeling their relationship is beyond professional and more personal. If you wanted to get to the Faceless Man, Skrenn would be your best bet. When you informed me, my first thought was Shulakh spies but it's still a little too early for them to be making moves, we're not even openly at war yet. We'll have to deal with them at some point though. I pray to Naul we've sorted this mess before then.' She paused. 'It doesn't strike me as a coincidence that this Herrick turns up then the next day bodies start dropping. This makes it all the more imperative that we find him, and quickly!'

'The man is proving hard to find. My search was fruitless. I doubt Thran and Reeva have fared much better. Speaking of Thran, have you spoken to him yet?'

'No. Not yet.'

'It may amount to nothing, but he's definitely holding back about what happened between him and Herrick.' confided Zel

'I'll speak to him tonight. Have they returned yet?'

He shook his head. 'They're due back anytime now. I almost feel sorry for the lad, he's muddled up enough as it is without you getting involved.'

'He's had enough time to come forward on his own. We can't have the Hand at odds with each other, especially now. I don't think Reeva is particularly happy with him at the moment either.'

'How you can know what that woman is thinking is beyond me. She's an enigma.'

'That's your only downfall Zel, reading people. And everyone can be read, even if it's only a glimpse inside the front cover.'

'Well that's why this Hand works so well, we cover each other's inadequacies.'

Sarfina's mind was far from inadequate but to Zel anyone's brain that couldn't keep up with his fell short of the mark. Trying to explain that to him was pointless, she'd tried once and decided it was a waste of time and effort. Sometimes talking to Zel was like talking to a brick wall. She was just about to reply when the door opened. 'Haven't you heard of-' the rest died in her throat as she saw who had entered. The Guild's second in command rarely visited the Hand's safe holds, Zel had never seen him before, Sarfina only a few times when reporting directly to him about urgent Guild business she herself couldn't handle. The fact that he was here meant that there was something wrong. Seriously wrong. Skrenn closed the door behind him and looked at them both.

'We need to talk.'

It was late by the time the trio had finishing talking, for there had been much to discuss. Sarfina was tired, all she wanted was her bed and a good night's rest, yet there was one final task that needed to be dealt with. She headed downstairs to find Drak drinking and chewing the fat with a couple of locals. The Tavern was pretty quiet tonight, dead bodies littering the streets would have that affect. People tended to stay home, stay out of Guild territory. Skrenn had followed her downstairs, he bade her goodnight before exiting the Tavern.

Drak's interest was piqued. While Tydon's vast trading network meant that people from all over Bellum ventured to its shore, it wasn't that common to see a black skinned man from the Slivannah Plains this far south.

'What's a Dresconii want with us?'

'I shall bring you up to speed at a more appropriate time. Have Thran and Reeva returned yet?'

Drak frowned for a moment. 'Erm, yeah I think so.'

'You think so?'

He nodded. 'I think so.'

'Well have you seen them or not?' Sarfina snapped, her patience wearing thin.

Sensing this Drak realised it would be a good idea not to push her further.

'I have. Dunno where Reeva is exactly but she's knocking around somewhere. You know what she's like. Thran went straight to his room and ain't been out since.'

'Thank you. Don't be too hung-over in the morning.'

It wouldn't matter if he was or not, Drak had long since mastered the art of being able to function with a terrible hangover. They both knew it, yet she still felt the need to remind him anyway, in the hope that he might curb his drinking ever so slightly.

'Night Sarf.' Was all he replied, his ever present grin widening.

Sarfina waited until she was out of view and heading up the stairs before letting her own mouth curl up into a smile.

Dam you Drak, I can't stay mad around you. Your cheerful demeanour is too bloody infectious.

He knew it too, which only made it worse. He was the one person who could crack the blank mask she constantly portrayed. There was nothing as infuriating as the person who you were cross with making you smile or laugh when you were in the middle of berating them. Yet for some reason, it only further endeared them to you.

She headed past Thran's room and towards her own at the far end of the corridor. She would be knocking on his door very soon.

* * * *

Thran barely registered the first knock that sounded on his door, it was only as the thumping became louder and much more insistent that he became aware of his surroundings once more. He'd been on the verge of making a decision and he couldn't help but feel a small surge of irritation at being interrupted. He lifted the small blade from the palm of his hand and tucked it away under his bed before calling for the visitor to enter. Sarfina slipped in and shut the door behind her, she smiled at Thran whilst he could only gape at her.

She'd changed into a plain white, short sleeved, nightgown that ended at her knees. It was tight fitting and clung to her shapely body. He gulped audibly.

'May I sit?' She asked innocently.

He gave her a number of short, sharp nods, not trusting his voice.

'Thank you.' She sat down next to him on the bed, close, so their thighs slightly brushed if either one of them moved.

'I just came to see how you were and how you got on today. I'm assuming you didn't uncover anything useful?' He shook his head. 'I thought as much. Herrick's proving to be more slippery than we thought he would.' He nodded. 'The main reason I came here was to make sure you're okay. We're worried about you.' She laid a hand on his thigh. 'I'm worried about you.'

Her touch was like a bolt of lightning zapping through his entire body. He was struggling to think straight. His hands were clammy, he had to stop himself from wiping them on his breeches because then Sarfina would know he had clammy hands, she was smart like that, and he couldn't have her knowing he had clammy hands. His heart was beating fast, so fast, too fast. How could a heart possible beat this fast and not give out?

'You've not been your usual self for a little while now, ever since the Pemtil contract. I know these are difficult times, stressful times, which is why we all need to stick together. As a Hand. Look after each other. If there is anything I can do to help just let me know.' Her hand slipped further up his thigh and closer to a bulge Thran was praying fervently to every god wasn't too prominent. 'Anything.' She stressed, giving his thigh a little squeeze.

Sweet Brioth I can't take much more of this.

Sarfina wondered if she was laying it on a bit too thick but poor Thran was as powerless to resist her as a fly trapped in a hungry spider's web. She'd picked up on his infatuation early into his recruitment, helped nurture it even. It was pitiful how easy this was.

'I hope you know that you can come to me about any problems you have. That you can talk to me, approach me anytime. I'm here for you. But the only way I can help you is if you let me in, open up to me and talk. Do you want that?'

'Y-Yes.' He tried to sound sure of himself but it came out squeaky.

'Good.' She smiled, gave him another squeeze. 'That's good.'

Please touch it.

'Because Zel was telling me-'

Touch it. Touch it. Touch it.
'-that he thinks that you're-'
Did she just graze a ball?
'-not telling the whole truth-'
I think she just grazed a ball!
'-about your conversation with Herrick.'
Drak's not going to believe this.
'Is this true?'
'Yes.' The word was out of his mouth before he realised what she'd asked.
Shit!
'Will you tell me the truth of what happened?'
And so he told her the truth about his conversation with Herrick. For the most part. He started off hesitantly, but once he got going it all came flooding out. He told her that Herrick had prophesied about him being the "Descendant" and that he had come on behalf of the god of Death. He told her Herrick believed he had this special power, this "Gift" because of his birthmark and that he was on a mission vitally important to a group called the Small Council. That Herrick would take him away to this Small Council where they would train him. He finished by telling her about today's encounter with the randomer sent by Herrick. He purposefully omitted his nightmares and the fact he did actually possess the powers Herrick thought he did. Sarfina sat silently and simply let him get it all off his chest. Thran was grateful that when he eventually fell silent she seemed satisfied that he'd told her everything.

'Do you feel better now?'

'I do.' It had felt good to unload his burden, even if it was just partially.

'I'm glad. I'm also glad we had this chat. Thank you for telling me the truth.' She knew it wasn't the whole truth, but that was fine. Sarfina suspected that Thran had gotten caught up in Herrick's delusions and was contemplating leaving with the madman but was too embarrassed to say so. More importantly a plan was starting to form in her mind of how they would lure Herrick out of hiding and capture him.

Sarfina draped both her arms around him, laid her head on his shoulder and gave him a firm hug. He could smell the scent of her hair, and feel her body pressing against his arm causing his heart to once again palpitate. Despite how uncomfortable he felt, he wished the moment would never end. It felt like no time at all had passed when she raised her head, told him to sleep well and planted a gentle kiss on his cheek. He was left staring at the door long after she'd departed his room.

When he finally looked down he noticed he was in dire need of a change of pants.

* * * *

The High Priestess was mad, furious in fact. Acolytes made sure to stay out of her way, not make eye contact and look busy as she stormed across the main worship chamber. Yet one unfortunate acolyte who was polishing the altar caught her eye and she stopped to chastise him.

'I want that altar to be spotless when I next inspect it! I want to be able to see my reflection in its surface!'

How he was supposed to make a stone alter shine in order to reflect her face was beyond him, but he set about vigorously scrubbing anyway.

'Spotless!' She reiterated before continuing on her warpath.

It brought her to one of the back rooms where a wounded man awaited her attention.

'Mortem!' She spat his name with disgust. 'You were under strict instructions never to come here.' He was entirely unfazed by her scathing tone.

'Well seeing as though I'm doing your goddesses dirty work, I figured the least you could do was patch me up.'

'Were you followed here? Did anyone see you enter the temple?'

'Don't insult me. Of course not. And as soon as I was let in I was shepherded straight here to await your hospitality.'

'What do you want?'

'There's no need to be so abrupt, we're allies after all.'

'Through necessity. I understand why my Mistress has called upon your services, but that does not mean that I approve!'

'Is the High Priestess questioning her goddess?'

'Be quiet.'

'As you wish.'

The High Priestess growled in frustration. 'What do you want?'

'I already told you, I need healing.'

'And why should I heal you?'

'Because I have secured the information you wanted.'

That grabbed her attention although she didn't want to imagine the methods he had used to obtain it.

'Well?' She demanded when it was apparent he wasn't going to elaborate.

'Healing first.' He growled.

'Fine. Show me your wounds.'

He removed his top to reveal a well-muscled frame that had seen its fair share of cuts. The High Priestess studied him with a frown of concentration. The wound on his side wasn't a problem, it was only a nick, but when she saw how deep the cut below his collarbone was she tutted. She placed a hand over each wound, closed her eyes and called upon her goddess. He couldn't hear what she was muttering and he didn't really care as long as it worked. At first nothing happened, and he began to suspect nothing would but then the skin under her hands began to warm and tingle and it took some restraint not to itch the two spots. The Priestess's incantations came to stop, and she removed her hands. Although he made sure not to show it, Mortem marvelled at her ability. He was totally healed, his torn flesh knitted completely back together. The only evidence that remained of his earlier encounter with the two assassins was a puckered white scar just below his collarbone and a thin line on his side.

'You'll make a believer out of me yet.'

'You jest but the power of the gods is very real as you have just witnessed for yourself. Now, please.' She spread her arms out invitingly.

'I know where we can find him.'

'Where!?'

Mortem, fresh in from the hunt, flashed her a smile that sent shivers down her spine.

'Sarfina's Tavern.'

Chapter 9

Zakanos was just about to tuck into his breakfast when he heard a knock at the door. He set down his fork with a sigh and went to open the door, already annoyed at the audacity of someone disturbing him at home at such an early hour. He intended to make that displeasure clear. Any official business could wait till official office hours, they were bloody long enough. As it was, he did not expect Zel to be the man waiting on his doorstep. He quickly ushered him inside.

'What do you think you're doing here?'

'We need your help.'

'I'm already helping.' Not bothering to hide the annoyance in his tone.

'There have been developments.'

'The murders?'

'The murders.'

Zakanos didn't answer straight away. 'Fine.' Footsteps sounded down the stairs. 'Leave now and I'll follow to the Tavern shortly.'

Zel shut the door behind him as the footsteps reached the bottom of the stairs. Zakanos turned to see his wife with their son swaddled in blankets in her arms, a look of concern on her face.

'Who was it?'

'One of my men.'

'What did they want?'

'I've been summoned to the Citadel.'

'So early?'

'There's been another murder.'

'Oh.'

She didn't have to verbalise her worry, it was written plainly across her face as her lips pressed together in a thin line. Zakanos crossed to her and slipped an arm around her waist.

'I'll be fine, don't worry.' He gave her a reassuring smile. 'It'll most likely be a boring meeting where the older Captains talk over each other about how they will catch the killer and how it was never this bad when they were growing up.'

'But you'll end up being assigned to catch him.'

'It's possible. But I doubt it. Somebody higher up will want that glory for themselves.'

'Well don't go putting yourself forward, you hear me?'

'I won't.'

'And try to be home a little earlier today if you can. This little tyke likes to see his daddy before he goes to bed, yes he does.' The end part was directed at the "little tyke" who stirred in her arms, almost as if he understood they were talking about him. Zak reached in with his free hand and gently caressed his son's chubby cheeks. A tiny hand gripped his index finger and he felt a surge of pride as he felt the strength in those little fingers that couldn't even encircle his whole finger.

That's my son.

The infant stared up at them through sleep filled eyes, wondering what all the fuss was about. He shared his mother's eyes, a fully black pupil that stood out sharply against the white. Although common among the Mirronese, it made the majority of people uncomfortable, which was why his marrying a Mirron woman had caused such a stir. Zakanos didn't care, he adored her, and the deep dark depths of her eyes he found so enchanting.

He placed a gentle kiss on his son's forehead before planting a firmer one on his wife's lips. 'Not even the Emperor himself could stop me.' He reluctantly broke free from their embrace and strapped his sword belt on. While he would be wearing plain clothes to avoid being noticed, there was no way he would venture out without his sword. He could pass as a merchant with it on.

'Are you not going to change into uniform?'

'No time, it's urgent. I'll change when I get there.'

He set off to Sarfina's Tavern with a heavy heart having left his family and now cold breakfast behind. He hated lying to Lia but he didn't really have a choice. At least not one that he could see anyway.

A rock and a hard place, he let out a bitter laugh, *a rock and a hard place.*

The Tavern was empty when he arrived save for two occupants. The serving girl behind the bar and a man sitting at a table facing the entrance, with a largely untouched tankard in front of him. He approached the girl, who seemed nervous, which didn't surprise Zak overly much. However, there seemed to be something "off" about the man at the table and he certainly wouldn't want to be left alone with him if he were in her position. Zak pushed it from his mind, he had more pressing matters to attend to. When asked, the girl informed him they were waiting upstairs for him in the room at the end of the corridor so he headed straight up.

Six figures were waiting for him in that room, two behind the table, with the finely crafted map of Tydon, and four in front.

That must have taken many an hour to carve.

He recognised half of them. He guessed the three standing next to Zel were the other members of the Hand, a man who Zak wouldn't want to pick a fight with, a blonde woman who was the only one not to turn around and face him when he entered and an apprehensive looking man. Sarfina was one of the two behind the desk, next to her stood a lithe, well-muscled, bald-headed son of a bitch.

'Skrenn.' He made the name sound like a curse. 'I should have known you'd be involved in this mess somehow.'

'Good to see you again Captain.'

'Two things I want to make clear before we begin. Never, *ever* come near my house again. I don't care what the circumstances are. And I want full disclosure of what's going on. Pretty soon the Citadel is going to take notice and launch Imperial inquires, I can't run interference if I don't know what I'm trying to deflect them from in the first place. I want to know who this man you had me searching for is, and why there's now a bunch of corpses strewn in his wake!'

Sarfina caught the slightest of nods from Skrenn in her peripheral vision. 'I think we can agree to those reasonable terms Captain. A man named Herrick approached me a few days ago with a contract that turned out to be a trap so he could capture my Hand. They broke free before he could commence with his plans, plans we were unable to discern before he slipped away.'

'Which is when you approached me.'

'Precisely. Herrick is an unknown, so I thought it best to go through both official and unofficial channels. However he is proving to be quite resourceful.'

'Resourceful enough to take out some of your people.'

'Five informants and two assassins assigned to another Hand to be exact.' Zak let out a low whistle. 'But we have reason to believe the murderer is not Herrick.'

'Then who is?'

Sarfina paused. 'We're not quite sure.' She admitted.

'It's a little too early for the Shulakh spies to be making their move.' Zakanos mused, scratching his cheek in thought, something he did unconsciously. 'But whoever attacked and killed those Hand members had to be well trained and equipped. Grellon and Mirron wouldn't jeopardise their trade ties with us and I highly doubt it's the Dresconii, not their style.

Which means this is more likely to be personal. Someone seeking revenge against the Guild, perhaps?'

'It's plausible. I've been searching through our contract logbook but it hasn't yielded any clues as of yet, although I've only had time to go as far back as three months ago.'

'So what's the plan? I doubt me and him-' he nodded towards Skrenn '-would be here if there wasn't one.'

'Yes well, now you are all caught up we can discuss why we are all here. How well do you trust your men?'

'Implicitly.' He replied, indignant his Company's loyalty was in question.

'Good, because we're going to need them to trap Herrick.'

'And how do you suppose you're going to lure him into this trap of yours?'

'By offering him irresistible bait.' She replied, gesturing to the apprehensive man.

* * * *

Things were beginning to get interesting, very interesting indeed. There'd been great risk in coming to the Tavern, especially so early in the morning when it was so quiet; meaning he was the only customer. Yet his risk had been rewarded with the appearance of the soldier. He'd been dressed in civilian clothes but Mortem knew he was a soldier, most likely an officer. The way he walked and carried himself gave it away. When you drill and exercise every day it becomes a part of who you are, it becomes second nature. A soldier could change his appearance all he wanted but that couldn't hide his military background. Even if he hadn't picked up on any of that, the sword was a big tell. While it wasn't uncommon for merchants and the upper classes to go around armed, their swords were much more ornate, made for show more than anything else. His had been a plain weapon, designed only for one thing; killing. A finely crafted sword too for he suspected it was a Grellish steel blade, hence his guess at the man being a ranking officer.

It amused Mortem to imagine them all scheming upstairs, unaware the cause of their problems was sat right below them, enjoying their hospitality. It made his next sip of cider that little bit sweeter. But he knew he mustn't tempt fate, for The Lady was a fickle bitch and he'd gotten what he came for.

I wouldn't want to overstay my welcome.

He drained the cup and took it over to the bar. The girl thanked him but barely glanced in his direction.

He walked outside and stretched, expecting to feel pain flare up across his chest and side but surprisingly all he felt now was a slight stiffness in his muscles instead. Being healed was a new experience for him, it would take some getting used to. The High Priestess was a valuable ally, but he would have to be careful. There were no guarantees she wouldn't try to kill him once his usefulness came to an end. He set off in the direction of the Citadel, for he had several things to do, but his primary goal was to now find out who exactly that soldier was. After all, he must have a real name.

He glanced up into the early morning sunshine. It was promising to be another lovely day in Tydon.

* * * *

Herrick rubbed his temple but it did nothing to alleviate the pain, the headaches were getting worse. He wasn't sure how much longer he could keep this up. He'd falter sooner rather than later and then it was only a matter of time before they caught him and he had no wish to endure that grizzly fate. If the Descendant would not speak to his master and be convinced of his destiny then Herrick would have no choice but to take matters into his own hands and take Thran by force. Although problematic; it was achievable. Perhaps it was time to call on his Brothers and Sisters. His brooding was interrupted by a knock at the door and a woman entered carrying a bowl of soup and half a loaf of bread, which she deftly set down on the table.

'Here you go father. Be careful, it's still quite hot.'

'Thank you.' He was about to tuck in when he noticed she was looking at him. 'Something wrong?'

'No, not at all.' She smiled. 'It's just nice to have you back after all this time.'

'It's good to be back.' He could sense she had more to say on the matter. 'But?' he prompted.

'Well, you, errr, just look different from what I remember is all.'

'My dear, time changes the way a person looks, but I'm still the same man who raised you.' He took her hand in his, trying his best to give her a reassuring squeeze, but when a fresh wave of pain spiked, his free hand instinctively shot up to rub his temple.

'Are you okay father?' Her misgivings now replaced by concern.

'I'm fine, just didn't sleep well last night.' He replied, giving her hand a firmer squeeze.

'Okay well just shout if there's anything else I can get for you.'

'I will. Thank you.'

The glamour was beginning to wear off, which meant that tomorrow he would have to find another place to lay low.

A shame he thought as he slurped his first spoonful of soup, *she's a dammed fine cook.*

* * * *

Thran hung back as everyone else left; he needed to talk to Sarfina about last night. He also needed to tell her that their plan wouldn't work, that Herrick wouldn't fall for their trap. But he didn't know how to tell her this without telling her about his Gift and that Herrick would only come out of hiding when he'd spoken to his master. The god of Death.

'Something I can help you with?'

Thran realised that he and Sarfina were the only two left in the room. He floundered for something to say before finally blurting out the first thing that came into his head.

'Why would Zakanos offer to run interference for us?'

'Because he knows if they were to find out what the Guild is up to, they would also find out about his past and present involvement with us.'

'Why would they find that out?'

Sarfina let out an amused snort. 'Because we would tell them. You really are quite naive sometimes Thran.' Colour rose to his cheeks. 'Now, what did you really want to talk to me about?'

'Am I really that transparent to you?'

'We've been together ever since the day I saw you bite that boy's ear off. I've known you for years. Seen you grow up, practically raised you. We've been, seen and done an awful lot together. I doubt you could keep anything from me.'

Thran suddenly realised something that shocked him. Sarfina might know everything about him, but he knew almost nothing about her.

I probably know as much about Sarfina as I do about Reeva.

A worrying thought.

'It's about last night...'

'Go on.'

'I feel used. You played on my feelings towards you.'

'What choice did you give me? You kept valuable information from the Hand.' She chided.

'I might have told you eventually.' He responded somewhat sulkily.

'Might is not good enough. The situation is dangerous enough without you keeping secrets from your own Guild members.'

'I realise that now and I'm sorry, but last night you took advantage of me.'

'Because in the grand scheme of things your feelings don't matter.' Her tone softened a little when she saw how much her words had stung him. 'Thran, your actions put Drak, Reeva, Zel and me in danger. As the leader of this Hand I have to put feelings to one side every now and then, regardless of who they are. My own included. I have to make tough decisions and do hard things, but if that keeps my Hand alive then it's worth it.'

'I guess I didn't think about it from your point of view.' He hesitated. 'What about, about...' He couldn't bring himself to utter the word *us*.

'Think about it logically Thran. If Skrenn found out, and he would, trust me, then best case scenario you get packed off to another Hand. Worst case, and most likely you get kicked out altogether and I get demoted. It would just complicate matters.'

Thran stiffened, and then gruffly replied. 'It seems that's all I ever do. Maybe when this is over it would be best for me to transfer to another Hand.'

'I don't think that's what you really want, and I don't want that either. You're a valuable asset and an integral part of this Hand. Why don't we talk again when things have calmed down and gone back to normal, okay?'

Thran nodded. He left Sarfina's room feeling dejected, yet for the first time in days, clear about the road that lay ahead.

* * * *

Zakanos had only just sat down when an aide knocked on his office door and informed him his presence was requested for a meeting.

'Can't they wait? I've only just sat down.'

'It's the Emperor himself, sir.'

'By the gods man, why didn't you lead with that information?!' He quickly gathered his gear together, made sure his uniform was presentable before gesturing for the aide to lead the way. 'Do you know what the meeting is about?'

'No sir. All the Captains have been summoned though. Rumour has it that it's to do with the recent trouble in the city.'

Zak cursed inwardly. While he'd been expecting this to happen, it was still too soon for his liking. It meant that technically he hadn't been lying to his wife earlier which helped ease his mind a little but it was still cause for concern. They exited the barracks and passed through the Soldiers Gate and into the Citadel without being stopped, the guards on duty knew Zakanos on sight. Catching his urgency, the aide hurried up the slight slope towards the main hall. It was here the Emperor held audiences and greeted dignitaries from other cities.

The slope levelled out as they reached a circular grassy area with a marble fountain in its centre. Four marble cherubs stood atop the fountain, each cheekily peeing down into the pool of water below. Buildings sprouted to each side of the fountain but it was the main hall that dominated the centre, dwarfing all around it. Eight mammoth stone pillars, four either side, holding up a triangular roof. They passed between the giant pillars which lead to gigantic oak doors that required four men to open and close. Thankfully they were presently open.

Inside the hall was a great show of wealth, everywhere you looked tapestries hung from the walls, beautifully carved statues of past Emperors in heroic poses lined the way every six or seven steps. Zak's particular favourite was one of an old Emperor called Ziolo who had ruled Tydon well over one hundred years ago. The statue depicted him in full armour, one foot on a rock, arm with sword in hand outstretched pointing toward some imaginary enemy with a fierce expression on his face as he encouraged his men forward. It was well documented that Ziolo had never once led his men on the field of battle. Yet here he stood, striking fear into all those who walked beneath the scrutiny of his stern gaze. It always brought a smile to Zakanos' face.

Toward the back of the hall on a dais stood the throne, currently vacant. In contrast to the wealth on display around it, the throne was of simple design, yet the deep brown mahogany it was carved from gave it a regal aspect. They headed past the throne and through one of the arched hallways at the back. They passed doors on either side of them, but Zak knew they were headed for the one at the end. When they arrived the aide paused outside and said:

'They're waiting inside for you, sir.'

Zakanos took a deep breath, readied himself, and stepped inside.

Chapter 10

The Tydon military consisted of ten regular Companies each led by a Captain. Each Company was made up of squads of ten led by a Sergeant. However the Elite Four Captains Companies existed outside the regular Companies and consisted of more men. The Captain of the Guard had one hundred and fifty men under his command, tasked with defending the citadel, whilst the Captain of the Elite Guard, personal bodyguards of the Emperor, commanded three hundred. The Captain of the Horse led five hundred mounted men, and was divided into two equal squads. The Captain of the Bow also led five hundred bowmen, but his were split into five squads of a hundred each. All thirteen other Captains had made it there before Zakanos, making his late entry painfully noticeable.

  The Captains were seated down the sides of a long table, which took up the majority of the space. The only light that entered came through big bay windows at the back of the room. Emperor Tavian sat in front of the windows at the head of the table. In his youth Tavian had been fit and strong, quickly rising through the ranks of Tydon's military, but now after many years of ruling Tydon in luxury, the muscle was giving way to fat. He had close cropped jet black hair with a smattering of grey creeping in. His cold, calculating eyes fixed on Zakanos as he shuffled his way past the other Captains. Most wilted under that hard stare. To the Emperor's right sat the Elite Guard Captain Remullus, to his left, Cyprian, the Captain of the Horse.

  The two Captains were polar opposites. Remullus was burly, powerful and quick to laugh whilst Cyprian was quick, concise, but more reserved, carrying himself with effortless dignity. Remullus' deep voice came from his thick belly, whereas Cyprian spoke in a much higher, almost effeminate tone. Both were extremely good Captains and leaders of men.

To Cyprian's left sat Corsca; Captain of the Bow. She was tall, taller than most of the men in the room with mousey brown hair that cascaded down to rest between her extremely broad shoulders. It required tremendous strength and years of training to pull back the longbow Tydon's archers used with such deadly efficiency. Instead of the olive tanned skin common amongst the Tydonii she had a pale complexion, hinting at mixed ancestry.

There were two empty seats at the table, although this was no surprise. High Alchemist Dyrox rarely attended such meetings, even important ones, for two reasons: firstly, he had no interest in matters of the state unless they related to alchemy, and secondly, he reeked so badly of chemicals that no one else wanted him there unless it was absolutely necessary. The Emperor moved meetings which included the High Alchemist to the great hall due to its open space and greater ventilation. The second empty chair belonged to the Admiral of the Fleet who was rarely in Tydon owing to his preference for the open ocean over stuffy offices and paperwork.

'Captain Zakanos, thank you for joining us.'

Zakanos sat down in his seat next to Remullus and pulled his chair up to the table, it scraped across the floor, making a screeching sound that made one of the Captains lower down the table wince. 'My apologies, I was attending to important matters that required my immediate attention.' He addressed the man who'd spoken; a smartly dressed nobleman by the name of Threm Sioll Celentine who stood behind Tavian. Zakanos disliked Threm immensely, something about the glorified merchant's constant smirking face just rubbed him the wrong way. It was like he knew a secret everyone else didn't and enjoyed lording the fact over them. He was popular among the ladies of the court but Zak reckoned he looked and sounded like the snake he was. Unfortunately as elected representative of both the Merchants Guild and the Nobles, Celentine wielded power and influence which he'd used to worm his way into the Emperor's inner circle.

'More important than the Emperor's summons?'

'Of course not. I-'

'Enough.' Tavian spoke for the first time. While he hadn't raised his voice, his tone brooked no argument. 'We have more pressing concerns. I want to know what is going on in my city.'

Cyprian answered his Emperor.

'My Lord, there have been a number of murders in the past couple of weeks. This is not uncommon in a city with an ever-growing population such as ours. However, many of the victims have clearly been tortured before meeting their end, suggesting we have a very unsavoury character roaming the streets. The torture also implies the victims were not targeted at random, but specifically chosen with the hope of extracting information. My Lord, I'm afraid to say these are not just simply killings, but rather assassinations.'

Disquieted mutterings passed from Captain to Captain as the ramifications of this news sank in.

'Who were these unfortunates?'

'Two were dock workers, one a fisherman, one a store owner. Then there was a baker and finally, three street peddlers.'

'What about that merchant who died around a month back? What was his name?'

'Pemtil Nozz Thoroes, my Lord. While he came to a bloody end, it was quick and clean. Without a doubt the work of the Assassins Guild. Not connected to the current set of murders.'

'Do we think the Guild is connected to the current set of murders?'

'Of course they will be!' Remullus rumbled. 'Those Guild scum are never far from the trouble that arises outside the Citadel.'

Tavian ignored Remullus' outburst and gestured to Cyprian to continue.

'We think they're connected, but not the cause. At the very least they will be scrambling to find out who is causing this commotion in their territory.'

Corsca spoke up. 'The Guild rules with a terrible efficiency. They will not take this level of disruption lightly; they will be keen to inflict retribution quickly, if they haven't already. The last few days have been without incident apart from a reported scuffle in the streets and another two dead. We found plenty of blood but no bodies. The Guild cleans up after itself.'

'And what of the spies currently operating in the city?' Tavian asked, switching tacts, directing his question to Threm.

'They've been quiet my Lord. Nobody's acting suspiciously. Well, no more than usual anyway.' He added drily. 'These attacks are not being carried out on behalf of the other cities. But something, or someone has drawn this killer to Tydon.'

'Find out!' Commanded the Emperor, before turning his steely gaze towards Zakanos. 'I'm tasking you with finding this degenerate and bringing him to justice. Alive if possible. Nothing appeases the mob quite like a public execution. We need to show the people we can protect them so I want your men to be clearly seen being proactive in finding this killer. Double the number of watches and have your men patrol with no less than four. If you can capture a Guild member or find what they're up to, do so. But finding this murderer comes first.'

'Thank you my Lord, for giving me this honour.'

'The Captains and men of the 5th and 7th Company are at your disposal if you require them. Do not disappoint me, Captain. Dismissed.' The Captains stood, clasped their fists over their hearts in salute, and then filed out the door. Corsca was the last out, she bowed to her Emperor before closing the door behind, leaving him alone in the meeting room. But not for long. Stones grated against each other as they parted, revealing a small gap in the wall wide enough for a hooded figure to slip through.

'Did you hear all that?' Tavian asked the newcomer.

'Of course.'

'Then do something about it! This situation is starting to try my patience.'

'We have it under control.'

'Make sure that you do. Keep the Captain in line and he should do the rest.'

'It's a dangerous game you're playing.'

Tavian offered him a rueful smile. 'Isn't it always? Hopefully we will be able to unite our forces once this threat has been dealt with.' He sounded almost wistful.

This statement brought a mirthless chuckle. 'You've been sitting on that throne too long, you're forgetting what it's like out there on the streets and rooftops. You're growing soft.' With this pronouncement, the figure turned to head back down the secret passage.

'Was she one of the two?'

The man paused, but didn't turn around. 'No. She's fine, for now.' He waited to see if Tavian would respond, but when it became clear he would not he disappeared through the gap, into the darkness of the passage. When the room was once more whole again and Tavian was truly alone, he slumped back in his chair and closed his eyes. He thought about what had been said.

Maybe I have, maybe I am. But I won't give it up!

* * * *

Three Captains walked side by side between the great pillars on their way out from the meeting.

'Well that was interesting to say the least.' said the first.

'Indeed.' agreed the second. 'It plays perfectly into our hands.'

'I can't foresee a more opportune time to make our move.'

'Especially given the time frame.'

'It would be best if we were in place before the inevitable conflict with Shulakh.'

'We must still be careful.' the third warned. 'We need to make sure we do not rush and make a mistake just because an opportunity has presented itself. Now let's go about our duties as normal and wait for word from *him.*'

The other two Captains nodded and went to see to their men while the third waited a moment longer under the last pillar. He laid a hand on the smoothly carved rock. A tough road lay ahead, but then he'd known that from the start, and for the first time, it looked as though the end might be in sight. He patted the pillar before moving on. He had a daily routine to keep.

* * * *

'Give it a rest Clipper, you're freaking out the newbie.'

Clipper lowered his toe from his mouth and spat out the nail he'd just bitten off.

'That so, Creak?' He glanced across to look at the "newbie" sitting on the bunk opposite him. 'I'm awfully sorry, Nozza.'

'I keep telling you, that's not my name!'

'It is now newbie, you'd better get used to it!' Creak said harshly.

'At least give me a proper name. I only worked for the Thoroes family briefly, I had nothing to do with them.'

'Still murdered em' though didn't ya.' Clipper sneered accusingly. 'Joined up so you could hide away.'

'I did no such thing, it was an assassin!'

'So you say.'

'There was an investigation, I was questioned and released.'

'I'd imagine you were pretty convincing.'

'Seriously, give it a rest.'

'We can change your name to Whiner if you want?'

'I'd rather you did not.'

Clipper laughed and mimed reeling in a fish on a hook. Creak snorted. 'Alright Clip, you've had your fun, leave him be.' She turned her attention back to Nozza. 'So why did you join up?'

'I might not have had anything to do with it but they still disposed of me. Didn't really have many options. I was drowning my sorrows when I bumped into a recruiter, so I decided to sign up. Seemed like a good idea at the time, but I'm quickly beginning to regret that decision.'

'What did you do to get assigned to the Guard Company?'

'I'm sorry, I don't understand?'

'A new recruit like you should've been sent to the 9th or 10th Company.'

'What she's saying newbie, is that you don't belong here.' Clipper sneered again.

'What I'm saying is,' Creak continued 'that to get this commission you've either got to have connections, bribed the right people, or slept with the right people, because you certainly don't have the skills or background for the Guard Company.'

'I did not do any of that. I was just assigned to this squad, I swear!'

'You're a spy then,' Clipper accused. 'come to stab us in our sleep!'

'Just be honest with us newbie, it'll be easier for you if you do.'

'I am being honest I swear! Why do I have to have a new name anyway? I was given a perfectly good one at birth.'

'Because it's symbolic. You're giving up your old name, your old life, leaving all former ties behind. Starting fresh. Whatever grudges, beliefs, relationships you held before are now redundant. Your new squad, your new Company replace all that. Having them choose your new name is supposed to help ease that process, help you feel a part of things.' At this comment, they all turned to find Sergeant Heelial standing in the doorway. 'Whether it works or not is another matter but that's the gist of reasoning behind it all. Satisfied?' Nozza nodded meekly as the Sergeant bit into a strip of meat. He noticed she had quite a few more strips held in her other hand. 'Good. Corporal, where's the rest of the squad?'

'Rolls n' Fingers are sleeping.' Creak answered.

'Wake them up. Scorch?'

'Not seen her, she'll be skulking around somewhere.' Creak said. 'Smokey and Owl were talking to a few other sappers in the mess hall. Oros only knows what they're cooking up.'

'Fetch them, and find Shriek too while you're at it.' Heelial called to Creak. The Corporal snapped a salute as she vanished out the door and headed down the hallway.

Clipper made to follow Creak. 'We've pissed someone off, Sarge, to be lumped with this worthless piece of shit.'

Heelial looked at the new recruit. 'Well I hope for all our sakes, you prove him wrong.'

'Uhm, Sergeant, ma'am, why are you gathering the squad together?' asked Nozza.

'Inquisitive aren't you. Because the Captain has orders for us. Have you met the Captain yet?'

Nozza shook his head. 'No not yet.'

'Well you're about to.'

It sounded very ominous to the newbie.

The 4th squad of the Guard Company stood to attention in front of their Captain.

'At ease.' They relaxed. 'As you are no doubt aware the Guard Company has been tasked with finding the killer who's been terrorising our streets over the past couple of weeks. The rest of the Company will be combing the streets, knocking on doors, making inquiries. However I'm giving the 4th a special assignment.' The Captain made to continue but suddenly paused, his eyes settling on the soldier three in from the left. 'I don't believe we've met.'

Nozza's heart was beating rapidly in his chest. He'd hoped to remain unnoticed during the meeting but now he was being singled out.

'Rumble got sick, couldn't shake it off. Carrion claimed him. This is his replacement.' Sergeant Heelial explained.

The Captain walked over to stand in front of Nozza and openly appraised him. He felt like a farmer's pig being judged to see if it was fat enough to survive the coming winter and had been found wanting. To Nozza's surprise the man smiled warmly at him and extended his hand.

'I'm Zakanos, Captain of the Guard.'

'Nozza.' He clasped forearms with the Captain. Zakanos' grip was firm and strong.

'Pleasure to meet you Nozza. Serve me well and I'll have your back' He released his grip.

'Thank you, sir.' Nozza mumbled, unsure how he was supposed to respond.

Zakanos stepped back to stand in front of his desk and once more addressed the whole squad. 'As I said, I have a special assignment for you. We've pieced enough of the puzzle together to suspect who the killer's next target will be; a merchant by the name of Kaprel Shellen who's agreed to help us. We're going to set a trap with Shellen acting as bait. You're going to act as his bodyguards. Half of you will guard him directly, the other half will be placed discretely near.'

The squad looked uneasy, especially the two heavies, Clipper and Rolls. Sergeant Heelial cleared her throat.

'I'm well aware, Sergeant, that this type of operation may make some of you uncomfortable. But if we do manage to capture this madman, it will curry great favour with the Emperor. He himself personally appointed me as lead Captain on this. The Emperor wants a public execution so only kill him if you have no other choice. You'll begin your duties this afternoon. We'll be escorting Shellen around Ritellis Square.'

They saluted and exited the Captains office and made their way back to where the 4th squad was billeted.

'This is bullshit. We shouldn't have to babysit some bloody merchant.' Clipper moaned to Rolls.

'It ain't proper soldiering.' She muttered.

'At least it's some action. We ain't seen any for quite some time.' Fingers pointed out.

'Still, we ain't cut out for this cloak and dagger stuff.' Creak shot back.

'The sooner we get back to war with Shulakh, the better! No offense Fingers.'

'None taken,' replied the Shulakhai warrior. 'I'm just as eager to settle old scores with Shulakh as much as anyone.'

'Soon you two, soon.' Rolls said as she slapped him on the back. The rest of the squad nodded their agreement.

They sounded like very solid blows to Nozza, but Clipper seemed to take no notice of them. All this talk of wanting to go to war made him wonder what he'd signed up for. The 4th squad members clearly had something wrong with them. Although he doubted the other squads were much different. Behind him he heard the two sappers, Smokey and Owl, speaking in hushed tones. Well, actually, it was Smokey doing all the talking, Owl just nodded excitedly to everything she said. He noticed Nozza watching them and, eyes bright, gave him a broad smile. It revealed the five teeth he had left and a scarred pink stub of what used to be a tongue. Nozza could only gape. Smokey was pulling on his sleeve so he turned his attention back to what she was saying.

'I found it quite unsettling at first too.'

Shriek had sidled up to him. At first Nozza had struggled to understand the Kidoshians thick accent but he was starting to grasp a little more of what the man said.

'How did it happen?'

Shriek screwed his face up, trying to remember. It made his brown weathered face look even more like cracked leather. 'Sapping accident by all accounts. Not like he will be able to tell us the specific details anymore. He was lucky, the other man caught in it died.'

Sappers ain't right in the head.

'Quit yer grumbling, the Cap'n knows what he's doing. Besides, probably nothing will come of this. The killer won't show his face.' They subsided at Heelial's words and carried on in silence. All except for Scorch, who was busy whispering in the Sergeant's ear. Nozza wasn't quite sure what Scorch's role in the squad was, but everyone bar Heelial seemed to defer to her.

They reached the squads room and each went to their bunk and prepared themselves for the so called special mission ahead.

To protect Kaprel Shellen.

Chapter 11

Ritellis Square was near enough in the middle of Tydon. Named after the architect who designed and built it centuries ago, as he had much of Tydon, the Square was a vast open space usually thronged with people. It was the central hub of activity in the city. Any newcomers arriving to the city by land only had to follow the main road straight up from the gates which led them to the Square. It was common belief that all streets eventually led back to Ritellis Square. In the centre of the Square stood a giant black obelisk with strange markings etched along its surface, the meaning of them long ago forgotten. Many claimed it was the exact centre of Tydon but such theories had never been proven. Today was a day much like any other, merchants had their wares laid out on blankets, mouth-watering aromas wafted through the air from the sizzling and spitting meat on offer from food vendors, musicians and jugglers performed for the crowd, hoping to earn some of their coin, whilst beggars outright pleaded for it. Taverns, inns and pubs surrounded the Square, all fine establishments.

  Thran felt uneasy and uncomfortable. In order to masquerade as the merchant Kaprel Shellen they'd dressed him in a white shirt with a blue jacket with golden trimmings sewn over the top, and cream coloured pants with green swirls up the sides tucked into calf length black riding boots. A silver rapier studied with gems hanging at his side completed the outfit. Thran thought he looked like a pompous fool.

  I guess I need to look realistic he mused.

  Thran had been instructed to hold himself with a straighter posture and pronounce all his words correctly. Any "slang" would give him away Sarfina had warned. Etiquette had been drilled into him from a young age before he'd been thrown out onto the streets and it surprised Thran how easily he slipped back into it after all these years. He reckoned he comfortably passed as a merchant; although the shirt collar felt tight around his neck and he had to refrain from trying to slacken it every other minute by undoing his top button. Compared to his usual loose assassin's garb, the merchant's attire felt tight and constricting.

He felt sorry for the woman they'd chosen to escort him around. However uncomfortable he felt in his clothes, she undoubtedly felt worse. She was in a full length light blue dress that was cinched tight in at the waist by a length of red ribbon tied into a bow. Her hair was tied up and a gold necklace adorned her neck. The only saving grace, in Creak's opinion, was that because the dress went all the way to the ground it allowed her to wear her military issue boots instead of some dainty little slippers she'd barely be able to fit her feet into. She cursed after stepping on the hem of her dress. Clipper and Rolls sniggered until she told them to shut up and keep their eyes out front. The two heavies led the way, followed by Thran and Creak. Fingers and Nozza brought up the rear. The four of them were acting as the "official" hired bodyguards for the merchant and the lady he was currently courting. Creak cursed again.

'Try taking smaller steps.' Thran advised her, receiving a glare in response. He did notice she listened to him however and after a while she said:

'Reth's teeth! I don't understand fashion.'

'Please stop cursing, it is not ladylike.' Another glare. 'I don't think anyone does. Understand fashion I mean. I think designers just make the most absurd dresses they can think of and see if the noblewomen will buy them, which of course they will because everyone wants the latest things and to set the new trend. Which only spurs the designers on to create things even more absurd, it's a vicious cycle. Don't worry though, I think you look nice.' This brought another snort of laughter from Clipper and Rolls.

'Save your chivalry for someone who gives a shit!'

'Okay, but you are going to have to curb your language, otherwise people will realise we're not who we're pretending to be.' Thran didn't notice his slip of including himself but Creak did. It made her like the situation even less. She glanced back to check on the two behind them. Fingers was whistling a cheerful tune, his eyes taking in the crowd around him, darting from person to person, never staying still. Nozza had his eyes firmly fixed on the back of Kaprel's head, a slight frown upon his lips.

'You okay newbie? You ain't asked a single question yet.'

'I'm fine. Just taking my rear guard job seriously.'

Nozza made a show of scanning the crowd for potential assailants until Creak turned away from him and went back to grumbling about her dress. Nozza couldn't help but keep staring at Kaprel. Something about the merchant seemed vaguely familiar but he couldn't quite place it. Of course he'd heard of the Shellen family before when working for Pemtil, but they'd never done any business with the Thoroes family, otherwise he would have remembered the name and face more clearly, so he could hardly be one of the more prominent merchants or from a noble family background. Yet he was obviously wealthy and influential enough to warrant being targeted by some deranged killer, as well as have them acting as his protection. He shook his head. Barely days into his new job and he was already involved in something dodgy. Trouble just seemed to follow him around. Sometimes he swore The Lady had it in for him.

"Kaprel's" uneasiness was growing by the minute as the day stretched by. He tried to relax by talking to the woman, what was her name? Crack? Something similar anyway.

Tydonii soldiers were called such bizarre things. What else could you expect when you let them name themselves? Talking to her just made it worse; the woman rejected any attempt he made to converse with her.

She might not like having to portray a lady, but she could at least be civil.

While Thran knew Herrick wouldn't show up there was a very real possibility someone in the Square was here to make an attempt on his life. Despite the protection he had the thought was still unsettling, he was the one usually doing the stalking. He didn't like being out in the open. Not one bit. The two heavies didn't seem overly bothered but whether that was because they were confident in their abilities or they simply didn't care; Thran couldn't tell. Whilst his disguised companion seemed preoccupied with her dress, at least one of the rear guards looked like he was paying attention. It was comforting to know that Zakanos and another two squads were on full alert, close at hand, ready to rush in if trouble arose. Most comforting of all, even though they weren't on particularly good terms right now, was that Reeva was also out there, keeping tabs on everyone.

Thran had wanted the rest of the Hand backing him up but Sarfina had rejected the idea, partly because they didn't know how deeply the Guild had been compromised by the killer and partly because Herrick had already seen Zel and Draks' faces. The latter stood out under normal circumstances anyway. Thran didn't like to admit it but he knew she was right. Only Reeva was allowed because it was impossible to find her if she didn't want you to.

As the afternoon slowly dragged on they moved around the square, visiting different stalls and making a few purchases with the money that the Guild had supplied. Nobody had bothered them; no suspicious types lurking around or following them. At times Thran forgot all about his life as an assassin, he was Kaprel Shellen, a wealthy merchant enjoying a lovely, peaceful day out in Ritellis Square with the woman he was currently courting. Although whenever he looked at Creak (he'd finally plucked up the courage to ask her real name) the spell was broken.

Bless her, she's trying.

* * * *

Sergeant Heelial eyed the piece of tender meat on the end of the fork, her mouth watering at how perfectly pink it looked. She slowly brought it towards her mouth and slid it from the utensil and onto her tongue. She waited a moment before taking her first bite. Her eyes automatically closed and a moan of unbridled pleasure escaped her lips as the warm, bloody juices swirled around her mouth.

Great Sollun above that's good!

She opened her eyes, after savouring every single chew, to find Scorch had sat down in the chair opposite her, an expression halfway between bemusement and amusement on her face.

'One day I hope to find someone who looks at me the way you look at meat.'

'Keep praying. You never know, Brioth might answer them.'

Scorch began to make her report but Heelial held up an admonishing hand. The squad mage had to wait till she'd finished every last succulent morsel.

'You done?'

Heelial leant back with a contended sigh, hands rubbing her full belly, and nodded.

'Good. There-' The Sergeant let out a loud belch '- there has been no signs of suspicious activity so far. If anyone is watching, they're keeping well hidden.'

'How's the rest of the squad?'

'Smokey wants to use her munitions on everyone and everything but Shrieks keeping her in check. Owls' fine. Although you never can tell, the way he's in a permanent state of happiness. He's made quite a bit of money actually. If I were him I'd be tempted to take up begging full time.'

'And what about you? What have you *sensed*?'

'There are a number of forces at play here. Powers are converging.'

Mages, always so bloody cryptic. 'Care to elaborate?'

'I wish I could but these forces are beyond my ability to discern. Which means there are gods involved. *Elder* gods.'

Cryptic and melodramatic. 'So? They're always meddling and scheming the way you mages talk.'

'Yes but never usually Elder gods.'

'Elder gods?'

'Yes.'

'You mean to say there are different types of gods?'

'That's one way to put it.'

'So these Elder gods are usually uninterested in what goes on?'

'For the most part.'

'But now they're somehow involved?'

'Undoubtedly.'

'And that's bad?'

'Of course it is!' Scorch said, almost shouting. She face-palmed in exasperation. 'They're extremely powerful, elemental beings who- why am I even bothering to explain, you won't understand.'

'It seems as though the Captain has involved us in something far graver than we'd originally thought.'

'Do you trust him?'

'I do. Although I think three of us need to have ourselves a little conversation about our concerns.'

'This so called merchant we've been sent to guard is not who he appears to be either. I think he may be Gifted.'

'Are you sure? He doesn't appear to belong to a temple faction and he certainly isn't military. Not many slip through the net of both.'

'As unusual as it is, yes, I'm sure. However, it's unclear from where, or who he draws his power from.'

'Perhaps he's an Elder god.' Heelial said, adopting a spooky voice.

'Don't joke about such things.'

'This has really got you worried ain't it?'

Scorch just shot her a look that said, *what do you think*? The mage stood up and scanned the Square, as if she feared a god would appear at any moment.

'One last thing before you leave, Scorch. Don't mention any of this Elder god and Gifted nonsense to the rest of the squad yet.'

'But we will.'

Heelial knew she had to choose her next words carefully or she might very well end up losing the mages trust. 'Aye, we will.' She agreed. 'But let's be clearer on the situation ourselves, first.' Scorch accepted this with a curt nod, before making her way into the crowd. Heelial signalled for the serving boy to come take another order, all this talk of gods had made her hungry.

* * * *

Sarfina was stood outside a house. The reason as to why would become clear, or at least she was hoping so. Skrenn had been vague as to his reasons for wanting them to meet here. The house itself seemed nothing special, just run down and dirty like the rest of the hovels on the street. Except that the homeless man camped opposite was a lookout.

'I do not like being kept in the dark.' She turned around, Skrenn stood behind her.

'I see your skills remain sharp. That is good. You will need them.'

'And why is that?'

He gestured to the door. 'Shall we?'

'You didn't answer my question.' Not that she'd expected him to.

'No, I did not.' He said over his shoulder, walking up to the door. It was unlocked and sprung open under his gentle push. Sarfina followed him in. The inside matched the out, a thin layer of dust and grime covered the floor and walls. It appeared long abandoned like it was meant to, the only give away that it was still in use were the many sets of footprints that were peppered around the room. The room was sparsely furnished, containing a single bed tucked to one side and a small table upon which a solitary candle stood. The bed looked like it had been slept in recently, probably by the lookout who she'd seen across the street, she surmised. Skrenn went over to the bed and pushed it to one side, then be began to prise the wooden floorboards up with a knife. He removed four and stacked them to one side, revealing a hole dug in the ground heading straight down. Sarfina leant over to glance down and wrinkled her nose at the smell that wafted up. It was not pleasant.

Metal spikes had been hammered into the dirt all the way down, two abreast. She could see that rope was tied between each spike forming a makeshift ladder leading into the darkness. Skrenn showed no hesitation and quickly clambered down and out of sight. With a grimace, Sarfina began her descent. Half way down the smell began to intensify. By the time she reached the bottom it had become so pungent she could almost taste it in the back of her throat. It took all her self-control not to gip. They were both immersed in darkness until a torch spluttered to life in Skrenn's hand; it illuminated the bracket he'd pulled it from and the immediate space around them. A thin trickle of sludge made its way down the centre of the tunnel that gleamed under the flickering glow.

'You really know how to court a lady Skrenn. Take her for a romantic walk through the piss and shit encrusted tunnels of the sewers.'

'Watch your step.' Was his only response.

The sewers under Tydon were a sprawling maze of damp, dark tunnels that emptied the population's waste into the sea. One could easily become lost down here but Skrenn knew exactly where he was going, he took every turn without hesitation. They walked for quite some time and Sarfina was pretty sure they were heading towards the richer side of the city but she couldn't be sure, being underground was messing with her sense of direction. She was tempted to press Skrenn further about what they were doing here but knew she wouldn't get a satisfactory answer to any of her questions. Finally, they came to a proper wooden ladder set against the wall. Skrenn set his torch in a bracket on the wall before extinguishing it, plunging them once more into complete darkness. The Dresconii started up the ladder and Sarfina waited till he was a few rungs up before reaching out to grab it, her fingers brushed the clammy walls causing her to shudder, before they finally found a rung. It was wet from where his boot had been. She heard him grunt, then after a creak and a clatter, a little light appeared from above.

They emerged into a basement filled with row upon row of wine racks. Whoever lived here had expensive tastes, and the wealth to satiate them, Sarfina pondered. It made sense for the benefactor of the Guild to be wealthy and influential. She'd always sensed there was someone above Skrenn, giving him orders to relay. The real question was how far ahead of her was Skrenn in the Guilds hierarchy? Was she finally about to meet the head of the Assassins Guild? The so called Faceless Man? She hoped so: it was about dammed time. Sarfina understood the need for secrecy, but keeping things from your own people at this high a level never ended well, and once sowed, mistrust was never easy to uproot.

They went upstairs and emerged into a kitchen as Skrenn took the lead, venturing further on into the house. Although to call it a house was a disservice, it was far larger, bordering on the size of two houses put together. Although there were no servants, which struck Sarfina as strange, they walked through different rooms and hallways, before finally halting outside a small sitting room. Skrenn stepped aside and motioned for her to go through.

The room was superbly furnished, yet Sarfina's eyes were drawn straight to the man standing with his back to her, gazing out the window. Skrenn shut the door behind her, leaving them alone together.

'Please, take a seat.' His voice soft, yet still carried clearly. Once she had complied with his request he turned around and took the seat opposite. He smiled at her sharp intake of breath. 'Yes, I'm told it can be quite unsettling.'

'Well, it wasn't quite what I was expecting.'

'And what were you expecting?'

'Something that lived up to the rumours that surround the Faceless Man, if that is indeed who you are.'

The Faceless Man chuckled softly. 'No one can ever live up to the rumours that surround them, imagination is often better than reality. Contrary to those rumours, and my moniker, I do actually have a face. Would you like to see it?'

The question hung between them. Sarfina gave the slightest of nods.

He slowly lifted his hand to the finely crafted marble mask that clung to the shape of his face. It was devoid of expression. Sarfina found she was holding her breath. The Faceless Man revealed himself.

A lot of things suddenly started to make sense to the Hand Leader, she understood the need for added secrecy, the reason why no servants attended him; he would be instantly recognised. They'd know who he was, *what* he was.

'Who else knows?'

'Only a select few.'

'Why now, why me?'

'I think you already know the answer for "why now". As for the "why me", we've always had big plans for you and your, *special*, Hand. Current events have propelled those plans forward somewhat.'

'How long has it been like this? How long have we served... you?' She couldn't bring herself to say his name.

'Almost from the beginning. The Guild already existed, but nowhere near its current scale. It was appallingly easy to take control.'

'Very clever, I must say. It makes a lot of sense. I can't believe I never guessed at it before.'

'Now, let us press on for we have much to discuss. But first, lest I forget my manners, would you like some wine?'

* * * *

'Well that was a waste of fucking time!' Rolls huffed.

They'd escorted Kaprel Shellen safely back to his fancy home before making their way back to the barracks, although unbeknownst to them the impersonator had slipped straight out of the back to re-join his Hand at the Tavern.

'When you say that, do you mean it's time you could have spent fucking people, or that it's a waste of time in general?' Shriek asked. 'Sometimes I struggle to pick up on your colloquial phrases.'

'Erm, both I guess.'

Owl hooted with what everyone assumed was laughter. It was hard to tell. The accident had not only removed his ability to communicate but had also scrambled his brain, reverting him to an almost childlike state. He was always happy to be involved. In some ways, to Nozza, he seemed like the squad's pet dog. Everyone doted on him, especially Smokey. Nozza wondered if they'd changed his name after the accident or it was just a coincidence that it fit perfectly with the sounds he made when trying to communicate.

'I just can't wait to get out of this bleedin dress!'

'It's not that bad.' Scoffed Heelial.

'That's because you spent the entire day stuffing your face full of meat!' Scorch countered. 'Some of us actually did work.'

'It wasn't easy eating my entire bodyweight in meat. It took a lot of hard work and dedication.'

Nozza felt a tug on his shoulder, he turned to find the rest of the squad hanging back.

'You're joining us for a drink.' Smokey told him, and although Clipper didn't look too pleased about it, he said nothing for a change. They slinked off as the mage and Corporal endured Heelial walking them through her struggle to get through her seventh steak.

'Where are we going?' Nozza asked nervously.

'The Haven.' The sapper replied.

Nozza nodded, made sense. The Haven was the most popular drinking spot for those billeted at the Barracks due to the fact it was within staggering distance come closing time. They made their way inside to find it was packed.

'Are these all off duty soldiers?'

Rolls laughed and clapped him on the back, knocking him off balance.

'They'll all claim to be.'

She winked at him, then proceeded to wade her way through the crowd to a table whose occupants greeted them warmly. They shuffled up so the 4th could join them. Nozza found himself seated between Owl and Shriek. Owl smiled and hooted at him, making it impossible for Nozza not to smile back. Horrible disfigurement aside, there was something childlike and endearing about the sapper. However, Nozza wanted answers to questions, so instead, he turned to the Kidoshian.

'Who are they?' He gestured to where Rolls and Clipper sat in conversation with the group who'd already been sat at the table.

'Wallow, Stump, Udders and Grimy. Heavies from 8th squad.'

'Guard Company?'

Shriek nodded.

'Sergeant Diallo's squad. Good squad.'

'Shriek… how'd you end up in the Guard Company? Especially seen as though you're a… well, you know, an outsider.'

'You mean because I'm not a Tydonii? Well, the Tydon military recognises talent, even if it's not sprouted from their own city. Corsca is mixed blood and look at her, Captain of the Bow. I got promoted through the ranks. 7th Company to 5th, then 3rd, then here.'

'Impressive. So they put you straight into the 7th when you enlisted?'

'Great Sollun above, no! I was a cut-throat.' Nozza gulped. He wondered how Shriek could sit there with a smile on his face whilst telling him he used to be a murderer in a friendly tone. 'I was part of a bandit group that raided out of the desert but we attacked the wrong caravan. I was captured and brought back to Tydon in chains. It was either slavery, death or service. I chose service.'

'Now you're in the Guard Company?'

He shrugged. 'As I said, they recognise talent.'

'I can understand recruiting Kidoshians, Grellons, but Shulakhii? Fingers is Shulakii isn't he?'

'Actually he's Shulakhai.'

'What's the difference?'

'Ask him yourself.' Shriek motioned behind Nozza who turned to find Fingers standing directly behind him, with fresh jugs and cups from the bar. The Shulakhai eyed him coldly before turning away and distributing the drinks. Nozza breathed a sigh of relief which turned out to be premature as Fingers returned and squeezed in next to Owl.

'Shulakhai are the Shulakii who have been chosen to follow the Reaper's path, the way of the warrior.'

'I thought all Shulakii followed the Reaper's path.'

'To this day, your city's ignorance of our ways astounds me. How can we share the same bloodline in our ancestry?'

'I'm not completely ignorant. I know that every time you lose in battle or a duel, your backs are marked in shame.'

'That is true.'

'So how many scars does your back hold?'

Nozza realised he'd made a mistake when he heard Shriek's sharp intake of breath and Fingers tensed. The others seemed unaware of the sudden tension, totally engrossed in a lively conversation with the heavies from Sergeant Diallo's squad. Only Owl looked on, still smiling away. One hoot from him seemed to break the tension and Fingers seemed to relax, turn his mind away from memories of his past.

'Fifty.' He said quietly. Nozza only just heard him. 'You're lucky Owl seems to like you.'

'I'm sorry, I did not mean to cause offence.'

Fifty times? Even I know that is a pathetic amount of scars for a Shulakhai to have.

'He's the best swordsmen in the Guard Company.' Shriek said softly. 'Recognising talent, remember?'

Oh. With fifty marks he's the best swordsman in the Guard Company? And we're on the verge of war with Shulakh? Reth below! Clipper is right, I don't belong here.

Shriek lifted his cup. 'To new squad members, different places of birth and defeating ignorance.'

Fingers and Shriek immediately threw back their cups and Nozza quickly followed suit. Shriek filled it again immediately. The new recruit feared he was in for a long night.

Nozza woke up the next morning in a sorry state. Shriek and Fingers knew how to drink and they expected him to keep up with them. He'd tried his best and now he was suffering the consequences, he'd vomited three times already, the third was just dry retching, having already heaved all his guts out. The two veterans, annoyingly, seemed unaffected by their night of drinking. Corporal Creak just shook her head when she saw the state of the new recruit, saying he looked like a walking corpse, which wasn't too far from how Nozza actually felt. Clipper laughed at him, claiming that half of soldiering was fighting, the other half was drinking.

The fresh air from the walk to merchant's house helped a little, but he still felt terrible. If Kaprel Shellen noticed his appearance, he didn't mention it. With Creak once again sporting a new fancy dress, they set off to Ritellis Square. If today turned out uneventful like the previous day, they'd move onto a different part of the city. Nozza prayed it would be so, he was in no condition to face the day, let alone a killer.

Please just let me have a quiet day of recuperation.

Nozza had always thought he'd been cursed by The Lady and his suspicions were only strengthened as the first screams sounded across the Square and smoke swirled into the sky.

I have the worst dammed luck.

Chapter 12

Shriek had walked a couple of paces further before he realised Smokey was no longer beside him. She stood with her nose upturned to the sky, sniffing away.

'What? What is it?'

'I smell smoke.'

'Well I can't smell anything. Are you sure?'

'Of course I'm sure, my nose is never wrong about these things. Somethings burning.'

'I still can't smell it.'

'Come on.' She headed off into the crowd towards the other side of the Square and he had no choice but to follow. Sure enough moments later her claims were proven true as the first shouts of fire erupted from the side of the Square they were heading towards. The sight and smell of burning wood quickly followed. 'I told you, my nose is never wrong. There's trouble!' She seemed too happy about that fact to Shriek, too eager to use her munitions. They fought through the crowd who were fleeing from the danger. Smokey was reaching into the satchel at her side.

'No! Not yet. Wait till the people are clear.'

'Fine. Hurry up then.'

He tried his best but it wasn't easy going fighting against the flow of the panicked crowd. Tall as he was, even Shriek couldn't get a glimpse of what was happening. Nor could he spot the other members of the 4th squad. He did, however, spot two hooded figures making their way through the crowd. He nudged Smokey and gestured, her gaze followed to where his finger was pointing. She spotted them and nodded. They set of after the hooded figures, fighting through the crowd with greater urgency. Shriek still couldn't spot the other members of the squad, where in the name of Naul were they?

Heelial was just about to tuck into her first steak of the day when the commotion started and people started rushing past where she was sitting. She sighed.
I'll have to rush it, what a travesty.
Before she could begin to eat the crowd spilled over into the seated area and knocked her table over. Time seemed to slow for Heelial as her lovely cut of meat soared through the air, juices flying in all directions. It hit the floor with a wet splat. Heelial could only stare in horror, her breath coming in ragged gasps. The unlucky man who'd been pushed into her table by the press of the crowd began to apologise but then she turned around and he saw the look in her eyes, quickly making himself scarce. She drew her sword.
That's it. Some cunts getting stabbed!
She waded into the melee. The crowd, as if sensing her murderous intent, gave her as wide a berth as physically possible as they fled by.

Clipper, Rolls and Fingers immediately drew their weapons and fanned out in a protective circle around Thran and Creak as soon as the first screams hit the air. Nozza followed their example seconds later. Thran had to refrain from drawing his knives, they were his last resort. He noticed Creak fumbling under her dress, she pulled out a crossbow that'd been strapped to her inner thigh, already cocked and loaded.

'I never go anywhere without my baby.' She said in explanation, stroking the stock of the projectile launcher. 'Keep your eyes peeled.' The words were barely out of her mouth before the first ambushers were upon them.

Nozza gulped and took a hesitant step forward to his first attacker, who, sensing his nervousness, came rushing in. He'd only had a few basic training sessions, he was nowhere near ready for this type of fighting yet. He wasn't used to the weight of the blade in his hand and he struggled to keep the tip upright. It felt awkward in his hand. Shriek had said most new recruits felt like that at the beginning but eventually it would feel second nature, like an extension of your arm. He just hoped he lived to see that day. He flung his blade up to parry a cut aimed at his head, the impact sent a jolt of pain flying through his whole arm. The man came at him again, driving Nozza back, trying to push home his advantage. So far he was managing to repel him but they both knew he wouldn't last for much longer.

  The man feinted towards his stomach before quickly flicking the blade up at his chest, having fallen for the feint Nozza's blade was too low to help him now, he jerked back just in time but the tip of the blade still sliced his chest and ripped up into his shoulder. He cried out in pain. His first reaction was to drop his sword and grab his injured shoulder, it clattered to the ground. Realising his mistake, Nozza could only look on hopelessly as his opponent drew back his own weapon for the killing blow. He sent a prayer to Jagreus, goddess of Life and The Lady, goddess of Luck, asking for a quick, painless death if it was his moment to perish. The blade sped towards him, he turned his head away and closed his eyes, ashamed that in the end, he'd not even been able to look his demise in the face. His last living moments would be those of a coward.

  Yet the blade did not skewer him as he expected, instead he heard something whistle past his head, followed by a thump. He opened his eyes to find a crossbow quarrel had slammed into the chest of his attacker. The man's eyes had widened in surprise, he tried to speak, his mouth flapping in a big "O" like a fish. He was dead before his body hit the ground.

'Don't worry newbie, I got your back.' Creak called above the rest of the noise, already reloading her weapon with an experienced hand. 'Now pick up your dammed sword and do the 4th proud!' He did so, without hesitation, and just in time as a new attacker filled the place of the dead one. Creak sensed an inner resolve in the man she'd never suspected existed.

We might make a soldier out of you yet.

She quickly glanced around and took stock of their situation. Clipper and Rolls were holding their own, no surprises there. Once planted, the heavies were pretty much immovable. Fingers, wielding his duelling swords, had a pile of bodies in front of him. He parried a lunge before his riposte took his attacker in the throat: another body added to the pile. The rest of the men seemed hesitant to attack him, having witnessed his speed and skill first hand. All the while Fingers had kept up whistling his lively tune which just seemed to unnerve them all the more.

Despite how well they were doing the situation was looking bleak. They were outnumbered already and she could see even more men pouring out of the rapidly thinning crowd coming towards them. 'You can drop the pretence, we could use your help.' In response to her words, twin long knives appeared in the pretend merchants hands and he dropped into a fighting crouch.

I knew it!

Creak managed to get a couple more shots away before attackers squeezed through and around their comrades and into the inner circle, forcing her to abandon the deadly crossbow and use the short sword she'd strapped to her other thigh. She put down her first opponent easily enough. The supposed merchant seemed competent enough, if the two bodies already laying at his feet were anything to go by. Good, one less problem for her to worry about. She had a moments reprieve and used it to check on Nozza. He seemed to be holding his own, although she had to step in and run through an attacker who was approaching on his blindside.

Creak clashed with another assailant. They were in real danger of being overrun; where was Zakanos with the backup squads? Where was the rest of her own squad for that matter?

Sergeant Heelial emerged into the centre of the square to find her squad entirely surrounded and in dire need of assistance. She charged headfirst into them, cutting down three before they realised they were under attack from behind. Their death cries fuelled Heelial's anger, and the enemy, even though they now faced her, wilted under it. She was screaming at the top of her voice, punctuating her speech with blows from her sword that she rained down upon them.

'YOU BASTARDS – MY MEAT – MY MEAT – HOW COULD YOU – YOU BASTARDS – MY MEAT!!!'

The attackers backed away, jostling with each other, wanting to get away from the crazed woman scything them down shouting about meat. A path opened up to her squad and Heelial took it, slotting in beside Rolls and Nozza, strengthening their protective circle and cutting off any easy route into the centre.

'You're a sight for sore eyes, Sergeant.' Creak said, once again loading her recovered crossbow now she wasn't being tightly pressed.

'How you all holding up? Good to see you're still alive, recruit.' Nozza could only offer her a blank stare in return. 'Where's the rest of the squad?'

'Not seem em. Scorch?'

'Holding back until she's sure there's no sorcery in play.'

'We sure could use her right now.'

They were still surrounded but their attackers seemed hesitant to push forward, although they would come again, of that Heelial had no doubt. They still had the greater numbers. They'd expected to quickly overwhelm the defenders and get straight at the merchant who was their main target. However, they'd been met with an unexpected ferocity and stubbornness, which, combined with heavy losses meant there was a sudden lull in the encounter. A welcome pause where everyone could catch their breath, especially the two heavies who were both sporting numerous cuts, yet neither had given a single step of ground.

A voice shouted, more threatening than encouraging, at the men surrounding them to charge in for one final push. Everyone inside the circle tensed, readying themselves for the incoming charge. Just as they were about to clash, twin explosions rocked the square, scattering the attackers, stopping any momentum.

Brioth bless sappers. Heelial thought with relief. The enemy were in complete disarray and she knew they wouldn't get a better chance than this.

'Form up on me. Charge!' She led them forward, flanked either side by Clipper and Rolls, aiming to bully their way out of the circle.

'Owl! Owl!' Smokey was worried; she'd not seen him since all the confusion had started. 'Can you spot him?'

Shriek shook his head. 'Maybe we should concentrate on helping the others first.'

'Not until we find him.' She cocked her head. 'There! I'd know that hoot anywhere.' They pushed through to find Owl still sitting in his lookout position beneath the obelisk. He greeted them with his usual broad grin and enthusiastic hoot.

'You ready to have some fun Owl?' *Hoot! Hoot!* Came the reply. 'Me too.' She reached into her satchel and brought out two small round objects made of clay which she then tossed to Owl.

Shriek's heart gave a lurch as they flew through the air. He'd never understood how sappers could be so careless with such destructive munitions. Thankfully Owl caught them otherwise the three of them would have gone up in flames. He gave a sigh of relief.

'You sappers are crazy.'

'Yeah we get that a lot. Now let's go help the others.'

Ritellis Square was practically empty aside from a few stragglers so it wasn't difficult to now spot the rest of 4th squad fighting for their lives. Although they'd seemed to repel the first wave without taking any casualties. The Sergeant had joined them but there was still no sign of Scorch.

'Time to even up the odds.' Smokey said with a glint in her eye.

In front of them stood the two hooded figures from before, berating their men to get forward and to attack once more. Smokey looked to Owl, he nodded. They both launched a clay ball towards the hooded figures. One ball fell short, exploding on impact it blasted one of the hooded men across the Square where they landed heavily and laid unmoving. Their companion was not so lucky, the other ball hit him high on the shoulder obliterating him into bloody little pieces. Only his lower legs remained whole.

'I love alchemy.' Sighed Smokey, already reaching into her satchel for more. Owl was jumping up and down, hooting repeatedly. Although he'd seen them in action before, Shriek still marvelled at the munition's destructive capabilities. It was hard to believe man could create such a thing, to be used for such means. As the ringing in his ears cleared he could make out the clash of blades as the fighting continued. Then out of the dust and smoke came Sergeant Heelial with Clipper and Rolls right behind her followed by Fingers.

'Smokey you beautiful son of bitch, you've got The Lady's own timing.'

'Good to see you Sarge. Where's the rest of the squad?'

'Right behind me. Or at least they were.' A quick head count revealed Creak, Nozza and the merchant unaccounted for. Heelial squinted through the smoke to see the outlines of people still scrapping in the centre of the Square. 'Looks like we're heading back in. Shriek you're still fresh, take point.' The former desert dwelling tribesman let out an ululating war cry before heading back into the fray, swinging his tulwar around his head.

Things were going poorly, just as he had told the High Priestess they would, but the stubborn cow had refused to listen so now they were caught in an obvious trap. Such was the way of the hunt and Mortem knew it wouldn't be long before reinforcements came to back up the targets. If he was to salvage anything from this, he would need to act soon, at the next half-decent opportunity that presented itself. He held back, waiting, watching the hired thugs fall one after another. The two imbecile acolytes the High Priestess had burdened him with were urging the men on, acting as though they had a clue what they were doing. He'd smiled when they were blown to pieces.

Maybe today hasn't been a total waste.

The woman rallied her men and started to lead them towards the opposite side of the Square and safety. He couldn't allow that to happen.

Thran's back was on fire. His birthmark was burning with a fierce intensity, reacting to all the bloodshed around him, demanding him to let loose and unleash his Gift. He was managing to rein it in so far, but barely, and with each body that fell it became harder and harder. He could hear, *feel*, the blood pumping through his veins, rushing around his body. He could just about make out someone shouting a name, although it wasn't his.

'Kaprel! Kaprel!' Creak shook him, bringing him to awareness. 'We're moving out, come on!'

Thran fell in behind Fingers, Nozza to his side, Creak brought up the rear, covering with her crossbow. Heelial and the two heavies were smashing their way through the dazed men still standing, meaning there was a good chance they'd all get out of this mess. He plunged into the smoke and dust and was almost through to the other side when he noticed movement. Thran pushed Nozza to the ground, saving his life as moments late a figure dashed through the space he'd occupied seconds before, knives flashing. The newcomer drove Thran back. He was far more skilled than any that had come before him and he carried himself in a confident and self-assured manner.

Finally the killer shows himself.

Having had the initial flurry repelled the killer edged back and the two began circling each other, waiting for an opening. Creak hauled Nozza to his feet, before they had to fend off new assailants who'd gained confidence from their leaders attack. They sensed an opportunity to get revenge for their slain who now littered the Square.

'Who are you? What do you want?' Thran tried to get his new deadly opponent talking, trying to buy some time for the rest of the squad to realise they were still in trouble. The man didn't bother answering, just flashed him a malicious grin. They sparred again, testing each other out, parrying, ducking and weaving, never fully committing. It seemed to Thran that this man was getting some perverse pleasure from their fight and was just toying with him. The man came at him again, forcing Thran back, and this time he kept coming. It seemed as though he'd had enough of playing and now intended to end it. Thran had no choice but to keep retreating, the man was quick and he was struggling to keep up with his movements.

His back hit something solid: the obelisk. He reached out a hand to steady himself. As soon as his fingers touched the smooth obsidian surface his birthmark sent searing white hot pain down from his shoulder, through his arm and into the black stone. He felt a pulse emanate from the obelisk and with it came visions. They sped through his mind, fleeting, yet he managed to catch glimpses as they flew past. Cities, deserts, plains, islands, jungles, mountains, caves, grassland all went by. Thran couldn't make sense of what he was seeing, or why he was seeing it. The only thing that linked all the different pictures together was the presence of a black obelisk with strange carvings in each one, identical to the one that stood in Ritellis Square. The images sped up, whizzing past him so fast they became blurs of motion, before he came to an abrupt stop in the middle of nowhere. Barren land stretched for leagues in every direction. The only deviation was another black obelisk, yet this one was not like the others, whilst they had all been pristine, this one's surface appeared worn and cracked, and the symbols almost unreadable.

'Are you listening to me?'

Thran spun at the sound of the voice. Two figures were next to the obelisk. Where had they come from? It was the female who'd spoken, but she wasn't addressing Thran, she was addressing the creature sat next to the obelisk. He wasn't quite sure how to describe it. It roughly resembled a human form but gigantic in size, its skin, for want of a better word was the colour and texture of red clay, appearing hewn from the very earth. *He's living stone* Thran thought in wonderment. The creature turned its gaze to him and sure enough, when it moved, it sounded like the very earth itself moved. They looked at each other, and to him the creatures eyes held a hint of great sadness that threatened to overwhelm Thran. Then the rock-man turned back to address the woman and Thran was once again speeding through the different landscapes back to Ritellis Square.

He tried to blink the dizziness from his vision but everything was still blurry. Had his physical body been transported? Or just his mind? Thran couldn't be sure, he was still getting his bearings. His water droplet shaped mark had stopped burning but still felt hot, as if it had been sated, for now. A body lay slumped at his feet, dead he presumed, killed by Mortem who was now fighting off Reeva. One of her knives was already jutting from his arm. Thran made to go to her aid but a hand grabbed weakly at his ankle. Seemed the fellow wasn't quite dead yet. He squatted down and turned the man, who groaned, onto his back. He gasped.

It was Herrick.

Chapter 13

The sun baked down on the dry, red cracked earth. No signs of life sprouted up from the ground and once again the woman who walked through this desolate wasteland found herself irritated at her journey. It was necessary she supposed, but still, it would have been much swifter if not for him and his... reluctance for the outside world. It would be worth it, even if she didn't get all she hoped she would from their conversation, so she kept on trudging through the bleak, never ending landscape. Eventually, after many hours and leagues, a small black dot appeared on the horizon. Whilst glad her destination was finally in sight, she still kept the same steady, measured pace. It would not do to rush now. The dot grew and grew, until she could make out its long rectangular shape poking into the sky. Finally, she stood in the obelisk's shadow.

'Will you not come out and greet your guest?' She announced into the nothingness that surrounded her. 'I have travelled rather a long way.' At first nothing happened, then the ground began to rumble beneath her feet, the cracks began to widen. A sound suspiciously like a groan to her ears emanated up from the dirt, and a being emerged from the depths of the earth. It pulled itself fully out of the ground before sitting back down but even so it towered over her.

'A touch dramatic, just for little old me.'
'What do you want?' It said in a deep, gravelly voice.
'That's no way to greet an old friend.'
'We are not friends. I told you never to come here again.'
'And I took that to heart. It's been centuries since my last visit.'

He just grunted in response. *That's the problem with immortal beings, their sense of time is all warped.*

'Well no one has bothered me since.'

'Are you not going to offer me refreshments? I'm parched from all that walking.'

'It's your own fault for walking.'

'I suppose you're right, but aren't you just a little bit curious as to why I walked here when I could have arrived much sooner by other means.'

'No.'

'Timing. Something you fail to comprehend but timing is very important. It's the key to everything. The difference between getting struck down by a passing cart and narrowly avoiding it.'

'You babble on about meaningless subjects.'

'Then I shall talk about something that will interest you.'

'I highly doubt it.'

'For that is why I have come here, to lift you from the depths of apathy.'

'You've come here to play your games.'

She smiled coyly. 'You wound me. My intentions are pure.'

'I care not for your kind's squabbles. The children of Jagreus were a grave mistake. They do naught but squander the gifts they were given.'

'He is returning.'

'So?'

'Do you not remember the mischief he caused when he was still alive?'

'Of course I do.'

'He's had time to mull over past mistakes and grievances. This time he will not be so easily quelled.'

'Assuming he makes it back.'

'He will. Unless you and the other Elementals put a stop to it.'

'You dealt with him before without me, you can do it again. It does not concern me. Which is why I did not take part in or bless your ritual. The children making a graver mistake than their mothers.'

'Are you really so naïve?'

'You've been caught up in his arrogance.'

'I'm the arrogant one? Says the one who deems him no threat despite-' she noticed his attention elsewhere. In her peripheral vision she could just make out a rent and the person withins shocked face as it closed on him. She allowed herself a quick smile of satisfaction. Once again her timing had been impeccable. 'Are you listening to me?'

His head swung to face her. 'No. What were you prattling on about?'

Despite his brisk manner, she'd just won a small victory. It was the first question he'd asked her. Progress. And sure enough, when their eyes met, she could detect just the slightest bit of interest begin to spark to life in his gaze. It was a start.

'I thought you weren't interested.'

'Don't be so facetious.'

'Then I'll be truthful with you. One has awakened who can bring him back. The danger is very real.'

'Ah, but dangerous to who?'

'That's the very heart of the matter isn't it? Just what has he decided to do?'

'Where has this awakened one stirred?'

'Tydon. It's-.'

'I am familiar with the name. The city by the sea, founded by one of those infernal brothers if I remember correctly.'

Now this did surprise her. *Clearly not as oblivious to all that goes on around you as we'd thought. I guess he has his own way of getting information, as we all do.*

'It is, although Tydon's influence is felt across the continent, including Mirron.'

But he was no longer listening, just scratching his side, lost in thought. His gaze swung back to where the rent had opened. 'Tydon, eh?' He muttered to himself.

'Well it seems you're obviously very busy, I shall leave you in peace.' But first she walked up to him and chipped off a piece of his body which she placed into her pocket. 'I can't be having to trail all the way back here if we need to talk. Besides, some company would be nice.'

'Yes, yes, goodbye.' He said distractedly. He was already summoning something up from the ground below. A huge black obsidian block emerged before him which he immediately began to work on. The woman began walking away, the sound of his chiselling like music to her ears. That had gone better than she could have ever dared hope. One of the vital pieces had just been put into play, yet there were still many more to nudge and nurdle into position before the games could begin in earnest.

She checked the sun's position above her. *I should just about make it to my next appointment in time.*

* * * *

His wounds were mortal, Thran wasn't entirely sure how he was still alive. Stubbornness he supposed, the man just refused to die, although he couldn't put off the inevitable much longer. His breath was shallow and ragged. So many questions came to Thran but he didn't know which one to ask first, his mind was struggling to comprehend what had happened.

'I see your Gift activated it.' Herrick was smiling thinly. Thran looked up to the obelisk above them.

I did what?

'That's good. Not even I could perform such a feat. Did you see a god?'

'I - I saw something. And a woman talking to *it*.'

'She wouldn't have been able to help herself.' Herrick began to laugh which quickly dissolved into a blood-filled coughing fit. His expression turned grave. 'Descendant – Thran – please, you cannot delay any longer. There will be more attempts on your life.'

'Who are they?'

'I do not have the time to answer all your questions, *he*, will be able to do so. I am not for this life much longer.' Herrick stared straight into his eyes. 'Do not let me die in vain. Promise me!'

Thran, moved by the raw emotion in Herricks beseeching eyes, felt tears forming in his own. How could he refuse the desperate, dying plea of a man who'd taken the dagger meant for his own heart?

'I promise.'

Relief flooded through Herrick. 'Thank you, thank you.' Thran realised Herrick hadn't been scared of death, the man served death's god after all, he'd been scared of his mission failing, scared that his death would be meaningless. *Aren't we all?* Now his dying words had sent the so called "Descendant" further along the road to his destiny. *He's found his comfort in the face of death. He'll face Carrion without regrets.*

Herrick grabbed at his shirt. 'Now hurry, you must finish me. Take out your knife.' He was insistent, brushing aside Thran's questions. 'Just do it! Now!' Thran reluctantly obeyed. 'Now draw it across your palm. Quickly!'

When Thran didn't move, Herrick grabbed the knife with what little strength he had left. 'May Death always be with you, but not for you!' He drew the knife across Thran's palm.

The moment the tip pricked his flesh his birth mark grew hot again, rapidly becoming a blazing inferno. The urge, the *need,* welled up insatiably inside him and he instinctively knew what to do. He placed his cut palm onto the open wound on Herrick's chest. Sharp shooting pains shot up his arm and into his head. His vision went white, it felt like ten blades were being repeatedly stabbed into his brain. He'd never known pain like this could exist, it was excruciating. His body was wracked by spasms, he could hear screaming - his own - sounding above those still clashing around him. Then it was gone, just like that, in the blink of an eye. His vision cleared and he was on all fours, panting heavily.

He checked Herrick but the man lay still, staring into the sky. He was gone.

What did you do to me?!?

His shoulder had cooled down somewhat but it still gently throbbed every so often, almost as if it were letting him know it was there, to be called upon if needed. Heat blasted the right side of his face as flames roared from one side of the Square to engulf the unfortunate men standing there. Their tortured cries, followed by the aroma of burning flesh was too much for Thran, he vomited the entire contents of his stomach onto the cobblestones. When he looked up, a woman in smouldering robes stood above him. Her arm was outstretched towards him, palm open, with arched fingers. Her thin lips were pressed together.

'What are you?'

'I don't know.' Thran answered truthfully.

Before Scorch could question him further a knife appeared at the mages throat. She lowered her arms and met Reeva's cold, hard stare. 'I only asked him a question.' The knife pressed in harder but Scorch stood her ground. The stand-off was broken by the arrival of Heelial with the rest of 4th squad in tow.

'What's going on here?' Heelial demanded. Reeva removed her knife from the mage's throat and moved to stand defensively in front of Thran.

'A good question, Captain.' Scorch replied.

'And who is she?' Heelial demanded from Scorch like Reeva's appearance was somehow her fault.

'For the love of the Twins woman, how am I supposed to know?'

'She's my personal bodyguard.' Thran ventured, but the words sounded hollow even to him.

Heelial spat like she was trying to get a bad taste out of her mouth. 'We've just bled for you, saved your life. Least you could do is tell us the truth.'

Thran was spared further confrontation by the arrival of Zakanos with the backup squads. He gave them orders to get the Square under control and check for survivors before making his way to the group stood next to the obelisk.

'Is everyone alright? Good work Sergeant.'

'Thank you, sir.' She replied curtly. 'If we're done here, I need to see to my squad.' She snapped a crisp salute and walked away before he could reply. The 4th followed, except for Smokey who had been carrying a body. She dumped it at her feet. 'This one was giving em' orders.' She said, giving a borderline insubordinate salute. She hurried off to catch up to the rest of her squad.

Zakanos scratched the bristles on his chin. 'Not sure how I'm going to explain this to the Emperor.'

'Then don't.'

Zak glanced sharply at Thran but he'd already turned away to gaze intently at the obelisk. Zak then looked to Reeva who just shrugged. His mind was clearly elsewhere. Thran extended his hand tentatively towards the black stone. When his fingers touched the surface, he snapped them back, as if expecting some sort of reaction. A confused expression on his face, he laid his hand flat on the obelisk, shaking his head. Zak wasn't quite sure what to make of his strange behaviour. He turned his attentions to the body Smokey had left for them.

He knelt to examine it. It was dressed in a full length plain robe, complete with hood. He pulled back the hood, but didn't recognise the face. She was pretty, well, had been pretty before one of the clay balls had sent dirt and shrapnel hurtling towards her. Scraping across the floor when landing had finished off the job. Her robes had been similarly affected. There were no identifying marks or insignia on her clothing. It wasn't until he lifted up the sleeves at her wrists that he found something worthwhile. Tattooed on her wrist was the symbol of infinity: a snake curled in a figure of eight eating its own tail. A common symbol but one mainly used by the follows of Jagreus as a show of devotion to their goddess who granted them everlasting life. Zakanos knew he wasn't making a big leap in thinking that they were somehow involved in all of this. How or why, he had no idea.

This whole mess just keeps getting more convoluted as the days go by.

'Thran, Reeva. You're going to want to see this.'

* * * *

'I told you it was a mistake.' Mortem growled as he pulled the knife from his arm. That blonde bitch had got him good, but only because he'd been preoccupied with his target and she'd caught him unawares with a throwing knife from across the Square. Given the chance, he intended to return the favour, with interest. Despite his scepticism it had almost worked. If not for that stranger who'd sacrificed his life by throwing himself in front of the boy, he'd be dead right now. The boy had been good, almost as good as Mortem himself, but had inexplicably dropped his guard when bumping into the obelisk. Mortem cursed the man vehemently. Whoever the fool was, he was dead now but his sacrifice had stalled him long enough for the blonde bitch to intervene and drive him away. When the mage had started burning down what little remained of his men he knew the opportunity had gone. He'd disengaged from the woman pressing him and slinked away with the rest of his fleeing men.

'Yes you've made that fact abundantly clear.' The High Priestess stood with her arms folded across her chest, her lips pressed tight in barely contained anger.

'Those hired thugs and sell swords were pathetic. Especially if they are the best Tydon has to offer.'

'You talk as if you didn't fail as well.'

'I came closest to succeeding and if those worms could have held their ground a little longer I would have finished him off. But you're right. The failure is mine also.'

'At least you don't have a goddess to answer to.'

Mortem let out a low chuckle. 'Ah yes. I'm sure the life giving goddess also has means to take it away.'

'You should not speak of matters you know nothing about.'

'But I stumble close to the mark, do I not?' She just glared at him. 'Now hurry up and heal me. We still have much to do.'

'Excuse me?'

'Heal me. This wound hinders my ability to operate.'

'And why would I do that?'

'Because you still need me. Because I know how to get close to the assassin.'

'How?'

'Ah-ah-ahhh. Heal me first.'

'How do I know you're not lying to save your worthless hide?'

'You don't. Just as I don't know if you'll deliberately botch healing up my arm. We're just going to have to trust one another.' He said, giving her a grin he knew would infuriate her. He could almost hear her teeth grinding together. Without another word she walked over to him and placed her hands over his wound. His skin tingled as she worked her healing magic, eyes closed and lips chanting. When she stepped away he was healed once more. He rolled his shoulder and flexed his arm.

'You're a marvel.'

'That is the last time I will patch you together.'

'Noted. It's not going to be easy, they'll be expecting us to make another move, especially after Ritellis Square failed so spectacularly. Which is why we're going to take a more...' he paused, as if searching for the right word. 'Subtle, approach.'

* * * *

'By the gods, what is that awful smell?' said Drak, wafting an arm in front of his face. The members of Sarfina's Hand were all together once again in the operations room.

Sarfina coughed gently into her fist, before clearing her throat. 'That's not important right now. What is, is that you're all safe *and* we have gained valuable information.'

'That's easy for you to say. It wasn't your life in danger!' Replied Thran indignantly. 'If it wasn't for Reeva I wouldn't be here.'

'Which is exactly why your life wasn't in danger. Reeva was guarding you for that very reason.'

'You also had the entire 4th squad protecting you, who more than held their own.' Added Zel. 'While I can understand why you're not overly enamoured by the situation, your protection was more than adequate.'

'Why don't you shove the situation up your backside!'

'That's physically impossible.'

'Enough! Quit your bickering.' They subsided at Sarfina's words. Reeva looked bored by the whole conversation. 'Thanks to Zakanos' find, we have reason to believe Herrick was a worshiper of Jagreus and those from the temple are the cause behind the abductions and attacks.' Thran shifted uncomfortably; he'd remained silent as Zakanos' men had disposed of Herrick's body along with the rest of the thugs and lowlifes, keeping Herrick's sacrifice to himself. He snuck a quick glance at Reeva to find she was watching him intently. She was the only other person there who could have identified him and thankfully, not unsurprisingly, had remained silent. Than knew he couldn't put off talking to her much longer. 'Which means,' Sarfina continued. 'That, Zel you're going to have to-'

'No.'

'Zel.'

'I'm not doing it.'

'Zel.'

'I refuse to talk to that imbecile.'

'Zel.'

'That man infuriates me!'

'Zel!' Sarfina voice had taken on a dangerous tone.

'Fine. Fine. But I'm not going alone. I don't see why I should be the only one to suffer.'

'Take Reeva with you.'

'Seriously? I would still have to bear the brunt of the burden. I don't think so. Thran can come with me.'

Thran wondered just who exactly could make Zel so flustered but before he could ask the door opened and Skrenn popped his shiny bald head through. 'It is time.' Was all he said before slipping back through.

'Time for what?' Drak asked the question all were thinking.

'For a meeting long past overdue. Now listen up, I don't want anyone making a fool of themselves so let me do the talking and for Naul's sake, don't gawp.'

She led them outside where Skrenn took over, taking them to the same nondescript house where he had met Sarfina last time. As he uncovered the secret entrance under the floorboards, Drak couldn't help but comment:

'By the gods, what is that awful smell?'

Chapter 14

Although Zakanos had braced himself for the inevitable tongue lashing coming his way from the Emperor after the violence in Ritellis Square; it didn't make it any easier to take. Thankfully the lesser Captains weren't here to witness his dressing down, only Remullus, Corsca and Cyprian were present, along with the weasel faced nobleman Threm Sioll Celentine. Zak still wasn't sure what he had done to worm his way into Tavian's good graces, but the Emperor seemed to be listening to his council more and more of late. Once Tavian had finished reminding him of his short comings and failure in the Square, he softened his tone.

'You have a bright future ahead of you Captain, let this be the only bump on an otherwise, smooth road. Remullus, you will be taking over from Zakanos.'

The huge Captain of the Elite Guard clasped his fist to his chest in salute. 'As you command, my Emperor.'

'And what of Zakanos' punishment?' asked Celentine. Zakanos glowered at the nobleman, but wisely, remained silent. 'Surely he must fall upon his sword.' he continued, answering his own question.

'You forget this is not a time of war, Councillor.' Cyprian countered, his voice cold.

'The Captain can count himself lucky in that respect.'

'It's the Emperors job to discipline his men.'

'Of course, of course. I was merely suggesting an option.' The nobleman turned his attention towards the Elite Guard Company Captain. 'Captain Remullus, may I offer assistance? I believe I may have some information that will be helpful to your cause.'

Remullus looked at the merchant guardedly before inclining his head. Corsca regarded Celentine with contempt. None of the Captains liked the nobleman being involved in military matters. She snorted and was about to comment when Tavian held up his hand for silence. 'I shall decide upon the Captain's punishment and mete it out accordingly. The rest of you may leave us.' Corsca and Cyprian saluted their Emperor. Threm wasn't happy about having to leave with the Elite Captains but adhered to Tavian's wishes none the less, flashing Zakanos a self-satisfied grin before leaving the room.

'And what am I supposed to do with you, Captain?'
'Sir?'
'A rhetorical question. I should punish you, yet you did commendably well. As well as any other Captain would have done, yet you ultimately failed. Tydon does not accept failure. In normal circumstances you would have been stripped of your Guard Company Captaincy and broken back down into the ranks. Yet, instead, I am going to reward you.'
'My Emperor, I don't understand.'
'I know Zakanos, but you will.' With that Tavian lapsed into silence, making Zak more and more uncomfortable as time went by. He wasn't entirely sure what was going on, or what he was supposed to do. What was Tavian planning to reward him with? Zak suspected it wasn't something he'd be overjoyed with. He'd just built up enough courage to ask a question when the wall began to rumble and break apart. Zakanos could only gape as a man emerged from the gap, Tavian on the other hand, seemed entirely unperturbed.

At first Zakanos couldn't understand what he was seeing. Skrenn had just walked casually into the room as if he belonged there. Tavian addressed Zakanos.

'Captain Zakanos, as I'm sure you've figured out by now, I am the Faceless Man.'

Skrenn inclined his head towards the Captain in greeting, but all Zak could manage in response was an incredulous stare.

How long have you been hiding this Tavian? And why?

'They are right behind me.' Skrenn answered the Emperor's unaired question.

'And the 4th?'

Zakanos realised this question had been addressed to him. 'Anxiously awaiting further instruction in the grand hall.'

'Good, bring them in.'

Zakanos left immediately, not wanting to irritate the Emperor further, speedily returning with Sergeant Heelial and her squad at the same time as Sarfina entered with the rest of the Hand through the secret passageway. 'Poleon's salty tears.' Heelial cursed as she saw the other occupants in the room. The rest of the squad echoed her sentiments with muttered curses of their own, Owl gave a nervous hoot. The assassins, aside from Skrenn and Sarfina, all looked decidedly uneasy.

'Please, all of you sit.' Tavian instructed them. For a moment, nobody moved, until Skrenn took Remullus' seat on the right side of the Emperor. Zakanos sat down next to him in his own and Sarfina sat opposite. The 4th squad and the Hand took their cues and followed suit. 'I'm going to talk, and you're all going to listen, *without* interrupting.'

'When I first seized power all those years ago, I knew that one day, someone would in turn attempt to take it from me. Betrayal inevitably leads to further betrayal. However, I have something the previous Emperors lacked; the Assassins Guild.' Heelial glanced towards the Hand but their faces showed just as much shock and confusion as her own squad, except for, Skrenn and Sarfina. Their faces were expressionless, unreadable. 'On the night of my ascendancy, the Guild made a… they… they made themselves known to me. I culled their ranks and placed Skrenn in charge as my second and became the Faceless Man. How better to monitor the seedy underbelly of my city than to run it myself. The Guild also acts as my protection against the military, should someone decide upon a coup. I'm putting that protection into play as of today, because there is a plot underfoot to remove me from the throne and I have reason to suspect many, if not most of Tydon's Captains have chosen to throw their lot in with the usurpers. I believe they are targeting the Guild to remove that protection.'

Zakanos breathed a huge sigh of relief. When he had first seen the assassins enter the room he had feared the worst, but now he understood what the Emperor intended, he felt like jumping for joy. His misbegotten dealings with the Assassins Guild had actually worked out in his favour.

Bless The Lady, what a stroke of luck! Although the irony was not lost on him. *My initial betrayal turned out to be the very reason he can now trust me.* Then another thought struck him, this one far more disturbing. *He's known all this time. He must have been the one to sanction it in the first place. Have my ambitions been groomed from the very beginning? Or simply tapped into?*

Either way, Zakanos had the unnerving idea that he'd attained the rank of Captain of the Guard through a contingency plan put in place by the Emperor for the very situation they found themselves in today. His respect for the Tavian increased.

You wily old bastard.

'Sergeant Heelial of the Guard Company, 4th squad. You are no doubt wondering why you and your squad currently sit at this table, after I have just spoken of the compromised military.'

Tavian paused, clearly expecting an answer so Heelial cleared her throat and prayed her voice would come out clear and steady. 'The, err, thought had crossed my mind, my Lord.'

'Captain Zakanos has proven his loyalty to me and has vouched for the 4th squad. Is his faith well placed?' Zakanos had to stop himself from snorting a laugh.

That's one way to put it.

'It is, my Lord.'

'You may well have to face comrades you have trained and fought with, men and woman you've known for years. Are you capable of striking them down?'

'They choose the traitorous path, my Lord, and so will have to suffer the consequences. If we are to be the, err. . .' She paused, searching for the right word.

'Arbiters?' Tavian prompted.

'Yes, if we are to be the arbiters,' she said only slightly stumbling over the word, 'of their punishment then so be it.'

'Good. You shall be suitably rewarded for your loyalty. I believe we have some openings in the Elite Guard Company.' Clipper, Rolls and Smokey seemed especially pleased. Promotion to the Elite Guard Company came with increased pay and perks. 'However, at the moment we must keep up appearances so you are to be punished along with Captain Zakanos for your involvement in the Ritellis Square debacle. You're all on latrine duty for the foreseeable future.' They liked that considerably less, but nobody audibly grumbled. 'Skrenn.' He gestured for the Dresconii to take over.

'Whoever is behind the attack in Ritellis Square is not acting alone and has inside information at their disposal considering they targeted the Assassins Guild. Yes, Sergeant Heelial?'

Heelial had been frowning in thought. 'Well, it's just that, how can we be sure it's not the Shulakhii stirring things up before they attack?'

Skrenn smiled. 'Our agents in Shulakh have assured me they can delay our enemies' armies from marching until next campaigning season. Although their own spies are no doubt reporting the bloodshed on our streets back to their masters.'

'And what of the Shulakhai sat in our midst? Can we trust him?' Sarfina spoke up for the first time.

Tavian glanced sharply at her. 'Explain yourself!'

'Sergeant Heelial, would you care to defend your man?'

The Sergeant's lips were pressed together in suppressed anger. However, before she could answer, a voice spoke up. 'I can defend myself.' All eyes in the room swivelled to Fingers who had stood. 'I make no secret of my origins, I hail from Shulakh but that is not where my loyalty lies.' As if to emphasise his point, he stripped to his waist, and turned so all could see the fifty marks of shame etched onto his back. The scars were almost identical, split into five neat rows of ten. 'I am an outcast from Shulakh. You question my loyalty? It belongs to my brothers and sisters of the 4th squad, to Captain Zakanos. None killed more than I in Ritellis Square.'

'Fingers is the Guard Company's most skilled fighter.' Heelial added.

'I would hope so too, living up to the Shulakhai legacy. Where you're born does not matter, only your current allegiances do. Why, we also have a Dresconii, a Grellon and a Kidoshian all sat round this very table. Add a Mirronese and the set would be complete.' Tavian quipped.

'We are not on the brink of war with the other cities, nor do we share with them the history we share with Shulakh.' Sarfina pointed out.

'You are quite correct Sarfina. However, we are all in this together now, we are committed. You all need to learn to trust each other implicitly, your lives *will* depend on it.' Sarfina bowed her head in deference. 'Besides, most worryingly about the Ritellis Square incident is Zakanos' discovery about the two servants of Jagreus appearing to command the attack. It appears our conspirators may have the temples backing.'

Scorch snorted in derisive laughter. '*Please*, the temples don't get involved in such petty affairs.'

Tavian's eye's narrowed but it was Skrenn who answered. 'So we originally believed, but according to Captain Zakanos, the tattoos he found on the body undeniably belonged to those who worship the goddess of Life. Isn't that right, Captain?'

'There was no mistaking the symbol.'

'Jagreus cares not who sits on Tydon's throne, so why should her followers?' Scorch countered.

'And what makes you the expert of the gods and their temples?' asked Zel.

'Seeing as I'm the only mage present in this room, it makes me the resident expert.'

It was Zel's turn to snort derisively. 'Mage's are just jumped up street performers, adept at tricks and sleight of hand.'

A ball of flame sprang to life in the centre of Scorch's palm. 'Does this look like some cheap trick to you?'

'You obviously have some complex system rigged together in your sleeve.'

'Then I shall strip naked!'

'Enough!' Tavian's voice sounded like a whip crack. 'What did I just say about getting along? We need to discern if the temples are directly involved or it's an attempt to mislead us.'

'We have a contact who Zel and Thran are due to meet tomorrow who may be able to shed some light on that.' Sarfina shared.

'I want to be in that meeting.' Scorch said immediately.

'Now wait just a minu-' Zel began.

'Agreed.' Tavian said. 'I want a mix of Hand and squad members working together on all outings. It will help build relationships. We've kept the 4th squad long enough now.' said Tavian. 'If we keep them any longer it will arouse suspicion. Keep your eyes and ears open, and be ready to be called upon at any moment. Dismissed.' Zakanos and his men saluted their Emperor and made their way out of the chamber, whilst the Faceless Man turned to address his own.

'Report to me at once with your findings tomorrow.' Sarfina acknowledged his order with a nod before leading her Hand out through the secret passage. Skrenn lagged behind momentarily. 'Can we trust the Shulakhii?' Tavian asked him.

'I believe so.' The Dresconii answered. 'But I shall watch him regardless.'

'Good. See that you do.'

The Emperor's expression changed, softened. He started rubbing his eyes with his thumb and forefinger.

'That was even more difficult that I thought it would be. Not once did she even glance in my direction.'

'She still blames you.'

'I know.'

'She will find a way to move past it. I will try speaking to her again.'

'Thank you, old friend.' Tavian grunted softly. 'It is now I who is indebted to you.'

'And that is why I stayed once mine was paid off, so you would know how it feels.'

The two shared a smile.

Not another word was spoken for quite some time as they shared a companionable silence, contemplating the past, and what now lay ahead.

* * * *

'Well.' Drak drawled, making the word sound like 'wheeeeel' as it echoed down the sewer tunnels. 'That's a turn up for the books ain't it?'

'What is?' Zel asked.

'Us working for that crafty bugger all along.'

'You mean you didn't already know?'

'Of course I bloody didn't!'

'I thought it obvious.'

'Not to me.'

'I thought everyone knew.'

'I think we would have mentioned it before now if we served the most influential man in all of Tydon.'

'I assumed it was an unspoken rule not to talk about it. Sarfina knew.'

Drak looked to Sarfina expectantly; there was a slight pause before she answered. 'I was aware of the Faceless Man's identity before today's meeting.'

'See, you big lummox. All it requires is a bit of thought.'

'Hey Thran, did you know?'

'Nope.'

'See, he's a smart enough lad and it wont obvious to him.'

Drak continued to air his thoughts on the matter as they exited the sewers and trudged back to the Tavern but Thran was no longer listening. He was lost in his own thoughts. Herrick had named him Descendant, did he mean the Emperor? Had they intended to overthrow Tavian and place him on the throne? Crown him Emperor? Thran dismissed the idea, why would the god of Death care who sits on Tydon's throne.

Besides, I have no wish for that burden.

He couldn't make sense of what was going on, every time he thought he'd made a decision about which path to choose, events steered him in the opposite way again. Perhaps it was time to talk to Reeva, get it all off his chest. He glanced over to her, padding silently beside him. Something seemed wrong, her jaw was set, and her eyes fixed ahead, hands balled into fists at her sides. She was angry, positively seething! Thran had never seen her like this before. What had gotten her this wound up? Thran resolved to speak to her. Clear the air between them, on his part anyway. *One less thing to worry about.*

When they finally reached the Tavern, Thran's only thoughts were for his bed, events at Ritellis Square had left him exhausted. He would speak to Reeva first thing in the morning, but right now, he needed to rest.

He didn't bother to undress, instead he just flopped straight onto the bed and immediately fell asleep. Thran had purposefully erased the memory of activating the obelisk with his powers, and so as sleep enveloped him, he found himself once more before the altar. Although this time the altar was not empty, sat atop it was a fully animated corpse, waiting, waiting for him, with a rictus grin spread across its ashen features.

* * * *

Zakanos was jubilant. He hummed a lively tune as he walked through the streets of Tydon back to his home, back to his family. Today couldn't have gone better. He was now part of the Emperor's inner circle, aware of his biggest secrets. Promotion to Captain of the Elite Guard was assured, despite Remullus still holding the position. He could always be disposed of. The Elite Guard, the military's most vaunted position. He could scarcely believe it. When the inevitable war with Shulakh erupts next summer, he might even be named Acting Wartime General. *Don't get ahead of yourself, keep your feet firmly grounded. There's still a lot to do, a coup to quash.*

He arrived home and closed the door behind him. 'Lia!' He called as he removed his cloak and hung it on a peg by the door. 'Lia! Where are you?' He expected her to admonish him for being too loud, that he'd wake little Nian. Instead he turned to find a man sitting comfortably at their kitchen table. 'Oh I'm sorry, I wasn't aware we had guests. Is Lia upstairs?' He voice trailed away. There was something awfully familiar about this man, yet they had never met, of that Zakanos was certain. Then it hit him, he remembered where he'd seen him before. His knees began to tremble. His future which had looked so bright moments earlier began to fade, turning to ash barely a bell later.

'Where is Lia!? Where is my son!?' Zakanos drew his sword and advanced at the man who still sat calmly at the table.

'She's safe. We had a lovely, interesting little chat, me and her, but I fancy it will pale in comparison to the one we're about to have. Now put that fine sword away before somebody gets hurt.' Zakanos let it slip from his grasp and clatter to the floor. He slumped down, dejected.

'There's a good Officer.' Mortem crooned. 'We wouldn't want anyone to suffer, now would we?'

Chapter 15

Even as young baby, he'd had vivid night terrors. He would wake screaming, night or day, until a maid came to comfort him. It wasn't until he was a little older that Thran realised he'd been having the same recurring nightmare about the corpse on the altar. His initial memories of the terrors were little more than a haze, and it wasn't until he grew to be around six or seven years old that he finally could recall them with any clarity. It had taken him another two years to realise his powers triggered the visions and by then he had developed a morbid fascination with assembling the corpse. Each night he would put more of the body together, resulting in the laughing corpse who had haunted his last trip to the altar. The very same body that now sat before him, whom Herrick had revealed as Carrion, the god of Death.

Thran had no idea what to say, so remained silent. In turn Carrion seemed to be content to regard him with a face and eyes devoid of expression. The silence, combined with the swirling blackness surrounding them felt heavy and oppressive.

Carrion deigned to break the silence first. 'You must have many questions.' His voice took Thran back a little, he'd expected a raspy, grating voice to come from the corpse but it came across true and clear.

'I- I do.'

'Then ask away.'

'Herrick named you Carrion. Are you truly the god of Death?'

'Yes and no. Yes, I am who you humans named and choose to worship as the god of Death. Am I worthy of such a title? A touch melodramatic I think, but no matter how true to the story a narrator sticks, he cannot help but embellish certain parts. And my story has been told, and retold, and retold countless times. As for being a god? Well that's certainly up for debate.' Carrion gave mirthless chuckle. Thran was taken aback, the god of Death was not acting like he had expected.

'You certainly seem different from what your ominous title would suggest.'

'That is the problem with titles, they attach expectation. I've known kings to greet guests like paupers, and paupers to greet guests like kings.'

'Herrick named me Descendant.'

This time the god's chuckle was genuine. 'More than a touch melodramatic, was Herrick.' Carrion's smile faded. 'He shall be greatly missed.'

'Who was he?'

'For want of a better word, a disciple of mine. The other gods have their priests and priestesses, their acolyte's and followers, I have my disciples. He was fervent and loyal to the cause as well as being extremely Gifted. Someone I called friend.'

'Gifted?' Thran prompted. He wanted Carrion to keep talking as much as possible, Zel often counselled to digest all the information you can to make sure you can properly assess the situation. Thran was glad he'd actually been paying attention to what Zel had been saying for a change. It would hopefully serve him well.

'Yes. Herrick was born with an exceedingly rare Gift that allowed him to manipulate people's perception of their surroundings. He could even plant memories, but only on a single target, and never for very long, although he was improving.' Thran considered the god's words. It was in line with what had happened to them on the night of the contract, they'd thought they'd been sneaking into their target's house but instead it had turned out to be a warehouse.

'If his Gift is so rare, why did he sacrifice himself for me?'

'Because while his gift is rare, yours is even more so. You're the first Blood-born for almost two centuries.'

'Blood-born?'

'Yes, that's the name for someone with your abilities.'

'Is that why someone wants me dead? Because I'm a... a Blood-born?'

'You pose a threat to the very gods themselves, because of what you may become.'

'The gods want me dead?'

'One does for certain. Jagreus, the goddess of Life means to kill you. I'm sure the irony of the situation is not lost on you.'

'But why? I haven't done anything wrong! To kill me over what I might possibly do in the future is absurd!'

'It used to be that everyone knew the story of the gods, but no matter how well the annals are kept, knowledge seems to erode away like a rock laid bare to the elements. The world is in a sad state of affairs, Thran. The temples are no longer beacons of light, drawing people from lands far and wide to its knowledgeable glow. Bellum is a shade of what it used to be.'

A melancholy came over Carrion as he contemplated his own words. Thran remained silent, sensing the god had more to say.

'For you to truly understand, we must go way back in time. Thousands of years in fact, to a time before the pantheon of gods there are today. I do not view myself as a proper god, because I was not there at the beginning. Poleon, Sollun, Reth, Naul, the Bestial Twins - Vittes and Vottres. They are the true gods. Those learned enough today refer to them as the Elementals, or Elder gods, especially in the Twins case. After much deliberation, the Bestial Twins decided to create life to occupy the lands and seas of the world. They created the animals, whose decedents roam the earth today. But they weren't satisfied with that. They poured all their energy into one final being: their daughter, Jagreus. Jagreus was their magnum opus, and the Twins loved her above all else, naming her the curator of all their other work. Upon seeing her parent's majestic and beautiful creations, Jagreus attempted to create something to live alongside them in her own image. She wanted them to be more self-aware and intelligent. Whether she succeeded or not remains to be seen, but the outcome was humans. They multiplied, advanced and spread faster than Jagreus could ever have imagined.'

'Fast forward a few hundred years and you have Mirron, the first major city of what would become Bellum. In those days it was much easier to speak directly to the gods, they weren't as reticent. The gods would bestow Gifts of power upon humans they found to be particularly pleasing. Very soon there were many Gifted members of society, and they formed the Council. Under the Councils guidance, Mirron and the Gifted themselves flourished. But there are always troublemakers. Some members of the Council abused the Gifts they had been given, dabbling in Blood magic, causing a rift between them and the gods.'

'It was not a good time to be Gifted, so many lost their lives needlessly. In the end the troublemakers were quashed, but their taint remained. A rift was sown between the gods and their subjects, a rift that continued to grow. The gods stopped visiting man as regularly, preferring to communicate telepathically, or through visions and dreams. They no longer bestowed Gifts freely, reserving them for only those who had proved themselves to be worthy. Eventually, some gods stopped their communication altogether, others were more lenient, some meddled from the shadows. All the while Bellum continued to grow and expand and develop into the city-state land it is today.'

'Then came someone who changed everything again. A young, ambitious pupil of the Council stumbled upon knowledge he should have left well alone. His name was Dragos and he single-handedly brought down the Council. How he accomplished that is another long tale for another time. In the aftermath some of the Council fled, but he followed relentlessly, intending not to leave a single one alive. They lured him to an old temple dedicated to Jagreus and set a trap for him. Many of them died but eventually they overpowered Dragos and killed him, or so they thought. Unfathomable to them, he had found a way to ascend, to attain the powers of a god. They killed his earthly body but his spirit, his soul, lived on.'

'I can see you are still wondering what this has to do with you, but don't worry, I'm getting to that. The Council returned to Mirron to find it in disarray, their disappearance had left a power vacuum that numerous groups had attempted to fill leading to a violent, bloody struggle for power. Many were expelled from Mirron and told never to return upon pain of death. Some went north and into the desert, some fled to the mountains, to build Grellon in its depths. Two brothers led a group further west, beyond the mountains. They would found Tydon and Shulakh. Among them was a woman who was with child. Dragos' child. It appears the child inherited his father's powers and when the boy grew of age, Dragos revealed himself to his offspring in his dreams. Father and son worked in secret towards the revival of his earthly body, but that meant returning to Mirron where the Council was making a recovery, lying in wait, although they shared power with a self-proclaimed king.'

'So they waited and schemed. Dragos' son took a family of his own, but the inherited power laid dormant in his children. Eventually his son made a move, journeying to revive his father. He almost succeeded, but the Council members still living from the time of his father thwarted his attempt. The

Council members knew they had to kill off all the remaining descendants of Dragos to insure he never returned, but his son would not betray the location of his family, instead taking his own life.'

'So the line of Dragos continued and the Council members knew they had to take precautions for the future. In the end they decided to betray their beliefs, their morals, and use the power they had fought against for their own ends. For good. They performed a ritual, a ritual to ascend.'

'How do you know all this?' The question had been bugging Thran for some time.

'Because I was one of them. I stood against Dragos, I helped stop his son. I took part in that unholy ritual.'

'But that means…'

'Yes. I'm old. So very old. And I'm tired.'

Thran thought he already knew the answer to his next question, but he wanted to hear it directly from the ascended Council member's mouth. 'Am I?…'

'Yes Thran. You are a descendant of Dragos, and the first in centuries to be born with his abilities.'

* * * *

Sergeant Heelial stood waiting outside her Captain's office. When she'd arrived his aide had told her he was already in a meeting with another Sergeant. She didn't have to wait long. Diallo, the Sergeant of 8th squad walked out of the office and closed the door quietly behind him.

He inclined his head in greeting. 'Heels.'

She returned the nod. 'D.'

'Sorry to hear about your squad's punishment.' If it had come from another Sergeant, Heelial might have suspected they were mocking her, but she knew Diallo was being genuine.

They got along. 'If you guys hadn't been in Ritellis Square, more innocents would have been killed.'

'Thanks, but unfortunately someone had to take the flak for what happened and we were easy targets.'

'Squad like yours, you'll be back in the good books in no time.'

'Here's hoping. Clipper and Rolls are already moaning and bickering like an old married couple.'

'Heavies ain't happy unless they're knee deep in someone else's guts. Or drink.'

'Ain't that the truth!' Heelial laughed in agreement. She lowered her voice. 'How's morale in the Guard Company at the moment?'

Diallo leaned in closer and also dropped his voice to a whisper so the aide couldn't overhear them. 'Fine. Usual grumbling and muttering, nothing out of the ordinary. Why?'

'No reason in particular,' Heelial lied. 'Just got a bad feeling, with war on the horizon. Keep alert, okay?'

Diallo nodded. 'Sure. I appreciate the warning. Your guts usually right, when it's not full of meat.' He flashed her a smirk before turning more serious. 'I'll return the favour right away. The Captain seems, well, dispirited. Be careful.'

The aide was glancing curiously in their direction. Heelial saluted smartly. 'Thank you for the advice, Sergeant Diallo.'

He snapped one back. 'You're welcome, Sergeant Heelial.' He turned and marched away down the corridor like he was on parade inspection. It took all her composure not to burst out laughing. She looked towards the aid, who was frowning at the departing Sergeant as he quickly turned round a corner and disappeared out of sight. He then turned his attention to Heelial.

'The Captain will see you in a few moments.'

Diallo's word about the Captain feeling glum didn't come as a surprise to her, the Captain was supposed to be acting as a man who'd just had his knuckles well and truly rapped by the Emperor. The Sergeant had just confirmed what Heelial already knew, that the Captain was playing his part to perfection. Time ticked away and she was pretty sure the aide was delaying her meeting as some petty show of power. *What a pathetic insect of a man.* Finally she was ushered through into the Captain's office.

She walked in and stood to attention before Zakanos who was seated behind his desk. The Captain did indeed look dispirited but she expected him to drop the act now it was just the two of them but when he looked up, it felt like his gaze went straight through her.

'Sergeant Heelial.'

She snapped a salute. 'Sir.'

'What do you want?'

That took her aback a little. 'You sent for me, sir.'

'I did? Oh yes, that's right. I did.' It was like she was talking to a small part of him, the other, larger part, was somewhere else, focusing on something else. 'What did we glean from the temple informant?'

'Nothing yet, sir. The meeting's this afternoon.'

'Of course, sorry. Report to me again this afternoon once Scorch returns.'

'Yes sir.'

There's no reason to keep up pretences with me. Unless?

'Captain?'

'What?' he asked, distractedly.

'I just wanted to say sir, there ain't no hard feelings in the squad. About all this I mean, towards you. We know you was duped and didn't have a choice in the matter.'

'What's your point, Sergeant?'

'Just that we're all behind you, sir.'

'Thank you Sergeant. Is that all?'

'Yes sir.' Heelial saluted. 'I shall report back to you this afternoon.' He barely registered her leaving. Outside the Captain's aide remained sat at his small desk like he'd been there all the time. There was no telling if he'd been listening at the door or not. *Little bastard.*

She headed back to the billeting quarters, or more accurately, to the latrine section of billeting quarters. She found her squad at work, shovelling shit. Clipper, Rolls and Creak were advising Nozza on how to curse properly.

'By the Lady's balls?' Nozza tried tentatively.

'No newbie! That was terrible.' Creak huffed. 'For starters, the Lady don't even have no balls, so it don't make sense. What did we tell ya?'

'A good curse is a simple curse.'

'And?'

'Just pick a god, pick a body part and put em together.'

'Exactly newbie. It ain't alchemy. It's piss easy.'

'Poleon's kneecap.' Nozza tried again, eliciting a groan from them all.

'It's hopeless Creak.' Rolls said. 'This is going about as well as his training.'

'Hey! I'm getting better. I handled myself in Ritellis Square, did I not?' He shot back, half defensive, half proud.

'All thanks to the Corporal and the Lady's own luck. You still wouldn't last two seconds in a proper scrap.' Clipper growled.

'It's better if the curse rolls of the tongue.' Creak continued in her lesson, ignoring the others. 'You want it to, ah, what did Scorch call it?'

'Illiterate?' Clipper ventured.

'No you idiot, that's what she called you.'

'Ah. She never did tell me what it meant.'

'Alliterate! That's what she said, something about alliteration, whatever that means.' Creak scratched the side of her head. Heelial decided she'd heard enough.

'Reth's teeth! Will you lot stop blabbering on and start working!' They all jumped, unaware of the Sergeant's presence and quickly became very interested in shovelling the excrement at their feet. Heelial watched them work for a little while. 'That's better you lazy layabouts. Corporal, has Scorch set off yet?'

'I believe so.' Creak answered.

She left them to it, but couldn't help overhear Rolls comment, 'See! The Sergeant knows how to curse good n' proper.'

'Can't believe Scorch got out of latrine duty, it ain't fair!' Clipper lamented.

Heelial arrived at the Soldiers gate just in time to see the squad mage walk through. *Hurry back and bring some good news with you.*

Something was eating away at the Captain and Heelial intended to find out what. Speaking of eating, it had been an hour since breakfast and she was famished. How was she supposed to think properly on an empty stomach? Concentrating took an awful lot of energy. She glanced again towards the gate but the mage had disappeared from sight.

She headed towards the mess hall.

Chapter 16

The trio were silent as they made their way through Tydon's bustling streets, each lost in their individual thoughts. Zel led the way with Thran just behind his shoulder, Scorch lagging a couple of paces behind. The mage wanted to keep the two assassins in front of her. Not that she suspected treachery, just old habits. They both seemed to be of a sour disposition. Scorch knew the origin of Zel's mood, he'd made his opinion about the forthcoming meeting abundantly clear. It was the younger assassin that interested her the most. He looked sleep deprived.

Something plagues his thoughts during the day and haunts his sleep at night.

He'd used some kind of sorcery in Ritellis Square, of that Scorch was certain. What kind however, she was still attempting to figure out. It was the main reason she'd asked to be a part of the meeting with the informant, but the mage also wanted to make sure the temples weren't causing any mischief despite her words at the meeting.

Zel finally stopped outside a small none descript building, sandwiched in-between two houses. 'This is it.' He said, but made no effort to make his way inside. Scorch glanced up and down the street. They were deep inside the Poor Quarter now, in a rather unsavoury area and while they could all handle themselves and were in no real danger, it would be better for them to remain unnoticed and away from any commotion. Scorch was just about to prompt Zel when the assassin sighed and headed towards the door.

A little bell sounded as they crossed the threshold and an enthusiastic voice called to them. 'Come in, come in, my most cherished customers, welcome to my shop.' The inside was cramped, tables and shelves took up the majority of the space, yet bizarrely, aside from a thick layer of dust, they were all empty, no wares, no products, no price tags: nothing. Scorch hadn't a clue what this so called shop had to sell. They weaved their way through to the back where a tall, skeletal man sat behind a counter smoothing down his sparse wavy hair that twisted and curled in every direction with one hand, while the other mopped the sweat from his brow with a plain white handkerchief. It was a warm day, but considerably cooler inside than out on the streets.

The man's sweating far more profusely than the heat warrants.

He recognised Zel and called to him with genuine warmth. 'Zelonius my dear friend, so good to see you again. I see you've brought friends. Has Zelonius' wagging tongue, which could put some dogs tails to shame, enticed you to come down to view my wares?' He gestured expansively towards the empty shelves. 'A pleasure to meet you both!'

'Hello Garbhan.' Zel already sounded weary despite the conversation having only just begun.

Garbhan? Where have I heard that name before? Then it came to her.

'Garbhan?!' Scorch spluttered, almost shouting. 'The mad priest Garbhan! He's your informant?'

'Ex-priest actually, I think you'll find. I, on the other hand, find the term "mad" to be quite slanderous to say the least. Just because my idiosyncratic nature is different to what the masses would define as "normal" does not make me mad. As for the definition of "normal", well what is normal for you is different to me. Surely it is defined by the individual, therefore we cannot apply it to someone because they do not conform to the masses. And who's to say that the masses are not mad themselves but for them mad behaviour is the norm. Am I an island of sanity trapped in a chaotic storm of madness that rages all around me? A most unsettling thought. I hope this news does not bring erratic responses or you may well find unwarranted labels attached to your names given at birth. And labels, my most esteemed guests, for good or for bad, alter the preconceptions of the masses, leading them to think you quite mad when in fact, you're quite normal. Depending on the definition of course. My other issues with such labels, they often end up being quite hyperbole.'

'Are you finished?' Zel asked, knowing full well he wasn't.

'For Sollun's sake! What do we hope to accomplish here?' Scorch threw her hands up in the air in exasperation.

'I do believe so. Although another thought strikes me, and this is purely hypothetical. Let us say I am indeed mad. Well, when did this madness come about? And how? Was it said so much that I actually started to believe it myself, and in turn act in such a manner that added weight to their allegations. Or, was I indeed mad from the beginning and they just brought it to my attention. Such questions require further pondering, but alas, at a different time.' The trio breathed a collective sigh of relief. Garbhan turned his attention to Thran. 'What is your name?'

'Thran.'

'Well it's an absolute pleasure to meet you Thran. Do you like chicken?'

'Erm, yeah I guess so.'

'Jolly good!' The priest beamed at Thran who looked to the other two to rescue him. Zel had his arms crossed, eyes toward the ceiling, looking thoroughly uninterested while Scorch was running a finger through the layer of dust that had settled on a table top. 'Now my fine fellows, before you keep me gabbing on all afternoon, what can I do you for? I'm sure you haven't come just to my shop to peruse my fine wares and have engaging, thought provoking conversation. I smell a specific reason, and my nose is never wrong. Well, rarely.

Sometimes. Only occasionally. Look, okay, it was right once, honest.' He wiped his forehead vigorously with the handkerchief.

'You truly are stark raving mad.' Scorch said, shaking her head.

'I do apologise for I have not asked your name yet.'

'Scorch.'

'Well then Scorch, I thought we had all come to an agreement on that subject matter of madness in our discussion earlier, but if you still have your doubts and wish to make a counter argument, I have no choice but to acquiesce to your wishes.'

'Discussion!?' Scorch exclaimed, incredulous. 'A discussion requires more than one person doing the talking.'

'ENOUGH!' They both quietened at Zel's rare outburst. 'Now listen up Garbhan. Do not say another word until I make it abundantly clear you may speak. Do you understand?' Words looked ready to burst out of the ex-priest's mouth, but he wisely remained silent. 'You may nod if you understand.' Garbhan nodded. 'Ritellis Square. We have reason to believe the temples were involved, specifically that of Jagreus. Is this true?'

Another nod.

'Were they the orchestrators?'

This time he shook his head.

'Then who was?'

He shrugged and made motions to speak. It was Zel's turn to nod. 'Perhaps these are questions you should be putting to Araxia. She's the High Priestess of Jagreus and currently residing in the city's temple.'

'So this Araxia, does she act on behalf of the goddess, or is she merely using the temple for her own ends?'

'The High Priestess would not dare act in such a way without orders from her goddess, or at least having her backing.'

'How can you be certain of this?' This from Scorch.

'Because I know, for certain.' His tone remained light, but he spoke with such surety that none of them deigned to challenge him further. 'Just like I know that the sky is blue, the grass is green, and an orange is orange. I also know which orange came first.'

Zel spoke again. 'So why does Jagreus care about who sits on Tydon's throne?'

'She does not. Whoever calls themselves Emperor or Empress of this city is not her concern, the goddess of Life's thoughts lie towards grander power struggles, the likes of which her children could not comprehend. A certain someone in particular has caught her eye.' It seemed to Thran that everyone glanced his way.

Maybe it's just my imagination? I hope so.

'That's if you believe certain rumours, of course. Rumours lead to labels which leads to expectations and judgement. The masses have much to answer for.'

'I could have told you all this,' Scorch fumed to Zel. 'In fact, I already have.'

'At least we know that means he's not lying.' Thran said in a feeble attempt to make her feel better.

'I would never lie to my good friend Zelonius.' Garbhan said in mock indignation.

'But you'd certainly bend the truth.' Zel countered.

The priest laughed. 'Ever quick witted Zelonius, ever quick witted. It's why I derive so much pleasure from our chats.'

'This High Priestess – Araxia – how will she receive us?'

Garbhan once again ran his handkerchief across his forehead. 'Well, that all depends on how you enter, doesn't it?' There was a hint of mischief in the ex-priest's voice.

They bade Garbhan goodbye and weaved their way back out to the entrance. The door opened, the bell tinkled, but suddenly he called for them to stop. They regretfully waited for him. Garbhan came panting up, somehow managing to squeeze through the thin gaps left in-between the tables and shelves.

'I forgot, I have a present for you Thran.' His hands held something behind his back.

'For me?' Thran said, surprised and apprehensive in equal measure.

Garbhan revealed what he'd been hiding behind his back: a chicken. 'You said you liked chicken earlier.' He sounded embarrassed, almost apologetic. 'Here, take her, she's quite docile.' It clucked, like it was confirming his statement.

'Thanks?' Thran said as he received the chicken.

Garbhan waved him away. 'It's nothing.' With that they finally left the mad priest and his shop of nothing. 'Feel free to drop by anytime my friends, it was a pleasure. I do enjoy our little chats.' He watched them walk up the road and out of sight, adding to himself. 'The vultures circle above this blood-stained city, waiting till only corpses remain to commence their feast.'

'I hope those musings weren't for my benefit.' He didn't turn at the sound of her voice. He knew full well she was there, sitting on the counter he'd vacated only moments before, her back against the wall. He continued to watch the streets and its occupants strolling up and down.

'My, my, my, I am overwhelmed with customers this fine afternoon. I can scarcely believe my *luck*.' His visitor chuckled. 'Greetings, most illustrious goddess of all: The Lady.'

'Come now Garbhan, no need to be so formal. A simple Lady will suffice.'

'How scandalous. You mustn't let the other ladies of the court hear of the boon you have granted me or their tongues will not stop wagging till winter.'

She ignored his ramblings. 'A Blood-born Garbhan, the first to be born for centuries. I was beginning to fear I would have to play paltry games for the rest of eternity. Being the generous, kind hearted person I am, I thought I would alert all the players. It's only fair, after all.'

Garbhan sighed, wiped the sweat from his temples. 'I will not make the same mistakes.'

'If you do something more than once, it's not a mistake, it's a choice.' He stiffened at her words. 'And our choices, Garbhan, seal our fate.'

'You always did fare better sparring with your words, than with your abilities. My mind is not as razor sharp, I do apologise.'

'You're far too modest Garbhan. You and Cipric kept things interesting, although you were always more pleasant.' Her tone shifted from playful to business like. 'A Shadow-Walker resides in the city. It may have to be taken care of.' It shifted back again. 'It sure does add another dimension though, Naul was ever aloof. Although I suppose he can't help that fact.'

'Do you not grow tired? For I am so weary, oh so weary.' He at last turned to face her, shuffled closer so his view wasn't obstructed by shelves. She didn't answer. Instead she took a small stone out of her pocket and placed it on the counter. There was no mistaking its dusty red hue. 'Collecting rocks I see. A new hobby?'

'Thought you'd be honoured to know you were second on my rounds.'

'When I was young, my brother and I used to go down to the lake and play. My favourite thing to do was skim stones. I'd spend countless hours searching for stones to skim across the lake's surface. It was all about finding a smooth, flat, stone that would get the most bounces. Sometimes I would find a stone too perfect that I couldn't bring myself to part with it, I couldn't waste it. I ended up with quite a sizeable collection. One day, as I was skimming some good one's I'd found across the lake, I saw a man watching me. He didn't say a word, didn't approach me, just stood there and watched. He left when I stopped. He was there the next day, and the day after that. On the fourth day when I arrived at the lake, I found him already there, attempting to skim like he'd seen me do. He wasn't having much success. His action was all wrong, he couldn't quite master the flick of the wrist. So I stood next to him and threw some stones. He picked it up and gradually his stones began to skim across the lakes surface like mine. We just stood there, silently skimming together. Enjoying the moment. The sun began to set, so we headed our separate ways without a spoken word, just a wave goodbye. The next day he wasn't there. I was disappointed, I had been expecting my skimming buddy. I tossed a couple but my heart wasn't in it, I doubt they even bounced twice. I headed home. The day after he was back and boy did he have a surprise for me! Next to him stood twin gigantic piles of stones. He'd spent the entire previous day collecting them. I jumped about excitedly, eager to get started. I grabbed the top stone from my pile and whipped it towards the lake but I hadn't checked to see if the lake was clear or not. It struck a duck square in the face. Quite a remarkable shot if I do say so myself. If I'd meant it, I hasten to add! Well, the man seemed distressed by this and started wading out into the lake, he got so far, but he could walk no further and just started thrashing and flailing around. Apparently he couldn't swim. I was no use, I was but a child, too weak to save him. He ended up drowning. Turns out he was a simpleton. He'd been kicked in the head by a horse and hadn't been the same since, scattered his wits it did. I never skimmed a stone across that lake again. Only ever went back once. Not sure what the point of this story is, I was just reminded because that stone looks like a good skimmer.'

'Tell me, have you truly gone mad like they say or do you just hide behind this persona you've created?'

'Honestly? At this point I don't even know. I'm simply me, and act as such.'

'Either way, you are grossly underestimated. I think some have even forgotten your existence. Tis a dangerous thing, to underestimate someone, especially you. How quickly we forget the past.'

'That's why the scholars of the world claim we are doomed to repeat it.'

'But you will not make the same mistakes this time?'

'I have chosen a different path. Perhaps I may finally complete the task set for me all that time ago. And what of you? What are your choices?'

She scooped up the red stone. 'Keep playing the game. Till we come full circle. Achieve balance.'

He nodded as if he'd expected such an answer. Ever stuck in her ways.

'Do be careful, Garbhan.' He was surprised at the genuine concern in her voice. 'I hope your choices do not cause our paths to cross on less, amicable terms. You're a source of such entertainment when we do meet.'

Am I really the closest thing to what you call a friend? Hmm, friend isn't the right choice of word. Ally perhaps?

'If only the Twins took greater interest in their daughters' ambitions, this all could be avoided.' She looked at him, her eyes cold and calculating. 'Or perhaps if they did, they would see that just because you can do something, doesn't mean you should. We all have our different parenting methods I suppose, all have different things we indulge.'

She fell silent and Garbhan turned back to look at the street once more. When she spoke again he was startled, he'd thought she'd slipped away.

'I will let you in on a little secret, Garbhan. I don't even believe in luck.'

He was still a moment, then laughter erupted from deep within his body. His long thin frame shook with each hearty guffaw. Once he started he couldn't stop. Tears started to stream down his face, he was now laughing at how much he was laughing. It hadn't even been that funny! Eventually he calmed down, although little chuckles escaped every now and then. He brought his handkerchief out and this time it mopped tears as well as sweat.

His door opened, the bell tinkled as someone stepped through and into his shop.

'Are you alright, Garbhan?'

'I am indeed my dearest Araxia, and all the better for seeing you once more. It's an absolute pleasure as always.'

Despite his words a sense of foreboding settled over him.

I have chosen, and in that choice sealed my fate. She said as much herself. This time I must do better. Will do better.

He would make sure this time some survived. To hope they all would, would be naïve and supremely arrogant, but he would make sure some did, at the very least.

Chapter 17

Thran had made his decision, now it was time to say his goodbyes. His talk with Carrion had been long and exhausting, but it had made his path clear to him. All his life he had been a problem, a burden to all those around him, now it was his turn to be helpful, be part of the solution. The god of Death had laid his options out before him, the likelihood of all eventualities, leaving, in Thran's mind, only one viable choice to make. Not that it made it any easier to swallow.

Sarfina and Zel were in a meeting with Zakanos and Heelial, discussing their next move against Araxia. Drak was downstairs helping himself to drink, making Reeva first on his list. He stood outside her door, hesitating, just like he had done all those nights ago. Except this time he would go in. He steeled himself.

You're putting them all in danger. Stop being so selfish!

Thran knocked on the door, waited a few seconds, then entered. She was half sat, half leaning against the windowsill, back perfectly straight, regarding him with the blank mask she always wore. Now he was inside the room, he was at a loss for words and the silence hung heavy between them. He attempted to talk twice but both times the words wouldn't come out. He'd never been very good at putting his feelings into words, never been good at expressing himself properly.

They always seem so inadequate.

So instead he just walked up to her and motioned for her to stand. She did so, albeit warily. He put his arms around her and hugged her tight. She immediately stiffened in his embrace and stood there awkwardly. Reeva wasn't one used to being hugged. Thran didn't care, he just continued to hold her, hoping his feelings would come across. The other Hand members were the closest things he had to friends, to family, and Reeva had played a massive part in that. Most misconstrued her silence for coldness and maybe that was some small part of it, but Thran knew she cared for them in her own way. She would always be there, always guarding their backs and had the knack of turning up to save them when they were in a tight spot.

    His eyes began to moisten. Reeva represented the security he'd come to find in the unlikely source that was the Assassins Guild, and he was about to leave that security, that comfort, behind. When his brother had thrown him out onto the streets all those years ago, it was Sarfina and the Guild who had taken him in, fed and clothed him, trained him to be the assassin he was today. He turned his thoughts away from his brother, he did not like dwelling on his youth. Thran knew he'd better leave before the dampness turned to real tears. He let go and stepped back to see something he never thought he would; a look of confusion, and perhaps, although it might have just been his imagination, a hint of uncertainty in Reeva's clear blue eyes. It made him smile.

    Without another word he left her and immediately bumped into Zel coming down the hallway.

    'Ah Thran, good, I was just looking for you.' Thran's smile widened. Typical Zel, oblivious to the obvious emotions of those around him.

    Ah my friend, feelings aren't as easy to process, are they?

    'What's up?'

    'Captain Zakanos wants you guarding his back while he goes to meet an informant who may be able to get us inside the temples for our long overdue meeting with the High Priestess.'

    One final mission. How fitting.

'Sure. When do we leave?'
'As soon as Zakanos comes out, he's just finishing up with Sarfina.'

* * * *

Thran should have known something was wrong. He should have known something was off about Zakanos, about the whole situation but he was too preoccupied with this own thoughts. On Carrion's offer to take his powers away.

'As a descendant of Dragos, you pose a very real threat to the gods. That is why Jagreus is so desperate to kill you, before he makes himself known to you and bends you to his will.'

'Why are you trying to help me?'

'We are stuck in an endless cycle. Ever so often a new Blood-born will emerge and we will scramble to kill them. I've lost track of the amount of bloodshed we've caused, most of it innocent. It has to stop. The cycle must be broken. Unfortunately, the responsibility has fallen to you.'

'And what if I don't want it?'

'Then you can run and hide, live out your life in loneliness. Jagreus will be relentless, she will not be denied. Anyone could be an agent of hers and any friends you do make, their safety will be compromised. A target used to get to you.'

Those words struck a chord within Thran. They'd been lucky to escape Ritellis Square unscathed, it was only a matter of time before they took casualties. The god of Death continued:

'If you ever have a family, well, one of your descendants will inherit your powers, and the same responsibility, because, I will beseech them to help me end this, just as I am with you now.'

Thran had paused, deliberating, although he was pretty sure what he would do.

'*How do we break the cycle?*'

The corpse's expression didn't change but Thran sensed the pleasure his words brought.

'*Are you willing to forsake your powers Thran?*'

'We're here.' Zakanos' words brought him back to the present. They were deep in the Poor Quarter, far from the Temple District.

'Why'd he want to meet out here?'

'Too dangerous to meet closer to the temple, we can't risk being seen.' Zakanos gestured down an alleyway. 'He should just be down through here. Take point.'

Thran drew his knives and advanced cautiously. There was always a possibility they were about to walk straight into a trap. Even Zakanos seemed a little apprehensive. Thran edged further along the alley. He could make out a figure stood waiting for them, hood drawn over his face. Thran purposefully came to a halt a few paces from him.

The figure removed its hood to reveal a twisted grin. An icy dread gripped Thran's stomach and began to claw its way up his body.

'Such a pleasure to meet you again.'

Thran caught a blur of movement behind him in his peripheral vision and reacted, but too late. A heavy blow stunned him, turning his vision black as the ground rose up to meet him.

Zakanos stood over Thran's crumpled form, sword drawn.

'I have done as you asked. Now keep your end of the deal.'

'I already have. See I know you're a man of your word Zakanos, a very rare quality these days. I knew you'd deliver, so I have already returned your precious wife and squalling infant to their home.'

Zakanos made no comment to this, instead he just stared intently at Mortem who returned his scrutiny. Eventually Zakanos sheathed his sword but made no other move.

'I would make threats at this point, but you know exactly what I'll do to you if you've harmed them.'

Mortem's smile deepened. Zakanos held his gaze, before turning and forcing himself to walk slowly back down to the alley entrance. He would not give Mortem the satisfaction. As soon as he rounded the corner however, he took off sprinting, praying to every god he could think of.

Mortem walked over to Thran and rolled him over so he was lying on his back.

So this is the one whose got everybody running in circles huh? Up close he doesn't look like much, although to be fair, he held his own in the Square. Mortem knew well it was not Thran's combat skills that was causing everyone to take an interest in him. He hunkered down on his haunches. It was time to get to work.

* * * *

Something was gnawing away at Sarfina's mind. She couldn't quite put her finger on it but there was a little voice in the back of her head that kept saying: *somethings wrong, somethings wrong.*

She had come to trust that niggly little voice implicitly over the years. The meeting with Garbhan had turned out to be fruitful and while his eccentric behaviour had caused them trouble in the past, he had never intentionally led them astray. No, it wasn't Garbhan she was worried about, or their forthcoming meeting with the High Priestess. It was this new informant Zakanos had brought to their attention. Why hadn't he mentioned this informant before now? Then there had been something about the Captain's demeanour, he'd not acted like his usual self at all. It briefly crossed Sarfina's mind that perhaps he was losing his nerve, but she immediately dismissed it. Not Zakanos. Once he committed, he would see things through to the end. He'd proven that all those years ago.

'Zel.' At the mention of his name he glanced up from the notes he was reading. 'See if Sergeant Heelial has departed yet, and if she has, go after her and bring her back,' she bade him. He didn't question her, just set about his orders. As her mind worked, her fingers absently traced the streets of Tydon carved into the table.

Thankfully Zel didn't have to go far. Just downstairs in fact. Heelial said she couldn't travel back to the barracks on an empty stomach so she'd stayed to taste some of the Tavern's questionable cuisine. After satiating her hunger, she sat amicably drinking with Drak, stating it was an important step in building relationships between the 4th and the Guild. When she walked in her steps were a little unsteady.

'You asked to see me?' She said with the faintest hint of a slur.

'Have you noticed anything different about the Captain?'

Heelial frowned. 'I have as it happens. He's been distant the last couple of days, very cold. Unlike him.'

'What could be causing it?'

'I'm not sure. It's hard to say. The Capn's a very private man. I'm only one of a few who knows about his family and even then, I don't have a clue what his wife's name is.'

His wife!

The words sent a jolt through her brain and dots connected. They were in trouble.

'Zel, send word to Skrenn to send a Hand to Jagreus' temple. Tell them not to enter till further notice but keep a tight perimeter. No one is to enter. Then take Drak and Reeva and head to the meeting place where Zak and Thran should be. Hurry!'

Zel leapt into action and Heelial, who sobered up when she heard the tone of Sarfina's voice, asked:

'What about me?'

'You're coming with me.' Sarfina said as she grabbed Heelial by the arm, pulling her down the hallway. 'And pray we're not too late.'

But Sarfina had a sinking feeling that they were far too late already.

* * * *

The door was wide open. That was a bad sign. Sarfina stepped through without hesitation, Heelial followed a little more cautiously. This was her Captain's private home, his sanctuary, it felt wrong to intrude without his permission but they didn't have a choice. The kitchen was empty. Sarfina padded across to the backroom and looked inside, she turned to Heelial and shook her head, downstairs was clear.

They both approached the bottom of the stairs and stopped. Sarfina looked expectantly at Heelial who just stared back noncommittedly. Sarfina pursed her lips, opened her mouth to speak but then thought better of it. She put her foot on the first step and slowly ascended. Heelial followed a couple of steps behind. A creak made them both stop, tense. Sarfina glared over her shoulder at the Sergeant who held up an apologetic hand. They continued up.

Sarfina reached the top and stood motionless. Heelial waited for her to continue but it seemed like the Hand leader wouldn't be moving anytime soon and her impatience got the better of her so she joined her on the top step. She immediately regretted it.

There was blood everywhere, pooling on the floor, smeared on the walls, even some dripping from the ceiling.

Whoever's done this is one sick fuck.

A large double bed dominated the centre of the room, with a cot to the right hand side which was clearly in view, the left hand side however, was obscured by the bed.

Plenty of blood, but no bodies.

An unnerving thought. She was just about to ask Sarfina if they could leave when she noticed the tips of military issued boots protruding around the side of the bed.

Captain!

She looked to Sarfina who'd also noticed them. The assassin stepped forward calmly into the blood, her face a blank mask. Heelial edged forward. Zakanos slowly came into view. He was slumped against the wall, staring at the far wall, staring into nothingness. His eyes were red and puffy, his cheeks still wet. Laid across his chest was his wife, in one arm he cradled his son. He held a knife in his free hand. Horror tore at Heelial as a shocking thought flashed into her mind, but it dissipated when she saw the knife was clean. Her relief was short lived as she realised what and who that knife was meant for.

Heelial tried not to look at the two bodies but her eyes betrayed her. They went to the little boy first. He almost looked like he was sleeping, but he was too still, too serene. Far too pale. The only wound she could perceive on his body was a single stab to the belly. The mind always looks for a bright side to help alleviate the suffering witnessing such atrocities bring and, in this case, Heelials was no different.

At least he did not suffer.

The same could not be said about Zakanos' wife.

Her face was bruised and swollen, her jaw was broken, hanging down slackly to reveal a number of missing teeth. A chunk of skin had been gouged out of her shoulder. Lower down on her arm the skin had been scraped and cut off from her elbow to her wrist. She was missing some fingers. That was as much as Heelial could take. Bile rose in her throat and she tried to fight it but was unsuccessful. She bent over and spilled the entire contents of her stomach onto the floor where it mixed with the blood. It took her a while to stop panting heavily and regain her composure.

    Sarfina remained still: standing there, taking it all in. Her face a stoic mask.

    You're one steel hearted bitch.

    Heelial admired her though, there was no way she could remain so composed in this situation. Not after what she'd just seen. Although she could just make out a hint of a grimace of disgust on the corner of the assassin's clenched jaw.

    She's not infallible.

    Heelial found the thought oddly comforting.

    Sarfina walked slowly towards Zakanos. He didn't even register her presence, even when she stood over him. She settled into a crouch, leant forward and started whispering softly into Zakanos ear. Heelial couldn't catch what she was saying. At first it seemed to have no effect, but after a while Zakanos' eyes seemed to focus once more. Taking in his surroundings. Sarfina reached for the knife and took it from his hand: he didn't resist. She held the knife out behind her for the Sergeant to take, all the while continuing to whisper into the Captains ear.

    Heelial steeled herself, darted forward, grabbed the knife and then retreated just as quickly. Zakanos was beginning to slowly nod in response to what Sarfina was telling him. He was nodding quicker now, but was still yet to speak. He was actually starting to look at Sarfina whilst she was talking to him, rather than at the wall. At nothing.

    His eyes quickly flicked towards her and Heelial was unprepared for the eye contact. It was the final straw. Her vision began to blur, she began to back away from the two of them. She turned and fled down the stairs, somehow managing to keep her balance and stay upright. She sped through the kitchen and into the street, trying desperately to suck in fresh air through large gulps. She vomited again, this time just bile, which stung her throat as it came out.

It had left her shaken to her very core to see him so broken. Eyes that once held such sparks of intellect and life were now dull and devoid of both. They weren't empty though. Even in that momentary contact she'd been able to see the deep well of grief and guilt that had threatened to overwhelm her, to drag her in and drown her. She felt her own guilt at running out like that when her Captain so obviously needed her, but she'd not been able to stay there any longer. Besides, what good was she? Very little at the moment. She thanked the gods Sarfina was there and able to be of some use.

She went back inside and sat at the kitchen table. She would wait here. There was no way she could make it back upstairs. A sound was coming from behind her, every few seconds. She turned towards it. Blood had come through the upstairs floorboards and was dripping down on the floor beneath.

Seems like there's no getting away from it.

She glanced out the door she had not bothered to shut. The shadows were beginning to lengthen, it would soon be dark.

Finally Sarfina came downstairs. By herself.

'He'll be down when he's ready. Just give him time. Now I must be off, this will not go unanswered. Stay with him, make sure he doesn't…' Sarfina couldn't bring herself to finish the sentence, she didn't have to; Heelial knew. 'I don't think he will now, but we can't take chances. I'll be back as soon as I can, or if events take over, I will send someone in my stead.'

She made to go. 'Sarfina.' She stopped, turned her head to look at Heelial. 'Thank you.' The assassin simply nodded, then disappeared through the doorway. The Sergeant wasn't sure how much time had passed when she heard footsteps on the stairs.

'Captain?' She asked tentatively.

He didn't answer as he came down the stairs. Didn't even look at her as he walked through the kitchen and out into the night. She scrambled after him.

Chapter 18

Captain Zakanos walked through the rapidly darkening streets of Tydon, Heelial followed in his wake. His pace was slow and methodical so she had no problem keeping up with him. The problem was, where they were heading, Heelial wasn't entirely sure but she had a pretty good idea. She wanted to run and fetch her squad but they were too far away. The Tavern was closer but the assassins wouldn't be there, they'd likely run into them if they held their current course.

The streets were mostly empty and the few people who were out paid them no heed as they hurried home through the lengthening shadows. Tydon's streets weren't the safest of places to be alone after dark and with the recent spree of vicious killings, the Emperor had enforced a curfew meaning the streets emptied very quickly as the sun descended past the horizon. It was mainly the fear that kept the people in their homes rather than the imperial decreed curfew. Yet Zakanos would not be dissuaded this night. His jaw was set; there was a grim determination in his eyes.

Heelial knew she was in for a long and eventful night, but she didn't mind. There was nowhere else right now she would rather be: her place was by her Captains side. Although she sorely wished there was something edible within reach. Her stomach was making noisy complaints. She supposed it was a good sign, it meant that she was recovering from what she'd seen in that room, that she was returning to normal.

Whatever normal means.

Zakanos picked up his pace, she altered her stride to match his. They were nearing their destination. When they'd first set out, she'd tried calling his name, but he'd simply ignored her and carried on. He stopped so abruptly she almost bumped into him.

'Are you with me?' He asked in a toneless voice, still facing forward.

'Always.' Came the reply, barely above a whisper.

He set off again, resuming his more measured pace. They were getting close. They'd entered the Gods' Way. It wasn't the correct name of the street but that's what everybody called it for the simple reason it was the main route to the Temple District. It started off quite narrow but eventually widened out as it progressed towards the temples. Shrines dedicated to different gods started to appear. At first they were infrequent, but about half way up the Gods' Way they became more and more numerous until soon there was a shrine every half dozen steps. Although they varied in size and simplicity they clearly displayed the identity of their chosen god to be worshipped and revered.

Heelial noticed that as well as widening, the path they were following was starting to gradually incline. All of sudden the shrines stopped. They were about to head up onto hallowed ground where no one dared build, unless it was sanctioned and blessed by the temples. Visibility was becoming increasingly poor as darkness crept forward to steal away the last of the light. The moon's creamy face peeked out from behind the clouds to shower them in its pale glow. This was the closest Heelial had come to believing in divine intervention, as it revealed two figures waiting ahead where the Gods Way gave way to an open expanse of neatly trimmed grassland where the temples all stood in a semicircle.

Thank you Naul!

There was a large amount of space between each temple and they were all individually fenced off. The only way in to each one was through a gate.

The two stood blocking their path and Zakanos came to a halt an arms length away.

'Are you going to let us past?' Zakanos asked, his voice still emotionless.

The one on the right shook his head. 'We're not supposed to let anyone pass.'

'I understand it's late and it's not usual visiting hours-' beseeched Heelial until their condescending laughter cut her off. At once she realised who they were and why they were here.

What a fool. I'm still not thinking clearly.

She switched tacts. 'We're allies of the Guild. We're partnered with Sarfina's Hand. We need to pass.'

'I know who you are, but we have our orders, nobody is allowed to pass. Friend or foe alike.'

'Please, we have to get past. It's very important.'

'Not happeni-'

Zakanos' sword was out and slicing into the man's throat before he could utter another syllable. His partner reacted quickly and dashed forward, knives drawn and flashing towards Zakanos who, overextended as he was, was wide open. Heelial hurled herself into the second assassin sending them both crashing to the floor. She felt a sharp edge graze her stomach and instinctively lashed out, landing a painful heavy blow to her opponent, although it did not deter him from bludgeoning the side of her head, making her vision swim. She tensed, waiting for the next blow. It never came. As her sight cleared, she could see Zakanos' had run him through with his blade. She stood up and felt the cut to her stomach, there was a fair bit of blood but it wasn't too deep, she'd be fine.

By the Lady we got away with that one. If there'd been a full Hand we'd both be dead. It did pose a worrying question:

Where are the other two?

No sooner had the thought crossed her mind when cold steel slammed into her lower back.

* * * *

Zel led the way, the rest of the Hand followed. They were all uneasy, but only Drak showed any outward display of this, chewing away on his bottom lip. Zel had scooped him and Reeva up and dragged them out of the Tavern without much explanation. It was clearly urgent. They'd gone to a small bar called The Final Jig. Apparently the bar took its name from when the building was used as holding cells by the local garrison before they moved to the main barracks. For the worst offenders it was the last place they would ever see before they met the hangman's noose.

The Final Jig was where Zakanos and Thran were supposed to be meeting their informant. Neither was there. Nor had the bartender, who'd sworn he'd been on all afternoon, seen anyone who matched their description.

The depleted Hand made their way back to the Tavern to find Skrenn waiting for them. He would not shed light on the situation. He sat in silence waiting for Sarfina to return. Drak was adamant they should be out searching for Thran and Zakanos but Zel argued against the notion. It would not do to wander the city aimlessly. It wasn't long before the Hand leader returned with her grave news. She filled them in as they made their way back out into the streets of the city.

'Did you do as I asked?' She asked Skrenn. The Dresconii nodded. 'Good.' The relief in her voice was palpable.

They turned a corner and found themselves at the bottom on a very narrow road. The beginning of the Gods Way. A slight crinkle in Skrenn's forehead was the only sign of his annoyance. He shared a knowing look with Sarfina. They should have been stopped by the other Hand by now. He let out a low whistle. There was no reply. As if on cue, everyone drew their weapons. Drak chewed his lip with more vigour. If they were to be ambushed, there was no better place than on the narrow Gods Way, and they all knew it.

      Reeva took point. There wasn't many who could sneak up and surprise her, even in the dark. Especially in the dark. Skrenn was next, then Sarfina and Zel, leaving Drak to bring up the rear. Gradually the street began to widen enough for Skrenn and Sarfina to walk side by side. If Reeva was concerned, she hid it very well as she continued to walk on, seemingly unfazed. The shrines began to multiply, spawning faster than breeding rabbits. Then all of a sudden they stopped. They'd come to the Temple District's entrance, and as the fenced off temples came into view, so did the bodies. There were four of them.

      They carried on past the fallen. There was nothing that could be done for them now, except to avenge them. With lips set in tight lines, eyes blazing with fury, hands tightened around each of their weapons, they silently vowed that retribution was going to be meted out, someone would pay, and pay dearly.

      Skrenn stopped and motioned for them all to do the same. He hunkered down, staring intently at the ground. He brushed his fingers along the grass; they came away slick with blood. Someone was bleeding. Heavily. He set off following the blood trail straight to the gate of one of the temples. It was wide open. A bloody handprint was smeared on the gate's latch. He quickly glanced at each one of his fellow assassins. They were all ready. He stepped through onto the path leading to the temple's entrance. They were on consecrated ground. Anything they did now might well incur the wrath of a goddess. Skrenn knew they had to be tactful, and hoped the damage had not already been done. The temple's great wooden doors had an image of Jagreus carved into them with her arms spread wide open, warmly inviting her children to receive their mothers love. Now they stood wide open, splitting the goddess in half. Another red smear stained her otherwise unblemished skin.

Inside they immediately encountered another body, this belonging to an unfortunate acolyte who'd been on duty. He'd been struck down where he'd stood. The room opened up towards the main alter and half way there lay another body sprawled face down. Most likely the unfortunate victim had come to see what all the commotion was about and who was making such an ungodly racket so late. Their confusion turned to horror as they spied the recently deceased acolyte on the floor and the killer advancing towards him, blood gleaming on their blade. They'd turned to flee. A slash wound from the shoulder to hip showed they had not made it very far.

Skrenn led them past the alter which appeared extremely well polished, towards the back rooms, hidden from the view of the worshipping masses. Skrenn cocked his head. Faint voices could be heard coming from one of the rooms. He honed in on them and opened the door slowly and soundlessly and came face to face with a waiting knife. Its wielder was in no condition to fight. She was swaying where she stood, eyes going in and out of focus.

Sergeant Heelial was on the verge of collapse.

Skrenn gently moved her aside so they could all enter. When Drak entered he passed the Sergeant over to the assassin who took her with care. She clung to him desperately for support.

Zakanos stood with his back to them, sword against the neck of a woman who undoubtedly must have been the High Priestess. Blood ran down her neck from where his sword was pressed against her skin. Whether it was from her veins or his blade, Skrenn wasn't quite sure. The High Priestess seemed calm to her credit, but when their eyes locked the Dresconii could sense the underlying panic ready to surface at any moment. He gave way deferentially to Sarfina. She stepped forward but kept a respectful distance from the pair connected by the sword.

'Zakanos.' She said softly, yet firm.

He didn't acknowledge her.

'Zakanos.' Firmer.

'Zakanos.' Firmer, insistent.

'Zakanos!'

'What.'

'Sheath your sword.'

'I intend to kill her.' He stated matter of factly. He could have been talking about the weather, or the price of fish down at the docks.

'And you will. But now is not the time.'

'I disagree.'

'She did not kill your wife and child. *He* did.'

Zakanos stiffened. The sword pressed further into her neck. It was definitely her blood that began to weave down to her collarbone. The raw emotion he'd been bottling up started to leak out.

'She all but wielded the knife herself.'

His words seemed to act like a slap across Araxia's face. 'I'm so sorry.'

'Be quiet!'

'I didn't know-'

'I SAID BE QUIET!' His anger was beginning to flow now. It was a tide that could not be stopped.

'You knew alright. You knew well enough what that man was capable of. Yet you let him off the leash regardless and now you dare claim *ignorance*?!' He spat the last word at her. 'Our actions have consequences, *High Priestess*.' He made her title sound an insult. 'And now you have to deal with those consequences, just like I have done.'

'He swore to me he would not hurt them, that it was the only way to force you into cooperating. Perhaps it was naivety, or that I did not want to believe what he was capable of doing, but I chose to believe him, and I regret that decision dearly.' Zakanos snarled. 'I know that means nothing to you. I know I deserve whatever fate you decide for me. But first Mortem must be stopped.'

'What do you mean? Stopped?' asked Sarfina.

The High Priestess smiled bitterly.

'He has betrayed my goddess and taken your friend.'

'You mean Thran's not dead?'

'No. I wish that he were. Willingly, tricked, coerced, either way he shall bring about a war unprecedented in Bellum's history. A war of the gods.'

'Don't be ridiculous!' Zel scoffed. 'How can a lowly assassin bring about such a calamity?'

'Because he is so much more. He is Blood-born. He is the Descendant.'

Zakanos raised the sword closer to her jaw. 'I couldn't give two shits what he is. Do you know where Mortem is taking him?'

'Yes.'

'Can you take us there?'

There was a slight hesitation. 'Y-Yes.'

'Are you sure?'

'I think so. I have not been there myself, but there is one who has.'

'Who?'

'Garbhan.'

'Garbhan!' Zel exclaimed. 'I should have known he'd be mixed up in this somehow. Conniving little shit, we'll be doing more than exchanging words next time we meet.'

'He is involved far more than you know.' Araxia replied. Sarfina wanted to question her further but Zakanos looked ready to shove her out the door.

'We're leaving. *Now.*'

'Zakanos.'

'I don't care what you have to say Sarfina.'

'Just look at Heelial.'

'Why?'

'Look at her!'

He craned his neck, he eyes widened when he saw the current state she was in. Barely conscious due to blood loss, her breath coming in ragged gasps. She looked like a child in Drak's arms. It drained away his anger. He finally lowered his sword from Araxia's neck.

'She's in no condition to travel, and neither are the rest of us. We need mounts, supplies and to somehow convince the Faceless Man about this expedition. Garbhan needs to be fetched. We will leave tomorrow morning, at first light. I promise you.'

He looked sceptical, but Zakanos begrudgingly nodded.

'I can heal her.' Araxia motioned to the Sergeant who had finally slipped into unconsciousness. She seemed desperate to help.

Everyone regarded her with open suspicion, but to Sarfina, the High Priestess had seemed genuinely contrite. She gave a curt nod. Araxia began to direct Drak. 'Lay her down on the bed, gently mind.'

'Sarfina, Zel. Come with me. We shall make the necessary preparations.' Skrenn turned to Zakanos. 'I know it will be hard, but try and get some rest.' Lastly he turned to Reeva who was leaning against the wall by the door. 'Make sure no one else enters, or leaves.' He looked over to where the High Priestess was carefully examining Heelial's wounds. 'And keep a close eye on her.'

Reeva shot him a look that conveyed her thoughts on his orders; that they had been entirely redundant. What else would she be doing?

Then the trio were gone.

Skrenn and Sarfina to face Tavian.
Zel to find Garbhan.
Both parties however, thought the other had the easier task.

Chapter 19

Dear Sir/Madam,

If you are reading this then it regrettably, unfortunately, terribly means I am out of Tydon on very urgent and important business. I have decided to take a long walk. Mother Nature calls me to explore her beauty. When will I be back? Who can say what fate has in store for me on this sojourn. I apologise whole heartedly with my whole heart for any inconvenience this has caused to my most loyal repeat customers who will be outraged, panicked and full of despair when the reality of my absence fully sinks in. As aforementioned in my previous sentence, I apologise! Now wipe those tears away, for I shall return. Although I am not sure when. However, I promise to rectify this horrendous turn of events caused by this calamitous walk of mine when I return. Although I'm unsure of when this will be. But now let us talk of more pleasant matters, like when I return, for I shall make it up to each and every single one of you, I promise. This can take form in any which way you desire. I can wash your feet and dry them off with my hair, or I can act as your personal mule for the day. Anything you can imagine. I am completely at your mercy. But when you think of all the terrible punishments to inflict upon me whenever I am able to return, please remember this dereliction of duty happened due to some very urgent and most *pressing business that called me away from Tydon and my duty to you customers. I just had to go on this walk. How long will I be gone? I really couldn't say...*

Zel stopped reading the letter he'd found pinned to the door of Garbhan's shop. 'It goes on for three more pages.'
    'Yes, well, I think we've heard more than enough.'
    'Were you more successful?'
    Sarfina nodded. 'He took some convincing. Without Skrenn, I doubt we would have swayed him.'
    'And Cyprian?'
    'Seething, even if he doesn't show it. Suspicious too, and rightly so, but what can he do? Emperor's orders.'
    'We'll have to keep a close eye on him.'
    'We'll have to keep a close eye on everyone. Are they ready to go?'
    Drak emerged at the top of the Gods Way with two packs slung over his shoulder, in answer to her question. He joined them at the gate to Jagreus' temple.
    'Fetch them.'
    He left the packs at their feet and headed inside. He returned moments later with Reeva and Araxia in tow. The High Priestess looked haggard. She'd spent the majority of the night tending to Heelial, only snatching a couple of hours sleep when her charge was stable and exhaustion got the better of her.
    'How's the Sergeant?' Sarfina asked her.
    'Fine.' Araxia answered after only a slight hesitation but it was enough for Sarfina to pick up on it.
    'Where is she?'
    'I-I don't know.'
    'What do you mean, you don't know?'

'She must have awakened and left while I was resting.' The High Priestess sounded embarrassed, but unapologetic.

Sarfina shot an accusatory look at Reeva who shrugged and calmly returned her gaze. She wasn't surprised by the Sergeant's disappearance, but it was frustrating none the less. It was starting to get lighter. Not good. They needed to be off while there were not so many prying eyes around. She led them down the Gods' Way.

They were heading to collect Zakanos who, despite being advised otherwise, had gone back home to see his wife and child. Drak had made a half-hearted attempt to stop him, but he would not be dissuaded, so the big man just let him go. Why the Captain would willingly torture himself so, Sarfina wasn't sure. Everyone deals with grief differently and perhaps this was Zakanos' way of trying to find closure.

Or saying goodbye. He knows there's a good chance he won't be coming back. Can't see a way of coming back.

So the little group, with Drak once again shouldering the packs, made their way to the once warm and welcoming family home that now offered only unspeakable horrors lurking within its sombre walls. Zakanos was stood outside when they arrived. His face was a cold mask but Sarfina could detect the steely determination in his eyes. She knew he would not stop, no matter what it took, how long it too, until he'd exacted revenge. He fell into step with them without a word.

They met Skrenn by the parade ground attached to the barracks. He'd procured their horses. There were far too many.

'Do we need this many horses?' asked Drak.

'They're not for you.' Heelial answered as she emerged from the barracks at the head of her squad. They'd all donned their leather armour as mail would have only slowed them down. They were fully armed. The Sergeant was walking stiffly, but unaided, and had regained some of her colour. She swung up into the saddle with some effort and sat there, daring any to challenge her. None did. The rest of 4th squad mounted up behind her.

Drak, Reeva, Zakanos and Araxia followed suit. The fourteen of them were ready to set off as Zakanos was growing more and more impatient by the second, but Skrenn had some final words to impart.

'Officially you're being sent on scout duty as part of your punishment. You have two weeks. The Emperor wants you back in time for the start of the Oros festival. You have enough provisions in your saddlebags to last a month.' The emphasis he put on this last sentence was not lost on all those gathered.

Zakanos tugged at the reigns and led them out of the parade ground. They weaved through the streets until they reached Ritellis Square, which was only just beginning to show the first signs of the hustle and bustle it would be rife with later in the day. From there it was straight down to the main gate. The guards had been notified of their departure and opened the gates. When they slammed shut behind the group, Zakanos eased them into a trot heading north towards Shulakh. Once they were out of view from the city, he upped their speed and turned east, cantering towards their destination.

Despite the early hour of their departure, multiple eyes noted Captain Zakanos and the 4th squad of the Guard Company leave Tydon. They also noted the three extra riders attached to the party.

* * * *

His mind struggled to break free from the darkness; it acted like quicksand, the more he struggled, the deeper he seemed to sink. Eventually he gave up and sank into the mire.

He slowly became aware of a dull throb, emanating from above. He homed in on this, clung to it. It was his way out of the darkness. It was coming from a head: his head. He could feel his bloodied hair matted around the cut. A cut? It came flooding back to him. The alley, Zakanos, Mortem. The fact that he could still feel the damage the blow from behind that Zakanos had dealt him meant that he was still alive which was surprising. Mortem had wanted him dead. In Ritellis Square he'd attacked with intent to kill. What had changed?

He wanted to probe his head wound to see how deep the cut was, but when he attempted to lift his hands he found himself unable. He twisted his wrists and felt the undeniable burn from rope. Not surprising. He patted his hands down and felt . . . fur? He realised he was in motion, swaying gently from side to side with the animal beneath him.

Thran slowly opened his eyes, expecting them to be assaulted by light. Instead he found it was dark. He could just about make out another rider in front of him. He turned his head but that brought about pain which made him wince and try to reach towards his scalp once more.

Oh yeah, my bonds.

Thran switched his attention from his cut to his hands. He was sure the damage to his head wasn't too substantial, head wounds always bled profusely, despite the size of the cut. He tried straining against the rope that bound his arms to the saddle of his mount, then he tried wriggling free but to no avail. They were too tight.

He settled back down into the sway and closed his eyes and soon found himself lulled back into the darkness.

When he next awoke, he was no longer mounted, no longer bound, no longer with Mortem. He was standing before a familiar alter where a corpse sat cross-legged staring back at him.

'Thran, how are you?'

The assassin couldn't tell if Carrion's tone was serious, or the god's sense of humour was incredibly dry.

'Just terrific. Couldn't be better. Some murderous maniac has me tied up and is taking me gods knows where.'

The corpse cocked its head and regarded Thran for moment.

'I do, actually.'

They regarded each other for a moment. Thran waited for the god of Death to continue.

'Thran, have you used your powers since Ritellis Square?' A shake of the head. 'When you do, you'll find yourself able to do things you weren't before, and it won't be as draining. Herrick's powers have bolstered your own. However you still fall short of the requirements needed for what is to come.'

'What does this have to do with Mortem?'

Carrion weighed his next words carefully.

'He was my, how can I phrase this delicately, insurance policy. I could not be sure of your decision or that your friends would not stop you from leaving. Mortem's intentions at the behest of Jagreus had come to my attention, so I made him a better offer.'

'That man is an evil monster.'

'A necessary evil, Thran. The world is, and always will be, full of them.'

'He has taken me from the city; I can be done with him.'

'Not yet, he is still needed. As I said, you are not strong enough, so a blood sacrifice is required. He will act as that sacrifice.'

Thran was so pleased about being able to exact revenge on the unwitting Mortem, he didn't stop to consider why a blood sacrifice was required at all.

'Mortem has instructions to take you to an old temple where he will end your life and gain powers as a reward. Instead, you will kill him with your powers, and lose them.'

'Why will killing him at this temple take away my powers?'

'When the Council first began to gather, discussions tended to get heated, and when powerfully Gifted men and women get heated, the outcome is less than desirable. So they created a temple with spells interlaced in the foundations, spells that negated the Gift. It worked for a time, yet the Gifted of that time were blessed with power and ingenuity. One of the more creative Council members worked out a way to access his Gift. So the foundations were added to, the spells reworked. If anyone tried to work their Gift whilst on temple grounds, it was drained from them and returned to the Elementals. The temple has long ago fallen into ruins, but the foundations, and the spells, remain strong.'

'Kill Mortem and be free of this curse. Return to the life of an assassin in Tydon. End the cycle, Thran.'

Thran awoke to find himself lying down, his legs tied together as well as his wrists. It was light enough to see his surroundings so he struggled into a sitting position and tried to gather his bearings. He couldn't spot Tydon in any direction, nor could he see the countless farms and villas that surrounded the city which worked tirelessly to keep the ever growing population fed.

'Glad you're finally awake. I began to wonder if you would at all.'

Thran turned to find Mortem relieving himself against a tree.

'How long have I been out?'

'A good number of days. Zakanos gave you a good whack, and then I slipped you a little something to keep you under. Wondered if I'd given you too much, but you're awake now.'

'I also need to piss.'

'Then piss yourself.' Mortem replied cheerfully.

'At least loosen my bonds, I can't feel my hands.'

'Sure, and why don't I give you a knife to stab me in the back while I'm at it?'

He did, however, toss Thran a water skin and a few strips of dried meat.

As soon as he was done, Mortem picked him up and shoved him towards their mounts: two donkeys.

'Why are you Tydonii so precious about your horses? Never known anywhere as difficult to procure horses. You'd think they were made out of Grellish steel.' Mortem grumbled as he hauled Thran into the saddle and tied him to it with a shorter length rope. A longer one tied the two donkeys together. Mortem mounted his own and set it moving. When the length of rope became taunt, Thran's docile beast began to plod along after them.

They stayed off the main road but followed it parallel at a leisurely pace. Mortem seemed to be confident they wouldn't be caught and as the day wore on Thran began to understand why. In the distance, the mountains were drawing ever closer. Thran had never been outside of Tydon, but like everyone else, he'd heard rumours of Grellon, the fabled mine turned city hewn into the mountain range running from one end to the other. Merchants and adventurers loved to claim they had scaled Mt Serpentine and navigated through the Endless Peaks instead of making their way through the city. They were always scoffed at, but everyone loved hearing fresh descriptions of the most famous mountain range in Bellum.

Once inside the mountain, inside Grellon, it would be near impossible for Thran's Hand to keep following their trail.

That's if they're coming at all.

While he was committed to seeing his power drained, it had still been comforting to think of his Hand rescuing him.

For the first time since awakening, Thran's spirits plummeted.

Chapter 20

He was too busy admiring the scenery to notice the goddess of Luck waiting for him further along the path until he was almost upon her. He stopped, pulled out a handkerchief and thoroughly mopped his wet, red forehead.

'I had not expected to see you again so soon.' He wheezed.

'I have time to kill.' A slight pause. 'And a proposition to make.'

'Well my dear, unfortunately time is no such luxury for one such as I. *I* must be on my way.' He set off in a quick, determined stride. She fell into step beside him, matching his tempo.

'And where might you be off to in such a hurry?'

'Oh, grave business, grave business indeed.' He told her seriously.

'Dare I ask?'

'I dare say you should. For it is a quest of upmost importance. One given to me by Mother Nature herself!'

'But I didn't ask.'

'I woke up with a calling, with a thirst in my heart only natural wonderment could quench. I knew I must make haste from that stone cesspool or feel my happiness wilt away like a flower denied the sun's life-giving rays.'

'The calling of a poet?'

'Only with the right inspiration, can I wax lyrical. Otherwise, I couldn't possibly hope to string two sentences together, let alone two verses.'

'I remember you once won a bet where you had to talk for an entire bell without stopping or repeating yourself. You were only just getting going when the time was up! So where is this calling taking you?'

'Through the mountains and beyond, I should imagine. Who knows? Certainly not me. Or should that be certainly not I? Me often get the two mixed. Me not sure. You see, me would make a poor poet, figuratively and literally. By that me mean I would have poor grammatical inconsistencies and there would be no coin offered for my ramblings.'

'You mean to intervene.'

'I haven't the foggiest idea of what you could possibly be trying to insinuate and accuse me of. I am simply travelling, taking in scenery often scorned.'

'You mean to intervene.' She said again, flatly.

'If I happen to come across fellow travellers, or heroic adventurers, then it would be my civic duty, even though I am currently outside the city, it's laws are ingrained into my very being, it would be my said duty to aid them by any means necessary.'

'I thought as much. Which is why I came with a proposition.'

'If memory serves, last time we spoke you did hope our intentions would overlap, therefore not causing you to have to squish me like the impudent bug I am. An irksome, irrelevant bug at that.'

'I do not recall phrasing it like that.'

'They call me mad, not stupid. It was implied.'

A half smile played across her lips. 'Yes, I suppose so.' They continued on in silence for a while.

'I would not enjoy having to squish you like a bug.'

'I know. There is often satisfaction in the initial act but the ramifications of the act is what takes the toll. By that I mean the clean-up, of course. Washing your hands, or boots, or whatever appendage you choose to deliver the squishing. It's a real inconvenience that we can't squish away without dealing with the mess.'

They lapsed back into silence. Every so often Garbhan would valiantly wipe his forehead in vain only for it to be glistening again moments later in the afternoon sun. Relief was at hand though as they walked forward into the shadow of the mountain. He let out a contended sigh.

Now if only Oros would bless us with a westerly wind. A pity we are no longer on speaking terms.

He glanced across at his companion who seemed absorbed in her own thoughts. He wouldn't push her, wouldn't pry, she'd make her proposition when she was ready. Garbhan already had a pretty good idea of what she would try to propose. He already knew his answer, as must she, but she was here asking regardless. All he could do was give her time, their past demanded that at least, and she had plenty to kill apparently. He looked across to her and their eyes met. Hers held a sadness which he knew mirrored his own. They looked away, unable to maintain the contact. Acknowledgment was one thing; acceptance was another matter entirely.

'The children of Jagreus wish for immortality. Whether they physically live forever or become immortalised through their deeds in history and folk lore, it matters not. They strive to make a difference in what they think is the small, insignificant, inconsequential time allotted them. They wish their time could be longer. Yet time is what gives their achievements context, what makes their accomplishments astounding. Because they managed it in the time given them. Am I immortal? I dearly hope not. I have lived an abnormally long life, which many would be envious of, but when I reflect on my time, do I see my achievements? Of course not. That's not to say I don't have any, but when I think about all the extra time I have gained, when I think about my life, all I can see is the time wasted, the opportunities squandered, the numerous failures. The mind is a marvellous tool that absorbs all our memories, yet it always seems to keep the regrets, the embarrassments, the hurts, close to the surface; to fling at us when we least expect it, over and over again. How many of these memories are accrued in a lifetime? Hundreds? Well, I have lived many lifetimes. In fact, I think I have lived for far too long. Give me ten years of accomplishments over one hundred misspent any day.'

He turned to face her once more. This time she would not meet his gaze but kept looking forward. He could see the impact of his words and pushed on.

'A famous theologian once pondered the question: "Do I serve a purpose, or do I purposely serve". Viella, these games you play, they serve no purpose.' He'd used her birth name, and not her godly one to hammer home his point.

She wiped at her eyes but when she spoke her voice was steady and clear.

'Deity or not, when you find one, you cling to it with all your being. Do I serve it? Or does it serve me? It's a moot point now, merely semantics.'

'Do you still wish to proposition me?'

'I believe you've already given me your answer.'

'Yes I believe I have.'

'Tell me Garbhan, did the famous theologian find an answer to his poignant question?'

'No one knows. After years of solitary contemplation he hung himself. Drove himself mad. Or perhaps he did find the answer to his question, an answer he did not like.'

'By the Elders, your stories are always so morbid.'

'I am no bard who changes the truth to fantasy so his audience can escape to a make-believe land where it's all sunshine and happy endings.' He hawked up some phlegm and spat out a thick green wad. 'I'm not built for walking, it does not agree with me, nor I with it. Animals exist for a reason, albeit the Twins created them for a different purpose.'

'You still have many leagues left to go.'

'Aye, that I do, but I have just remembered a tale of a man who stared at the sun for a whole hour. The ending is not quite as morbid as you might expect, and it will help the leagues pass.'

'Another time, unfortunately I must now hasten to make other arrangements for what is to come.'

'Do not seek them out Viella, they cannot be trusted.'

'Who said anything about trusting them?'

'To deal with the Twins is madness, even for you, goddess of Fortune, Luck and Favour. And if the Mad Priest Garbhan is claiming your adventure is folly, then Elders help you lass.'

'Who says they're not already? Sometimes madness serves a purpose. Do you still mean to continue your journey?'

'But of course, there is so much more of Mother Nature to explore and discover.'

'Yes I thought you might say that. Be careful.'

'Ah but the Twins bring about such an unpredictability and excitement that not even the much-vaunted Lady can match. It would be madness to miss out on such a spectacle.'

Despite his bravado, Garbhan's hand began to shake. He mopped his brow in an attempt to hide it. He needn't have bothered as Viella was already gone.

He sighed.

'Garbhan just wants a simple life, where things aren't so complicated. A life where he doesn't have to walk so far for days on end. Garbhan would like that very much. Well Mother Nature, it appears to be just I and thee once again. Would you like to listen to my tale of man verses the Elder god Sollun? To pass the time of course.' He cocked his head, then broke out into a beaming smile. 'I'd be even more delighted. Make yourself comfortable, let Garbhan's dulcet tones take you away.'

'There was once a man named, hmmm let's see, what should we call him? Bertillious. Let's call him Bert for short. Now Bert was a thrill seeking sort and one day he bet his friends he could stare directly into the sun for an entire hour. "Nay Bert" they cried! "Your eyes will fry like an egg". But Bert had a cunning plan…'

* * * *

It was hot and humid inside the blacksmith's shop, beads of sweat were rolling down Skrenn's bare dome. He signalled with a flick of his hand for them to continue, he was impatient to be finished.

The victim's hand was held down firmly across the top of an anvil, and with Skrenn's permission the assassin hefted the hammer and brough it swiftly down. The assassin's aim was true, the hammer caught his index finger square on the nail. He screamed but the rags stuffed inside his mouth muffled them. He struggled but two more assassins held him firmly down on his knees. The fourth Hand member was keeping watch outside, making sure they were not interrupted.

Skrenn gestured once more and the rags were removed. The man gasped for air and began to writhe in panic when he saw the blood seeping from his crushed fingertip. Skrenn squatted down on his haunches so he could address the apprentice blacksmith at eye level.

'We know you've been stealing weapons from your master and selling them. What we don't know is who you've been selling them to. So… if you will kindly disclose this information we can be done with this unpleasantness.' He looked pointedly at the man's mangled finger. 'And you will still be able to continue being a smithy's apprentice.'

'They'll kill me!'

'I don't think you understand the severity of your situation.'

Skrenn motioned with his hand, the hammer swung down once more. The apprentice's cries were cut short as the rags were stuffed back into his mouth.

'For them to kill you, would require us to leave you alive. To do that, we'd need an incentive. Understand?' He nodded. 'Now are you prepared to give us an incentive?' The apprentice nodded furiously, attempting to speak but the gag stopped him. 'Stealing from your master, how cowardly! Yet it also took courage, bravery even. It took balls, big balls.'

As if sensing what was to come, the apprentice started thrashing about, desperate to be free from the assassins' grip. They held him steadfast. The assassin holding the hammer tugged at the man's pants, managing to haul them down despite his frantic squirming.

Skrenn let out a low whistle.

'Big balls indeed. So, courage or cowardice? Let's find out if you deserve them.'

They shoved him forward so his genitals lay over the anvil, the hammer came down to rest gentle on a single big ball. Skrenn wrinkled his nose as the man pissed himself. Tears were streaming down the apprentice's face.

'Please… please… I'll tell you what you want to know.' Came his muffled sobs.

'But they'll kill you!' said Skrenn with mock concern, removing his gag.

'It was a Captain, I don't know his name, but one of the men with him accidently let slip he was their Captain. I'd know his face if I saw it, I swear. I can help you find them!'

'Seems you are a coward after all.'

The hammer began to slowly rise into the air.

'NO! PLEASE! I CAN HELP YOU!'

Skrenn turned his back, ignoring the desperate pleas and began to walk away. The hammer stopped at its zenith.

'PLEASE! PLEASE! I TOLD YOU WHAT YOU WANTED!'

The hammer retraced its arc, considerably swifter.

As Skrenn exited into the cooling wind, shrill screams tore into the night.

* * * *

'I've seen enough tortured confessions to know when a man is genuine or he is just telling you what you want to hear. The apprentices was genuine.'

Tavian leaned back and took a sip from his cup of wine. He sighed.

'This is why I was against sending Sarfina's hand on a wild chase after the abductor.'

'We still have Venustus' Hand. And Lagatha. They're of the same calibre.'

'True enough old friend.' Tavian looked reproachfully at the Dresconii. 'But we are still missing our best assets.'

'Half our best assets.' Skrenn corrected. 'Give me Sarfina, Zel, Venustus and Lagatha and I will see to this wayward Captain.'

'*Captains.*' Tavian corrected. 'There is no way this Captain is acting alone. Did you get an accurate description?'

'Accurate enough for us to narrow it down to three potentials.'

'There's no way a regular Captain would do this without the backing of someone powerful.'

'You suspect the Elite four?'

'I always suspect the Elite four. They wield too much military power and influence. And we only have Zakanos in our pocket. His absence further complicates matters.'

'I'm not sure how much help he would have been, were he still here, given the state he was in.'

'You're right, but the 4th are handy to have in a scrap. And the rest of the Guard Company would have thrown their lot in with the Captain.'

Tavian took another sip of his wine, offered a cup to Skrenn who accepted and drained it in one go.

'It's just the timing, with the festival of Oros fast approaching. There'd be no better time than the height of the festivities.' Skrenn mused, scratching his smooth pate.

'Which leads me to suspect a nobleman's hand in this, or a merchants, or both.'

'Celentine?'

'He's content suckling the Empire's teat at the moment, but it won't be long before we'll be having to deal with that greedy pig.'

'The merchant's guild?'

'They're conniving little worms, but we've bought or threatened enough of them to keep them quiet.' Tavian drained his cup, refilled it, and then reclined on the couch once more.

'If only the taxpayers knew their hard earned money was going into the pockets of merchants. They'd tear the city apart.'

'Maybe we should let them, start again from scratch. Let them deal with Shulakh.'

'Don't let your daughter hear such talk, you know what she'd say.'

'Ha! Nothing, and that's the problem, she won't talk to me, she won't talk to anyone. How did things go between the two of you?'

'Unfortunately, I have not had chance to speak to her, with recent events taking precedence.'

'Of course, forget I asked. We digress. I shall give you both Venustus' and Lagatha's Hands with Sarfina and Zel attached. Sarfina shall act as your second.'

Skrenn bowed his head in acknowledgement.

'But first refill your cup with wine and keep me company a little while longer.'

* * * *

No matter how much Thran shifted and fidgeted he couldn't get comfortable on the cold, hard floor. He cursed Mortem's name. He'd refused to stay in the guest rooms sporadically placed along the tunnel stretching right through the mountain, where guests could take their rest in proper beds. Mortem had a distrust of communally sharing a room with any other travellers.

So they had stopped for the night, if it was night, it was rather difficult to tell under the mountain, in the darkness in-between the gas lamps that lit the tunnel every thirty or so paces. Thran had heard merchants talk of Grellon's gas lamps but had never had the chance to see one up close until now. The concept was quite strange to him: how could the air burn without any fuel? With no cloth or timber? To Thran the Grellish were ingenious inventers of marvels.

Which was why he had been sorely disappointed he wouldn't get to see Grellon, the fabled city lying underneath the heart of the Endless Peaks. Sprawling across countless caverns, the mining station turned city was said to hold an ethereal beauty caused by the glow of the gas lamps. Thran remembered one merchant describing arriving at the stairs leading down to the caverns as looking upon the stars in the night sky, but from above.

They had passed through the great steel gates guarding the mountains posing as down on their luck merchants, not that the guards paid them much attention, especially when Mortem told them they'd be using the fast track directly through the mountain and not visiting the main city. The fast track was the nickname for the passage that went straight as the crow flies through the mountain but even so it would take a day and a half of travel to emerge out of the other gate. It was usually favoured by merchants who couldn't afford to travel by ship, hauling their goods between Tydon and Mirron. There was a toll of course, but everyone was willing to pay that because it saved those days of extra travelling skirting around the Endless Peaks, and that bandits dare not operate within Grellish territory for fear of retribution and being trapped in the mountain.

Thran cursed Mortem's name again.

At least I got to see Mt Serpentine.

Mt Serpentine had grown and grown with every step until it dominated the horizon, stretching unassailably into the sky. They'd finally passed into its shadow where they had to crane their necks upwards to see its flat headed tip.

'Quit your mumbling! If we get spotted camping in the darkness there'll be questions, and I'll have to start killing, turning this whole thing messy. So keep your trap shut.'

Thran spat out one last curse before shifting into a semi-comfortable position and attempted sleep.

He was rudely kicked awake. He felt groggy, worse than if he'd not slept at all. His body ached. How long he'd been asleep was hard to say, being underground was also messing with Thran's perception of time. Mortem had already readied the donkeys so as soon as he manhandled Thran into the saddle, they were away.

The fast track was packed with merchants and traders, all making their way to Tydon to make profit at the festival of Oros. Aside from the odd traveller they were the only ones travelling in the opposite direction, and the further they progressed into the mountain, the quieter it became, only seeing stragglers whose journeys had been delayed.

'You seem even more sullen than usual today.' Mortem remarked sometime into their journey.

'I do apologise, I wasn't aware kidnapped people were usually joyous travelling companions.'

'Well there's no need for sarcasm. I'm not just a heartless killer, I'm more attuned to people's emotions than you might think.'

'Well I'm sure that's real comforting to your victims' families: at least it was an empathetic killer.'

'And I suppose the families of your victims are comforted by the fact you did it for money.'

Thran had no immediate comeback.

'At least when we kill, it's quick and painless. Instant. Why do you kill?'

'For the pleasure of it.'

'A tad contradictory, Mr. Empathy.'

'I knew you wouldn't understand.' Mortem sneered.

'Then by all means, enlighten me!'

Mortem seemed about to do just that when a voice boomed down the enclosed space.

'HO TRAVELLERS!'

Both instinctively reached for their weapons. Thran swore when his hand grasped thin air where his knives should have been. Mortem had unsheathed a knife of his own, keeping the naked blade down by his thigh, so it was obscured from view by his donkey.

'HO!' The merchant cried again, waving his arms in the air, attempting to flag them down.

Mortem glanced behind them but could see no others approaching. Yet they may have been back there, hidden in the darkness between lamps. He waved back at the merchant while at the same time discreetly cutting Thran's bonds with a flick of his wrist. Thran winced as the blood flow circulated in his hands for the first time in days. He rubbed them together in an attempt to bring the feeling back quicker. He met Mortem's eyes, saw the threat and question they were simultaneously posed and nodded his understanding.

They stopped well short of the merchant who seemed not to notice their hesitancy.

'Thank goodness, someone has come along at long last. I began to fear the worst. As you fellows can see my left rearmost wheel has become lodged in a crevice and refuses to un-lodge itself. I thought I would be stuck here forever! And miss the tidy profits to be made at the festival. Would you kind sirs help me?'

'Of course.' Answered Mortem friendly enough, but his gaze kept sweeping the darkness. They dismounted and headed over to the merchant. As they approached Thran noted how tall and broad shouldered the man was. He had the unmistakable pale complexion, blonde hair and blue eyes of a mountain dweller. He must have noted Thran's expression for he laughed.

'First time seeing a native Grellon, eh? I thought as much. It's a common misconception that living under the mountains stunts our growth. We're bred strong and strapping! I'm considered to be on the short side.'

Thran could only wonder how big the Grellons were who were considered to be tall.

A city of giants!

He felt another pang of regret at not being able to see it for himself.

On the way back, he promised himself, *on the way back. If I go back.*

The sudden thought surprised him. He'd always just assumed he would make his way back to Tydon and take his place in the Hand. Yet seeing Mt Serpentine, travelling under the Endless Peaks, had opened his eyes to a whole new world outside of Tydon he'd never imagined or experienced before.

After my responsibilities as this so called Descendant are over, I think I've earned the right to be a little selfish. Indulge my own desires for a change. And I desire to see the rest of the world. The Guild will continue without me. I'll be replaced in no time, if not already.

In the end they had to unload all the merchants' belongings off the back of his wagon. Mortem and Thran heaved the wagon up while the merchant coaxed his two horse team forward, the wheel just about scraping over the top of the crevice. They loaded the wagon back up. Afterwards the merchant slapped them on the back and shook their hands, all the while smiling warmly.

'Thank you both so much, honestly, got me out of a spot of bother there! I'm in your debt. If you're ever in Grellon again, ask for the merchant Bisher and I shall see you properly rewarded! That is, when I've come back from making a small fortune in Tydon at Oros' festival.' He added with a wink.

Thran felt an instant liking towards Bisher. He had an open, honest face and a genuine warmth in his smile, which he almost constantly wore. Thran was positive he would make a small fortune in Tydon.

'Well perhaps we could take a small payment now, and replenish our dwindling supplies?' Mortem asked.

Bisher laughed. 'Your companion is a shrewd man.' He told Thran, giving his back another round of hearty slaps. 'Of course, of course, help yourselves.'

'It'll be nice to not eat dried meat for a change.' Thran admitted.

They bade their goodbyes to Bisher and went their separate ways. The merchant had rubbed off on him a little and his spirits had lifted. Mortem didn't bother to re-tie his bonds, evidently satisfied he would not try to escape. It was time to focus on the upcoming ritual.

It was time to do as Carrion suggested.

It was time to test his powers.

Chapter 21

Nobody had warned him about the saddle sores. Nozza dismounted gingerly, getting the feeling the horse was just as glad for him to be getting off, for in truth he was a poor rider. He'd always ridden in the carriage with Pemtil anytime they'd ventured outside the city, which was few and far between.

Zakanos set a gruelling pace, pushing their mounts to their limit. Each day they were up before dawn and set up camp well after dark. Despite the dangers riding at night posed, none dared complain. The first few days had been the worst. His thighs were red raw and bleeding, making sleep elusive despite his exhaustion. When they halted for the third night, Nozza had already made up his mind to ask the healing Priestess to see what she could do to help ease his pain now that Heelial no longer needed her supervision. He could already picture and hear the rest of the squad's sneers and jeers at his weakness.

'Pull down your pants.'

He'd just stared at her blankly.

'I need to see your thighs to access the severity of your sores.'

Grinning sheepishly, he'd pulled down his pants, cupped his modesty with both hands and glanced around hoping the rest of the camp wouldn't notice. She bent for a closer inspection, clucking her tongue all the while. She gently pressed a particularly angry looking welt with her index finger. He winced.

'I'll tell you exactly the same as what I told the others. There is no point in me healing you every night because you will end up in the same predicament. Better to let your skin harden into a natural toughness. There are some salves, but I don't have the necessary ingredients.' With that she'd gone to her bedroll to turn in for the night. She called over her shoulder. 'You can cover yourself now.' Which he promptly did.

'You look like a merchant who's just fleeced a whole village out of their meagre savings.' Creak told him as he approached the fire.

'Eh?'

'You look like a slimy little weasel.' Clipper said, spitting out a chewed up toenail.

Creak rolled her eyes. 'No, you just appear rather pleased with yourself.'

'I don't know what you mean.'

'Well you can swagger over to Rolls and relieve her, you've got next watch.'

The truth was he was rather pleased with himself and not even having to stand watch dampened his mood.

I wasn't the first one to approach the Priestess.

The overall mood was a different matter. That little bit of bantering was the most they'd had on the journey. Zakanos kept to himself and barely acknowledged them, only allowing Reeva to ride near him and approach him with meals when they'd camped. Araxia was practically a recluse. They still didn't trust her even though she'd healed Heelial and nursed her back to full strength, only approaching her for medical matters. The 4th squad shared a few words between themselves at night around the fire but the subdued atmosphere ensnared them all. The other assassin had ingratiated himself into the squad seamlessly and seemed friendly enough, almost like an extra squad member.

Shriek acted as a scout roaming ahead of the group seeing as he was the most comfortable in the saddle, which wasn't surprising given the fact Kidoshians learnt to ride before they could walk. His job was to sniff out any potential trouble. Not that they expected any because the city-states of Bellum were at peace with each other. For now. Any bandits roaming the area would be foolish or desperate to attack such a heavily armed band when there was much easier prey to be had. Usually this time of the year the traffic on the road was heavy with merchants heading to Tydon with goods to sell at the festival of Oros. No, they weren't expecting trouble until they reached their destination. Which was still a mystery.

All Nozza knew was that it was beyond the mountains they'd reached on day two, having been ordered to ride around and not go directly through, which had cost them several more days. He'd been confused at this seeing as though time seemed to be of the essence if the Captains gruelling pace was anything to go by. When he'd said as much to the Sergeant, she'd just thrown him a look of contempt. Creak had been kind enough to spell it out for him.

'Look, *newbie,* they ain't gonna let over a dozen well-armed men just go riding through their gates and into their precious city. They'll think were trouble. Which is true. Which means we'd have to explain that we're troops from Tydon and not low-life brigands. Which means they would want to know what we were doing this far from Tydon and where we were heading, which is none of their bloody business! So we ride around.'

So they'd ridden around. That was two days ago. Once past the mountains Zakanos increased the pace beyond what Nozza had thought possible. When they finally stopped to camp, after a brief consultation with the High Priestess, Captain Zakanos spoke up.

'Tomorrow morning we arrive. Prepare yourselves. No fires tonight.'

He retreated back to his solitude leaving the squad staring at each other. Fingers and Shriek stood up, stretched, drew their swords and started to run through numerous exercises. Reeva was nowhere to be found. Heelial, Scorch and

Araxia took themselves off from the rest of the group, whispering furtively.

'I want to know what the fucks going on.' Clipper grumbled.

'We'll find out what we need to know, when we need to know.' Creak scolded him. 'Although it would be nice to have some idea.'

They were all quiet, contemplating the day that lay ahead. Owl hooted a couple of times, then lay down in his bedroll, wheezy snores soon followed. Rolls huffed, unable to settle she stood up, eyes narrowing in on her prey; 'Hey, big man.'

Drak looked up from where he'd been picking at blades of grass.

'Come with me.'

He grinned and followed her into the night.

'Where are they going?' Nozza asked. The rest of them just looked at him. 'Oh… How can they think of doing that right now?'

'It's amazing how potent an aphrodisiac the threat of imminent danger and death can be.' Smokey said.

'And Rolls'll sleep with anyone.' Added Creak.

'She once told me she had two rules. One, they have a pulse. Two, they have a penis.' Clipper said in all seriousness. 'Although she's been known to be lenient on the second rule.'

'She never did!'

'Honest she did. I swear by the warmth of Sollun.'

'I'm going to ask her in the morning.'

'Okay she may not have used the word rules, more like guidelines, but it's the gods honest truth.'

'There's nothing honest about the gods.'

'Then I swear on my good name.'

'There's nothing honest about yours either!'

Nozza left Clipper and Creak to their debate, dragged his kit away to a quieter spot and attempted to sleep. It eluded him. He couldn't settle his nerves, it would be his second taste of real combat.

His mind kept spinning around the same thought like a whirlpool: *we won't be using practice wooden swords tomorrow. It'll be real steel biting into my flesh, just like in Ritellis Square, which I was lucky to survive. Brioth's blessings, why did I think it would be a good idea to enlist?*

It was at the sound of his name being spoken that drew him out of his morbid thoughts. He looked up to find Smokey standing over him, a blanket wrapped tightly around her.

'Having trouble sleeping?'

'Yeah, can't help wondering what tomorrow will bring. You?'

'It's the cold that's keeping me awake.' Nozza frowned. While it was certainly milder this side of the mountains, by no means was it unbearably cold. Summer was only just waning. 'Especially with no fire. So I thought that instead of shivering my arse off alone, we could attempt to share some warmth together.'

He looked up to see her grip on the blanket had loosened, and in the pale, dim moonlight he could she was naked beneath. He nodded, mouth drier than a desert as she slipped under his blanket and pressed her body against his.

A potent aphrodisiac indeed!

His final thoughts that night were not of the coming battle. He didn't think of how the fear would grip him, how it could coil in his belly like a snake and make him sweat so profusely his vision would blur. He didn't think about how some of them would most likely be sleeping permanently this time tomorrow, himself chief amongst them. Instead, his final thought was this:

Perhaps soldiering isn't so bad after all…

He was kicked awake by Clipper.
'Get up newbie.'
He sat up and rubbed the sleep from his eyes. Despite only snatching a few hours he felt rested, but not quite as refreshed as he'd have liked. There was no Smokey sleeping next to him. She must have gone before the rest of the camp stirred. He sat down to breakfast with the rest of the squad. It consisted of stale bread and salted meat washed down with a few warm mouthfuls from his water skin.
The conversation was about as exciting as their food. Clipper attempted to lighten the mood.
'You have fun last night?'
Nozza almost chocked on the piece of meat he'd just bitten off.
'Not bad. Middle of the road.' Rolls replied. 'What's wrong with you newbie?'
'Nothing.' He managed to wheeze out in-between coughs.
'He's just thinking of the good old days, when he used to be the merchants private whore.' Clip teased. Nozza went to object but caught Smokey's gaze out the corner of his eye. She winked. He could feel his face turning crimson. 'Ya see! I was right! He was Pemtil's little bitch.'
'I'm sorry, I don't understand. How could he be the merchant's dog?' Shriek asked.
This brought a little laugh from the group. It helped ease the nerves and the tension. The dialogue felt a little less forced afterwards.
'I wasn't! I accidently choked on some meat.' Nozza shot back defensively.
'I bet you did!' Creak quipped.
This time the laughter was genuine and lasted longer. Owl hooted loudly.

'Speaking of dogs, you've done it now Rolls.' Smokey said when it had quietened down. 'That big'uns' been making puppy eyes at you all morning.'

'What did you do to him?'

The question even drew Fingers attention, which had previously been devoted to cleaning his fingernails with a knife.

'Nothing.' The squad made their disbelief known. 'I'm serious. He just experienced what it was like to have a real woman, with an appetite.' Rolls smiled wolfishly.

'What did she do to me?' Drak wondered aloud as he watched the 4th squad sitting around chatting to each other. Had he been paying attention to Reeva he would have noticed her eyes roll.

'I feel weird. Different. I've never felt this way before. It feels so . . . so . . . *foreign.* I don't understand. I can't really describe it, but, if I could only sleep with her for the rest of my life I'd be okay with it. In fact I'd be more than okay with it. What did she do to me? She must be an enchantress. Or a succubus! Oh shit! Reeva, did I fornicate with a succubus? Has she ensnared me for eternity? Once you've done the deed there's no going back. They own you, body and soul. Am I to be a slave to her desires? Her whims? There must be a way to undo this perverse pact, there's always a way to undo curses…'

Reeva patted him gently on the shoulder.

'Gather round you ingrates! 4th and Guild.' Heelial waited till they were all before her. 'We've been busting a gut up until this point, but now we're gonna take it nice and slow. Now I don't know what it is we're expecting exactly, but it'll be trouble. But we ain't expecting trouble until we reach the trees. From which point on the Priestess will be leading the way.'

That raised a few eyebrows.

'We'll be leaving our mounts at the treeline. Without a guard. Can't spare a single soul, so tie em' up tightly. If we don't take any of them back, we'll have to listen to them horsefuckers complaining for months.' It wasn't much of a joke, but it got a few smiles and grunted laughs. She looked over them all, meeting every single person's eye. 'We're here for different reasons, we're from different backgrounds, but working together, we're gonna kill that sonofabitch and get vengeance. And get our missing person back!'

Hardly awe inspiring, but it'll have to do.

'Now get your shit together and get ready to move out.'

* * * *

Araxia preferred it when they'd all ignored her. It was better than feeling a dozen pairs of eyes bore into the back of her head. She did her best to ignore the mutterings.

Concentrate! You have a job to do. And wrongs to right. Not that you can.

She'd already made her mind up about what to do once this little escapade had reached its conclusion. If she lived to see its conclusion. Although she supposed her life was no longer her own. She'd given that right up when turning a blind eye to Mortem's atrocities.

She laid a hand on the trunk of the great sprawling tree that rose before her. Oak she supposed, although she wasn't really sure. Nature wasn't particularly her strong suit. It signified the start of the forest, and her time to start leading their little group deeper into its murky depths. Into a convergence of power that gave her goose bumps and made her hairs stand on end.

Araxia, High Priestess of Jagreus, the Elder goddess of Life, took a deep breath, exhaled slowly, and stepped into the forest.

* * * *

At her vantage point high up in a tree, The Lady waited patiently, surveying the clearing before her. That was the key to most plans: patience. It was a virtue she'd learnt to master, although when she'd been a mortal, it was something she seemed to have little of.

Funny how living for a few hundred years changes your perspective.

She stretched her back, before settling once more against the trunk, her legs sprawled out before her on a thick, sturdy branch. Judging from its humongous size, The Lady reckoned the tree had seen a few hundred years itself. Nature's sentinels she liked to call them, and they ringed the clearing in a crooked circle. In the centre lay the ruins of a temple overgrown with moss and lichen. Hardly impressive; yet it was not the ruins she'd planned this little gathering for, it was what lay beneath.

Not what: who, she corrected herself.

She could sense him stirring below, knowing they were close at hand. His presence, even after so long imprisoned, was palpable. Even more reason this needed to play out exactly as she planned. Yet this wasn't the cause of her underlying unease. It was her bargain with the Twins. Oh she'd gotten exactly what she wanted, *needed*, from their little palaver, it's what they'd demanded in return. It had surprised her. She didn't like being surprised. She knew they would demand something in return, as was their right, but it hadn't entered into her reckoning how much they would demand of her! It had been insightful, indicative of their plans - she'd gained useful information without prying, it had been freely given and that was what worried her.

Perhaps I should have listened to Garbhan's warnings after all. Yet I still met with them regardless and accepted their help even after they listed their terms. I could've walked away, but that would have meant intervening directly and that's not something I'm prepared to do. Yet.

So she'd accepted and would deal with the consequences once today's show was over. Speaking of which, here came the first two actors, trudging cautiously out from underneath the sentinel's protection to take centre stage by the ruins.

The presence from below the ruins began to intensify, as if preparing to play its part in the upcoming entertainment.

* * * *

Sarfina sensed the mood shift as the Tavern door opened and a group of four sauntered in and claimed a table. A few locals, already knowing that trouble was brewing, gulped down their drinks and made for the exit. A few choose to stay. Whether it was through ignorance of the situation or a desire to see how it played out, Sarfina wasn't sure. She was mildly offended, and disappointed. Only four? They didn't bother with any pretences of ordering food and drink, they just waited for the Tavern to clear. No witnesses.

No new customers filtered into the Tavern either, meaning they had someone posted outside making sure anyone who approached kept on walking. One by one, the Tavern began to clear. Sarfina went about her normal duties, pointedly ignoring her hostile guests.

The night was still young when the four were the only customers left inside the Tavern. A fifth man entered and stood by the door.

That's more like it.

She headed over to the table, their eyes tracking her every move.

'Good evening gentlemen. I know why you're here.'

They all shared a glace.

'Is that so?'

'Oh yes.' She replied with a lascivious grin. She lifted a leg and placed it on the table's edge. 'In fact, it's your lucky night.' Sarfina began to lift the hem of her dress, revealing a shapely leg. 'Well, actually, let me correct myself.' All eyes were on her hands as they slowly went higher. 'One of you is getting lucky tonight.' Her dress was now above knee level. 'The others, well…' The garment swept past mid-thigh to reveal- 'I don't need you alive.'- a concealed dagger which she pulled free whilst simultaneously kicking the table over in one fluid motion. It tipped over, taking the two sitting opposite Sarfina with it to the ground.

As the table fell, Sarfina was already in motion, her dagger slicing across the throat of the thug to her left. Pivoting, she reversed her grip on the weapon so as to hold it by the blades tip, pulling her arm back, she released. The dagger whipped across the room, taking the man by the entrance in the chest. He hit the door he was supposed to be guarding and slumped to the floor.

She was now facing the only assailant left standing, who rushed forward to try and grab her. She surprised him by stepping forward, sending a full forced open palmed blow into the centre of his face, crushing his nose and stunning him. She followed this with two quick elbow blows to the temple. Sarfina then swept the dazed man's legs from under him and brought her foot sharply down on his throat, crushing his windpipe.

The final two had regained their feet as Sarfina turned to face them. She cocked her head and said. 'So which one of you is going to be the lucky one?' This elicited the desired response as they let out growls from snarling mouths and charged.

By the time Zel entered, a fourth man had joined his lifeless companions and the fifth was face down, whimpering, as Sarfina gripped him by the hand twisting his arm at an unnatural angle.

'What took you so long?'
'You had the situation under control.'
'That's not the point!'
'We don't have time for this, let's get to work.'
'Gladly.' She replied, twisting the hand even further.

Chapter 22

'Well…' Mortem said as he kicked over some loose rubble. 'This is rather disappointing.' He stood in the middle of the clearing, surrounded by what little remained of the temple. 'I was expecting something a little grander.'

Thran said nothing.

This is it. This is where it stood. The temple I've been dreaming of. I stand amongst its remains.

He stopped following Mortem, who carried on further into the ruins, his features holding a look of haughty contempt.

'Although I suppose we're far from Tydon now.' Mortem continued, seemingly unaware, or unconcerned that Thran was no longer directly behind him.

Thran could sense the power below him. Feel it in the air around him. Heavy, oppressive, almost reducing him to his knees, he could not help but marvel at the ancient spells of the Council members, still so powerful after all this time.

This is it. Where I lose my powers. Where all this madness ends and I can go back to living a normal life in Tydon. Without having to keep secrets from everyone. If I go back.

Mortem turned around to face Thran.

'I've got to say I'm also a little disappointed in you, *assassin.*' He sneered.

There's no going back. My powers will be gone forever.

'I was hoping you would fight. Make things interesting, not meekly submit to your fate.'

This is it.

Thran balled his hands into fists.

'That's more like it!' Mortem said, his eyes gleaming.

'Why?' Than asked quietly.

'What?'

'I said why! You are going to tell me why you are doing all this.'

'And why would I do that?' Mortem replied, half smiling.

'Because I'm going to make you.'

Mortem's customary grin returned in full force.

'Is that so?'

'And then.' Thran stared Mortem straight in the eye. 'I'm going to kill you.'

* * * *

Six sets of eyes swung to the door as they heard the body thump and slide down the wall outside. The mixture of Captains and Sergeants reached for their weapons. The door opened to reveal a woman dressed completely in black. It made her white hair and gloves stand out in stark contrast. Her pupils were completely black, the only visible sign of her Mirronese heritage.

'Hello boys and girls.' She purred, striding confidently into the room, like she'd extended them the invitation to this little gathering. 'Lagatha. A pleasure I'm sure.'

None of them had moved, thrown by the newcomer's confidence and unsure of her intentions. White knuckles gripped hilts in readiness.

'Now I'm not so arrogant as to believe you've all heard of me.' Lagatha continued as she moved towards the table they were all sat around. Despite her plumpness, she was graceful, moving with the fluidity of a trained killer. 'However I'm sure you will have heard of my current employer. The Guild I work for. May I?' She sat in the empty seat. 'She'll no longer be joining us, is the answer to your unaired question. But seeing as though we're all here, why don't we get started?'

They didn't answer her, their faces strained. She shook her head.

'Loose ends.' She tutted. 'When you're planning on carrying out something this dangerous, on such a big scale, you really can't be leaving loose ends. Perhaps you are unsure of what constitutes a loose end? Well let me tell you, a young, loose lipped apprentice definitely qualifies. The gods forbid if you were actually going to be successful and overthrow the Emperor because Tydon would be doomed. The key to ruling, and something which you are severely lacking, is ruthlessness. Being ruthless is a trait that our Tavian has in abundance, hence why I am here.'

'I said I'm not so arrogant as to believe that you've heard of me, but there is a chance you've heard of what they call me, what is whispered fearfully into the darkness. The "White Raven".' A few of the Captains shared a quick glance. Lagatha smiled. 'Ah, I see that you have. Good. If you've heard of the White Raven, you will have heard of her little rituals. Well, they're more like habits really. You see, I cannot stand uncleanliness. I know, I know, odd, given the nature of my work, but I abhor dirt, dust and grime, anything that contributes to filth. It's why I wear mostly black, so when my work becomes complicated, it's not as easily visible. I do however, allow myself one treat: my pristine white gloves, so beautiful and pure. It matches my hair so wonderfully and reveals the nature of my spirit.'

'So before things get messy, I remove them to keep them clean. Now as you can see, I have removed one. The question is... do I need to remove the other?'

The Captain nearest her stood up, and spat at her. The goblet landed on Lagatha's gloved hand. She stared at it, then stared at the Captain whose mouth it had come from. Speaking as she slid the sullied glove from her hand, she said:

'How... repulsive...'

'I'm going to have to burn them now, they're completely ruined!' Lagatha lamented.

'You have like, three hundred of pairs of exactly the same gloves. You single-handedly keep that tailor in business.' Venustus muttered as he rolled his eyes.

'That doesn't mean I shouldn't mourn the passing of a perfectly good pair.'

'You're not right in the head. Focus up, here comes Skrenn.'

Skrenn padded softly towards them, his gaze sweeping the rooftops around them. The Assassins Guild owned the rooftops, and vigilant sentries patrolled them regularly, yet despite this Skrenn could not shake his unease.

'White Raven. Report.'

'There's seven officers who won't be turning up for duty tomorrow morning. They knew nothing we didn't already suspect. They did confirm it will take place during the festival of Oros. I lost a pair of perfectly good gloves.' Lagatha added with a huff.

Skrenn grunted. 'Venustus.'

'Somehow word got out. Only two showed, same as Lagatha.'

'The both of you, follow me.'

They worked their way down to street level, to the same building Skrenn had taken Sarfina to not so long ago. He uncovered the secret entrance into the sewers and clambered down.

'I'm not going down there!'

'Don't think you have a choice.'

'I'm not ruining another pair of gloves tonight.'

'Have you still got the ruined pair on your?'

'Yes, I've not had the time to properly dispose of them.'

'Then put them on.'

'Absolutely not.' She shuddered.

'It's the only way.'

'I'm not putting them on, and that is final!'

'Well it's either that, or you go down bare handed.'

With that he followed Skrenn downward. Lagatha stared after him, before sighing resignedly. She took off her pristine white gloves, carefully folded them and slipped them inside her pocket. She brought out a cloth which she unfolded to reveal the soiled gloves and begin to put them on.

'How… distasteful…'

* * * *

Araxia paused until the rest of the group had caught up with her. Zakanos who had been walking beside her carried on for a few more paces, before finally stopping. His impatience was written across his face.

'We are close. Squad mage, please may I have a word?' asked the Hight Priestess.

Scorch separated herself from the rest of the squad and they walked through the trees out of immediate earshot, but still within eyeline. Sergeant Heelial was right beside them.

'If you think you're keeping me out of the loop on what we're about to walk into then you're seriously mistaken. It's fallen on me to keep this squad safe, which I intend to do.' Heelial glared at them both, challenging either to defy her.

'Of course Sergeant, I did not mean to cause offense.'

'None taken, now what the fuck is going on?'

The High Priestess looked to Scorch. She raised an eyebrow.

'I'm assuming you can sense what is ahead.'

'I can.' Scorch replied tersely.

'I know you do not like me, or trust me, and I completely understand that. However, if we are to survive what is to come, you need to put those emotions to one side. I was not referring to the temple ruins, but to what lies in wait for us below it.'

'What are you talking about?'

'Ignore the temple. Do not get drawn towards it like a fire in the night. Search the darkness.'

Scorch closed her eyes and was silent. 'I feel it.' She opened her eyes and looked directly at Araxia for the first time. 'You're right. I'm sorry. What is that?'

'I believe it is a creature spawned by the Bestial Twins. Why it is here, I cannot fathom, but it stands in our way.'

'No I think you're right, it definitely has the scent of the Twins. Why does it not mask itself?'

'Because it does not feel the need.'

Her words sent a chill through the other two.

'Would you two care to explain this magic nonsense to me?' Heelial asked.

'To be brief, at the beginning of times, when the Elder gods were young and the world in its infancy, the Bestial Twins, Vittes and Vottres decided to create creatures in their image to fill the empty lands and seas. The animals that we see today are their descendants. They decided to create a sentient creature; a curator to look after their work. Jagreus. They came to regard and love Jagreus as their daughter. The Twins' creations began to breed at such a rate that Jagreus needed help. Like her parents, she decided to make her own creations, in her own image, to help her with the task set by the gods. They were our forefathers. The first humans. We worshipped Jagreus as our own creator, and set about our duties with diligence and reverence.'

Araxia paused for a moment. When she began again, it was with a profound sadness.

'The problems began as our own population swelled at a faster rate than the animals. Soon we began to outnumber them. Fights began over resources. It wasn't long before we started hunting and killing what we had been sworn to protect. The Twins were enraged and demanded their daughter destroy all the humans for what they had done, but Jagreus could not find it in herself to wipe out her own children. Vittes and Vottres dared not upset their daughter for whom they cared so much by wiping us out. Instead the Twins created protectors of their own, to fight back against the humans. Terrible creatures, monsters created out of malice, designed to tear people apart. The humans and these creatures fought incessantly, slaughtering each other. Distraught, Jagreus pleaded with the Twins to end the violence, to which they did, recalling their creatures back. Restrictions were placed upon the humans. There are parts of this world we may not enter, unless bestowed with the blessings of the Twins.'

'I do not divulge the secret past of my Mistress lightly. The reason I tell you all this, is so that you are all fully prepared for what is to come, for I believe one of those creatures lies ahead in waiting for us.'

Heelial nodded. 'Right… okay then.' She marched back over to the others. 'Right, everyone listen up. There's a big angry creature up ahead that can tear us all into little pieces, so here's the formation we're gonna use to kill it. Heavies up front with Scorch. Shriek, Fingers, you're bringing up the rear with the big assassin. The rest of us are gonna form a nice, tight compact centre. Creak, crossbow at the ready. Smokey, Owls, get out your nastiest surprises. High Priestess, you stick by the Captain and no matter what happens, get him to that fucking temple.'

'Is everyone clear?'

There were a mixture of nods and grunts.

'Good. Now salute like the proud soldiers of Tydon you are!' They all saluted, fists thumping against chests, apart from the assassins, the High Priestess and the Captain.

Heelial put on her best parade voice.

'GUARD COMPANY, 4TH SQUAD, MOVE OUT!'

Scorch, flanked by Clipper and Rolls, set off through the trees once more.

* * * *

'You're going to kill me?' Mortem's harsh laughter cut through the air. 'As I said, you disappoint me. All these gods taking such an interest in you, all that happened in Tydon was because they wanted you! And you just meekly followed me here, even after I let you free from your bonds. I was testing you, to see if you had any fight left in you to escape. Only now you finally show some fire in your eyes, when it's too late and it's going to be my pleasure to douse it. You're not worthy of the powers bestowed upon you. First the goddess of Life chose me to kill you, then the god of Death himself sought me out as he recognised I was worthy. Worthy to ascend and join the godhood.'

'You're crazy!'

'I pity you. You still don't understand, I'm free. Ever since I was young I've been able to hear the gods whispering to me, choosing me to be the vassal of their will. I've been called crazy many times before. I made them understand, and I will make you understand. See, I thought it was just me the gods had chosen, that only I could hear them, but I was wrong. They give everyone a chance to break free from society's chains and join the calling. That voice in the back of your head telling you to steal from that merchant, to throttle your neighbour and take his wife because you deserve it. To take what's yours. That's the gods!'

'You're not only crazy, you're also delusional.'

Mortem sighed. 'You're no better than I. In fact, you're worse, a hypocrite who claims to kill only for coin. Why did you become an assassin?'

'I had no choice.'

'There is always a choice. It's just easier for you to hide behind that lie. The truth is that you love the killing, live for it. You revel in the feeling of power that it gives you, and there's nothing wrong with that. It's what the gods want, they want you to grasp that power. To become their vassal and rise above the rest. People become like ants. We can be merciful, we can be kind, or we can crush them, because it is our god given power to do so, if only we accept it. My parents abused me from a young age, I was going to take the cowards way out, when I first heard their whisper. That night I locked my parents in the farmhouse and set fire to it. As their screams rose into the night, I knew I was free. Ever since then I've never looked back, listening only to the gods. I have been dutiful. I have earnt my ascension, I will kill you and claim your power as Carrion's reward. It is my destiny.'

'You're so deluded I almost feel sorry for you, but what you did back in Tydon is unforgivable. You are right about one thing though,' Thran admitted, 'I'm going to enjoy killing you and being done with all this. Enough talk, let's end this.'

Mortem smiled and drew out two knives before throwing one, point first, into the dirt at Thran's feet. 'Try not to die too quickly, I too, want to enjoy this.'

As Thran bent to pick up the weapon, Mortem sprang forward, knife flashing.

* * * *

As Skrenn entered the wine cellar from the secret sewer entrance, he instinctively knew something was wrong. As Venustus and Lagatha came in behind him, he made swift hand gestures. They both immediately drew their weapons and dropped into a fighting half-crouch. He slowly made his way up the stairs before coming to a halt before the door to the kitchen. The Dresconii rested his ear against the door, straining to see if he could hear if anything lay beyond the door. Deathly silence. He inched the door open and peered through. Nothing. He slowly opened it fully and crept through into the kitchen, beckoning for the other two assassins to follow him. The three of them stood in the kitchen for quite some time, waiting, listening. The two Hand leaders were unsure what was wrong, but they trusted Skrenn and his judgement implicitly.

Maybe I was wrong...

Just as the thought entered Skrenn's head, he heard it; the muffled sound of a weapon being drawn.

We have been betrayed.

He signalled to retreat, hoping that it was not too late. They began to back towards the cellar as the first assailants charged into the kitchen through the opposite door. Venustus surged forward to meet them.

'Go! I will buy you some time.'

With the sound of clashing blades in their ears, Lagatha and Skrenn fled down into the basement only to be met by more attackers climbing up out of the sewers. The White Raven met the first one just as he rose out of the entrance, sidestepping his thrust as she sank her blade into his neck. She shoved him backwards so that he fell into those below who were ascending. Grunts and curses echoed up from the sewer as Lagatha glanced down to see more shapes beginning to make their ascent.

'We can't escape that way. There's at least a dozen down there.'

Skrenn cursed, his mind racing. He hurried over to one of the larger wine racks near the sewer entrance. 'Help me.' He grunted as he pushed against a big wooden rack, moving it into place. Lagatha joined him and together they heaved it over just as a woman stuck her head out of the hole. She screamed as the wine bottles tipped onto her followed by the rack, sending her plummeting back down into the darkness.

'Now what?' Lagatha asked.

'Now we make a stand, take as many of those bastards with us as possible.' Came the grim reply.

She nodded. They made their way back to the stairs just as a body came tumbling down to land at their feet. It was Venustus. He'd been run through the side several times. His killers were pounding down the stairs, although they stopped short when they spied the two assassins unharmed at the bottom waiting to face them. They'd be expecting the group from below to be pressing the assassins hard. Skrenn used the pause to push Venustus' body up a few steps, putting him between them and their attackers. He joined Lagatha in taking a defensive stance.

'Let me through!' A voice snapped in irritation. Those in front shifted to the side to let a squat, but powerfully built woman through. She stood at the front of her men, eyeing Skrenn and Lagatha with hostility. 'Thanks to that whoreson, I already lost more men than I wanted to, so why don't you just surrender and we can call it a day?' Neither deigned to answer. 'Look, you must understand your situation. You're trapped, there's no escape, so unless you want to end up like your friend, throw down your weapons.' When she still received no answer, she growled in frustration, half turned and snapped a couple of orders to the soldiers behind her. The orders were relayed back until something was passed very carefully forward until it reached the woman. 'I was going to send in the heavies, but I think I prefer this.' She held up a small clay ball that made those around her shift uneasily. 'You're gonna burn like a sacrifice to Sollun, assassin scum.' With that she hurled the clay ball down the stairs. Both the assassins dived out of the way as the ball smashed into the space they had just vacated, spitting fire in all directions. The woman retreated back up the stairs along with her remaining men. 'Make sure they don't escape. When the fire reaches the kitchen, pull back to the street. Watch it burn down. I'm heading back to make my report.'

I lost more than I would have liked, but overall, the mission was a success.

She made her way briskly back to the Citadel and went straight to where the Elite Guard Company was billeted and was immediately admitted to her Captains office.

'Ah, Sergeant Flick, I hope you bring more good news!' Remullus' deep voice filled the spacious room.

She snapped a smart salute. 'I do indeed, Captain.' She gave her report.

'Ruthless as ever Sergeant, ruthless as ever. I expect the butcher's bill on my desk by tomorrow morning.'

'Yes sir.' She saluted and left.

The Captain of the Elite Guard rubbed his hands together gleefully.

'Finally! After all these years I'm finally going to cleanse the Guild from the city. I must say, when you first told me I could get them all in one swoop across Tydon, I thought you were making a fool out of me. I can't thank you enough.' Remullus was addressing his guest who stood looking out the window, his gaze towards the main hall of the Citadel.

'The pleasure is all mine, Captain.' Threm Sioll Celentine said as the nobleman turned round with a smile on his face.

* * * *

Skrenn could feel the heat from the flames even as he rolled away from the explosion. Lagatha had jumped in the opposite direction as the clay incendiary flew at them, she appeared unscathed, having avoided direct contact with the flames, but they were spreading fast, soon they'd hit the wine bottles and they'd both meet a fiery end.

The wine bottles!

They'd given Skrenn an idea, but first he needed to get across to Lagatha's side, as fortunately for her, and unfortunately for him, the flames now separated him from the sewer entrance. He knew he had to act quickly, he backed up as far as he could, braced himself, then charged forward and leapt over the growing flames, feeling them lick at his legs as they hungrily snapped up at him. He looked over to his fellow assassin.

'You okay?' She nodded. 'Good. I need your gloves.'

She slipped them off as the Dresconii moved to the nearest rack that hadn't as yet caught fire. He grabbed the four largest wine bottles in sight and took them back to Lagatha. He gestured for her to hand the gloves over which she did. 'Remove the corks from these bottles, I'm going to need your other pair.'

The Hand leader realised what he was planning to do.

'Aww Skrenn come on! We can make do with two.' He shot her a stern glance. 'Okay, fine!' She produced a second pair of pristine white gloves. 'For the love of Naul, could this day get any worse?' Lagatha grumbled as she set about removing the corks from the bottles. Skrenn took the two sets of gloves and held them, fingers first, to the stairs as the fire spread up them. When they'd caught alight, he brought them back and, one by one, stuffed the unlit end of a glove into the opened bottle. He admired his make-shift munitions, they'd do nicely. He passed two of them to Lagatha. He moved over to the wine rack they'd overturned and slipped his fingers underneath and began to lift.

'Quickly woman!' He said through gritted teeth as he heaved away. 'It's heavy!'

As soon as Skrenn had lifted it enough for her to get underneath, she slipped in and tossed the first bottle down, quickly followed by the second. Lagatha backed up, grabbed the next two bottles and went underneath once more. She could hear cries of confusion and screams of pain from below. The last two bottles were added into the mix. Figures scattered to avoid the flames, whilst two had been unlucky enough to be directly below the holes entrance and were now desperately trying to put out or remove the clothes that were on fire. Their shrill screams echoed down the tunnels as the flames devoured their flesh. She then moved to help Skrenn, lifting the rack from the hole and standing it upright once more. The two of them glanced at each other, nodded, then readied their weapons. Skrenn jumped down first, followed quickly by Lagatha as the first wine bottles exploded behind them.

Chapter 23

Araxia paused as she briefly spied a figure ahead in the trees. Heelial held up her arm and the group stopped behind her.

'What's wrong, Priestess?'

'There's something ahead.'

'The creature?'

'I'm not sure. I don't think so.'

'Then where is it?'

'I'm not sure, I can no longer sense it.'

'Great! Let's keep moving, if that thing shows up, you take the Captain and you get him to that temple. You understand? You take him and just go, we'll take care of whatever the Twins can throw at us.'

'I understand, Sergeant.'

Did Heelial's ears deceive her or did the High Priestesses voice hold a hint of sadness?

'Good. Now move!'

Scorch, along with Clipper and Rolls continued to lead the way. They kept a tight, compact formation, or tried to, as much as the trees allowed. They were getting close. Araxia could feel the dread power of the god of Death seeping in all around her, settling on her shoulders like an oppressive cloak. She shrugged involuntary, trying to shake the growing sense of unease. She knew that the Twins Guardian was out there, stalking them. She glanced back at the squad mage, the practitioner of Sollun. The woman was trying to hide it, but Araxia knew she felt exactly the same.

Her thoughts were interrupted by a roar that shook her bones as the creature burst through the trees to their right. Standing upright on two hind legs, it towered over them, the most freakish abomination of all the Twins' creations. It had a lithe, well-muscled, wolfish body with razor sharp claws. It snarled at them, teeth gleaming, promising bestial fury. Twin horns jutted from the top of its head and its huge feathered wings were tucked into its back. Below them, a scaled tail coiled around itself, ending with a serpent's head, alert and dripping venom.

Heelial was the first to react. 'Go. Now!' She ordered Zakanos and the Priestess as the Guardian eyed them hungrily. Araxia made to protest but the Sergeant shoved her. 'GO!' The two of them set off running through trees drawing the attention of the beast.

I don't think so.

'4th squad, time to earn your pay! Heavies, on me.'

She moved to intercept the beast as it made to chase down her Captain. Much to her pride, Clipper and Rolls didn't hesitate, they came together, shields up, sword tips presented at the creature. That pride soon disappeared as it effortlessly batted the two heavies off their feet, sending them cartwheeling into nearby trees. The Guardian turned its attention to her and she locked gazes with the beast.

Such anger.

As the creature lifted its claw back, Heelial had a sudden realisation:

I'm going to die.

The paw whistled through the air, claws raking into the ground where the Sergeant has stood just second earlier had Creak not pulled her back just in time. She nodded her thanks to the Corporal and gathered her scattered wits. 'Scorch! Smokey! Set that monster ablaze!'

'If we're not careful this whole forest will go up in flames.' The squad mage warned.

The beast came again, growling in frustration. This time Fingers stood in its way, except he didn't try face it head on. The Shulakhii renegade was quick, but even he was struggling to evade, parry and deflect the Guardians attacks. Shriek backed him up, swinging his tulwar up at the creature's face whenever it tried to nip in for a bite.

'Right now, burnings preferable to being eaten!' Heelial retorted.

'What can we do?' Drak asked, gesturing to Reeva at his side.

'Help the sappers.' She gestured to Smokey and Owl who were both rooting around in their munitions boxes. The assassins went over and were handed clay balls.

'Just aim and throw, don't drop them.' Smokey told them.

Heelial looked expectantly at her squad mage.

'If we can lead it over there, I'll have enough space to cast.'

'Okay, any ideas on how we do that?'

'I do.' Creak butted in. 'Me and the newbie will lure it with my crossbows, once it's in position, torch the bastard.'

Heelial nodded. Fingers and Shriek were still somehow keeping it distracted, but barely, and tiring fast. Creak shoved her spare crossbow into Nozza's hands and began dragging him over to the space they were trying to lure the Guardian into. He'd been stood, staring slack-jawed at the beast ever since it had emerged. 'Wake up newbie, we got work to do.' She admonished him. 'You shot one of these before?'

He nodded. 'In practice.'

'Yeah well this is the real deal, make sure you hit the fucker.'

They set up by a large, felled tree on the other side of the now open space where the Guardian had come crashing through, propped the crossbows on its length and took aim, pausing briefly for the others to get into position. Once the trap was set, Heelial gestured and fingers curled around triggers. Creak could see Nozza struggling to keep his hands steady.

'Deep breaths newbie, deep breaths. Steady your breathing. That's it. Hitting him 'll be a piece of piss. Aim low, you'll probably jolt upwards with the kick back, so aim low and you'll hit it. Keep your breathing steady. I'm gonna count down and we pull the trigger on fire, got it? Good. 3... 2...1... fire!' Twin bolts sped towards the Guardian. In a blur of movement, its tail uncoiled and intercepted Creak's bolt sideways on and snapped it in half with its fangs, however it couldn't intercept the second bolt which, despite Nozza's best efforts, only grazed the Guardian's shoulder, maybe nicking it's wing on the way past. Thankfully it was enough to grab its attention. The beast was growing frustrated at the mere humans' continued ability to repel its attacks for so long. Feeling a thin flare of pain lace through its shoulder, the Guardian spun on its new foes, let out an enraged bellow and charged them on all fours. Fingers and Shriek sank to their knees, spent, resting on their planted swords and shared a look of relief, both knowing they'd only been moments away from death.

'Good job newbie!' Creak cried, clapping Nozza on the back. 'Oh shit!' The Corporal continued to let out a string of curses as the creature barrelled towards them with unbelievable speed. Nozza prayed fervently to all the gods, hoping that at least one of them would hear and answer his desperate pleas. Instead of divine intervention, he heard his Sergeant snap out an order and munitions whizzed towards the creature. Two from each side, it had no chance of avoiding them all. It twisted its body in a vain attempt and managed to dodge all but one. The Guardian made the mistake of trying to swat it away. Upon impact with its claw, the munition exploded, blowing chunks of flesh and bone it all directions. Shocked, the beast shrieked in pain, causing them all to wince. The other munitions landed around the creature, one exploded, sending dirt everywhere, the other two spit out flames. Owl jumped up and hooted in delight. It was the last thing he would ever do. The creature, now in a frenzy, tensed its hind legs and pounced. Owl didn't have time to move as the Guardian's jaw closed around his head with a sickening crunch.

Smokey let out an anguished cry as her fellow sapper, and long-time friend, had his head ripped from his body right in front of her eyes. His body, now headless and spurting blood, twitched, then slumped to the floor. Scorch had not been idle whilst all this had been taking place, she'd manoeuvred herself behind the creature, and having just witnessed her squad members' brutal death, she was determined to make it pay. Arms upraised, hands extended, flames began to swirl from her fingertips, gathering into a small blaze. The squad mage gathered all her sorceries and poured it into this one effort, sending it coursing towards the monsters exposed back with a snarl. The flames washed over its furry back, causing it to howl in pain once again. Hearing this encouraged the mage, she stepped forward, putting her everything into the flames, straining every last sinew. It was a fatal mistake. The serpent tail shot out through the flames, extending full length and buried it's fangs in Scorch's face. The top set of fangs entered in through the mages left eye, popping it on impact; the second bit up into her cheek. Both of them immediately began pumping deadly venom into her body. The squad mages flames disappeared instantly as her body began to spasm in unimaginable agony. Every single nerve ending screaming at her, as she in turn voiced her own.

    Drak moved towards Scorch but felt a restraining hand on his arm, he turned back to see Reeva shaking her head. The half-Grellon drew her own weapons.

    I didn't want to, but I guess I have no choice.

    The assassin stepped into Drak's shadow and disappeared. The huge Tydonii could only gawp in bewilderment at where his fellow assassin had stood moments before. She emerged from the beast's shadow, knives flashing, chopping down into the serpent's neck, just below the head which was still biting into Scorch. It took a couple of blows, but Reeva was finally able to hack its head clean off. The tail started to flail, thrashing with increasing aggressiveness. Reeva rolled out of its way, came up sprinting, darting underneath the creature. She moved swiftly, knowing she didn't have much time until the creature reacted. Aiming for the left leg, she drove her blades forward, one into the hamstring, and the other into the ankle, severing tendons. The creature collapsed, the left side of its body falling down upon the assassin who appeared to be trapped underneath the smouldering fur. She seemed to sink into the ground, into the creature's shadow, popping up by its right leg this time. Once again she tore into its tendons with surgical precision before seeping back into the shadows and away. She reappeared in the shadow of a tree to the right hand side of Sergeant Heelial who stared at her wide-eyed.

    The Guardian, now a cut-up, burnt mess, tried valiantly to keep itself propped up with its right arm. Smokey, tears streaming openly down her face, approached it clutching a clay ball in her hand. The creature stared at her, fangs bared. She could see a feral madness in its eyes induced by the pain of its wounds.

'This is for Owl.' Smokey cried hoarsely. She ran towards the creature, loosening a shrill cry. It waited till she got in close before opening its jaw to engulf her. This is what the sapper had been waiting for. Without stopping she wound her arm back and hurled the clay ball at the Guardian. Her aim was true. The munition flew in-between the beasts set of fangs, hitting the back of its throat. Upon impact it sent flame spouting in all directions, seeking escape. Some rocketed down the beast's throat into its lungs and stomach, cooking its insides. The rest was spat out through the mouth into the oncoming Smokey. The sapper twisted but to no avail as her side, face and hair were all set alight. Heelial surged forward, desperately trying to put the flames out as her squad member screamed in pain as the flames tried to devour her. Thankfully they were able to extinguish the flames with a mixture of Smokey thrashing around on the floor and Heelial frantically slapping at anything in sight that was alight. Stepping around the now corpse of the creature, Drak came, carrying Scorch in his arms. Her body was still spasming uncontrollably and she crying out in pain. The assassin had at least managed to remove the serpents head from her face, revealing the gruesome gouges the fangs had inflicted. The assassin shook his head.

'I don't think she's going to make it, even if we could get her to the High Priestess.'

Heelial nodded. It was clear for everyone to see.

'I don't mind putting her outta her misery.'

It was the Sergeants turn to shake her head. 'Scorch was part of my squad, it's my duty.'

Drak laid the mage gently on the ground and offered Heelial his dagger. She took it, lined it up over Scorch's chest, and plunged it straight down into her heart. Scorch stiffened, sighed, and then lay still. Heelial removed the weapon.

Be at peace.

A sudden eerie silence settled upon the group, interrupted by the occasional moan from Smokey. Fingers and

Shriek came, dragging the two heavies behind them. They dumped Clipper and Rolls next to Smokey before wearily sprawling out on the floor. Creak and Nozza came next, the Corporal's pleased expression souring when she saw Scorch.

The smell of cooked flesh was pungent.

'How are they?' Heelial asked.

'Unconscious but alive.' Fingers replied between breaths. 'They'll be sore when they awake, maybe a few broken bones, they've had worse.'

'Good.' Heelial looked at Reeva. 'Thank you. If not for you, we'd all be dead right now.' The assassin just shrugged off the compliment.

Drak clapped her on the shoulder. 'You've got some explaining to do lass. Been holding out on us all this time!'

A loud crash grabbed everyone's attention.

'Maybe I spoke too soon.' The Sergeant said as another Guardian emerged into view. Similar in appearance to its now dead brethren, this one had a scaled torso, its wings a wiry membrane. It stood on cloven hooves with a lion's head. Its roar was sorrowful as it saw its slain kin. Just as it was about to set upon them, a gangly figure came puffing into view.

'My, my, what in the name of all that is holy is going on here?' huffed Garbhan, mopping his forehead with a handkerchief. 'Here I was, taking a lovely walk, through these beautiful, serene woods, when I harkened to hear the sounds of battle. That can't be right I said to myself, who in their right mind would conjure up battle in the middle of such a peaceful place. Investigation is required I told myself. I must find out who would dare besmirch Mother Nature's integrity. Thus, here I find myself, face to face with the perpetrators. The aggressor seems obvious. Someone is in need of a good walk themselves. What do you say boy? Care to join me enjoying Mother Nature in all her splendour? Ah, you seem to be becoming more irate. Are you in fact a girl? Pardon my ignorance but it is hard to tell, Garbhan just requires clarification on the matter is all. Come, we can discuss it at length on our walk. You'll feel better for it, trust me. Come along then. Good day to you fellow nature enthusiasts, I trust the rest of your journey will be uneventful so you truly get to enjoy your surroundings.'

With that, Garbhan tootled off into the trees once more. The Guardian hesitated for a moment, glancing at the surviving Squad and Hand members as if sizing up who was the bigger threat, before dashing after the ex-priest. The sounds of a frantic chase slowly faded away, leaving them all staring at each other, dumfounded.

Sergeant Heelial was the first to speak.

'I'm not sure what just happened, but if we ever run into that mad bastard again, I'm buying him the finest cut of steak I can afford.'

'I'll treat him to as much as he can drink.' Drak added in agreement.

'Right.' Heelial assumed an authoritative tone once more. 'Let's get to that temple.'

* * * *

Sergeant Diallo couldn't shake the growing sense of foreboding that had been steadily growing over the last week or so. Firstly, Captain Zakanos had disappeared overnight taking Sergeant Heelial and the rest of 4th squad with him. Official word was that the Captain was on an urgent scouting mission in Shulakii territory, but Diallo didn't buy it. Scouting was the Horse Companies territory, or spy work, not the job of the Captain of the Guard Company and a single squad. It just didn't make sense. And it was the manner of their departure. Just gone, overnight, without a briefing, without orders, no planning. Something had to have happened to make the Captain need to be gone that quickly. He knew the other Sergeants of the Guard Company shared his unease.

Not just any Captain either, he's the Captain of the Guard for Naul's sake.

Secondly, was the Assassin Guilds' string of murders. For some reason they'd targeted officers, Sergeants and Captains alike across all the companies. Then had come Remullus' brutal, yet efficient response. His company had all but obliterated the Guild across Tydon, targeting well over fifty safe houses, storefronts and hideouts. Anything even loosely associated with the Guild had been raided. The Captain of the Elite Guard had long been vocal of his distaste for the Assassins, so his response had come as a surprise to no one. What had been surprising was the speed at which it had come, almost instantly. Diallo wondered where his accurate intelligence had come from. The Sergeant doubted that the Captain had been biding his time, gathering information, and waiting for the chance – the excuse – to exact his revenge. Remullus wasn't a schemer, he was a man of action. If he'd had the opportunity to strike before now, he would have done. So who had given him that opportunity? Diallo understood Remullus' motivations. What he didn't understand was the Guild's. An uneasy truce had held for years, a mutual understanding to stay out of and not interfere with each other's business. Now that truce was well and truly shattered, and for what? Diallo couldn't figure it out. The power balance in the City had been forever shifted, there was no going back.

Why do I get the feeling that both the Guild and the Companies were cleaning house? Zakanos leaving the city, the recent spree of killings, the turmoil and unrest it was causing, not to mention the threat of war looming large. Diallo was sure it was all connected somehow, he just couldn't quite put it all together. He knew it was all going to come to a head, and soon. He wasn't going to be caught unprepared. That's why he'd asked Corporal Stubbs to gather the 8th squad.

'Even Buzzard?' The sapper had asked.

'Yeah, even Buzzard. Go wake him.' Diallo had replied.

The sapper had been surprised, but set off to do as his Sergeant had asked. They'd gathered on the parade ground under the pretence of extra drills, and he'd explained his unease to them.

'So none of you will be partaking in any of the coming festivities. I want you all sober and alert, you understand?'

The squad started to grumble as he'd expected them to.

'That ain't fair Sarge! We got plans!'

'Not anymore. Stump, Nut, Wallow, Grimy, Crutch, Udders, I meant it, no drinking!'

'Why you singling us out?' demanded Udders.

'Because we all know what you lot are like when you get into your cups. I can trust Buzzard, Puddle and Stubbs to behave themselves. If any of you disobey me, you'll be docked pay and put on latrines for the foreseeable future. Do I make myself clear?' Diallo got a mixture of reluctant grunts and nods. 'I want you to remain armed, and don't trust anyone outside this squad right now, until we know how things stand.'

'That all, Sergeant?' Buzzard asked.

'That's all.'

'Then I'm off back to bed.' The veteran yawned. 'Wake me when all the excitement starts.'

Diallo watched the rest of his squad wonder away, muttering between themselves. Let them be unhappy he thought, rather than be dead. Whatever happened at the festival of Oros, he would be ready and waiting. All that was left was to figure out which side he was on.

* * * *

Thran could feel the slim fire of pain flair across the back of his hand where Mortem had sliced him as he'd reached for the weapon in the dirt. He grimaced. He wasn't sure if he had just been quick enough to pick up the knife, or if Mortem had allowed him to do so. Thran thrust it from his mind, it didn't matter.

Concentrate. One misstep here and you're dead.

'Looks like I've drawn first blood.' Mortem sneered.

'Attacking me whilst I try to arm myself, even the gods would view that behaviour as petty and pathetic.'

The sneer settled into a thin frown. 'Trying to goad me into recklessly attacking? You'll have to do better than that.'

Despite his words, Mortem settled into a fighting stance, bouncing lightly on the balls of his feet. Thran followed suit. Mortem advanced but Thran did not give any ground. Instead he focused intently on the weapon in his opponent's hand and his feet, watching where and how he shifted his weight. That would be the real indicator as to when Mortem would spring into his real attack. Mortem launched a series of feints, testing Thran's defences, but he stood firm, not falling for any of them. Thran was happy to let Mortem do the pressing for now, let him get overconfident and overextend. A slight weight shift and suddenly Mortem's blade shot through the air and into Thran's midriff. Years of training took over, muscle memory kicked in and the assassin from Tydon twisted just in time. Now off balance he dove out of the way of the next attack. Turning into the roll he was back on his feet in one fluid motion, flashing his blade behind him but Mortem had not pressed the attack so the blade whistled harmlessly through the air.

'That's better!'

Once again they settled into stances opposite one another, this time slowly beginning to circle, each waiting for the other to show an opening, misplace their weight or glance away for even a second. Thran decided to press the attack. He closed in, knife dancing in front of him. Mortem parried or evaded the attacks with ease before launching a counter attack forcing Thran to step back and disengage. Mortem followed, not giving him any respite, pressing his advantage with a flurry of attacks now that Thran was on the back foot. Thran gave ground, doing his best to repel the blows raining down on him whilst trying to find an opening to exploit, but Mortem was not presenting any. Deciding to gamble, Thran threw all his force into his next counter, taking Mortem by surprise, but the assassin reacted quickly to avoid taking fatal damage. Blood now gushing from the gash in his side, Mortem lashed out himself, catching Thran across the chest.

They both stepped back to collect themselves and slow their breathing. Thran assessed the wound to his chest. Again, not too deep, however he could feel a thin line of fire when he moved. He hoped it wouldn't impede his movements too much. He looked across at Mortem who was probing the slash in his side with his fingers. His birthmark began to heat up, calling to him with its usual intensity. He could feel, *smell,* the blood calling to him from the wound. He pushed the calling back down inside him, it wasn't time yet.

It's not enough. I need more!

'Much better indeed! But you're waning from the loss of blood. This is over.'

Thran spat in reply and advanced once more. He knew that he faced a more skilled opponent and that if he were to carry on facing Mortem outright, he would lose, but he had his Gift to fall back on, if he could just catch him enough times before his strength left him. Thran willed his body forward for another burst. If he failed, he would die. The two clashed once more, however this time the grace and fluidity of their movements were diminished. It was no longer just a test of skill, it had become a test of endurance, who could take the most punishment and stay standing. Kicks and punches now flew alongside the knives, aiming to batter the opponent into submission. Time and time again they drew apart momentarily before launching at each other with frightening ferocity, trading blow for blow, wound for wound.

The next time they drew back, neither were inclined to dive straight back in. Thran had taken a cut above his left eye. He tried to wipe away as much blood as possible but it kept trickling down to obscure his vision. His whole body was a mixture of aches, cuts and numbness. Mortem was similarly afflicted. Thran's gift, his birthmark was screaming at him; begging to be unleashed. Yet instinctively he knew that it still wasn't good enough.

One more push!

Thran staggered towards Mortem who let him come, bracing himself, favouring his left leg as his right had taken a blow. They came together, grappling with one another, fighting for purchase. Despite his best efforts, Thran was being overwhelmed, he'd lost too much blood, and his strength was failing him. He knew what he had to do. It was a huge risk, but if he didn't do something soon, it would all be over. He let his grip on Mortem's wrist go. Even though he had been expecting it, the blade sliding into his stomach sent shockwaves rippling through his body. He almost collapsed there and then but

Mortem's momentum had carried him straight into Thran, keeping him upright from underneath. Locked in a twisted, deathly embrace, Thran, just like all those years ago when Sarfina had first found him, sank his teeth into flesh. This time, like a wolf, he bit into his prey's throat. Mortem started to panic and gripped Thran's head with both hands, trying desperately to prise him off. This freed up Thran's other hand which contained the knife. He blindly slammed it into Mortem's side. Despite lacking the strength to do real damage, he felt it scrape across rib-bone. His elation at this success was short lived as Mortem's fingers found his eyes, applying pressure. He unclamped his jaws lest he end up blind. Besides, the damage had already been done.

The two staggered back from each other and collapsed. Thran knew the knife in his belly was fatal, but if he were to die, he would make sure that Mortem went before him. He dragged himself up, slowly, agonisingly, to stand, albeit unsteadily, somewhat hunched, to his feet. His vision blurred as he rose but Mortem eventually came into focus. He'd rolled onto his uninjured side and gripped the handle of the knife. Grunting, he pulled the blade free with a wet squelch. He rose to lean on one knee, gingerly tracing the teeth marks on his neck. His fingers came away dripping with blood. Thran could see that his habitual, mocking smirk had gone. It had been replaced with pure rage.

'The gods gave me this one final test and test me you have. But it is finished. I will take your life and *ascend*!' Mortem's voice had a borderline hysterical tone to it.

Thran half-smiled. 'You're right, it's finished.' He raised his right arm, pointing directly at Mortem, who began to laugh.

When Mortem had removed the knife from his side, blood had started to flow more freely from the wound and Thran knew it was enough. His Gift, his birthmark, now an inferno on his back told him it was time. It was more than enough. All through the fight he'd been suppressing it, pushing it deep inside of him. Now he unleashed it, set it free. He could feel it flooding through his body, taking over, consuming him.

It coursed through him with reckless abandon, revelling in its freedom. This power, *his* power threatened to overwhelm him. He couldn't believe how much it had grown since Herrick had sacrificed himself in Ritellis Square. Thran was not sure he would be able to control it, but if he could channel it for just one moment, it would be enough to see his purpose met.

Focus. You can do this. Form the image in your mind. Will it into being!

Mortem's derisive laughter abruptly stopped as even he, Ungifted as he was, felt the power begin to stir beneath his feet.

'What is this? What are you doing?'

Thran began to form the image in his mind, force the blood to his will.

'Stop!'

The call that had built up inside Thran echoed through him to Mortems body. The blood from his wounds responded to the call. Single, perfect droplets answered the cry, heeding the demand. They pulled away from the assassin, drifting towards Thran's outstretched hand. Reaching him, they swirled lazily around his hand, awaiting further command.

I need more!

The droplets turned to thin strands streaming from Mortem's body, all the thin cuts he'd taken in the duel to the deep gash in his side, blood streamed from him to form a pool around Thran's hand.

'Stop! Stop this! STOP! STO-'

His cries cut off as he started chocking on the blood streaming up his throat and out of his mouth. Thran's bite had caused bleeding not only on the outside of his neck, but internally too. All the streams joined, flowing into the ever-growing pool.

There was nothing Mortem could do except watch in fear, rooted to the spot as his life force was drained from him, pulled from him, in front of his own eyes.

The pool began to pulse as strands shot upwards, spiralling, roping together. As he wielded his Gift, Thran felt a complete sense of purpose. This was his birth rite; the power he had been born to wield. Thran closed his eyes.

Focus. Bend the blood to your will!

He opened them to find the blood had been transformed into a hiltless crimson sword. The blade seemed alive, although the liquid held its form, it was constantly shifting and flowing. He clutched the naked blade in his hand, feeling no pain. They were one and the same. The blade was an extension of himself. In his greediness, Thran had taken too much from Mortem, so that the excess flowed down into two wavy streams hanging from the bottom of the blade. Thran quelled his elation, he was not finished yet.

The blade solidified, hardening like tempered Grellish steel.

Thran knew instinctively that the bloodsword was razor sharp. Sunlight danced along its length as the assassin examined the blade, twisting it back and forth. He looked at Mortem. He was barely conscious. Still kneeling, slack-jawed, he stared with vacant eyes into the sky. His skin had lost its colour. Thran mustered what was left of his strength and shuffled forward until he was standing over Mortem. He could feel the knife in his gut with every step.

To Thran, it felt as though the bloodsword were alive in his grasp, humming with vitality. It was demanding more from him. His birthmark screamed for more. His soul wanted more. He would have his vengeance and then pass into the afterlife. He would never see Reeva, Sarfina, Drak or even Zel again.

I'm sorry, but this is bigger than me, bigger than us. I have made my peace.

Now held in two hands, Thran raised the crimson weapon above his head and reversed his grip. He mustered what was left of his failing strength, and brought down the bloodsword.

Chapter 24

The bloodsword stopped a hairsbreadth from running Mortem through. Thran frowned in confusion. *Why?* Something was gripping his arms, stopping him. *Am I delirious? Hallucinating from blood loss?* Thran thought he saw Captain Zakanos by his side, preventing him from killing Mortem.
'He is *mine.*'
Thran was in no position to argue with the apparition. The bloodsword wavered, holding its solid form for a moment longer before returning to its original state. Blood splattered down over Thran and onto the dirt, with a few droplets splashing onto Zakanos. Finally pushed to his limit, the assassin plunged into unconsciousness. He stood before the alter in the temple yet again. For the final time.
How can I be here? I'm not dreaming.
The realisation hit him like a blow.
I'm dead.
Than wasn't quite sure what to think. Life after death, if there was one, was the topic of much debate. A plethora of beliefs, theories and hypothesis sparked endless arguments, and although Thran had never really given it much thought, he'd assumed that Carrion, the proclaimed god of Death, would have been here to greet him. He'd fulfilled all that the god had asked of him after all. He'd used his power to kill Mortem, well, he was as good as dead, even though Zakanos had intervened at the very last moment, Thran had been connected to Mortem through his draining blood and knew that he was not long for this world. As he'd activated his Gift, Thran had felt the ancient powerful spells activating below him, hungrily rushing upwards to strip him of his power.
Not that it matters now anyway, I'm dead. The line of Dragos ends with me. My power cannot be passed down.

Thran wondered where the god of Death could have been. Every time he'd visited the temple, Carrion had been here in one form or another, yet here at the time of his actual death, Thran stood alone.

I guess it's foolish to expect anything from a god.

Yet Thran couldn't shake this uneasy feeling. The gods absence made him uncomfortable, but he wasn't exactly sure why. He just knew that Carrion should have been here, like he always was. Trying to shake the feeling, his thoughts turned once again to Tydon and those in the Guild he'd left behind. They were the closest thing to a family he had. His parents were both dead and his brother had abandoned him to the streets once he'd become the new head of the family. He'd thought often of his brother over the years and would keep an ear out for any scraps of news regarding him. Apparently, he'd done well for himself and advanced the family name further than their father ever could have dreamed of. He had dreamed of confronting his brother, fuelled by righteous anger, Thran would stand boldly before him and his brother would weep and beg for forgiveness, but he would not be granted it. Instead, he would be made into a servant and attend to Thran's every wish or, depending on the assassin's mood, killed on the spot. When the Guild finally rescued him from the streets and equipped him with the tools to make his revenge real, Thran always made up some excuse as to why he should hold off, not return to his childhood home.

I was scared. Scared of the confrontation. Years of anger at his betrayal, jealousy at his success. The Assassins Guild helped train me to push those emotions down, drown them in detached efficiency. I was scared of dredging up all those repressed years.

Suddenly, Thran's stomach began to feel warm, his flesh began to tingle. The darkness around him lifted, white light began to pour in from above, briefly revealing the rest of the temple and the kneeling worshippers scattered throughout. Before he could bring them into focus, the light grew brighter, blinding him.

Thran opened his eyes to find a strange woman kneeling over him, her hands clasped over his knife wound.

'Wh- Who are you?'

'Ah, you've regained consciousness, that's a good sign. You're resilient. Now hush, be quiet and let me finish healing you.'

His whole body in pain, Thran was happy to close his eyes once more and let the warmth from her hands seep into his body.

'There, all done. Now sit up, gently mind, so I can have a look at the rest of your wounds.'

'I thought I was dead.' Thran admitted.

'You very nearly were. If we had arrived any later, you would have been too far gone.'

'Guess I'm just lucky.'

The woman glanced at him sharply. 'This has the Lady's meddling written all over it alright.'

Thran sighed. 'Well I'm sick and done with the gods' meddling.'

'Well whether you like it or not, they're not done with you.'

Thran snorted. 'And what would you know of the gods intentions?'

She raised an eyebrow. 'Quite a bit, considering I am the High Priestess of Jagreus.' She felt him stiffen. 'Relax. She no longer wants you dead. You have already brought about what she desired to stop.'

'I was about to die, why would Jagreus want you to save me?'

'She didn't. He did.'

Thran looked behind him to where the Priestess had nodded. Captain Zakanos stood over Mortem's prone form with his arms folded, staring into the trees.

'Why would the Captain want to save me? He betrayed the Guild and set me up in the first place.'

Before she could reply, Zakanos interrupted.

'Priestess.' His tone was cold. 'If he's talking, he's fine for the time being, finish seeing to this one.'

Araxia did as she was told. She began to heal Mortem.

'What are you doing!?!' Thran exclaimed, shooting unsteadily to his feet, fingers instinctively searching for a weapon.

'Stay out of this!' Zakanos' sword was out of its scabbard in an instant. 'I told you, he's mine. I consider my debt to you paid, so if you try to intervene, I will kill you.'

'What do you intend to do?'

'What he did to Lia, *tenfold*.'

Those words sent a shiver down Thran's spine. He could well imagine what the twisted assassin had done to the Captain's wife. Thran held up his hands in supplication.

'I won't get in your way. He has it coming.'

'He's starting to come around.' Araxia informed them, taking a step back from him.

Moving closer, Thran could see that Mortem's hand and feet had been bound. Mortem opened his eyes, saw his captors and immediately began straining against his bonds. Realising it was hopeless, he laid still.

'Well what a lovely little gathering we have here.' Mortem tried to adopt his usual haughty tone, but he couldn't quite keep out the slight hint of panic creeping in. His eyes settled nervously on the Captain. 'Zakanos, it is especially a pleasure to see you again. I never did thank you for allowing me to spend that amazing time with your wife.'

The Captain's jaw clenched, but he remained unmoved. Thran admired his iron will. Had he been in Zakanos' position, he'd have lost all self-control and would have been clawing Mortem's eyes out the moment he opened his mouth.

'Her hands were shaky at first, but once she felt my stiffness in her palms, your wife really let herself go. I didn't even have to tell her to get down on her knees. I guess she just wanted to take a real man in her mouth. I couldn't believe how wet she was, and that was before I'd even started to make her *bleed*.'

Zakanos' sword flashed, its tip held at Mortem's throat.

'I know you want to goad me into flying at you in a fit of rage and give you a quick death.' The tip pressed further, drawing blood. 'But I'm not going to do that.' He withdrew the sword and squatted down so he was face to face with Mortem. A cold smile spread across his face that would have been better suited to the other man. 'I'm tempted to cut out that tongue of yours first, seeing how you love to wag it so much, but we're going to be together for a long, long time. I don't want anything to impede your screams. Your ability to beg, because, you. Will. *Beg.*'

He stood, sheathed his weapon and grabbed Mortem by his hair.

'Let's find somewhere a little more private, shall we?'

'No! You can't do this to me! I'm chosen by the gods! I'M CHOSEN BY THE GODS!'

Mortems protests faded as he was dragged out of the clearing by Zakanos. This left Thran alone with the High Priestess. He wasn't sure what to say. Thankfully she took the lead.

'My name is Araxia. Why don't I tell you what's happened while you've been gone whilst I finish healing you?'

Thran nodded. As she lay hands of him, Araxia told him how Jagreus had commanded her to hire Mortem to find and kill the descendant of Dragos. How they had become aware of Herrick's presence which had led to the rushed attack in the square, how Mortem had found out about the Captain's involvement and had blackmailed him into handing Thran over. Lastly, she told of Mortem's betrayal, Zakanos' bloody retribution at the temple and their frantic ride out to rescue him.

'I'm sure you have many questions.'

'I do. Why did Jagreus want to kill me instead of taking my powers? I would have given them up if she'd asked instead of trying to kill me.'

'It is not so simple. The gods, mainly the ascended ones, not the Elder, all have a vested interest in you. Jagreus had to act before they could get to you, and historically, assassination has been the most effective method. I do not approve of such a method, but I understand the necessity. The gods have been dealing with Dragos' descendants for centuries.'

'How can you say that after all that Mortem has done?'

'Yes, well, he is an abhorrent man. Do not think that this decision was taken lightly and without reluctance by my Mistress, or myself.'

'Carrion said that some of the gods are actually ascended Council members, is this true?'

'Yes.'

'Do they all want me dead?'

'I don't know. Not all, I think. The Lady certainly seems to have taken a liking to you, which I would argue is actually a bad thing. Even amongst the rest of the Council members, she has the reputation for being the most fickle and manipulative.'

'Why was Carrion the only Council member who wanted to save me?'

This brought a sad smile from Araxia. 'He didn't. Carrion brought you here for his own purpose. He was never a Council member. Carrion and Dragos, they are one and the same.'

Thran was stunned, but suddenly things started to slot into place, make a little more sense. *My dreams! Why didn't I realise it before? He could only come into my dreams when I awaked my Gift; his dormant blood within me.*

'Carrion, or Dragos rather, brought you here for his resurrection.'

'You said earlier that I had already done what Jagreus wanted to stop.'

'We're not entirely sure but we know that his resurrection requires a sacrifice and a Gifted descendant to use his powers.'

'But I didn't kill him.'

'True, but open your senses and search below.'

'The power that I felt earlier… it's gone!'

'I don't know where, but it seems that whatever transpired here was enough for Dragos to escape from his prison.'

'What a fool I've been.'

I'm no more than a new toy for the gods to squabble over. They don't care, they only want to use me. We're treated like cattle, not humans!

'If my purpose is fulfilled, why can't the gods just leave me be? I'm no use to them anymore.'

'I'm afraid that's not true. Now that Dragos is free in some capacity, your unique powers could play a vital part in what is to come. The god of Death will come for you too. Except next time it won't be in your dreams, it will be in the flesh.'

'I just want be left alone, to go back to my life in Tydon, or travel, take in the world.'

'You could, but they will still come after you. Your bloodline does not give you a choice.'

'So where does your goddess stand in all this?'

'She is putting on a feigned indifference towards you now, but I think she's just as curious to see what you are capable of. You are still a child of hers after all.'

Thran stared down at his hands and recalled forming the bloodsword.

What exactly am I capable of?

'Priestess! Priestess!' They turned to see Heelial striding into the temple grounds. 'We got injured!'

Immediately Araxia was on her way over, directing them where to lay the injured so she could attend to them. Thran let out a cry of joy as he saw one hulking figure laying a body down on the ground. Drak looked up and grinned. Catching movement in his peripheral vision, Thran turned to find Reeva beside him.

'Reeva! When did-'

She surprised him with a quick, but fierce hug that left him startled. Reeva was not usually so tactile, especially in front of others. It was a little different when he came to her alone seeking comfort. She stepped back, looking down, avoiding his gaze. Before he could do anything else, he was being swept up in a crushing bear hug.

'It's good to see you lad!'

'Drak! Stop, stop, you're going to break my ribs!'

Thran felt himself smiling as Drak set him down, on the verge of bursting out laughing. The big Tydonii was as infectious as ever.

'It's good to see you too, both of you. I can't believe you're here.'

'What?' Said Drak in mock indignation, giving Thran a dig on his shoulder. 'Like we were never going to come rescue you. You're part of our Hand. We're family, simple as that.'

Reeva, still looking everywhere but at Thran, nodded in agreement. Feeling tears beginning to form, he tried to change the subject.

'Where's Sarfina and Zel?'

'Back in Tydon. There's some serious trouble brewing lad. There'll be more killing before this is done, mark my words, there's treason in the air. If anything, they're in more danger than we are.'

Glancing over to where Araxia was working, Thran said 'Seems like you ran into some of your own trouble.'

'Nasty business that lad, nasty business. We ran into a monster, and I mean a literal monster, horns, teeth, claws, the lot! If it hadn't been for Reeva here, we'd have all been face to face with Carrion right now.' Thran couldn't help but wince at Drak's choice of words. 'You should have seen her lad, I've never seen anything like it before. She was jumping through shadows, slicing that beast good n' proper. It was incredible.' Reeva was staring intently at the ground. 'It took everything just to kill one of the bastards, then another came crashing in and I thought we was all done for, until that mad priest came and it started chasing him instead.'

'Garbhan? What on earth was he doing there?'

'I don't think the gods even know. He's a strange one, but we owe him our lives.'

The conversation was interrupted by Sergeant Heelial who'd made her way over.

'Where's the Captain?'

Before Thran could answer, screams drifted through the temple grounds.

'He's getting his revenge. I don't think he wants to be interrupted.'

She simply nodded and left without saying a word, going back to oversee her squad who, on Araxia's advice, were setting up camp at the treeline, rather than on the temple grounds. Thran suddenly realised he was exhausted and ravenous.

'You guys got any food?'

Slinging an arm around Thran, Drak guided him over to the camp. Reeva followed a couple of paces behind.

Thran awoke in the middle of the night. He looked around to find everyone else asleep, even the two man watch that Sergeant Heelial had set up.

This is not normal slumber.

He stood gingerly, still feeling the effects of his struggle with Mortem. He attempted some gentle stretches before walking back onto the temple grounds. Instinctively he veered off before entering the ruins and made his way over to the treeline to his right. He stopped a few yards from the gnarled roots of a grand oak where, sat up in the branches, a woman rested comfortably against the trunk. There was nothing distinctive about her; all in all, Thran thought her rather plain, yet he could feel power emanating from her, power similar to what he'd felt below the temple as he'd activated his Gift.

'You're an ex-council member too, right? A goddess they call the Lady?'

'Yes. I thought it was about time we had a face to face chat.'

'That my friends had to be asleep for?'

'Well, not all of them. Come on out, I know you're there, skulking around in the darkness.' Reeva appeared out of nowhere by Thran's side, startling him. He'd sat and ate whilst Drak talked incessantly, describing their fight in great detail and despite it explaining a lot about her, Thran had a hard time thinking about Reeva as Gifted too. Their joyous reunion had been dampened somewhat by the 4th squad's mood, which Thran could understand, seeing as though they had lost two and had three injured, one of those critically. The assassins had tried to be as respectful as possible. Mortem's screams periodically drifting through to them hadn't helped either. One of the squad members, the new recruit, had been eyeballing him in particular, although Thran couldn't fathom why. After eating and talking with Drak, exhaustion finally got the better of him, so he'd wrapped himself up in a spare cloak and sank into a dreamless sleep.

'You can put away your weapons, there will be no fighting.' Perhaps it was the reassurance, or her authoritative tone, but Reeva obeyed readily.

'Why are you here?' asked Thran.

'As I said, to have a chat.'

'What if I don't want to listen to what you have to say?'

The Lady snorted, she smiled but there was a slight annoyance in her pressed lips.

'Is that any way to treat a goddess who saved your life?'

'I doubt that you did that out of the kindness of your heart. You gods only serve yourselves. I'm finding that out very quickly. I'd be dead right now if it had suited you.'

'True, but can we agree that you would rather be alive than dead right now? You should be grateful that I was inclined to want you alive.'

'Well I'm not currently inclined to give you my gratitude, I'm sick of being used.'

'I would hardly call keeping you alive, using you.'

'But that's what you plan to do now, isn't it? Use me.'

'No. I plan to continue keeping you alive.'

Thran wasn't sure what to say back to that. How could he trust what she said, she was after all the most notoriously fickle goddess. 'What do you want in return?'

'Nothing.'

It was Thran's turn to snort. 'I don't believe that.'

'If I keep you alive, you will do what I want of your own free volition, not because I've *used* you, or demanded a service from you. That is why I will keep you alive.'

'How can you be so sure I will do what you want?'
The goddess only smiled at his question.
'What about Dragos?'
'I will keep you safe from him.'
'That's not what I meant. Did you want to bring him back?'
'Why would I want that? He poses a threat to us all if he returns to full power. He is a god-killer. The Council feared him with good reason.'
'If he is powerful as you say, how do you plan on protecting me? I hardly think your blessing will be able to stop him.'
'I don't plan on blessing you, it would only draw unwanted attention. I will provide for you, put things into play for you.'
'So you will meddle from the shadows, while we suffer the consequences.'
'I also have to suffer the consequences of my actions. Do you think I have no empathy? That I am some emotionless being just because I am a god? You forget I was also human before I ascended. By all means, be angry with me, but do not assume you know how I feel. I don't do what I do for the fun of it, I do it because it is necessary. Why do you always assume those consequences will be negative? Do you regret meeting Sarfina that day? Being accepted into the Assassins' Guild? I have been looking after you for far longer than you realise.'
'You had no right to do so!'
'I equipped you with the skills to be able to face what was coming, for your own good.'
'You caused me to be cast out from my family!'
'No. That was your own power, Dragos' blood manifesting in you. You consumed your mother from the inside, draining her life-blood as she birthed you. If you're looking for someone to blame, for someone to focus your hate on, it would be him.'
'How can I trust what you're telling me is the truth?'

'Then let me prove my integrity to you. Give you the opportunity to not only save your friends, but for the Shadow-Walker to have some closure with her estranged father.'

Reeva bristled at his side, her fingers slipping around knife hilts.

'Speak plainly.' Thran said on her behalf.

'At the height of the festival of Oros, a faction of the Tydon military, backed by the Merchants Guild and a faction of the nobles, will attempt to remove the Emperor from his throne.'

'What! Why?'

'Goddess I may be, but not even I know everything.'

'Why are you telling me this? The festival has already begun, we'll never get back to Tydon in time to stop it.'

'About an hour's walk due north of here, straight as the crow flies, is an obelisk twin to the one in Ritellis Square. You will encounter a god - a real god - who can transport you back to Tydon in time.'

She threw something down to Thran. He caught it and when he opened his palm, he saw that it was a piece of red stone.

'What am I supposed to do with this?'

'You do like to ask questions, don't you? Now, off to bed with you, you have a long day ahead tomorrow and could use the rest. Don't worry, I have a feeling you will sleep well and deeply. Take your hedgehog with you.'

It took him a second to realise the Lady meant Reeva. They began walking back to the camp together.

'Look,' Thran began awkwardly. 'I don't trust her at all, but if what she's says is true, we're going to have to do as she says. I won't pry into your personal business, but you've always been there for me, so it's my turn now. I'll get you back to deal with your dad.'

Reeva acknowledged his words with a slight incline of her head.

It was enough.

Thran laid back down and immediately drifted back to sleep without noticing the faint screams still echoing through the dark.

Chapter 25

Despite the Priestess' attentions, Smokey could still feel the fire in her wounds. She probably would for the rest of her life, wherever there was puckered white flesh, of which there was plenty. It hurt to talk as her skin felt tight across her cheek. The munitions were a feat of modern science and alchemy, created to destroy, disfigure and obliterate their targets. Smokey's case was no different. Running her fingers gently over the ruined flesh, tears began to form at the corner of her eyes. She'd never considered herself to be beautiful, especially not when she was covered in muck from sapping, but she scrubbed up well, and when she smiled, it brought out her best features. She'd done alright.

I look like a half melted candle. She would have laughed had it not been so painful. *They're right, if you become a sapper you're either insane, or unlucky. I wonder where my sanity went?*

Nozza settled down beside where she was laid.

'Hey, how're you feeling?' A withering look was her response. 'Okay, stupid question, I'm sorry. Didn't know what else to say. Not really my strength, this sort of thing.'

'I don't need your pity.' Smokey tried to move her lips as little as possible, but it still hurt.

'It's not pity. I mean, yes I feel bad for you, but who wouldn't? The rest of the squad are worried about you.'

'They know to leave me alone. Just because we spent a night together, doesn't mean anything. It was just a fuck before a battle. I don't want your pity.'

'Well maybe it meant nothing to you, but it meant something to me.'

'For Naul's sake newbie, you really are pathetic.'

'Yeah, well, that's me. If caring means I'm pathetic, then I'm glad to be pathetic.'

'Pathetic and hopeless.' Nozza thought he could see the hint of a smile creeping on her face, but maybe that was just wishful thinking, it was more likely to be a grimace. 'You like this with all the girls who give your pickle a tickle?'

Nozza laughed despite himself. 'Not heard that one before. Joining the army has really been an eye opener for my ears. Such uncouth language.'

'Hopeless.' sighed Smokey.

Nozza cleared his throat.

'The Sergeant sent me over. Probably wouldn't have had the courage otherwise, but she wants me to look after the munitions. I'll be a poor substitute for you and Owl, but I'm useless with everything else so Heelial said I could at least make myself…' He trailed off as the tears once again came and this time, they rolled unashamedly down Smokey's cheeks. Nozza inwardly chastised himself for using Owl's name, throwing salt on an open wound. 'So, uhm, I'll do my best till you're back on your feet.'

The sapper was silent, eyes closed. Then she surprised him by suddenly bursting out laughing, which quickly turned to sharp intakes of breath to try deal with the pain. When she was in control again, she asked Nozza:

'Are you sane, newbie?'

'I used to think so. These days, I'm not so sure. Can you stay sane when all you seem to be surrounded by is insanity?'

'Unlucky then.'

'What?'

'Never mind. Welcome to the sapperhood. Fetch my box of munitions and I'll talk you through 'em. Be careful though, don't drop it! You've caused me enough pain already today.'

Nearby, Rolls was also dealing with an unwanted visitor.

'Is there anything else I can do for you? Another cloak? Back rub? Foot rub? Anything at all, just let me know.' Drak asked sweetly.

'Well, I could do with a piss, so why don't you go on over to those trees, whip out your little pecker, 'n start streaming away.'

'How about I escort you over instead?'

'What am I, twelve? I don't need no escorting.'

'Never said you did.'

'What's it gonna take for you to leave.'

'If you really want me to go, then I will, but I only wanted to help. Make you feel better.'

Rolls cocked her head and weighed something up in her mind.

'Fine. I'll take the foot rub.'

Enthusiastically, Drak began to knead away at her exposed soles. Despite herself, Rolls began to moan.

'Sweet Brioth, that feels good.'

The big Tydonii grinned, although it was quickly wiped away by Rolls next comment.

'Shame you couldn't use your fingers to make me moan like this the other night. I didn't say stop, carry on.'

Across the camp, Clipper sat sulking as the assassin continue to massage Rolls feet.

'No one gives a shit about me. No one asked if I'm okay. I'm fine by the way!'

Creak glanced over to him. 'That's 'cuse you're a miserable bastard. We know you're fine when you start grumbling again.'

'Any chance of a foot rub Creak?'

'Fuck off.'

'This ain't fair! Us men need to be taken care of too!'

'I'll take care of yer open trap if ya don't shut it. I'm trying to listen to what they're saying.'

A little away from the others, but not quite on the temple grounds, Thran was holding council with Sergeant Heelial and High Priestess Araxia. It looked like he was desperately trying to convince them of something. Heelial looked sceptical, while Araxia seemed exhausted but concerned.

'Hey Shriek, you got good ears. Can you hear anything?'

Usually the Kidoshian would have been exercising, running through his sword forms with Fingers, but the fight with the Guardian, despite its briefness, had exhausted him along with the man from Shulakh. They were both laid down in between two roots, rolled up in cloaks on a bed of leaves. He sat up, bent his ear to the air and announced quite seriously:

'They appear to be moaning.'

With that he laid back down, rustling away until he settled in a comfortable position.

'Oros above! Rolls, shut it!'

'Can't help it Creak.'

'Oi, big man, cut it out or I'll fire a crossbow bolt where the sun doesn't shine!'

Drak backed off, but it was too late, the conversation was done and the Sergeant was heading their way.

'Corporal, get the squad ready, we're leaving.'

'What about the Captain?' Creak said, asking what they were all thinking. Whilst the screams had stopped some time during the night, Zakanos had yet to return to camp.

'The Priestess will be staying put to wait for the Captain. She'll look after Smokey till she's well enough to travel, then they'll collect the horses and head back to Tydon. The Priestess says she can stop the bodies from rotting for a time, so we'll give Owl and Scorch a proper send-off when they get back.'

'Why the rush to get back?'

'Because the assassin tells me we're needed.'

'For what?'

'I'll tell you if he's right. I'm not convinced.'

'So we're leaving the Captain on a hunch? That don't sit right with me Sarge. 'Specially after we came all this way.'

'The Captain would want us to go. Now get up off your arses and get moving. Bring only essentials, prep for battle.'

Had he not been looking for it, Thran would have walked straight past the obelisk as it was almost completely hidden by overgrowth. The symbols were so worn and faded, he could barely make them out. He wasn't quite sure what he was supposed to do next, the Lady had said he would encounter an Elder god, but there didn't appear to be one in sight. He thought about shouting "hello" into the forest but decided against it. The Sergeant was already sceptical in believing him that this would be a quicker way back to Tydon, and her patience had worn thin as it'd taken them longer than the hour he'd promised to arrive at the obelisk. Now that they were here, he needed to fulfil his part. He could feel the eyes of the 4th squad on him along with Drak and Reeva's.

He laid his hand on the black marble as he had done in Ritellis Square but it did not respond to his touch. At a loss, Thran reached into his pocket and brought out the stone that The Lady had given him. As soon as his fingers brushed it, the stone began to pulse, sending out waves in all direction. Thran glanced back. No one seemed to sense them apart from Reeva who gave him a slight nod. Thran wished the Priestess were here and not back at the camp, she was far more knowledgeable than him with these type of things. Thran removed his hand from the obelisk and the pulsing immediately stopped. He waited for a few moments, but nothing happened, so he placed it back on, where upon the pulsing immediately resumed once more.

Heelial's impatience got the better of her. 'You have no idea what you're doing, do you?'

'No, but something's happening. Just wait a little longer.'

The words were barely out of his mouth when the ground began to rumble and tremble around them. A hole appeared at Thran's feet and he was swallowed whole by the earth beneath him. The strong smell of dirt filled his nostrils. Thran could see nothing in the darkness and could not move as the compact earth smothered him from all sides. He panicked, fearing suffocation, before realising that he was still drawing air into his lungs. He also realised that he was moving. Like an arrow shot from a bow, Thran was being propelled through the earth by the dirt behind. He barely had time to marvel at the strange sensation before he was spat out into the middle of nowhere. As far as the eye could see, Thran was surrounded by barren, dry, red cracked earth. The earth began to heave and it was all the assassin could do to stay on his feet.

This must be an earthquake!

He'd never experienced one before, only heard of them through rumour, but the way the ground was screaming at him, Thran knew it could be nothing else. Great rents began to snake outward, jagging unpredictably, yet miraculously, the ground around Thran remained firm. From the fissures, mounds of earth flew upwards. He could only stand in awe. A giant wall of earth, stretching leagues wide, had been erected before him out of nothing in a matter of moments. The softer soil began to mould itself into a detailed face that stared down on him with such an intensity that Thran could only quail beneath it.

Such raw, primordial power! This is an Elder god!

'What does she want now?' The voice boomed across the plain. Standing this close, Thran felt it in his bones.

'W-who?'

'Don't play your goddesses' games with me boy! What does she want with me now!?'

'You mean The Lady?'

'Who else would I mean? You called me using the part of me she took. It is not something she would readily part with, and I doubt you are strong enough to take or steal it from her, so you are here on her behalf. So I will ask you one final time, and if you do not answer me, I will crush you. What does she want now?'

'I don't know, and that's the gods honest truth. Not that that counts for much.'

'Yet she has sent you here.'

'She has.'

'Why?'

'So that you would help me.'

'Helping you means helping your mistress, something I am not inclined to do.'

'I do not serve The Lady!'

The laughter that resounded from the face in the cliff was deafening.

'I do not serve her willingly! At this moment, I do not have a choice.'

'Given the choice, what would you do?'

'Honestly, I don't know. I just want to be left alone.' The face in the cliff seemed to soften at Thran's words.

'Tell me properly then, why are you here?'

'I have companions back at the obelisk who need passage to Tydon as a matter of urgency. The Lady said you could provide this.'

'I can, but why should I? I do not care for the needs of Jagreus' children.'

'I don't have a good reason, I'm not sure how to convince you. I was sent here by a goddess I distrust, and there's a squad of the Guard Company who has no faith in me waiting back at the obelisk. Most of the other gods want me dead, or to use me for their own ends. I just want to go back home, sit in the Tavern with my friends, and be left alone!'

'I too wish to be left alone, yet more and more I am intruded upon by the likes of you.'

'Tell me Reth, you are the Elder god Reth, right?' The face in the cliff shifted in what Thran took to be a nod. 'What about your followers? All the other gods, Elder or otherwise, have priests, acolytes or disciples. What about you?'

'My followers are safe from the likes of your kind, deep in the bowels of the earth, beyond the reach of those who wish them harm. You are the first human I've spoken to in centuries, aside from Viella, who dwell on the surface. I still have those who worship me who stride the land, but they are few in number. What they do does not concern me.'

'Why have you cut yourself off from your followers above ground?'

Reth snorted.

'You are funny. How can a human with such a fleeting lifespan, hope to understand the action of an immortal being whom they cannot comprehend?'

'We might surprise you, even if it just for a short while.'

'I very much doubt that. Before I closed myself off, I spent many years amongst your people.'

'Then you weren't with the right people. I agree with you, most of us are a waste of time. We're selfish, hateful, spiteful, impudent and all the rest. You don't give a toss about them, and they sure don't give a toss about you. But when you find those people who accept you for who you are, take you in and treat you like one of their own, those are the people you hold onto and try to protect. They make it all worth it. That's why I'm doing this, for the people I care about. You can take all the rest of them in an earthquake.'

'You would discard the rest of your kind so easily?'

'Well, right now, I'm not exactly a fan of the goddess of Life or her work seeing as though she's spent the last few weeks trying to kill me.'

'You think you could become one of these people to me?' Reth scoffed.

'Me? No, of course not. I've had enough of you gods to last my lifetime. Someone else can do it.'

'You left out arrogant off your list earlier.'

'That came under "all the rest".'

'Now you're starting to sound like The Lady.'

'Not intentionally, of that I can assure you. So now what?'

'Now I send you back, and transport those by the obelisk to Tydon. I shall also grant you the solitude you so desire, mortal.'

The face melted back into the cliff face and the wall of earth withdrew back into the ground as quickly as it had arisen, leaving behind a new, pristine, black marble obelisk. Thran moved towards it but had barely taken a step before the ground opened up to devour him once more.

* * * *

Sarfina tensed as the door to Garbhan's shop opened, but it was only Zel and the White Raven returning. Skrenn shifted impatiently beside her, although it was partly to do with his wounded side and not being able to settle into a comfortable position. With the Guild compromised, this was the only safe place left in Tydon that Sarfina could think to hide on such short notice. After the fight at the Tavern, Sarfina and Zel had rushed to intercept Skrenn at the mansion before they ran into the trap. They'd arrived too late, the sewers were already crawling with soldiers, laying in ambush for the assassins. Unsure of what to do next, they'd waited and watched until Skrenn and Lagatha came fighting their way out, right into the waiting soldiers. Looking like they'd be quickly overwhelmed, Sarfina and Zel rushed to their aid, surprising the attackers from behind, forcing an opening for Skrenn and Lagatha to slip through and make good their escape together. Fleeing aimlessly to be rid of any pursuers, it was by chance that they passed the street on which the mad ex-priest had his shop and the inspiration to hide in there struck Zel. The four of them had waited a few hours for darkness to fall, plotting their actions. Once dusk approached, Zel and Lagatha had been sent out for reconnaissance.

Lagatha was shaking her head, but it was Zel who delivered the report.

'It's not looking good, Sarf. They hit us effectively and efficiently. All our hideouts, covers and safe houses simultaneously across Tydon. That's a huge operation, I've got to say I'm impressed. Aside from us, there's only a handful of survivors that haven't fled the city or gone deep underground.'

'What are our exact numbers looking like?' Sarfina asked.

'We're all that's left in the city that are still operational, the rest are too wounded, or dead.'

Nothing was said for a little while as the depth of the Assassins Guilds' destruction sank in.

Sarfina turned to Skrenn. 'There's no way Remullus is capable of organising this alone. You know the political situation in the Citadel better than anyone, who could be behind this? I also think it's highly likely that someone in the Guild has betrayed us. How else could they have gained such extensive knowledge of our operations?'

'Agreed. Remullus does not hide his long standing hatred of the Guild. If you approached him with a way to eradicate us he'd take it in a heartbeat.'

Lagatha spoke for the first time. 'So why now?'

'Because with the Guild gone and Captain Zakanos away, the Emperor is exposed.' Zel answered.

Skrenn nodded. 'This is true, but whilst Remullus hates the Assassins Guild, his loyalty to the Emperor and Tydon is unquestionable. As for Corsca and Cyprian, it's possible they may have had their heads turned, but not without backing. Remullus is Captain of the Elite Guard for a reason, he's well respected and holds sway with the majority of the lesser Captains. I doubt they would go against him unless they had the support of the Merchants Guild or the nobles.'

Sarfina looked up sharply. 'What if they had both?'

Understanding came to Skrenn. 'Celentine!'

'He holds considerable clout with both camps as well as being a close adviser to Tavian. I thought you said he was unaware of the Emperor's connection to the Guild.'

'He is, the Emperor kept him out of all Guild affairs. It seems we have underestimated him, we did not think he would be a problem this soon.'

'So how do we get to Tavian? They know about the sewers, and we can hardly just knock on the Citadel's doors and ask to be let in. Is there anyone left in the military we can trust?'

'Potentially, but making contact will be difficult, everyone will be under close scrutiny.'

'Why don't we go after Celentine?' Lagatha asked.

'He'll be too well protected.' Zel replied. 'Our chances would be far greater if the rest of our Hand were here, especially Reeva.'

'We can only work with what we have,' interjected Sarfina 'So let's concentrate on what we can do.'

'We have to get to the Emperor at all costs.' Skrenn stressed.

Zel began pacing as an idea struck him.

'Celentine may be well protected, but what of the other conspirators?'

* * * *

Sergeant Heelial blinked as she emerged into the light once more. She reached up to clear her eyes and brushed away some remnants of dirt. She looked around her and stopped dead: they were in the middle of Ritellis Square in full flow at the height of the festival of Oros. It helped to mask their miraculous entrance. As they'd sprouted from the ground in front of the obelisk the majority of people had been busy eating and drinking their fill at the tables and benches set throughout the square, or being entertained by the numerous musicians and street performers trying to earn extra coin during the frivolities. The few who did take notice thought it was some clever trick and gasped and clapped in amazement.

We need to move before the wrong people realise we're here.

Heelial was still struggling to understand how that'd come to be. Thran had been sucked into the ground, causing them all to draw their weapons and back off. The Sergeant had been all for leaving Thran to his fate and heading back to Tydon on horseback, but the big assassin – Drak – had convinced them to stay for a least a little while longer. It had helped that the silent assassin had backed him up. After how she had taken down the Guardian, the 4th squad feared and respected her in equal measure. So they'd stayed. At first, nothing happened, then the ground began to shake and her squad began to be swallowed before her eyes. They'd tried to flee, but there had been no escape, the earth had taken everyone into its depths, into the darkness. What had followed was strange sensation as if she were floating through the dirt, yet Heelial had known she was moving and they'd ended up in Ritellis Square. She wasn't sure how long they'd been in that state, being underground in the darkness had messed with her sense of time, but now they'd arrived, and they had a job to do.

She looked round to find her squad coming to their senses and looking to her for direction. The big assassin was there, but of the blonde there was no sign. Heelial gestured and set off through the crowd, they fell in behind her. All around her, the people of Tydon celebrated joyously, thanking Oros, the goddess of the seasons, for a bountiful harvest and asking for her future blessing, that she would continue to provide good weather to see the fields full of crops. Heelial knew that the majority of the populace used the festival as an excuse to eat and drink as much as they possibly could at the Emperor's expense, but she knew the goddess had to be kept appeased as Tydon relied on the fertile ground surrounding it to keep the City fed. Anything extra was stockpiled or sold to add to the city's treasury. They made a tidy profit as Tydon was the main source of grain throughout Bellum. The Sergeant was not surprised that the festival of Oros had still gone ahead despite the recent unrest; all throughout summer the festival was much anticipated and talked about, if Tavian had cancelled it there could very well have been rioting in the streets, not to mention petitions from the Merchant Guild who stood to make considerable profits from the festival.

They left the Square where the majority of the public celebrations would be taking place, making their way towards the Citadel, weaving through crowds spilling out from houses, restaurants and taverns. Heelial had decided the best course of action would be the direct approach so when they neared the Barracks she strode right up to the Soldiers Gate which was closed, raising her suspicions. She called up to the guards on duty to let her in, but instead of answering her they muttered to each other before calling for the Sergeant in charge. In the silence that followed, she thought she could hear the faint clash of arms, but she couldn't be sure. Heelial tried to hide her impatience, especially as time dragged on before the Sergeant arrived. She knew there would be trouble as soon as his face appeared above the parapet, looking down on them with a haughty expression.

'You know the rules,' he sneered. 'If you wanted to stay the night in the Barracks, you had to be back before the sixth bell. Find somewhere in the city to stay.' He turned to leave before Heelial had time to respond.

'We've not been out enjoying the festival.' She called after him. 'Sergeant Heelial, Guard Company, 4th squad. We've just returned from a scouting mission.'

'Still can't let you in, I've got my orders. The Soldiers Gate is shut for the night, same as the Heralds.'

'We were told by the Emperor himself to report directly back to him once we returned.'

'Is that so?'

Heelial nodded. The Sergeant scratched his chin, as if in thought, then gestured to his men in what Heelial took to be an order to open the gate. She was wrong. Moonlight glinted off metal as crossbows were levelled at the 4th squad.

'Run!'

'Fire!'

She heard the bolts whistle and skitter around them as they turned and fled back into the safety of the streets. She brought them to a halt a few streets later. Shriek was limping due to his thigh being nicked and Clipper, overseen by Drak, was removing a bolt embedded in Rolls' back, but aside from that the rest of them were unscathed. The Corporal stood next to her Sergeant.

'Can't believe they opened fire on us.'

'I know. Things must be worse than we anticipated for them to be so brazen.'

'So what do we do?'

'We try the Heralds Gate, but I imagine we'll get a similar reception.'

'We've got company!' Fingers called from the street corner where he was posted as lookout. Heelial let out a string of curses, she hadn't expected them to be able to mobilise a force to send after them so quickly. Fortunately the alley they had stopped in was only wide enough for two to approach at a time.

'Clip, to the front, you, big man, take Rolls place next to him.' Rolls made to protest but Heelial cut it short with a chop of her hand. 'You can't fight properly until you get bandaged up. Fingers, I want you right behind them. Creak, ready your crossbow. The rest of you fall back behind me, newbie I hope you know what you're doing with those munitions, they're our last resort if things get dicey.'

The pursuing squad came round the corner and halted as they saw the 4th waiting for them, weapons at the ready. Heelial recognised the Sergeant straight away as he stepped forward in front of his men with a frown on his face.

'Is that anyway to greet a fellow squad of the Guard Company!?' The new Sergeant demanded in a stern tone. Heelial pushed forward to clasp forearms with him.

'Diallo!' She greeted the Sergeant of the 8th squad with genuine joy.

'Heels.' His frown turned to a grin. 'It's good to see you! Things have gone crazy around here, can't trust anyone.'

'Tell me about it, the squad guarding the Soldiers Gate opened fire on us.'

'Yeah we saw. I had Crutch on lookout at the gate, as soon as he saw you approach, he came and got the rest of us. When you fled, I volunteered my squad to chase you down. We were through the side door before they could stop us.'

Heelial shared his grin. 'Good work D.'

'Thanks.'

'So what now?'

'Well, I have an idea, but I'm not sure if you'll like it…'

Chapter 26

Thran eased himself from the saddle, glad to be stopping even though they'd only been going for a few hours since this morning when Reth had sent him back to the obelisk near the temple and he'd emerged to find himself alone. He'd rushed back to the temple to find Araxia clearing the camp as Zakanos was putting together a makeshift litter for Smokey by tying the squads sleeping rolls to lengthier branches. They'd shifted Smokey into the litter and carried her through the forest as gently as possible. It was slow going and Araxia made a few trips back and forth with the squads' gear before they reached where the horses were tethered and rigged the litter to one of the horse's saddle so it could drag the sapper along behind it. Whilst the High Priestess loaded the horses, Thran and Zakanos collected the bodies of Scorch and Owl and tied them securely to the back of a mount each, then they were off, riding back to Tydon, albeit with less haste than when they had originally set out. Nobody spoke as they plodded along. Captain Zakanos rode a few yards ahead of them, brooding, and Araxia seemed content to keep her own counsel so Thran rode quietly beside her. The only person to make any noise was Smokey who couldn't stifle all her groans, the occasional one slipping through clenched teeth to mix with the clip-clopping of hooves. Now, as the sun reached its zenith, Zakanos just stopped, slipped from his saddle and began handing out rations. Thran went to check on Smokey to see how she was holding up but only received a curt response telling him she was fine, so he sat down next the other two and began to eat and drink. Thanks to the rest of the squad leaving their packs behind, they wouldn't have to worry about food or water for the journey back. Thran thought the silence would carry on throughout lunch but Araxia suddenly spoke.

'Captain, I've been thinking, and now that you have enacted revenge upon Mortem for his actions, it's time for you to punish the other culprit responsible for what happened to your family. If you wish to take it, my life is yours.'

Zakanos continued to chew the meat he'd bitten from the strip in hand. He swallowed, took another bite, chewed, swallowed. Thran began to think that he would never answer. Finally he glanced at the High Priestess, who sat calmly awaiting her fate.

'Then I shall have it.'
'Very well, I understand.'
'However, there has been enough bloodshed. There isn't any amount that will be able to fill the void inside me, so instead I will have your servitude. The 4th has recently lost its squad mage. You will fill that vacant position.'

Araxia, a little taken aback by the proposition, quickly regained her composure.

'I accept.'

Smokey spoke up from her makeshift litter. 'Welcome to the Guard Company.' She laughed, although they quickly turned to agonised moans.

'What of your goddess?' Zakanos asked.
'We are… at odds with each other right now, although I sensed her approval when I offered you my life.'
'And when you accepted my offer instead?'
'She understands that to have declined would have tarnished my honour as High Priestess.'

Zakanos seemed to accept this as he said nothing and went back to taking bites from his strip of meat. Thran however wasn't convinced, he knew the honour of the gods meant nothing, which meant by default so did the High Priestesses. However it was not his place to question Zakanos' judgement, he was the Captain after all, and it would fall to him to deal with Araxia and her goddess if she had ulterior motives. Araxia turned to Thran.

'Have you decided what you're going to do next?'
'Why does everyone keep asking me that?'
'Because we all want to know.'
'It's none of your business, or that of your goddesses.'
'Agreed.'

'Then why ask?'

'I told you, everyone wants to know.'

'What are Jagreus' intentions?'

'Honestly, I'm not quite sure what her true intentions are, but she will try to stop Dragos regaining his full power.'

'Why?'

'Fear.'

'Is he really that powerful?'

'Potentially.'

'And what will he do with that power?'

'That's the thing, no one truly knows. He's been trapped for centuries, alone, scheming, waiting for the chance to exact his revenge. You're one of the few people to actually talk to him. Others, gods included have tried but he ignores them. You'd know his intentions better than anyone else.'

Thran thought back on his conversations with Dragos, or Carrion as he'd known him.

'Yeah I can see revenge, but why is Jagreus so concerned? I thought it was the Council that imprisoned him, not the Elder gods?'

'So most believe, but it happened so long ago, and time muddies the clearest of waters. Most of the Elementals were present during his imprisonment ritual.'

'If Carrion wants the rest of the gods dead, why did the Lady seem like she wanted to bring him back.'

'Who can understand the conniving mind of the Lady of Luck? She thrives off the chaos of pitting god against god, but even for her it seems madness to start a war she can't predict or control. And you Thran, are the crux of that unpredictability.'

'Even for a High Priestess, you seem incredibly well informed.'

'I serve the goddess of life, I've been around longer than you may think.'

Zakanos, his frugal meal finished, stood and started packing. Thran and Araxia followed his cue and soon they were mounted once more on the long road back to Tydon.

* * * *

Kaprel Shellen fidgeted in his chair before the fireplace. Tonight was the night. He called for a drink to settle his nerves. A small, fastidious man, Kaprel uncharacteristically missed the fact that the servant who brought him a glass of wine was not a usual member of his household staff.
'Leave the jug.' He said absently.
The servant settled the jug on the small table next to the merchant, before pulling up a chair of their own.
'What in the name of the gods do-'
The rest of the sentence stopped dead in his throat as the imposter sat opposite him.
'Do you know who I am?'
Kaprel nodded.
'Do you know what they call me?'
He nodded again.
'Tell me.'
He didn't answer.
'Tell me. What do they call me?'
'T-the White Raven.'
'Yes. The White Raven of the Assassins Guild. A Guild that you believed to be completely wiped out, correct?' Another nod. 'Well, unfortunately for your fervent hopes, they were not thorough enough.' She could see the hate and anger start to build up and swirl within the fear in his eyes. 'Do I need to remove my gloves?'
This time Shellen shook his head.
'Good, I was hoping to settle this betrayal amicably.'
'Betrayal!?' The merchant started to find his voice. 'The Guild put me in a perilous position when they decided it would be a good idea to parade around Ritellis Square using my name! I came under intense scrutiny from the rest of the Merchants Guild and had to answer a lot of uncomfortable questions regarding my relationship with the Assassins Guild.'
'For that, we are truly sorry, but it was a necessity. However, your inability to inform the Guild of its impending butchering is something that cannot be overlooked.'

'I already told you, the Guild was watching me the entire time, I couldn't take a shit without the other merchants knowing.'

'That's not the only reason though, is it? You wanted to be rid of us and our hold over you. You always viewed us as unhappy bed mates. When the Merchant Guild discussed our eradication, I bet you were ecstatic, couldn't believe your luck.'

'I've been nothing but loyal to the Guild.'

'Reluctantly, Kaprel, reluctantly.'

'My willingness has nothing to do with it. I've done your bidding time and time again.'

'Yet not at this most crucial of times.'

'If you're here to kill me, get it over with. You can't stop the Guild or the noblemen now.'

Lagatha smiled. 'That's where you're wrong, Kaprel. You're going to help us do exactly that. Ah, finally, your other guests have arrived.'

Skrenn, Sarfina and Zel came in dressed in the livery of Kaprel's household guard. The merchant quailed as he realised how they'd been acquired. Sarfina tossed a spare set to Lagatha, who promptly checked it for any stains, blood or otherwise.

'This will have to do.' She sniffed. 'Now, Kaprel, avert your eyes, even the White Raven has her modesty.'

Kaprel's fingers shook as he curled them into a fist and knocked on the finely wrought iron doors. He knew there was little chance of him surviving the night. A slat was pulled back to reveal narrowed eyes.

'State your business.' Came the gruff voice muffled behind the metal.

'My name is Kaprel Shellen, I have urgent business with your master.'

'He ain't expecting any visitors.'

'I was not expected, however I must see your master.'

The eyes flitted from Shellen to his four bodyguards and back again.

'We're under instructions not to let anyone enter tonight. At all.'

'Wise precautions that I fully understand. Please, tell your master I have come to see him.' Kaprel could see his reluctance to disturb the noble. 'Tell him I have important information he must hear about a certain Guild who could still yet interfere with our plans.'

The slat closed. Kaprel sent prayers to Sollun above that the guard would carry his message to the nobleman, or he was dead at the first hurdle. He was all too aware of the four assassins acting as his bodyguards standing behind him. All four would take his life without a moment's hesitation. Time seemed to stretch and drag, Kaprel willed the slat to re-open with all his might. He regretted agreeing to this mad plan, almost wishing he'd just been murdered instead. He wiped the beads of sweat from his head. Finally, after what had seemed like an age, the guard came back and slid back the opening to the peephole.

'You and one other. The rest stay outside.'

Kaprel sighed in relief. Lagatha, Sarfina and Zel looked to Skrenn who nodded almost imperceptibly at Lagatha who moved to the merchant's side. Shellen could hear the click of a lock and, to his surprise as it had rested seamlessly inside the main door, a wicket door opened. The guard impatiently beckoned them inside. Once through, they were immediately surrounded by guards on all sides. Kaprel handed over his dagger, which he only wore for show anyway and the White Raven handed over the sword strapped to her hip. To his surprise, she also handed over her hidden weapons too, although he soon understood why. They were both patted down thoroughly. He noted the guards hands lingered longer on her than they did on him. Shellen pitied the man, he'd unknowingly marked himself for death. The fool leered and winked at the assassins dead eyed stare. The wicket door had closed behind them, they were inside. All Kaprel could feel and hear was his heart going into a frenzy as they were led up through the sprawling gardens to the humongous main house. This was the trickiest part of the plan. Up marble steps and through grand twin doors, they entered the foyer which itself was larger than Sarfina's Tavern, flanked on both sides by guards. However, the foyer was as far as they got. Stood in pure white robes, cinched at the middle by silk strips, the nobleman Perro Lier Ulp Thoroes stood with furrowed brows.

'What do you want, Shellen? Tonight of all nights.' His strong, authoritative voice brought the merchant to a stop.

'Ah, well, it's about tonight, actually, your lordship. You see... the Assassins Guild, they weren't completely wiped out.'

Perro visibly stiffened at the mention of the Assassins Guild. Skrenn had chosen him as he'd been actively seeking out the Guild or any information about their involvement in the death of his older brother, Pemtil. He was one of the most outspoken noblemen against the Guild and instrumental in their collaboration with the Merchants' Guild and the Elite Guard Company to push the purge ahead. It was said that he and Captain Remullus were childhood friends. Skrenn, Sarfina and Zel were all in agreement that, because of his personal involvement, he would be most likely to take the bait.

'How do you know this?' asked the nobleman, his voice taut.

'They came after me, your lordship! In my own home they came for me. Thankfully I'd hired local sellswords to up my protection, otherwise I'd be dead right now.'

'Why would they target you, of all people? An insignificant, coin-counting merchant.'

'Be-b-because I was an informant for them.'

'I KNEW IT!' Perro roared. Kaprel shrank from his ferocious outburst. The guards grabbed Shellen and forced him to his knees, a naked blade to his throat. They also grabbed hold of Lagatha, who made no move to escape or struggle. Perro advanced on Kaprel. 'You pathetic excuse of a man, you wretched little cur, you gave them information on my brother, didn't you!?'

'I did not.'

'DO NOT LIE TO ME!'

'I swear I did not, my lord!'

'I will set my dogs upon you to rip you to pieces, I will see you staked for this, you will stand in the garden for days while ravens pluck out your eyes and feast on your flesh.'

'My lord please, I had nothing to do with your brother's murder. They came after me because I did not warn them of what was to come. They want me dead.'

'And you thought I would spare your life? You really are a fool.'

'My lord, I came to make amends. You can exact your revenge, I know what the Assassins are planning.'

'How?'

Kaprel knew he had to sell Perro the lie completely or he was dead.

'When they attacked, they were dressed in the uniform of the 7th Company. It's how they were able to get so close without anyone realising. They plan to use the disguises to gain entry to the Citadel through the Heralds Gate and stop the assassination of the Emperor.'

'Why would they want to stop their own assassination attempt?'

'Because the Emperor is the true head of the Guild.'

Perro was visibly shaken. Skrenn had been right, Celentine had not been completely honest with the nobles.

'What are you talking about?'

'I'm telling the truth, the Emperor is the one who controls the Assassins Guild. Think about it, it's how he keeps both the Merchants Guild and the nobles in check.'

'If what you're saying is true, then Tavian has the blood of my brother on his hands.'

'He has the blood of many, my lord. Countless nobles and merchants.'

'And the assassins are making a last ditch attempt to save him?'

'I swear it lord, the assassins are trying to save him from being dethroned.'

The inner conflict was written all over Perro's face. He turned to the nearest guard.

'Have my carriage prepared immediately, gather my entire force, we head for the Herald's Gate.' He turned his attention back to Shellen. 'Get up, you're coming with me.'

'Yes my lord, thank you.'

The guard bundled him back outside through a hive of activity as Perro's personal troops mustered quickly and efficiently. The White Raven was released and moved to stand beside him. A large carriage pulled by a team of six horses soon pulled up to the main entrance. Perro emerged, a humongous axe strapped to his back. He climbed into the carriage, motioned Kaprel up alongside him. The merchant climbed in and sat opposite the nobleman, looking anywhere but at the youngest of the Thoroes brothers. He'd barely had time to sit down and they were off, racing down the path with Perro's troops trotting smartly behind the carriage. Shrugging, Lagatha fell in behind them. When they got beyond the finely wrought iron gates, the rest of the assassins joined Lagatha. As they jogged along behind the carriage towards the Heralds Gate, Lagatha filled them in, quietly so she wouldn't be overheard, as to what transpired inside the nobleman's expansive manor.

* * * *

Sergeant Diallo's squad stopped and snapped smartly to attention before the Heralds Gate. Diallo lowered his salute waiting for the guards to challenge him. The rest of his squad stood behind him, their swords out and at the necks of their prisoners. Heelial's squad, including Drak, stood with their arms bound, disarmed and helpless. Diallo held his nerve and finally one of the guards called down to him.

'You know the order. No one's allowed inside past curfew.'

'I know.' Diallo answered. 'However, we are here under orders.'

'The curfew order came from the Emperor himself.'

They all knew he was lying.

'My orders supersede that authority.'

'State your name, rank, and reason for being here.'

'Sergeant Diallo, Guard Company, 8th squad. The person behind me is Sergeant Heelial, also of the Guard Company. The men my squad have captured are her 4th squad. They were sent on a covert mission by the Emperor, and we found them sneaking through the city trying to infiltrate the Citadel. We were one of many squads sent to find them and bring them in for interrogation.'

'You taking them to the Barracks?'

'Yes.'

'Then why are you here and not at the Soldiers Gate?'

'We found them closer to this Gate, figured it would be best to bring them straight in rather than go around to the Soldiers', just in case.'

'Wait here.' The guard turned to his companion and spoke loud enough for Diallo and both squads to hear. 'If they move at all, shoot them.'

For the second time tonight, Heelial found crossbows levelled at her and her squad. 'You'd better hope this works, D.' She muttered under her breath.

'Have some faith. We've been in worse situations. Remember the winter training camp in the mountains?'

'How could I forget… Down to a quarter rations, it was torture.'

'We almost froze to death, but all you cared about was a full belly.'

'I have my priorities straight.'

'Stubbs lost a couple of fingers and toes to frostbite.'

'I was so tempted to eat them and pretend they were sausages.'

'To this day his balance is still off.'

'Give me a crossbow bolt to the head any day over starving to death, slowly wasting away. Couldn't think of a worse fate.'

'What would you pick for your last meal?'

'I'd pick a whole banquet hall clean.'

Diallo had to suppress a laugh. 'Of course you would.'

'What about you?'

'What would I have for my last meal?'

'Yeah.'

Before he could answer, the sound of pounding hooves reached their ears and a huge carriage screeched to a halt beside them. Troops in the livery of the Thoroes household came after the carriage, trying not to show they were out of breath in front of the City's military. The Sergeants' looked on with interest.

'Open the gates!' Ordered the driver of the carriage.

'On whose authority?' The remaining guard demanded.

The carriage doors slammed open and the nobleman Perro stepped out and drew himself upright in the pompous way only those born into wealth and title could.

'Mine! I am Perro Lier Ulp Thoroes, you will open these gates or face the consequences!'

The guard blanched at the announcement, glanced around in the hopes of finding someone else to make the decision. Seeing he was on his own, he quickly caved and called for the gates to be opened. Perro finally took note of the two squads waiting next to the carriage.

'What are you doing here?' He asked, eyes narrowed.

Diallo snapped another sharp salute despite Perro not having any authority over him.

'My Lord, we're escorting these traitors for interrogation.'

'Traitors you say?'

'Yes, my Lord.'

'Traitors to who?'

The question took Diallo off balance, he took a few heartbeats before carefully answering:

'Tydon, my Lord.'

The nobleman looked long and hard before nodding his head.

'Good. Follow my men through.'

He disappeared back into the carriage, and it set off through the now open Heralds Gate. His men followed and then tacked onto the rear came four more dressed differently and Drak almost involuntary shouted as he recognised his fellow assassins. Not one of them spared a look in his direction and he understood, they did not want to give anything away. They would meet up inside. Diallo barked orders so that as soon as they passed, his squad would shove Heelial's quickly through the gates so there would be no chance they would be shut with them still on the wrong side. Once inside they quickly set off away from the gate and further up into the citadel grounds. The sounds of fighting echoed all around them, the sound of steel on steel. The stench of munitions hung in the air. Skrenn, Lagatha, Sarfina and Zel began to lag behind the nobleman's troops as if struggling to keep up with their superior fitness in order for Diallo's group to quickly catch up with them. Once they were out of sight of the gate's troops, they cut Heelial's squad free and returned their weapons.

'Much better.' Heelial exclaimed, rubbing her wrists. 'Still, never thought I'd be glad to see a group of assassins.'

'They're members of the Assassins Guild?' Diallo asked in surprise. 'Rumour was they'd all been wiped out.'

'Aye, they're Assassins Guild alright. Don't worry D, we're on the same side. We've got a lot of catching up to do, which we can do when you treat me to a ten course meal, in the meantime, lets finish this.'

Drak couldn't hold back his grin as he made his way over to the Guild members.

'It's good to see you guys!'

'It's good to see you too Drak.' Sarfina flashed a brief smile before concern took over. 'Where's Thran and Reeva? How did you get back here so quickly?'

'I'm not quite sure what happened to Thran, but we saved him. He's safe, I think. He's the reason we got here as fast as we did, but I don't really understand it. Reeva's here, she came back to the city with us. My bets that she's already up there.' He nodded towards the sound of fighting.

'Okay, good. Sergeants, we're going to need your help. We must fight our way through to the Emperor and get him to safety.'

Together, the last makeshift Hand of the Assassins Guild and two squads of the Guard Company set off together. The Emperor's last hope.

Chapter 27

As soon as they pushed through the cobbles into the heaving mass of celebrations and merriment Reeva was in motion, leaving Drak and the others in her wake. Weaving through the crowd, she was soon out of Ritellis Square and into the streets. Feeling a rising sense of urgency within her, she ducked into a deserted side alley and shadow-walked. Sliding from shadow to shadow, she made her way up to the rooftops, and skimmed her way to the Citadel in moments. She knew it was risky, but any who could sense her would most likely be preoccupied or have their attention drawn to the group still coming to grips with their surroundings in Ritellis Square. She crouched on the rooftop opposite the Citadel, scanning the battlements for an opening. This was the risky part, her timing had to be impeccable to split the patrols and avoid detection in the brief moment in between shadow hops, that is, if there was another shadow within range for her to use. A patrol passed, she waited, she counted, another patrol passed, she waited, she counted. There was enough time. The next patrol passed, she moved. She dove into the street below, entering into the shadow the building cast as if it were a tranquil pool, its surface undisturbed by her passage. She shot out of the shadow provided by a guard tower, tucked into a roll and came up into a crouch, just out of torchlight and exposure. Not waiting to see if a cry of alarm would sound, she swung up onto the crenellations, spied her next camouflage spot and stepped off the battlements and into the darkness beneath.

    Reeva knew the way around the Citadel, knew the route she had to take to get to the Emperor. Many a night she had shadow-walked into the Citadel just as she had done now to figure out the best way to get to him. A few times she had even gone so far that the only thing that separated them was the final thin wall to his chambers. Of the numerous times before, she'd reached for the handle only to stop, pull herself back and flee into the night. Tonight was different. Tonight the choice might be taken from her. Tonight she would open that door. Flitting from shadow to shadow like a phantom in the darkness, she ghosted to the main entrance of the great hall. A battle was ensuing, Tydonii against Tydonii, the coup was in full swing. The attacking force was larger and swarming over the defenders who were heroically standing their ground, as steadfast as the giant pillars they stood between. Reeva knew they would not last much longer. She made her way around the back of the hall, keeping out of sight. Sidling up against the back wall she crouched and felt along the bottom of the wall until her fingers brushed against a brick that was ever so slightly sticking out ahead of the rest. She pushed it back into place. The wall groaned and split before her. Reeva slipped straight in and pressed another brick to close the gap behind her. Darkness enclosed her, but that presented no problems to a Shadow-Walker of Naul, it barely made a difference. Built in between the walls of the great hall, the secret passage would have been tight for any Grellon, tall as they were, but Reeva was of mixed blood, the shorter, squatter genes of the Tydonii came to her rescue here. The passage split off in different directions, leading all over the hall, but Reeva knew which path to take. This time, when she reached the door, she didn't hesitate, she reached out and twisted the handle, opening the wall directly into the Emperor's private chambers.

'So you've come. I hoped you would...' Tavian expressed no surprise that the assassin had come through the secret passage into his bedroom. The Emperor was dressed for battle, adorned in full mail, short sword at his hip. The only sign of his station was the thin gold circlet nestled on his head. 'Are you here to kill me?' He asked softly. Reeva stared at him before slowly shaking her head.

'A pity. If I'm to go, I would've liked for it to be you. To try to, well, to try to...' Tavian trailed off and for a while he said nothing. 'Ironic, really, that my reign will end how it began: in betrayal. A military coup. Maybe ironic isn't the right word, fitting perhaps.'

Tavian took a step towards Reeva who still hadn't moved from the passages entrance.

'It is time for you to end your vow, no matter what happens tonight. You must move on.' Reeva stiffened, her jaw clenched. 'That's not how I meant it. Honour her memory, but stop punishing yourself. Keep punishing me, I understand that, I deserve that, but not yourself, not anymore. It has gone on long enough.'

He took another step forward.

'Promise me.'

He took another step, now just out of arms reach.

'I want to hear you say it.'

His glistening eyes pleaded with hers.

His voice barely a whisper.

'*Say it.*'

She opened her mouth, only to close it again. She swallowed but the lump in her throat would not go away. Quivering, her lips parted to release the first words they had uttered in a very long time.

'My Lord!'

The cry came as the Captain of the Elite Guard burst into the Emperor's chambers. Remullus looked worse for ware, dishevelled and sporting numerous cuts, he'd only managed to pull on half his armour before the assailants had struck. Upon seeing Reeva, he rushed forward, sword raised.

'Assassin!'

'Stop! Remullus, I am in no danger. This is my daughter, Reeva.'

That brought the Elite Captain up short. Unsure what to do, he half bowed to Reeva.

'Milady. My Lord, we can't hold them much longer, they've pushed us back into the main hall, and we'll soon be overrun.'

'Then that is where I shall make my stand. Draw my weapon in battle one last time.'

'Sir please, let me take you to safety, if you escape, there is still hope.'

'What kind of Emperor, what kind of man would I be if I abandoned my men now. Go, strengthen their resolve, tell them their Emperor comes to stand beside them in battle and is honoured to do so. I'll be right behind you.'

Remullus saluted and left. Tavian turned back to Reeva. He was about to pick up where they had left off, but the moment was ruined.

'We will talk when I get back, okay?'

Reeva nodded, accepting the lie they both knew he was telling.

'That night, it should have been me, we both know it, that's who they were after, yet they took your mother instead. I can't change the past, and I can't make up for it, but your mother, she'd be damned proud of you. A Shadow-Walker, just like her.'

The sounds of battle intensified, coming closer.

'I love you, my daughter. I always have, I always will.' A tear rolled unashamedly down his cheek. 'I would have liked to hear you sing one last time.'

With that, Tavian turned and strode towards his death without looking back.

Reeva watched him go, took half a step after him, then stopped, conflicted. She knew when he'd joined the battle because of the Elite Guard Captain's cry of 'For the Emperor!' which was quickly taken up by the rest of the loyal soldiers. She knew it would sway the fight in their favour, albeit only temporarily, the opposing numbers were just too great. Her mind made up, she left the private chamber and made her way to the great hall, where the Emperor fought in the front lines before his throne. He fought bravely, valiantly, with Remullus by his right side, but the betrayers swarmed around him greedily, their prize within striking distance. She arrived just in time to see the fatal blow take her father in the throat. He staggered, blood beginning to flow freely, lifting his sword to block another incoming attack. Buoyed by the sight, the betrayers doubled their efforts. Remullus stepped before his Emperor, trying to shield him with his bulk and sheer force of will, but it was too late, a glancing blow on Tavian's shoulder was enough to spin the Emperor around before he fell onto his back. News of his fall rippled down the line and the fighting ground to a halt as both sides waited to hear if their reason for fighting still existed. The Elite Guard Captain stood in front of his fallen Emperor, sword raised in challenge which none of them accepted. The rest of the troops stood still in shock. The only one in motion was Tavian's kin. Reeva was by his side in an instant. She lifted his head to hers, but the light in his eyes had already faded.

She bent her lips to his ear and whispered haltingly with a voice hoarse from disuse.

"M-my... v-vow...is...b-b-broken."

Feeling all eyes on her as she rose from her father's corpse, Reeva felt hot tears start to roll down her cheeks. Not just from sadness or sorrow, but anger. An overwhelming anger. Those nearest her took half a step back as if her feelings were a physical force emanating from her. Her knives slipped into her hands, knuckles white on the grip. Her gaze swept all around her, like a butcher assessing where to make the first cut. Even Remullus quailed as his eyes met hers, for to look into them was to see Carrion, death itself, staring back. Then she was amongst them. To her they were all guilty; there were those who had succeeded in their attempt to kill her father, and those who had failed to stop them. They were all guilty, and she would mete out their punishment.

The first few to die saw nothing, a blur of movement as she went past, slicing throats and severing arteries. She cut open those around her with surgical precision, her movements graceful as she pirouetted and danced her way around the great hall. Foes became allies as they all sought to trap the death dealing demon in their midst. Whenever they closed on her she would shadow-walk to safety to begin the slaughter once more. Confusion reigned, fear and panic spread through both sides as Reeva moved through them like the wind. Those near the edges began to flee, but this only served to bring them to her attention. They were hunted down. All thoughts of fighting back evaporated into every man and woman for themselves. They fought each other in the desperate attempt to escape, doing Reeva's work for her as they struggled. The most unfortunate were trampled to death beneath their comrade's boots. Remullus could only watch in horror and awe as Reeva scythed down his troops, many of them Tydon's finest. He looked down at his fallen Emperor.

Your daughter, your bloodline is destroying your life's work in a matter of heartbeats. She is all that is left of your legacy now.

With a start he realised that Reeva now stood before him, plastered in gore, blood dripping, corpses strewn in her wake. Some, the lucky few, had managed to escape, but most who had entered the hall would never leave again, their bodies weaving a tapestry of violence and bloodshed in front of Tydon's empty throne. The assassin lifted her stained weapon to point at his throat. He did not resist. He knew it was pointless, he could not match her speed or her skill. He understood. He had failed her, failed his Emperor, and failed his city. The ensuing slaughter was his punishment, his torture for failure. It had been Remullus' greatest honour to serve in Tydon's military, an even greater honour to be named Captain of the Elite Guard. He had failed his post, his troops. All he could do now was to try and reclaim some of that honour.

He would face his death with dignity.

* * * *

Outside the entrance to the great hall, beneath the mighty pillars, another battle raged. The betrayers had left a portion of their forces to guard the doorway to make sure that any of the Emperor's remaining loyal men couldn't come to his aid. They'd already repelled one disorganised attack, but then Corsca, Captain of the Bow arrived with her bowmen to organise another assault. First she peppered their ranks with volley after volley, then once their numbers had been thinned and their ranks looking ragged, she personally led the charge to break them. Just when it looked as though they would overwhelm the betrayers, Perro arrived with his troops. Believing them to be the assassins in disguise he ordered his men to charge, crashing into the exposed backs of Corsca's squads. Trapped between the two forces, their lines lost all cohesion, and they began to take heavy casualties. Corsca, her tall frame easily visible even in the masses, tried valiantly to rally her troops and organise them into line once more, but it was to no avail. Her numbers were quickly being whittled down.

    Sergeant's Heelial and Diallo arrived with their squads and immediately ordered their heavies forward to form a line. Clipper and Rolls took the centre, with Wallow, Udders, Stump and Grimy flanking them. Trusting the heavies, Diallo and Heelial formed the second rank with Creak, Shriek, Fingers, Buzzard, Crutch and Nut. Nozza found himself at the back with the assassins and two members from the 8th squad. He was at a loss as to what to do, this was his first real taste of proper battle. He clutched the munitions that Smokey had given him, trying desperately not to look as nervous as he felt.

    'Stubbs' is the name, sapping is my game. This here is Puddle, our squad mage. I can see we're in the same trade, but don't recognise you.' The sapper beamed as he introduced himself, although it faded. 'Don't think we'll be seeing any action though.'

    'I'm Nozza, new recruit, stand in sapper. Why won't we see any action?'

    'Well we will, we'll be fighting, but we won't see any fun action, no munitions.'

    'You're not planning on using your munitions?' Nozza asked in surprise.

    'Of course not! Look at how packed the ranks are, we'll take out half our own if we do. Sollun above lad, even us regular sappers ain't that reckless.'

    'Oh, yeah, guess I didn't think it through.'

    'Itching to use em' though, we'll make a real sapper of you yet.' Stubbs clapped him on the shoulder and Nozza caught a glimpse of his hands. They were missing a number of digits. He gulped and made sure his grip on the munitions was absolute.

Heelial was barking orders to both squads and despite his seniority, Diallo deferred to her.

'Right, listen up. We hit 'em quick, we hit 'em hard. We punch through and strengthen the line. These jumped up nobleman guarding wanna be soldiers will turn tail when we show them what it's like to be in a real battle. Then we face those traitorous bastards and show them how loyal fucking soldiers fight! FOR TYDON! FOR THE EMPEROR!'

The squads took up the cry which alerted Perro's guard to their presence, but it was too late as the heavies barrelled towards them and smashed down those attempting to turn to face them like a scythe through wheat. Those who escaped the heavies' punishment were picked off by the rest of the squad following up and the odd one that somehow managed to avoid both met an assassin's blade. Skrenn, Sarfina, Zel, Lagatha and Drak were all fanned along the backline, behind even the sappers and spare squad mage. Their momentum carried them straight through Perro's thin lines and soon they were face to face with the remains of Corsca's squad. At first they clashed blades before Heelial ordered a stop, shouting over the din of battle that they were on the same side. Corsca's troops refused at first, suspecting a ruse, another betrayal. It was the Captain of the Bow herself that gave the order to let them through. She knew it was gamble, but it was her last throw of the dice, but tonight, auspiciously, The Lady was on her side.

The two squads of the Guard Company, fresher than both sets of troops around them, rallied once more and carried the fight to the traitors, relishing in their ability to strike directly at their former brethren. When they first struck they pushed the front line back, piling pressure on the defensive force, but the betrayers soaked it up and stood their ground. The line buckled but held firm. They knew that to lose here meant certain death. The fighting grew fierce and casualties were mounting on both sides but neither relented, each gap that opened was immediately filled from the ranks behind.

Zel was conscious that the defenders were eating up precious time, they had to break the ranks and quickly. The quickest way would be to use the munitions regardless of the damage it did to their own troops, but he didn't bother to voice this because he knew there was no way the Captains or Sergeants would ever go for such an abhorrent idea. Zel and his pragmatic thinking be dammed.

Out of the corner of his eye, he noticed Perro trying to rally what was left of his troops, waving his big axe about frantically. He'd gathered about a score of them by his wagon and more were limping over, he'd also become a threat if not dealt with. Then Zel had an idea, the noble has just provided a solution to his problem.

'Drak, come with me. You, sapper, you're coming too, prep a fire munition.'

Nozza took a moment to realise that the assassin was talking to him and quickly scrambled after Zel who was making a beeline for Perro, Drak sauntering in his wake.

'I'm going to need that axe Perro.'

'I will have you flayed for such insolence!'

'Just give us the axe and you can all live.'

In response Perro just growled and raised his weapon above his head, behind him his men readied their own. Zel didn't look the least bit concerned, he just turned to Nozza.

'Torch the carriage sapper.'

Nozza had at this point not managed to find what had been asked of him so instead he just grabbed the nearest clay ball and lobbed it at the carriage. The resulting explosion blasted those nearest off their feet and sent bits of wood flying in all directions. Zel and Drak both lifted their hands to protect their faces. The poor horses still tethered to the carriage panicked and quickly took off, dragging the smouldering remains with them.

'By the gods! I only asked you to set it alight, not blow the damn thing up!'

However, it still had the desired effect, all the fight had gone from Perro and his men. The nobleman threw his weapon down at the assassin's feet and Drak scooped it up, appreciating its heftiness and craftmanship.

'I want you to break their line Drak, force your way through as fast as you can.' Zel ordered.

The big Tydonii nodded and trotted towards the fight, picking up his pace he bellowed for his allies to make way as he charged the enemy. He hadn't fought with an axe before, he had no skill with the weapon, but it didn't matter, he wielded it like a crude club, bringing it down time and again, splintering shields, breaking limbs. The members of the Guard Company stepped back to give him space to swing and hack across the line, causing havoc.

Invigorated by the ferocity of his attack, Corsca and Heelial urged their troops on for one final push. The weary, outnumbered betrayers gave more and more ground, the holes in their line no longer being replenished. The first of them began to edge away and seek escape, but their only option was into the great hall. One and two soon became three and four, until all resistance fell away and they were all fleeing inside. Howling in victory, Corsca and Heelial's troops showed no mercy, righteously chopping at exposed necks and backs. The betrayers were butchered as the battle turned to slaughter. It was like looking into a mirror, as those escaping the carnage outside ran into those escaping the Shadow-Walker inside.

The battle-joy, the euphoria that unbounded killing brought did not last long as word of the Emperor's fate filtered back through the ranks. Everyone stood still, unsure of what to do next. Corsca once more took charge, ordering her troops to round up the remaining betrayers while she made her way into the great hall to see the "Shadow-Demon" that was now supposedly rampaging. Skrenn pushed forward, forcibly shoving anyone who remained in his path. The rest of the assassins followed. They arrived slightly ahead of Corsca to see Reeva kneeling over the Emperor's body, his but a drop in the sea of death that surrounded her. Remullus stood, alive, but broken. Corsca made her way carefully over to her fellow Captain.

'She would not even grant me an honourable death. I am left with nothing.' He muttered as she offered her support.

'NO!' Skrenn's anguished cry tore through the hall, echoing his sorrow back at him. 'No, no, no, no, no, no, no! What have you done!?'

Reeva looked up and blinked, as if a veil and been lifted from her eyes. She looked around the room as if seeing it all for the first time. She stood, tottering slightly. Eyes darting between men and woman she had only moments ago cut down.
'What have you done!?'
Reeva shook her head. She couldn't look at Skrenn, couldn't face him. She just kept shaking her head as if she could shake the grim reality before her away. Sarfina stepped towards her.
'Reeva.' She said softly. 'Reeva, drop your weapons.'
The Grellish assassin looked down in surprise to see her hands still tightly clutching her weapons. Painfully, and with great effort, she uncoiled her fingers to release her grip but the knives stayed there, stuck to her by the blood of her victims. She shook her hands and finally they clattered to the floor. Sarfina took another step towards her, Reeva backed away.
'Reeva, just stop. Stay. We can help.'
Skrenn lurched forward which was enough for Reeva to break.
She fled into the nearest shadow and was gone.
The Dresconii, his concern only for his fallen friend, knelt by Tavian's side and sobbed onto his chest as the two Elite Captains and the remaining assassins looked on.
The man from the Slivannah Plains rose with the Emperors body draped in his arms and walked to the throne, seating Tavian on it one last time. The gold circlet still adorning his head, he almost looked alive, slumped in his throne, about to give a decree or pass judgement on a dispute. Yet Skrenn knew the truth he did not want to face.
Tydon's Emperor, his long-time friend, was dead.

Chapter 28

Thran sighed as he walked through the streets of Tydon: the city he had returned to was not his own, not the one he had left. Once so full of life, the streets thronged with people going about their lives were now empty, with only the brave, mad or destitute to be seen. Even as they'd ridden towards the city, Thran could tell something wasn't right. He could sense the atmosphere. The fear and uncertainty hung over the city like a smog, encircling all in its smothering embrace.

A cheerful voiced pierced through the murk of Thran's musings like a ray of light. 'HO TRAVELLERS!'

Thran looked up to find a beaming Bisher pulled up by the side of the road, laid across his wagons driver's seat, enjoying the morning sun. The merchant sat up and climbed down from the carriage. Zakanos and Araxia looked at him quizzically but he gestured to them that it was all okay and dismounted. He strode over to the Bisher and was once against struck by the merchant's size. Smiling, the Grellon clapped the assassin on the back.

'It is good to see you again my friend.'

'You too.' Thran replied, surprised to find that he actually meant it.

Bisher cast an appraising eye over the horses, Zakanos, Araxia and the stretchered Smokey. 'Where is your other friend?'

'He was no friend of mine Bisher, he was an enemy. I was his captive. These are my rescuers.'

'Well met, rescuers. I must admit, there was something in his demeanour that struck me as dangerous.'

Keen for the subject to change, Thran asked: 'What are you doing by the side of the road?'

'Enjoying the morning sun after a late breakfast. I left Tydon in haste this morning to make sure I was one of the few able to leave the city.'

'What news of the city, Bisher?'

The smile the merchant had worn since Thran had met him disappeared.

'Grave my friend, grave. Some nights ago there was a coup in the city, violent slaughter in the Citadel. Thankfully it barely spilled out into the city so the festivities continued unhindered, meaning my profits barely took a hit.'

Sensing the Captain's interest from behind him, the assassin asked:

'Bisher, what happened in the Citadel?'

The merchant spread his hands. 'I'm sorry my friend, I cannot tell you because I do not know. According to most rumours, the Emperor was killed, slain by a conjured demon. The next day nobody was allowed out of Tydon, since then they've only allowed so many in and out, all subject to thorough searches.' The merchant glanced again at Thran's companions. 'My friend, I can't help but notice that those horses are tacked with Tydonii military harnesses.' Zakanos' hand reached for the hilt of his sword. 'There is no need for violence, I was merely making an observation.'

'Your observations are correct.' Thran replied, looking to diffuse the situation. 'He is military and needs to find out what happened in the city. Who controls the gates?'

'The soldiers at the gate had a Merchant Guild official overseeing them, taxing us higher than usual.' Bisher spat. 'The Guild's greed knows no bounds.'

Thran shared a look with Zakanos and Araxia. The news wasn't good.

'We need to gain entrance to Tydon.'

'Perhaps I can help with that, my friend.'

'Why would you do that?' Thran asked, his suspicions raised.

'I am a man who pays his debts, I still owe you for helping me out when my wagon was stuck. If not for you I would not have amassed the small fortune I acquired at the festival. My friend, it's the least I can do. I have an idea.'

Under Bisher's guidance they loaded Smokey carefully onto the back of the wagon, along with all the saddles removed from the horses except for two which the Captain and High Priestess would continue to ride. Thran would sit beside Bisher at the front of the wagon.

They continued onto Tydon for just shy of a bell until the city loomed before them. They joined the ragged line to enter the gates.

'By the time we reach the city's gates, the Guild stooge in charge should have switched. Let us pray for a favourable change.'

'Tell me Bisher, what deity do you pray to?'

'To be honest Thran, I'm not very religious, but no sane merchant forgets to keep the goddess of Fortune appeased with offerings.'

Thran bit back a bitter, bark of a laugh.

Of course, I should have known. There is no coincidence anymore, only her.

'We are in luck, my friend.' This time Thran did not hold back his bark, of which the merchant seemed to take no notice. 'I know the Guild representative. HO REJAN! REJAN!' Bisher waved frantically at the woman overseeing the ins and outs of the city. She looked up, saw Bisher and waved him forward, much to the annoyance of those who had been waiting longer.

'Bisher, good to see you.'

'You too Rejan my friend, you too.'

'Not like you to miss the Oros festival.'

'Indeed it is not, yet I received some information I had to act upon. It's not often the Dresconii will part with their precious mounts.'

Rejan eyed the horses with open desire. 'Fine mounts you've got there too Bisher, they'll fetch plenty of coin.'

'They certainly will, and mine they will stay until I sell them.' The merchant slipped a hand inside his tunic and removed a heavy pouch which chinked loudly when he sat it in her open palm.

Rejan cackled. 'That's what I like about you Bisher, you understand business.'

Thran hadn't been listening to the exchange, instead he'd been focused on the two guards monitoring those who entered the city. Thankfully they were uninterested in their party, happy to leave it to the Guild representative. Something about the pair conversing with each other seemed vaguely familiar.

'What's wrong with you?'
'Nothing.'
'It's not nothing.'
'It's nothing if I say it's nothing!'
'It's obviously something. You've been miserable ever since the Oros festival ended, which doesn't make any sense because your plan worked! Beyond all reason, the maidens picked you! Yet since you emerged from that temple you've barely said a word. What happened inside that temple?'
'I can't talk about it.'
'Can't, or won't?'
'...Both...'

Then Rejan was waving them through and into Tydon.

Lining the main route on either side of the main road up to Ritellis Square were stakes with people impaled upon them. The poor souls had been stripped naked, had a spike shoved up their rear end and left upright to rot. The unlucky few who were still alive, slumped onto the stake, resigned to their agonising fate. Only one called out to them, but his desperate cry was weak and they knew he was not long for this world. It was a poor way to go and Thran was thankful that so far he hadn't seen anyone he recognised, member of the Assassins Guild or otherwise. He'd said his goodbyes to Zakanos, Araxia and Bisher before they'd made it as far as Ritellis Square so he could head straight to the Tavern. The Captain and his latest recruit continued on towards the Citadel with the merchant in tow who was promised a reward for his services. His farewell with the Grellon was warmer than the other two. In truth they'd made poor travelling companions, with Zakanos barely saying a word to either of them and the High Priestess happy to keep her own council. The days had passed in almost complete silence.

He rounded a corner and the Tavern came into view and Thran let out a breath he hadn't realised he'd been holding. Sarfina's Tavern looked to have been largely untouched. It stood as it always had, giving him a sense of reassuring normality. However, that was quickly shattered as two soldiers stood guard outside. Thran flattened himself against the building and cursed himself for being so careless, putting it down to weariness from the road. He'd been too eager to get back to the Tavern and see everyone. He risked a glance at the Tavern; it appeared they had not clocked him as they remained in place. Judging by the insignia that he squinted to see clearly, they were Elite Guard Company soldiers.

This makes no sense. Why are Elite Guard Company soldiers guarding our Tavern!?

The Tavern door opened and out stepped Drak, two mugs of beer in hand which he then offered to the two guards. One took the mug straight away but the other refused, shaking his head. Drak clapped him on the back, said something to him and offered it again. Thran couldn't make out what the huge Tydonii was saying, but heard his hearty laugh as the second guard finally accepted the drink. Drak made one last comment and headed back inside. Still confused, Thran stepped out into the open. The two guards noticed him instantly, but kept sipping their drinks, eyeing him cautiously. Thran approached slowly, hands in the air at shoulder height to indicate he came peacefully, even though he could have a dagger in each hand in a split-second. He stopped a few paces from them. He nodded, they nodded back.

'You Thran?'

'Erm, yeah.'

'Head in, we were told to expect you.'

With that they promptly ignored him and went back to their beers. Wondering what to expect when he went inside, Thran opened the doors. More Elite Guard Company soldiers were inside, Thran reckoned there to be two squads worth, considering there would be more guarding the back entrance. A few eyed him up, but most continued to go about their own business. He scanned for Drak and found him sitting opposite a well built and intimidating Sergeant with a scowl on their face. The Tydonii assassin was gesticulating as he spoke to the Sergeant but they remained unmoved. They were the only two at the table yet there was an empty chair with an untouched cup of ale in front of it. He sat down without much fanfare and took a swig from the cup.

Now that is what I'd call inconspicuous.

'THRAN! By the gods it's good to see you! Thought it was about time you got back.' Drak beamed at him. Thran tossed back the remaining contents of the cup.

'Good to see you safe and sound Drak, and especially good to wash the road from my throat.'

The Sergeant's scowl had deepened and turned its attention to Thran who stared coolly back.

'You're Thran?' She asked.

'I am.'

'Huh. Thought there'd be more to you.'

'Well that's the point.'

'The point of what?'

'Being an assassin. Not standing out. Drak doesn't count.'

She didn't answer but instead dipped a hand into a pouch at her side, withdrew a few coins and flicked them across the table to Drak who scooped them up gleefully.

'Your big friend here had faith that you'd be back. I thought you'd end up dead. Turns out his faith was rightfully placed.'

Sensing Thran's burning question, Drak flashed him one of his infectious grins.

'This here is Sergeant Flick of the Elite Guard Company, she's here to protect and serve.'

'I'm here to babysit.' She didn't sound particularly pleased about the assignment.

'Why?'

'Well.' Drak puffed out his cheeks. 'That's a long story, one worth telling over a few jars. Don't worry lad, I'll pay, just had a real recent windfall.' He shot Flick a wink, who replied with a deepening of her perpetual scowl. 'Get em' in and I'll recount the tale.'

Thran did as he was bade, and was soon seated comfortably. Drak drained his cup and replenished it, scratched the side of his head with a finger and then nodded.

'Right, well, where to start. When you left us is probably as good a point as any. The ground ate you up, and pretty soon it ate us too, sucked us right in and shot us all the way to Tydon. If I hadn't experienced it myself, I wouldn't have believed it. Travelling underground like that, it were weird. Surreal. Spat us out right in the middle of Ritellis Square at the height of the Oros Festival. The Lady must have been smiling on us, 'cos everyone was either too drunk or wrapped up in the festivities to give us much notice.'

Drak was too busy telling his story to notice Thran's grimace at the mention of the goddess, but Sergeant Flick picked up on it. Drak told Thran how they'd gone to the Soldiers Gate, been fired at and hooked up with Diallo's squad and tried to get access to the Citadel via the Herald's Gate.

'So we gets there, all disarmed and at the mercy of Diallo and his squad, it's getting dicey, then this jumped up asshole of a nobleman comes and ends up saving the day. What was his name again?'

'Perro Thoroes.' Flick answered.

'Right, that's him.'

'Seriously? The head of the Thoroes family? What was he doing there?'

'I'm getting to that. So anyway, he turns up with his personal guard demanding to be let in, spouting off about his privilege and all the usual tripe. Luckily for us, they bow under the pressure and let him in and us along with him. And, you'll never guess who's attached to his personal guard but Skrenn, Sarfina, Zel and Lagatha. Couldn't believe my eyes!'

'Why were they with Thoroes?!?'

'I'm getting to that, so stop interrupting me and fill my cup. So, turns out that whilst we'd been gone, the Guild was getting close to uncovering a coup led by the nobles and the Merchants Guild. So Celentine, the ringleader in all this fed

Remullus information about us and he organised a City-wide raid and effectively wiped out the Guild. Skrenn and those with him when we met up with Perro were all that survived, or resurfaced after. The Sergeant here led the raids.'

Thran's cold gaze locked with Flick's whose showed no emotion. She shrugged.

'Orders.'

Thran couldn't believe Drak was sat here drinking with the woman who had slain so many of their fellow Guild members and said as much.

'Well, I'm getting to that. Besides, we've killed a lot of theirs over the years, we can hardly claim their retribution was unjustified.'

'What happened to the others?'

Drak shot him a look. Thran held up his hands in supplication. The Tydonii caught him up on what the Guild members had been doing in all of this and the final desperate fight to gain entrance to the grand hall, telling Thran with pride how he'd smashed through the lines. Here Drak paused, and when he continued, his voice was softer, he spoke more hesitantly, like he'd lost his enthusiasm for the tale.

'We got inside and there must have been more than fifty bodies surrounding her. It was Reeva. Thran, she'd... she'd slaughtered them all. Cut every single one of them down despite who they fought for. Sergeant Flick here was one of the lucky ones to survive. I've seen some sights lad, believe you me, but that... it was the look in her eyes. The Emperor was dead, his daughter had avenged him.' Seeing the disbelief on Thran's face, Drak nodded. 'Aye, we couldn't believe it either, turns out we've been living with royalty all this time.' Drak's smile was as weak as his attempted joke.

'The only other living person left inside was the Captain, Remullus. When we approached, Reeva fled. She ain't been seen since.'

Drak was silent for a while.

'Tydon's fucked. The military has taken heavy losses and nobody trusts each other. Remullus controls the Citadel but the nobles and merchants control the city, although they're also bickering between themselves. Celentine controls most of them, but some have sided with Perro who wasn't happy that the truth was kept from him and some of the others. So it's a three way fight for power. Although Remullus doesn't want it for himself, here's the craziest part of it all. He wants to put Reeva on the throne.'

'What!?'

'Yeah we couldn't believe it either. That man follows his own code of honour. So here we are, unlikely allies, despite the Captain's hatred of the Guild, we're the only link he's got to Reeva. Plus we were actually loyal to the Emperor all along.'

Thran puffed out his cheeks. 'So what's Skrenn going to do?'

'He's gone, lad.'

'Gone?'

'Yeah, he took the death of Tavian hard. Said his loyalties were to the man and not the throne and left. Gone back to the Slivannah Plains is Sarfina's guess. She runs the Guild now, or what's left of it. She's upstairs with Zel. White Ravens out paying Shellen a visit. He slunk off when all the fighting started and nobody was paying him any attention. Still got our reputation to uphold. The rest of us have just been waiting for something to happen, it's been a tense few days, cooped up in here, and tempers are starting to fray.'

'Nothing a little scrap wouldn't sort.' Flick opined.

'See, the Sergeant here understands, we speak the same language, although she could do with brightening up a bit.' She didn't return his smile. 'Anyway lad, it's your turn. Tell us how you got here.'

Thran shrugged. 'Not much to tell, I got swallowed up by the ground, it spat me back out at the obelisk near the temple ruins but you were all gone. I caught up with Zakanos and Araxia and we hurried back. They went straight up to the barracks.'

'Well it's good to have you back, we need you, now more than ever. You should let Sarfina know you're back, she'll be pleased.'

Pleased to see me? Or pleased that she has another assassin left from the Guild?

'Yeah I think I will do.'

'Not before you back me up though.' Drak swung his attentions back to Flick. 'Just out of curiosity, who's the biggest, meanest bastard here?'

'Me.' She stated matter of factly, without a hint of arrogance or boastfulness. 'But I will not be seen scrapping with the likes of you.' She nodded to a heavy heading out of the back to take a piss. 'He's your man.'

Drak rubbed his hands together. 'It's settled then, time to make some new friends. Come along Thran.'

Thran made no move to follow the big Tydonii who headed out after his unsuspecting opponent.

'A wise decision.'

It was Thran's turn to scowl at the Sergeant, whose frown disappeared, which was the closest thing to a smile her mouth ever got. Shouting sounded from outside and moments later Drak came crashing back into the Tavern, the heavy barrelling in after him. Soldiers were up and surrounding them in an instant, egging the fighters on and placing bets. Drak and the heavy closed, grappling and pummelling each other with blows. Thran glanced at Sergeant Flick to see if she would break it up but she looked on, uninterested in the fight. Instead her attention was captured by the figure weaving her way through the mob to stand at their table.

'Thran.' Said the White Raven without looking at him. The assassin's gaze was locked on the Sergeant's, who stared back, unperturbed. Sensing the tension between them, Thran stood up.

'Lagatha. I was just leaving actually, need to see Sarf.'

Neither of them watched him go, Flick casually sipped from her cup. The White Raven remained standing opposite the Sergeant. With Thran gone and everyone else's attention occupied by the fight, it was like they had the entire Tavern to themselves.

'I could kill you right now.'

'You could try.'

'You killed Venustus.'

'I don't know who that is.'

'Yes you do.'

'Nothing personal, just following orders, just like you followed Skrenns.'

'I don't trust you.'

'Understandable.'

'Watch your back.'

'Of course.'

Lagatha seemed like she was about to say something else, but instead grunted and folded her arms.

'Care to join me?'

'No.'

'You might as well. Easier for you to gut me if you're next to me, especially after a few drinks. Easier for me to keep an eye on you. Better for the both of us. Look, even they're drinking together.'

Drak and his adversary had ended their contest. Unclear who'd won, they were both bruised and bleeding, an arm around each other's shoulder and a cup in the other, surrounded by the rest of the troops. They were laughing like old friends. All the earlier tension and frustration gone.

Lagatha eased down into the seat opposite Flick who slid a spare cup her way.

'Help yourself. Although you might want to take those pretty white gloves off first.'

'I don't remove my gloves unless I'm about to get my hands dirty.'

'Not dirty, wet.'

The White Raven reached over and poured herself a drink.

'As you can see, my hands are quite steady.'

'That's what I'm counting on.'

A flash of understanding passed between them.

'Ah, I see.' She began to slowly peel off her pristine white gloves and lay them on the table. 'You're quite right, I would not want to ruin such fine craftsmanship by getting them carelessly damp.' The two shared the table and cups for the rest of the night.

* * * *

Upstairs Thran was laid on his bed, mind racing, still struggling to digest all that Drak had told him. The news about Reeva was startling, to think she had been the daughter of the Emperor all along, but when he thought about it, it wasn't that much of a surprise. No one really knew where she had come from, she'd always just been part of the Guild, mute and accepted. Once they'd learnt Tavian had secretly been running the assassins through Skrenn it wasn't that hard to imagine his daughter being hidden amongst their ranks. The night of his rise to the throne was no secret. What had unsettled him most was Celentine.
Threm.
Brother.
His upbringing seemed like a different lifetime ago, almost as though it belonged to someone else. After he'd been kicked out, he'd faced rough years on the streets, then the Guild had become his new home, his new family. Once he'd become an assassin, become competent and confident in his own skills, Thran had often thought about going back to pay his brother a visit in the night, but each time he'd set off to the Celentine manor, he'd never made it inside. As he grew older and Guild business took over, he thought about his brother and old life less and less, until it was no longer a thing of importance. He paid no attention to the rumours and gossip about the nobles or Merchants Guild, in fact he actively ignored them. He had initially craved it, although he knew that his brother flourished by all accounts, propelling the Celentine name further than their father ever had. Now he could no longer ignore him, pretend he was not a Celentine. Thran wondered if this was also the Lady's doing and cursed her vehemently.

He tensed as he realised he was no longer alone. Sitting up, a figure stood at the bottom of his bed. Reeva shuffled forward and Thran involuntarily recoiled from the sight of her.

Crusted blood mapped her entire body, she looked haggard, standing in a semi-delirious state.

She can't have slept since that night.

Seeing his reaction, Reeva turned to go.

'Wait! I'm sorry.'

She turned back.

Shuffling down, he beckoned her over. She came willingly, desperately. She laid her head on his lap and curled up into a ball on the bed. He said nothing, just stroked her blood-encrusted, straw-like hair as best he could as she cried silently. Thran tried to console her as best he could as she had always done for him, but seeing her like this was a shock. Usually so composed, a rock, unmovable, staunch, this was a side to her he had not seen before and it shook him more than he thought it would have. Yet in a strange way, he was happy that she had chosen him, allowed him to see her in such a vulnerable state of weakness, of despair. So, he would give her this night of consolation, because there would be scant going forward. After all, she was the Empress elect.

What a mess. Drak is right, this is all fucked.

* * * *

As the ragged corpse shambled into view, The Lady let out a grunt of pleasure tinged with relief. Even her legendary patience had been tested whilst she'd waited for him to emerge from the trees. Although given the state of the body, she shouldn't have been surprised. It dragged one leg uselessly behind, while both arms hung limply from its sides. It was a wonder it could stand at all seeing as though most of its toes were missing. The goddess continued to watch as the corpse dragged itself tirelessly into the ruins and stood amongst them for some time.

'And so our star finally takes centre stage.'

The body turned to look up at the goddess sat up in the tree, gazing at her with empty sockets where eyes had once sat. Its face expressionless, she could feel the hate oozing from him as palpable as the pungent scent of death emanating from his decomposing body. Mortem's once fine features had been ravaged by revenge and animals where his body had been left to rot.

'You,' the voice grated. 'It's always you.'

The Lady pouted. 'I don't know what you mean.'

'What are you doing here?'

'Why, to see Carrion, the gruesome god of Death arise and walk the earth once more!'

'I hate you, Viella.'

'Dispensing with the godly titles? Such informality, how indecent. Very well, I shall reciprocate... Dragos.'

'You're going to be one of the first to die by my hand.'

'You'll need to get one that works first.'

She beamed her best smile, knowing it would infuriate him. He glanced down at his decrepit body.

'I take it this is also your doing?'

'But of course.'

'What of my chosen vessel?'

'What of him?'

'You can't possibly hope to control him, just like the Council couldn't control me.' Dragos let out a cruel, hacking laugh that sent ice running through The Lady's veins and raised the hairs on the back of her neck.

'Do you think me naïve? I have contingencies placed around him.'

The corpse laughed again, although this one more out of genuine amusement.

'You were never naïve, Viella, never, I'll give you that. Your weakness was your hubris, and still is, judging by my resurrection. You and your games. The rest of the Council will not let your actions go unpunished. You might even stir the Elders out of their apathy.'

It was the goddesses turn to laugh.

'Much has changed during your imprisonment, Dragos. The world you once knew has long since gone.'

'Oh I know, goddess of Luck, I know.'

His tone unnerved her.

'Been chatting to the soil and stone all these years have we, gaining valuable information from them?'

'That's between the buried and me. Enlighten me though, if you will: why?'

'Why what?'

'Oh please. You do nothing on a whim. For what reason have you helped bring me back?'

'Balance.'

'Balance?'

'They call me the goddess of Luck, The Lady, but in reality I am the goddess of Balance. Hmm, no that doesn't sound quite right. I am the Balancer.'

'Speak plainly.'

'The universe around us, this world, has a delicate balance, an equilibrium that must always be maintained. It is my duty to maintain that balance. Life has death, darkness has light. Scholars like to cite good vs evil in this bracket too, but they're two sides of the same coin, with everything else in between. Everything has a counterbalance. If one is gone, things become lopsided and chaos reigns. The humans cannot comprehend this, so they put it all down to chance, down to luck. When all I do is maintain the balance. If someone wins at dice, there must be a loser. Two men stand side by side in a hail of arrows, for one to live the other must die. Balance.'

Dragos snorted. 'I told you hubris was your weakness. Delusions of grandeur so that you feel you have some divine purpose. Did the Elder gods beg you to take the position, due to it being too great for them? So I will ask again, O great Balancer, why have you aided in my resurrection.'

'If you were listening, I have already explained. Although I suppose it's difficult when you only have one ear left.'

'Your tongue fires barbs that sink into dead, nerveless skin.'

'Skin that life begins to bloom in once more. I wouldn't let it heal over the barbs, they're all the harder to dig out.'

'Look at us, a lifeless corpse inhabited by a soul, talking to a soulless body full of life.'

Viella laughed and clapped her hands.

'Oh I have missed sparring with you Dragos, you truly are a student of Esser.'

'What about your spindly little pet Garbhan?'

'Yes, well, unfortunately I think him and sanity had a parting of ways and they've not quite reconciled yet.'

'You make it sound like they were close to begin with.'

'Levity aside, I brought you back for balance. Life and death. As I said, you've been gone for a long time, god of Death. Time to even out the scales.'

'I shall tip them in my favour.'

'You will undoubtedly try, I'm counting on it. If you had secured your vessel, you might well have been able to, but in this current state.' She shrugged, gave him a coy smile. 'Good luck.'

'Stick to your barbs, they land better than your jokes.'

Viella laughed and clapped her hands again.

'Oh, god of Death, you are aptly named, for I am slain.'

'You will be *goddess*.' He spat the title. 'Next time we meet and I am restored.'

With that he turned and began to drag himself towards the opposite treeline and away from her. Tempted as she was to reply, she decided not to give him the satisfaction of a retort and watched him toil away until he was out of sight.

Viella reclined in the tree for a little while longer before dropping to the ground, smoothing her skirts and brushing off any stray leaves. As she did a skeletal figure huffed into view, halting by her side, panting hard, struggling to catch his breath. He defiantly mopped his brow with a handkerchief, which was also sopping wet with sweat, to no avail. It could not stop the deluge that seeped from every pore.

'C-can't… stay… here long…' He wheezed. 'Guardian coming.' He desperately sucked in air.

'Compose yourself. I can't believe I'm about to utter these words, but I prefer it when you can speak properly. Besides, the Guardian won't be hunting you any longer.'

The man didn't reply until his heart stopped threatening to break through his ribcage and his breathing had somewhat stabilised.

'Oh good. Nasty little creatures, although I suppose there's nothing little about them. Nasty big creatures doesn't sound right thought does it? Big, nasty creatures, ah! Now we're onto something, that sounds better, more intimidating. Big, nasty creatures bred for one deadly purpose: weight loss. My fat has all melted away. Blobs lay discarded on the wayside, wherever they were shed, left to fend for themselves. My poor little babies. If I had ventured by the sea, they'd be mistaken for seals and clubbed to death for meat, fat and blubber. Oh the injustice! I know how the seas were created. The Twin's set the Guardians on poor old Poleon and they chased him round and round in a big circle, the god sweating all the way, until eventually they were no longer running, they were splashing, then paddling, then swimming. Haven't you ever wondered why the oceans are salty? There you have it. Poleon's sweat. Garbhan's unconventional methods yield ancient truths that have stumped scholars for centuries, I must write up my thesis at once!'

The mad ex-priest looked much the same to her as when she'd last seen him. She was tempted to say as much but decided against it. It would only unleash another tirade.

'Does this mean you're heading back to Tydon then?'
'Oh I think not!'
'I want you in Tydon.'
'The learned members, or should I now call them scholarly brothers, will tear me apart if I can present no evidence to support my bold, yet truthful, claims. Tell me, what does the goddess intend? To rest upon her laurels? To celebrate the culmination of her plans?'

The Lady sighed.
'She goes to uphold her end of the bargain with the Twins.'
'Distasteful business by the sounds of it, but excellent news for this budding academic. The written testament of two gods will carry much weight within the scholarly halls, they are

wise men after all. Although I do begin to see potential risks. What if the Twins cannot write? They are bestial after all. Perhaps I can jot their words down and then they can sign with an inked paw. Would that be accepted as a valid evidence? Hard to prove it's not a forgery. Hmm, I have much to ponder as we begin our journey.'

'You're not coming with me.'

Garbhan looked at her and blinked rapidly.

'Of course I am. This is an opportunity I cannot pass up.'

The Lady shook her head, relenting.

'Come along then Garbhan, let us be gone. I shall be glad of the company, even if it is you.'

The two set off together, seemingly in no particular set direction or haste. After a dozen or so paces, Garbhan asked:

'Would you like to hear a story?'

'It seems today is your lucky day, I'll allow it.' She said to him with a sly smile, which to her surprise, was unreturned. Viella grunted. 'First Carrion, now you. Does no one have a sense of humour anymore?'

'Just like the Guardians did to me, you have run those jokes into the ground.'

'I guess you're right. After all these centuries, I need to work on some new material.'

'But first you must listen to my tale, and listen with an open mind, free of prejudice, free of your preconceptions of what is possible.' He paused for dramatic effect.

'I once knew a man who claimed he could lick both of his elbows at the same time, without holding them together... impossible I hear you claim? Well, I thought so too, until one fateful night. This man, this long tongued deviant, let's call him... Bertillious! Bertillious walked into the local bar that night with a swagger I've never seen the like of again...'

Epilogue

The figure knelt before the altar as if in prayer, although in truth he was simply meditating, calming and clearing his mind. The god to which he appeared to prostrate himself before was The Reaper, god of War. A stone carving of The Reaper stood upon the altar. The carving stood in a pose of victory, resplendent in full mail armour, his legendary giant two-handed great axe, Skull-Splitter, held aloft in one hand. His helmet was tucked under the crook of his other arm so that the god's snarling face was clear to all his enemies. His left leg firmly planted, his right stood atop the severed head of a fallen foe. A blood red cloak billowing from his shoulders. Before the god was a wooden bowl filled with blood, which worshippers anointed themselves with on the forehead and chest above the heart. The meditating man was shirtless and bare footed, only wearing breeches to cover his lower half. He sensed a presence behind him but made no attempt to acknowledge it, simply kept meditating.

'I'm still not sure this is wise.' The presence said, after a while.

'Do you doubt my abilities, Deyander?' The kneeling figure replied.

'Of course not.'

'Good.'

'There is nothing wrong with having insurance.'

'You will not intervene.'

'Just-'

'You will not intervene.' His voice took on a dangerous tone.

'Okay. Even if you are about to die?'

'Even so.' The matter settled, the kneeling figure moved on. 'Have the Dresconii emissaries arrived?'

'Yes, two of them.'

'Good. Make sure they have a good view, and keep an eye on them.'

'Of course.'

'What do you make of them?'

'Hard to tell. I don't trust them. They're hiding something. Whatever is going on out in the Plains is driving them to us, and not out of choice.'

'I fear you are right, yet it presents us with an unprecedented opportunity, one I mean to grasp.' The figure stood, his movements smooth and measured. He retrieved his twin duelling blades, his hands fitting perfectly around the well-worn handles. Already unsheathed, the blades stood naked and proud. Wrought from Grellish steel, they were perfectly balanced killings tools of beauty.

They both left the altar room which led into a narrow corridor and parted ways. The man with the duelling swords headed left, towards where the sun streamed through an arched entrance. He halted just before the entrance, on the edge of the shadow. It was nice and cool inside the corridor. Two steps and he would be out into the open, upon the hot sands of Shulakh's oldest fighting pit. Despite it not being midday yet, the sun had been beating down on the pit for a few hours and he knew that the sand would burn the soles of his feet.

He could hear the crowd, packed to the rafters in their thousands, voicing their excitement. Today was not to be missed. The grandest of spectacles their city's famous fighting pits had ever seen. Yet he intended to deny them of that spectacle. They were here to witness two of Shulakh's finest, if not the finest warriors, fight and contest their skills and he planned to do exactly that. Demonstrate his unquestionable superiority and put an end to questions of his leadership. He didn't need anyone's help, after all, he was unscathed. No one had been able to best him in duels to the death or in exhibition. His back bared no scares, no marks of defeat or shame. That alone should have secured his right to lead, yet still there were mutterings against him and the way he desired to conduct war. They claimed it was not the Shulakhai way. They were right of course, but if Shulakh was to finally conquer their most ancient of enemies, the Shulakhai way would have to change and adapt.

Those voices aired against him would end today, one way or the other.

He stepped out onto the sands.

The noise from the crowd subsided. Tense anticipation. The time had come.

He was kitted out in much the same way as his opponent, wearing only breeches, twin duelling blades in hand. Both had shaved heads and faces, as was the Shulakhai way. The only difference between them was that his opponent bore a single scar upon his back. They stood a few sword lengths apart.

The pit herald's trumpet sounded shrilly into the sky. The two combatants settled into their fighting stances which seemed to waken the crown from their slumber. Whispered murmurings, shouts of encouragement mixed with final bets being placed swirled together, creating a whirlpool of sound flowing around the sands as the pit herald's trumpet sounded for the second time.

The combatants closed. Blades flashed. Silence reigned once again.

Most who claimed to have witnessed what happened during the exchange of blades that day were liars, for all but the keenest of eyes could not follow the Warrior King's movements. His opponent dropped to his knees as his own weapons dropped from his hands. His wrists had been sliced, he would never wield a weapon again, or be able to grip anything for that matter. He looked up in awe at the monster standing above him. He did not have to plead, he knew the King would grant him the mercy of death. The path of the warrior was now closed to him, his life held no meaning. His decapitation was done in one quick, seamless swing. The head stayed on the body for a few heartbeats until the body followed the head as they slumped to the sands which thirstily drank of his lifeblood as it seeped onto the ground.

The King stood motionless in the centre of the storm of silence. He plunged the crimson tips of his duelling blades into the sands so that they quivered by his sides and waited for the blades to still. His shout smashed the tranquillity like a stone through a glass window.

 'SHULAKH! HEAR ME!'
 'I AM RULLOR THE UNMARKED.'
 Arms upraised, he turned, showing them all his scarless skin.
 'SHULAKH! HEAR ME!'
 'I AM RULLOR, YOUR WARRIOR KING!'
 'SHULAKH! HEAR ME!'
 'WE MARCH TO WAR!'

 The fighting pit shook as the crowd erupted like a volcano, sending the name of their Warrior King into the heavens, chanting it over and over again. Their rancorous support swept over Rullor, who stood there soaking it all in. He took up one of his swords, held it aloft while he placed his right heel on the head of the slain, imitating the most popular depiction of the god of War. This was not lost on the Shulakhii as it sent them into a frenzy, creating a cacophony of sound that could be heard from leagues away. His eyes scanned the crowd until he found Deyander who inclined his head, acknowledging this masterstroke.

 Rumours of the fight rapidly spread, rumours that Rullor was The Reaper's marked King, that he had chosen him to be leader of not just Shulakh, but of all. He would be the legendary Warrior King to finally lead them to eternal glory, to the slaughter of Tydon and the sacking of Mirron. Some even claimed that he was the god of War reincarnate, although not many believed it as Rullor did not wield the axe Skull-Splitter. He did nothing to dispel such rumours, in fact he would do what he could to actively encourage them. It would help in the months to come when he laid out his war plans. There would still be outrage that it was not the Shulakh way, that is was blasphemous, but he would forge on regardless. It was the only way to finally bring Tydon to heel.

 A burning sensation flared on the right side of his temple, just above the eye. There on the side of his head, was a red welt, the shape and size of a water droplet. He was not in pain, just slightly surprised that it had taken this long to awaken as it had been doing more often as of late. He took it as a sign that this day was indeed ordained.

He smiled, a gods confidence flowing through him.

Shulakh was going to war…

Printed in Great Britain
by Amazon